PENGUIN BOOKS

FATAL ERROR

Acclaim for Michael Ridpath's international bestsellers:

'A gripping story of murder, corruption and intrigue . . . the thriller everyone has been waiting for' *Daily Telegraph*

'Taut, strongly plotted . . . provides a rush of blood to the head and stings your page-turning fingertips' *Independent*

'Riveting reading' *The Times*

'Ridpath . . . has cornered the market in intelligent, fast-moving financial thrillers' *Sunday Times*

'Thrillers . . . [that] never fail to deliver satisfaction and excitement' *Daily Mail*

'Sheer entertainment . . . I read it in one gulp' *Observer*

'It'll send a shiver down bankers' spines' *Mirror*

'Well written, pacy and informative . . .' *Punch*

'It's hard to put down and difficult to stop thinking about . . . an excellent, fun thriller. Read it and enjoy' *Punch* online

'Ridpath's financial thrillers are remarkable for having their finger on the pulse' *Mail on Sunday*

Fatal Error

MICHAEL RIDPATH

PENGUIN·BOOKS

PENGUIN BOOKS

Published by the Penguin Group
Penguin Books Ltd, 80 Strand, London WC2R ORL, England
Penguin Putnam Inc., 375 Hudson Street, New York, New York 10014, USA
Penguin Books Australia Ltd, 250 Camberwell Road, Camberwell, Victoria 3124, Australia
Penguin Books Canada Ltd, 10 Alcorn Avenue, Toronto, Ontario, Canada M4V 3B2
Penguin Books India (P) Ltd, 11 Community Centre, Panchsheel Park, New Delhi – 110 017, India
Penguin Books (NZ) Ltd, Cnr Rosedale and Airborne Roads, Albany, Auckland, New Zealand
Penguin Books (South Africa) (Pty) Ltd, 24 Sturdee Avenue, Rosebank 2196, South Africa

Penguin Books Ltd, Registered Offices: 80 Strand, London WC2R ORL, England

www.penguin.com

First published by Michael Joseph 2003
Published in Penguin Books 2004
1

Typeset by Rowland Phototypesetting Ltd, Bury St Edmunds, Suffolk
Printed in England by Clays Ltd, St Ives plc

For Hugh Paton

PART ONE

I

'Are you ready?'

Guy was smiling at me. A smile that held confidence and anxiety in equal proportion. The confidence was there for all to see. Only I, his friend for seventeen years, could see the anxiety.

I glanced around the large room with its white-painted brick walls and blue pipes, its cheap desks bearing expensive computers, its chairs in bright green and purple, the table football and the pinball machine, both at rest, both ignored, and the whiteboards covered with scribbles detailing flow-charts, timetables, schedules and missed deadlines. The room was bustling with young men and women in T-shirts and combat trousers tapping away at keyboards, staring at screens, talking on telephones, rushing from desk to desk, pretending that this was just a normal day.

It wasn't.

Today we would find out whether ninetyminutes.com, the company Guy and I had founded a mere five months before, had a future.

'I'm ready.' I gathered together the papers I would need for the board meeting. 'Do you think he'll go for it?'

'Of course he'll go for it,' said Guy. He took a deep breath and smiled again, banishing the anxiety, pumping up the self-confidence, winding up the charm. Guy had charisma, and he would need it today, even for his father. Especially for his father.

He was thirty-one, just a few months older than me. He looked younger, boyish even. He had short blond hair, high cheekbones, bright blue eyes, a mobile, delicate mouth. He dressed cool: white T-shirt under a black designer suit. But he had an edge. Something sharp that lay just beneath his finely structured features. It was a hint of danger, a hint of unpredictability, a touch of cruelty perhaps, or perhaps melancholy. It was difficult to say exactly what it was, or even how it was betrayed, whether by a glint in his eye or a hardening of his mouth. But everyone saw it. Women, men, children for all I knew. It was what attracted people to him. It was what made people follow him.

It was how he usually got his way.

The boardroom was a glass-encased bowl at one end of the open-plan office. The table could seat twelve, which was eight too many for our board. There were only four directors of Ninetyminutes: Guy was Chief Executive Officer, I was Finance Director, Guy's father Tony Jourdan was Chairman and the fourth director was Patrick Hoyle, Tony's lawyer.

Although Guy and I ran the company, Tony had put up most of the money and held eighty per cent of the shares. He also held eighty per cent of the votes. Patrick was there to say 'Yes, Tony,' whenever necessary. There were other shareholders, all Ninetyminutes employees, including Guy's brother, but none of them had a seat on the board. It was up to Guy and me to fight their corner.

This was our second board meeting. They were held on the third Monday of the month and Tony and his lawyer had flown to London from their homes on the French Riviera to attend. We were already settling into a pattern. It began with Guy outlining the company's progress. Which was good. Astoundingly good. We had founded ninetyminutes.com the previous April with the aim of creating the Internet's number-one soccer website. Somehow we had managed to get a site up and running by the beginning of August. It provided commentary, gossip, analysis, match reports and statistics about every club in the English Premier League. It had been well received, with great coverage in the press. More importantly visitors were flocking to the site. In our first full month on-line we had had 190,000 visitors and the numbers were climbing strongly week on week. We now had twenty-three employees and were aggressively hiring more.

Guy went into our plans for the rest of the year. More writers, more match reports, more commentary. Alliances with a bookmaker to enable our visitors to gamble on soccer results. And the gearing up of e-commerce. We were planning to sell club and national kit off the site as well as ninetyminutes.com's own branded clothing. This was Guy's big idea: build a brand on the Net and then make money from selling fashionable sportswear on the back of it.

Tony Jourdan listened closely as Guy spoke. He had been a spectacularly successful property developer in the seventies, but had retired at an early age to the South of France. Too early. It was clear that he missed the cut and thrust of business, and he took his duties as chairman of Ninety-minutes seriously. He looked much like his son, but smaller. His own fair hair was turning a sandy grey. He had the same blue eyes, twinkling out of a deeply tanned face, and the same easy charm that could be turned on at will. But he was tougher. Much tougher.

It was my turn. Guy had done the easy stuff. Now Tony was warmed up it was time for the crunch.

I referred everyone to the board papers. 'As you can see our loss this month will be slightly less than budgeted. I'm hopeful we'll manage to keep that through to the end of the year, especially if we begin to see some good advertising revenues come in.'

'But still a loss?' Tony said.

'Oh, yes. That was always in the plan.'

'And when do you expect to turn in a profit?'

'Not until year three.'

'Year three? That's 2001, isn't it?' Tony said, a note of mockery creeping into his voice.

'Probably 2002,' I answered.

'Our funds won't last that long.'

'No,' I replied patiently. 'We'll have to raise more.'

'We'll need cash to gear up for the e-commerce phase,' added Guy.

'All of this was in the plan,' I said.

'And where is this cash going to come from?' asked Tony.

'Actually, we have an idea for that,' Guy said.

'Really?'

'Yes,' I said. 'Over the last few months we've been talking to a firm called Orchestra Ventures. They've seen what we've been doing and they like it. They want to invest ten million pounds. It'll be enough to finance our growth plans and take us through to next year.'

Tony raised his eyebrows. 'Ten million, huh? And what do they want for their ten million?'

'It's all here,' I said, passing copies of a term sheet to Tony and Hoyle. The sheet outlined the terms under which Orchestra Ventures would make their investment. They were the product of several days of hard negotiating.

Tony scanned it quickly. Then he tossed it on to the table. 'This is crap,' he said. His blue eyes were cold. No sign of the famous Jourdan charm. 'The way I read this, my equity stake goes down from eighty per cent to twenty per cent.'

'That's right,' I said. 'After all, they're putting up ten million quid. You invested two.'

'But management's stake is sticking at twenty per cent.

6

Do Orchestra Ventures expect me to give up some of my equity to you?'

'Well, that's not quite the way it will be done.'

'But that's the overall effect, isn't it?'

'Yes, I suppose so,' I admitted.

'Why on earth do they think I should do that?'

'They think we need a decent equity stake to give us an incentive.'

'They do, do they?' Tony let his contempt for that idea show. 'But I was the one who stumped up the cash when you came begging to me. When you'd been to everyone else and no one was prepared to touch you. I deserve to make a decent profit.'

'You will make a profit,' I said.

'And Ninetyminutes will have the funding to take us on to the next stage and beyond,' said Guy.

Tony leaned back in his chair and folded his arms. 'You boys don't have a clue about this, do you?'

If Tony was trying to bait me, he nearly succeeded. But I just managed to keep control. 'And why is that?' I asked through gritted teeth.

'Because you give away everything to the first mug who's willing to back you. Now that's fine when I'm the mug. But not when it's my equity stake you're giving away.'

'So what do you suggest?' Guy asked.

'Bootstrap it,' Tony said. 'Get some cash flow into the company. Then use the cash to expand. Better yet, borrow on the back of it.'

'But that'll be too slow!' Guy protested. 'If we're going to dominate this space, we need cash now. And more in six months' time.'

'Not on these terms, you don't.'

'So where do you suggest we get this cash flow?' I asked.

'Skin.'

'Skin?'

'Yeah, skin. You know. Pics of women without clothes on. And men, for that matter.'

I flinched.

Tony ignored me. 'Last week I bumped into an old friend from my property days. Joe Petrelli. Smart guy. He has a nose for cash flow, always has. He tells me the only money being made on the Internet at the moment is in skin.'

I had heard that too. But I didn't like it.

'People rack up a fortune on their credit cards download-ing dirty pictures,' Tony went on. 'It's a licence to print money.'

'I can't see what this has to do with us,' said Guy. But I was sure he could.

'It's a perfect fit,' said Tony. 'Sign up the punters with football, and then reel them in with links to a porn site. Joe can put us in touch with the guys he deals with in LA.'

Guy and I sat stunned.

'What do you think, Patrick?' Tony asked.

'Great idea, Tony,' Hoyle said. 'These losses worry me. We have to do something to turn them around. Footie and totty, a great combination.' He gave a deep chuckle at his own skilful use of language, a low rumble that shook his broad shoulders. He was a huge fat man with several chins and a sweating brow. His merriment just seemed to underline the sleaziness of the whole proposition.

'If we turn ourselves into a porn site we'll never attract respectable investors,' I protested.

'We won't need them,' said Tony. 'We'll have our own cash to spend. Guy?'

We all turned to Guy. I prayed that he would be able to come up with an effective response. I had less than no desire to count the credit card payments of sad men downloading computer porn, however much money there was in it.

Guy stared hard at Tony. It was a cold stare, lacking the affection or even the respect of a son for his father. If Guy was angry, he was controlling it. It was the stare of someone assessing an enemy, thinking through his weaknesses, weighing options.

Eventually, he spoke, 'Let's stand back a bit here,' he said. 'My objective when I first dreamed up this company was to make it the foremost soccer website in Europe. If we can do that, the site will be worth hundreds of millions, given the valuations we're seeing at the moment. That's much more important than a few hundred thousand in the P and L. I can see a link to a pornography site would help our cash flow,' he nodded towards his father. 'But it would make it that much harder to reach our objective. It would take the whole site a long way downmarket. So I don't think we should do it. We're better off going for outside investment.'

'From Orchestra?'

'Yes.'

'The bunch of crooks who want to steal my equity?'

'Tony,' I said, 'you'll end up with a smaller slice of a much larger pie –'

'Don't give me that apple-pie bullshit,' Tony snapped. 'I heard it dozens of times in my property days and I ignored it every time. You know what, Guy?' He was speaking to his son now, his voice hard. I was out of the picture. 'I always kept the pie. The *whole* pie. And I got rich as a result. That looks like a lesson you need to learn.'

'So are you saying no to Orchestra?' Guy said, struggling successfully to keep his tone reasonable.

'I'm not just saying no. I'm saying I want you to get hold of Joe Petrelli and find out what he does and how he does it. We'll discuss it at next month's board meeting. Sooner if need be.'

This was worse than we had expected. We had known

Tony would be unhappy with the dilution of his equity stake, but we hadn't expected him to start dictating the strategy of the company. And in such a repulsive direction, too.

'This is *my* company,' Guy said in a low voice. 'And I decide what we do with it.'

'Wrong,' said Tony. 'I own eighty per cent of the shares. I decide what gets done. You do it.'

Guy glanced at me. The anger was burning in his eyes. 'That's not acceptable,' he said.

Tony held his son's stare. 'That's the way it's going to be.'

There was silence for what seemed like an age. Hoyle and I watched the two men. We were no part of this. This was about much more than who controlled Ninetyminutes.

Then Guy closed his eyes, slowly, deliberately. He took a deep breath and opened them again.

'In that case, I resign.'

'What!' I exclaimed before I had a chance to control myself.

'Sorry, Davo. I have no choice. I'm determined Ninety-minutes is going to be the best site in Europe. If we don't take on more equity we haven't a chance of getting there. We'll just be another also-ran site with a particularly sleazy image.'

'But one which makes money,' Tony said.

'Frankly, I don't care,' said Guy.

Tony weighed that up. 'That, Guy, is your problem,' he said. 'But I think you should reconsider.'

'And I think *you* should,' said Guy.

'I'm in London until Thursday,' Tony said. 'I'll give you until that morning to decide. Now, gentlemen, this meeting is closed.'

Ninetyminutes' office was on the fourth floor of a converted metalworking shop in a quiet street in Clerkenwell. The Jerusalem Tavern was just over the road. Usually cramped and crowded in the evening, it was cool and empty at that time of the afternoon. Guy got in the beers, a pint of bitter for me, a bottle of Czech beer for him.

'Bastard,' he said, shaking his head.

'He'll back down,' I said.

'No, he won't.'

'He'll have to. He can't run Ninetyminutes without you.'

'He'll figure out how.'

'There's got to be a way through this,' I said. 'We can come to some kind of compromise.'

'Maybe,' said Guy. 'Just maybe we could this month. But next month it'll be more of the same. He'll come up with ideas for how Ninetyminutes should be run that he knows I won't like. He'll dangle them there in front of me for a while, and then he'll force them through. To show who's smarter. Who's the better businessman. Who has the power.' He took a drink of his beer. 'Did you ever play snakes and ladders with your father?'

'I don't know. I suppose so.'

'Who won?'

'I can't remember. I think I did. Perhaps he did. I don't know.'

'I played snakes and ladders with my father a lot and he always won. That made me really angry when I was four. And even angrier when I got older and realized that snakes and ladders is a game of chance. The only way you can win every time is by cheating. Pretty sad when a father has to cheat to beat his four-year-old son.' Guy stared at the label on the bottle in front of him, as if an answer was written there. 'I knew it was wrong to take his money.'

'We had no choice.'

Guy sighed. 'I suppose not.'

He was slumped over his beer, his eyes gloomy, almost desperate, the vitality that had been his constant companion over the previous few months nowhere to be seen. An aura of pessimism emanated from him, dragging down my own spirits. The change frightened me.

We had gone through a lot over the last few months, Guy and I. We had worked long hours, evenings, nights, weekends. We had achieved so much. Getting the site on-line in such a short space of time had been a miracle. Scrabbling together the funding. Recruiting a team of totally committed individuals. I had had a lot of fun. And I had learned a lot about myself and about Guy during that time. I didn't want it to end.

'We have to fight him, Guy. We've worked too hard for too long for it all to finish like this. What about all your plans for covering the major European leagues? What about the e-commerce? What about the ten million quid Orchestra Ventures have put on the table? Yesterday you were more fired up about this than anyone.'

'I know. Yesterday I was acting as if Ninetyminutes was my company. I was ignoring my father, ignoring the meeting today, pretending they didn't exist. But I was deluding myself. They do exist. I can't hide from the reality.'

'We've faced obstacles like this before and you've never quit. You've always found a way over them or under them or through them. If it was just me, I'd have given up long ago, you know that.'

Guy smiled.

'I've learned a lot from you,' I went on. 'I've learned to believe in you. Don't tell me I was wrong.'

Guy shrugged. 'I'm sorry.'

'Is it because it's your father? If it was anyone else you wouldn't just roll over.'

'I'm not just rolling over!' Guy snapped. Then he got a grip of himself. 'No, you're right. It is because it's my father. I know him. He's determined to turn Ninetyminutes into my failure and his success. And he has all the cards. As usual.'

'Don't give up.'

'I'm sorry, Davo. I already have.'

I looked at him. He meant it.

We sat in silence. I could feel the edifice that we had all worked so hard to create over the last few months crumbling around me, as though Tony Jourdan had removed a vital keystone that kept the whole thing up. It was so bloody unfair!

'We have to tell them back there,' I said.

'You do it. I can't face them. Go on ahead. I'll stay here.'

So I left him, shrouded in his own darkness.

2

There was no sign of Guy in the office the next day, Tuesday. I called his flat in Wapping with no reply. My contact at Orchestra Ventures rang me three times but each time I avoided talking to him.

I was drumming my fingers on my desk, wondering what to do next, when Ingrid joined me. Ingrid Da Cunha had known Guy almost as long as I had, but she had been with Ninetyminutes for only two months. She had joined as publisher of the website, and she had been the final ingredient that had made the team work together. I liked her. And I respected her opinion.

'So, we're going into the glamour business, are we?' she said.

'You are. Not me.'

'You should stick around. Chartered Accountant of the Month. Mr October. We could really use you.'

'Thanks.'

'Of course, with my ancestry this should be the perfect job for me. Copacabana babe. Swedish au pair. I could do it all.'

I couldn't help smiling. Ingrid had big pale-blue eyes, a wide friendly smile and thick chestnut-brown hair. But I had seen her in a bathing suit, and although she didn't look bad, she was hardly page-three material.

She caught me. 'What are you laughing at? Sure, my bum's too big. And my thighs. But I could get cosmetic surgery on the company now. It's just a question of moving things around a bit. Tony will pay for it. I'm sure my father could fix me up with a surgeon in Rio. You wouldn't recognize me.'

'What about growth hormones?'

'What do you mean? I'm five foot two. Five foot five in the right pair of shoes.' She punched me on the arm.

'Ow!' When Ingrid hit, she hit hard. 'Don't get too excited. I think all Ninetyminutes will be doing is providing the links to some seedy little studio in Los Angeles. You'll have to keep focusing your talents on the football.'

'Arbroath nil, Hamilton Academicals nil,' Ingrid said, in an appalling imitation of the results announcer on *Grandstand*. Ingrid had an accent like none I had ever heard before, although she probably spoke like every other woman in the world with a Swedish mother, a Brazilian father and a British education. Her tone became serious. 'I just wanted to say that you don't deserve this.'

'None of us do.'

'Tony isn't going to give in, is he?'

'I don't know. I doubt it somehow. But it has to be right to try to get him to change his mind. We can't give up without a fight.'

'No, we can't. But if it does all fall apart, you should be proud of what you've achieved. Guy would never have got this far without you. He has his own problems with his father to sort out. You were caught in the middle. It wasn't your fault.'

She was right. I knew she was right. And it was exactly what I needed to hear at that moment.

'I've been talking to the others,' she said, 'and nobody wants to hang around here if you and Guy leave.'

'There's no need for that. You've all put money in. If you stick around you'll still be able to make something of the site.'

'But if we leave, Tony's screwed, isn't he?'

'I don't know.'

'Think about it. No technical support, no writers, just a bunch of computers, some crappy old desks and a website that will be out of date within a week.'

I thought about it. She had a point.

I looked around me at the bodies beavering away. 'Will they really do that?'

Ingrid nodded. 'Yep. I think we should tell Tony, don't you?'

I smiled. Tony was a stubborn bastard, but it was worth a try. Well worth a try. I picked up the phone and called him at his flat in Knightsbridge to ask for a meeting. He was quite businesslike. He agreed to see Ingrid and me at nine o'clock the following evening.

Owen Jourdan strolled in at about midday, clutching a big cup of coffee. I was surprised to see him: if his brother had gone AWOL then I thought he would have too. Owen and Guy had an odd relationship that I had learned to understand over the years. In the normal course of things they hardly spoke to each other, but if one of them got into trouble the other was there for him. Always.

Owen stalked over to his computer and turned it on, ignoring everyone around him as usual. I went over to his desk, pulled up a chair and sat down. He didn't say anything, but stared at his computer screen powering up, and sipped his coffee.

Although Owen was Guy's younger brother, he looked nothing like him. It was as though some freak hormonal imbalance had stimulated the growth of some parts of his body while ignoring others. He was well over six feet tall and must have weighed close to seventeen stone. He was bulky without being fat, with an oversized head that gave the impression of immense stupidity. His tiny eyes were deeply set beneath full eyebrows. His mop of short white-dyed hair was uncombed and he looked as if he had just crawled out of bed. He was wearing what he always wore, long shorts and a ninetyminutes.com baseball cap. It was September and the weather was getting cooler. Owen would soon have to get himself a new pair of trousers.

'How's Guy?' I asked.

'Pissed,' he answered.

'By pissed, do you mean pissed off, or pissed drunk?'

'Probably both.' His voice was high, almost squeaky. Guy and Owen's mother was American and they had both spent a fair bit of time living there, but Owen's accent was much more pronounced than his brother's.

'And how are you?'

'Me?' For the first time Owen turned towards me, his tiny eyes showing a sudden interest in my face. 'What do you care about me?'

'He's your brother. You've worked as hard as any of us in starting this company. It's your father who's shutting it down.'

Owen turned away from me, and began tapping passwords into his computer. He ignored me for a whole minute before he finally spoke. 'I guess I'm pretty pissed too.'

'Guy seems to have given up,' I said. 'But the others haven't. Ingrid says they're all willing to resign with him. Your father will have to back down, won't he?'

Owen didn't answer, but tapped away.

'Won't he?' I repeated in exasperation.

'Dad won't give up,' said Owen.

'But why not? You're his sons. This is his chance to support both of you.'

'Because he's a total asshole,' said Owen. His high-pitched voice contrasted strangely with his size and the words he was saying. 'He doesn't give a shit about either of us. Never has. Never will.'

He must have seen my surprise at the sudden vehemence

17

of the response. 'I used to worship him. So did Guy. Then he walked out on us. Left us with that bitch of a mother. Never saw us, never asked for us. When we did go to stay with him in France he still ignored us. Especially me. And when I saw that slut he left us for, I couldn't believe it. *You* know she was a slut,' he said.

I could feel myself going red.

Owen noticed and smiled to himself. 'After all that screwing around in France I knew he was a total waste of space. It's taken Guy a bit longer to figure that out. You know, I think Dad's scared of him?'

'Scared of Guy? That doesn't make any sense.'

'It does to Dad. Guy represents everything he used to think he was good at. Chasing women, making money. Dad needs to prove to himself he can still do all that. That's why he screws women half his age. That's why he's screwing Ninetyminutes now.'

'But he's made much more money than Guy.'

'He did when he was young, yes. But that was a long time ago. I know for a fact he's made some bad investments these last few years. It's not surprising – he doesn't concentrate on them. But it, like, bugs him. I can tell it bugs him. Now he wants to prove he hasn't lost his touch.' Owen's eyes glowed with a black fire deep beneath his brows. 'He's a selfish pig, my dad. He hates us. Both of us. So I'm not at all surprised he wants to destroy Ninetyminutes.'

The strength of all this bitterness took me aback. 'Where's Guy?' I asked.

'I don't know,' said Owen. He had shared a flat with Guy in Wapping, but once Ninetyminutes had established itself he had moved out and found himself his own place somewhere in Camden.

'Will he be coming in today?'

'No idea.'

'Do you think he'll change his mind?'

'No point. I told you. Now, I got a line of code here I need to fix.'

I left Owen to it, reflecting that I had had just about my longest conversation ever with him. And it hadn't changed my opinion of him one jot.

He was strange. Very strange.

There was no sign of Guy on Wednesday, either, and I didn't even try to ask Owen about him. Ingrid and I worked till half past eight in the evening, and took the tube to Knightsbridge. She was more confident than I, bristling with arguments and justifications to win Tony over before the next morning's deadline. I was going to try, but I was much more sceptical of our chances of success. Funnily enough it wasn't Guy's defeatism that worried me most, it was the unalloyed certainty of Owen's hatred for his father. This was not a family about to forgive and forget.

Clutching an *A to Z*, I led Ingrid through a maze of small streets just to the north of Harrods to where Tony's flat should be. I paused under a streetlamp to check the map. I was pretty sure I was in the right place, a narrow one-way mews. I looked around for a street sign. A century ago the houses had been inhabited by horses. Now they were inhabited by humans who probably paid at least a million quid for the privilege.

I saw the sign obscured by a car on the other side of the street. I moved a couple of yards down the road to get a better view. I was in the right place. There was a man in the car who caught my eye for a second and then looked away. I wondered briefly what he was doing sitting in a car in the dark. Waiting for someone, presumably. Then I looked for Tony's flat, which turned out to be the top floor of one of the mews houses.

We rang the bell. Tony answered.

'Ah, the deputation,' he said. 'Come in. I'm afraid you can't stay long; I'm meeting some friends for dinner in half an hour.'

We sat on pale leather armchairs in his expensively decorated living room. There was no sign of anyone else in the flat. I suppose I had secretly hoped that I would find Guy there negotiating an arrangement with his father.

Ingrid came straight to the point. 'We've come to ask you to keep Guy on.'

Tony raised his eyebrows. 'Well, I can try to persuade Guy to stay, but it's his decision. There's really nothing I can do about it.'

'Oh, come on, Tony,' I said. 'We all know why Guy is resigning. You won't let us raise more money to fund Ninetyminutes' expansion. I was there. I saw it.'

Tony held up his hands. 'There's no point in discussing this now. Let's see what happens tomorrow morning, shall we? We can talk about it then.'

'No,' said Ingrid. 'We talk about it now. You see, if Guy resigns the rest of the team will resign also.'

'That's up to you,' said Tony calmly.

'But if we all leave, how are you going to run the site?'

'I'll hire people.'

'That won't work,' Ingrid pointed out. 'You need people who are up to speed with the content, the design, the site software. You can't just get bodies off the street to do it.'

'Are you trying to blackmail me?'

'No,' said Ingrid. 'I'm just trying to explain what will happen to your two-million-pound investment if Guy resigns tomorrow.'

'You *are* trying to blackmail me,' said Tony, a patronizing smile playing on his lips. Then his expression changed: all traces of humour disappeared as he leaned forward, deadly serious now. He spoke with a low measured urgency that commanded our total attention. 'Let me tell you something. I don't respond to threats. No one in my entire working career has threatened me and got away with it. Whatever happens, Ingrid, you won't have a job tomorrow. Neither will you, David. Now, it's time for you both to leave.'

I could see Ingrid was furious, but I caught her eye, and we got up to go.

'Creep,' muttered Ingrid as we strode down the mews towards Knightsbridge and taxis.

'Never mind,' I said. 'It was worth a try.'

'Guy was right,' she said. 'We never should have taken his money.'

'No, we shouldn't. Big mistake.'

My mistake.

We passed the man in the car at the end of the street. He looked as if he had fallen asleep. With a jerk, he seemed suddenly to wake up and start his car. As we turned the corner, I looked over my shoulder and saw Tony coming out of his mews house.

'I never liked that man,' said Ingrid. 'Ever since we stayed with him in France, I knew he was a scumbag. He gives me the creeps every time I look at him. He thinks he's a super-suave playboy, but he's just a dirty old man. He always was. Do you know what I'd like to do to him?'

I never found out what Ingrid would like to do to Tony. Instead I heard the roar of an engine from the mews, and a cry, abruptly cut short.

I glanced at Ingrid and ran.

I rounded the corner and saw a body splayed out at an unnatural angle on the pavement just in front of Tony's house. As I came closer, it was obvious who it was. I recognized the clothes. I recognized the shape and size. But when I reached him, I couldn't recognize his face. His head was a bloody mess.

A second later, Ingrid arrived at my shoulder. She looked down at the body on the pavement and screamed.

Ninetyminutes had lost its chairman.

PART TWO

3

July 1987, twelve years earlier, Dorset

I began running from the edge of the penalty area just as Guy kicked the ball, aiming for the far post. I leapt at the same time as Phil, the 'keeper. The ball drifted an inch above Phil's outstretched fingers and struck my head, ricocheting between the posts and into the brambles guarding the ditch behind.

'Yes! Nice one, David,' Torsten cried. 'Five–four. We win!'

I glanced over to Guy, who wore a quiet smile of satisfaction on his face. Guy seemed able to place a football anywhere on the pitch with perfect timing.

I trotted off to retrieve the ball from the brambles, and joined the others picking up items of discarded clothing and ambling back towards the house. It was a lovely evening. During the game, unnoticed by the players, the sky had turned to a deep blue-grey and the small puffs of cloud to inky black. Rooks kicked up a fuss in the copse running along the side of the playing field as we made our way down to Mill House, the converted watermill where forty of us boarded. The sprawling modern campus of Broadhill School itself was still visible a mile and a half over peaceful cow pastures to the east.

Evenings, which until that week had been crammed full of revision for exams, were suddenly free for pick-up games of football. Nearly all the O and A level exams had finished. I had only one maths paper left and thought my brain deserved a rest. In three weeks' time my life at Broadhill would be over. The race from thirteen-year-old new boy to eighteen-year-old adult would be finished. At that moment, it seemed like a shame.

I caught up with Torsten and Guy. 'Nice cross,' I said.

Guy shrugged. 'Your head is difficult to miss, Davo.'

We walked three abreast along the short stretch of country lane to the house.

'I spoke to my dad earlier,' Torsten said. Torsten Schollen-berger was a tall, clean-cut German whose father owned a network of magazine publishing interests throughout Europe. 'He wants me to work in his office over the summer. In Hamburg.'

'What? That's inhuman,' said Guy. 'After exams and everything?'

'I know. And I'm going to college in Florida in September. I deserve a break.'

'So, you won't be coming to France?'

'It doesn't look like it.'

'Man, that sucks. Can't you just tell him to piss off? You're eighteen. You're an adult. He can't make you do what you don't want to do.'

'Guy, you've met my father. He can do what he damn well likes.'

I walked next to them in silence. My parents were taking the caravan down to Devon again that summer. They were hoping I would come with them. I probably would. The caravan was very cramped, but I actually liked my parents and I liked Devon. I enjoyed striding over the moors with my father. He, too, had offered me a summer job working in his office, a small branch of a building society in a Northamp-tonshire market town. He would pay me sixty quid a week. I was planning to take it. I needed the money.

None of this, though, did I feel like mentioning to Guy and Torsten.

Broadhill was a unique school. It was one of the most expensive boarding schools in England and had superb facilities. But it also offered scholarships to a large minority of pupils, and not just for academic ability. I had an academic scholarship, but Phil, the goalkeeper, was an accomplished cellist from Swansea. I knew Guy's father paid full whack, although Guy's sporting skills at soccer, cricket and tennis could have secured him a sporting scholarship. Torsten probably paid double.

The result was an eclectic mix of boys and girls, from the super-rich to the quite modest, from geniuses to the almost illiterate, from international swimmers to concert pianists. There was also a fair quota of slobs, yobs, idlers and rule-breakers. Alcohol and tobacco were widespread. Other even more forbidden stimulants occasionally circulated. But for some reason, despite the presence of adolescent boys and girls together in one boarding school, there was very little sex.

I could never work out why. I made a few attempts to change this situation myself with very little success. There were, of course, school rules banning it, but it seemed to be the pupils themselves who enforced this celibacy. Eventually I developed a theory that might explain it, a sort of extension of Groucho Marx's dictum that he didn't want to belong to any club that would accept him as a member. There was a rigid and well-defined hierarchy of boys and girls in the school. It was beneath the dignity of an individual pupil to be seen with a member of the opposite sex at or below his or her level in the hierarchy. We all had to strive for higher. This meant a great deal of frustration for ninety-nine per cent of the school, and an embarrassment of choice for the lucky one per cent.

And who was at the top of this hierarchy? Well, Torsten was close, but right at the top of this totem pole was, of course, Guy.

He and I shared a room that year. Valentine's Day is an embarrassment at any school, but it had been particularly humiliating for me that February. I had received one card, from a sad girl with glasses in my maths class who went on to become a top equities analyst at an investment bank. Guy received seventy-three. Most of them were probably from thirteen- and fourteen-year-olds he didn't know, but even so. He had played the lead in an unofficial production of *Grease* the previous summer, and had made an impression on the female half of the school that had endured until the following February. Tall, dark and unremarkable, I knew I was no competition for Guy, but my ego, not for the first time, was crushed. What really annoyed me was that he didn't even seem pleased. He took it as his due.

Although I shared a room with Guy, he was very discreet about his love life. I assumed that he had 'gone all the way', but he didn't brag about it. His relationships did seem to form a pattern, though. He would be seen charming a gorgeous girl of sixteen or seventeen, chatting her up, making her laugh for a period of weeks, or even months, and then he would suddenly drop her. Within a couple of days he'd be chasing someone else.

His current interest lay with a girl called Mel Dean, who was also in her last year at school. She wasn't as classically beautiful as some of his conquests, but I could see what drove him on. She wore tight clothes and a permanent soft pout that suggested availability, yet she had a reputation for chastity. 'Fit but frigid' as the schoolboy parlance would have it. For Guy, an irresistible combination.

I stayed up late that night, trying to fight my way through a few more pages of *War and Peace*. I now wonder at how foolish I was to try to read that book in the same term I was taking my A levels, but I had a self-image as an intellectual to protect.

Guy clattered into the room and got himself ready for bed. 'Come on, Davo, I'm knackered. It's past eleven. Can I turn the light out?'

'Oh, all right,' I said, in mock irritation. But in truth I had been reading the same page for ten minutes, and it was time to put it out of its misery. The book fell with a thud to the floor by my bed and I lay back on my pillow. Guy turned out the light and flopped on to his.

'Davo?'

'Yeah?'

'Do you want to come to my dad's place this summer?'

At first I didn't think I had heard right. The idea of Guy inviting me to stay with him and his father in the South of France came as a total surprise, a shock in fact. We liked each other, even respected each other, but I had never counted myself as one of Guy's friends. Or not that kind of friend. Guy hung around with the likes of Torsten, or Faisal, a Kuwaiti prince, or Troy Barton, son of Jeff Barton, the film star. The kind of people whose families had millions of pounds and several homes scattered around the world. Who met each other in Paris or Marbella. Not the kind who went to Devon in a caravan.

'Davo?'

'Oh, sorry.'

'Well? You'll like it. He's got this great place on the cliffs overlooking Cap Ferrat. I haven't been there myself yet, but I've heard it's amazing. He asked me to bring some friends along with me. Mel's going, and Ingrid Da Cunha. Why don't you come?'

Why not? He meant it. I didn't know where I would get the cash to get there, but I knew I had to go.

'Are you sure?'

'Of course I'm sure.'

'OK, then,' I said. 'Thanks. I'll come.'

4

I raised the champagne flute to my lips and looked down at the ancient volcanoes of the Massif Central twenty thousand feet below. It turned out I hadn't needed to find the cash for the plane fare. We had all met at Biggin Hill, an airfield to the south of London, and boarded Guy's father's jet. Within minutes we were in the air, heading for Nice.

Mel Dean and Ingrid Da Cunha were in the seats behind me, with Guy opposite them. Mel was wearing tight jeans, a white T-shirt, a denim jacket and a quantity of make-up. A streak of yellow ran through her long dark hair, which wound around the back of her neck and tumbled over her shoulder towards her chest. And what a chest. Her friend Ingrid was wearing baggy trousers and a sweatshirt. I barely knew either of them; Mel had been at the school for five years, but we had never been in the same class and I had scarcely spoken to her in all that time. Ingrid had arrived at Broadhill only the previous autumn, half way through the sixth form.

I said hello. Mel's lips betrayed the tiniest of twitches in acknowledgement, but Ingrid gave me a wide friendly smile. I left Guy to do the chatting up: judging by the peals of raucous laughter from Ingrid, he was doing it well. I leaned back into my deep blue leather seat. It was the first time I had ever flown. This was the life.

Guy moved up to the seat next to me. 'You haven't met my dad before, have you?'

'No,' I said. 'I don't think I've even seen him. Apart from in the papers, of course.' Tony Jourdan had been a wunderkind of the London property market. My father knew all about him, although by the time I had begun to read the newspapers he was less often in them. I had seen a couple of articles in *Private Eye* accusing him of bribing a local council over the planning application for a shopping centre, and of ruthlessly ousting his former business partner. But mostly he rated a mention in the gossip columns, not the business pages.

'He's only been to Broadhill a couple of times. I haven't seen much of him myself in the last few years. But you'll like him. He's a good guy. He knows how to have a good time.'

'Excellent. Has he married again?'

'Yeah, a few years ago. A French bimbo called Dominique. I've never met her. But forget her. Prepare to have some fun.'

'I will.' I hesitated. I was looking forward to visiting the bars and restaurants. Now I was eighteen I wanted to exercise my legal right to drink to the full. But there was one problem. 'Guy?'

'Yes?'

'I don't actually have that much cash on me. I mean, I might have to duck out of one or two things. You'll understand, won't you?'

Guy smiled broadly. 'No I won't. Dad will pay. Believe me, he'll want to. He's always been generous, especially when it comes to having a good time. And if you do get caught short, just ask me. Really.'

'Thanks.' I was relieved. For five years I had managed to survive on a fraction of the allowance of some of my contemporaries at Broadhill, but I was worried that it would be much more difficult in the outside world. And the joys of a student overdraft still lay several months in front of me.

The jet skimmed over the tight green folds of the Riviera's hinterland, passing above a town dominated by two extra-ordinarily shaped apartment complexes that looked as if they were built of Lego. Once over the deep blue of the Mediterranean, it turned eastwards towards Nice airport, an incongruous rectangle of unnaturally flat reclaimed land jutting out into the sea.

Tony Jourdan met us in the terminal. He must have been forty-five at the very least, but he looked younger. I was struck by the resemblance to Guy, not just in the way he looked, but also in the way he moved. He welcomed us with Guy's winning smile, and threw us all into the open back of his yellow Jeep.

He drove us through Nice, along the Promenade des Anglais lined with hotels, apartment buildings and flags on one side, and palm trees, beach, sun-worshippers and sea on the other. We turned inland, battling through the heavy traffic to the Corniche, the famous coast road that wound its way towards Monte Carlo. We climbed ever higher, the Mediterranean beneath us and the coastal mountains above us, drove through a tunnel and then swung on to a narrow winding road. We continued climbing until Tony stopped outside a ten-foot-high iron gate. 'Les Sarrasins' was inscribed on one of the gateposts. He pressed a remote control, the gate swung open, and the Jeep pulled up beneath a pink-washed house.

He leapt out of the vehicle. 'Come and meet Dominique.'

We made our way up some stone steps that led around the side of the house and were struck by the most spectacular view. On three sides was the powerful deep blue of the Mediterranean, stretching towards an indistinct horizon where it merged with the paler blue of the sky. We seemed to be floating high in the air, suspended a thousand feet above the sea, which we could just hear breaking on to the beach below. I felt disoriented, dizzy, as if I was about to lose my balance. I took a step back towards the house.

Guy's father noticed and smiled. 'The vertigo often gets

people, especially when they're not expecting it. Come and look.' We edged towards a low white marble railing. 'Below us is Beaulieu, and that's Cap Ferrat over there,' he said, pointing down to a crowded little town and a lush green peninsula beyond it. 'Behind that is Nice. And over there,' he pointed to the east, 'is Monte Carlo. On a clear day, when the mistral has blown all the muck out of the air, you can see Corsica. But not in July, I'm afraid.'

'What's that?' asked Guy, pointing to a crumbling wall of thin grey brick perching on a rock at the end of the garden, next to a lone olive tree.

'That was a watchtower. They say it's Roman. For centuries the locals used this place to look out for Saracen raiders. Hence the name Les Sarrasins.' Tony smiled at his son. 'So, what do you think?'

'Nice, Dad. Very nice,' Guy said. 'Not so handy for the beach, though, is it?'

'Oh yes it is. Just hop over these railings and you'll be down there in ten seconds.'

We leaned over and looked down. Far below we could just see a strip of sand, next to the coast road, the Basse Corniche.

'*Allo!*'

We turned. A few feet back from the railings was a pool, and by the pool was a woman lying on a sun chair. Topless. I stared. I was eighteen: I couldn't help it. She waved and slowly sat up, reached for her bikini top and slipped it on. She stood and walked over to us, hips swaying. Long blonde hair, dark glasses, swinging figure. I still stared.

'Dominique, this is my son, Guy. You finally meet!'

'Hello, Guy,' Dominique said, extending her hand. She pronounced it the French way, to rhyme with 'key'.

'Hello, Mum,' said Guy with his best smile, and she laughed. Guy's father introduced her to Mel, Ingrid and me.

I couldn't say anything apart from a pathetic 'Nice to meet you, Mrs Jourdan,' which also seemed to amuse her.

'While you're staying here, I'm Tony and this is Dominique,' said Guy's father, smiling. 'Call me sir, and I'll toss you over the cliff.'

'OK, Tony.'

'Now, you and Guy are in the guest cottage over there,' he pointed to a small building tucked behind a bed of tall lavender on the other side of the pool. 'The girls are in the house. Why don't you go and take your things in and then come out here for a drink?'

We gathered around the pool an hour later. A tiny grey-haired man in a crisp white jacket served us all with Pimm's from a pitcher stuffed with lemon, cucumber and mint. The girls had changed into light summer dresses, Dominique had wrapped something around herself, Guy and Tony were wearing white slacks and I wore my scruffy jeans, preferring them to my only alternative of an old pair of black cords.

The sun was hanging low over Cap Ferrat and the air was still. I could hear the hum of bees in the lavender, and of course the sea below.

'Gorgeous,' whispered Ingrid next to me.

'Yes it is,' I agreed.

'Not it. Him.'

I realized that she was referring to a gardener carrying some tools back towards the house. He was young, Arab-looking, probably North African, and the muscles of his bare smooth chest were perfectly defined by the late-afternoon sunlight. He caught Guy's eye, and smiled at him.

'You're in there, Guy,' Ingrid said as the gardener disappeared round the corner of the house.

'What are you talking about?' said Guy. 'He was smiling at all of us.'

'I wish that were true, Guy, but it wasn't. He was all eyes for you.'

Guy scowled. He had the kind of looks that attracted admiring glances from men as well as women and I knew he hated it. There was nothing he could do about it, though. 'What are you grinning at?' he growled at me.

'Nothing,' I said, exchanging a glance with Ingrid. 'Let's get a drink.'

The Pimm's slipped down very easily. Despite our pretended sophistication none of us was used to spirits, and the drink soon had its effect. I didn't say much, but watched the others, a pleasant buzzing caressing the edges of my brain. It was clear that Guy didn't know his father well, but equally clear that they were both doing their best to be nice to each other. Tony soon had the girls giggling, especially Mel, who seemed quite taken with him.

Just then Guy's brother Owen shambled into view. For a fifteen-year-old he was big. His muscles were unnaturally well developed, and his large head appeared to belong to someone much older. But he seemed uncomfortable with his overgrown body. His walk was hesitant and stooped, as if he was trying to reduce his size. Of course it didn't work. His mousy brown hair lay in greasy coils on his scalp, and he had pretty bad acne. He was wearing an Apple Computer T-shirt and black rugby shorts. Everyone ignored him.

'Hi, Owen,' I said out of politeness.

'Hi.'

'Been here long?'

'Couple of days.'

'This is a fantastic place, isn't it?'

'It's OK,' he said, and wandered off. End of conversation with Owen.

Tony appeared, bearing a pitcher full of Pimm's. 'Want some more?'

'Yes please, sir.'

'David. I warned you about that. One more time, and it's over the cliff.'

'Sorry. Tony.'

He refilled my glass. 'Good stuff, isn't it?'

'It goes down very easily.'

'Yes. It's the one English thing I find that translates well to France. Even Dominique likes it.' He looked over to where Owen was pouring himself a Coke. 'You're in Guy and Owen's house at school, aren't you?'

'Yes. Guy and I share a room.'

'How's Owen getting on?'

'Hard to say, really. I think he's OK. He doesn't have many friends, apart from some computer types. But he seems happy enough. He spends most of his time in the computer room. He reads a lot. He keeps himself to himself. But no one messes with him, Guy makes sure of that.'

'Yes. Guy has always looked after him,' Tony said. 'Owen took the divorce quite badly. I don't think his mother has much interest in him, apart from making sure he stays away from me. And I'm on record as the world's lousiest father. Guy's really been all he's had. What about that rugby incident? Did you hear about that?'

'Yes, I did.'

'Did he do it?'

I tensed. This was difficult ground. 'I don't know, sir. I mean, Tony.'

'Sorry. That's an unfair question. But what do people say? Do they think he did it?'

Owen was a good rugby player, a prop-forward for the Junior Colts. But there had been trouble on the pitch earlier that year. A boy from another school had lost part of his ear in a ruck. There were teeth marks. Owen had been suspected, and for a few days his future at the school had been in doubt, but they were not sure enough of their ground to expel him. He had been dropped from the team, though.

'Nobody knows.'

'That's the thing with Owen, isn't it?' Tony said. 'You never know.'

'That's true.' Owen was a mystery but, unlike his father, I was quite happy to leave him that way. Most people were.

'Any girlfriends?'

'Owen?' I said, unable to suppress a smile.

'Fair point. What about Guy?'

'Now that's a different story. And a constantly changing one.'

Tony laughed, a thousand crinkles appearing around his bright blue eyes. He glanced appreciatively towards Mel, who was listening to Guy with rapt attention as he told some tall story about a mishap on the Cresta Run in Saint Moritz. 'Is she his current girl?'

'No.' I paused. 'At least, not yet.' But watching her, I was pretty sure Mel was hooked. So, I thought, was Tony.

'Well, I'm glad to see my son has good taste.' He smiled. 'This house was built to impress women. I hope it works for Guy.'

'Somehow I suspect it will.'

'What about you? How do you like Broadhill?'

To my surprise, I found myself answering Tony at some length. He wasn't at all bothered by my relatively humble background and he had a genuine interest in the school and how it worked. It was certainly not like talking to my own parents, but it wasn't quite like talking to a contemporary. The questions were less superficial, and there was none of the probing for image or status that goes on when two eighteen-year-old strangers talk. It was quite refreshing. I was charmed.

As the sun set red over the hills towards Nice, lighting up

the calm sea in a blaze of gold, we climbed some steps to a terrace above the pool for dinner. A goat's cheese salad and fish cooked in a delectable sauce, washed down with the best white wine I had ever tasted, it overwhelmed my senses. I was intensely conscious of the presence of Dominique beside me, so conscious I could barely turn my head towards her for fear of staring.

Eventually, she spoke to my shoulder. 'You are very quiet this evening.'

'Am I? I'm sorry.'

'Is everything all right?'

'Oh, yes,' I said, turning my head reluctantly towards her. 'This is all so . . . I don't know, lovely.'

For the first time I was able to look at her properly. She had an angular face and I noticed lines around the side of her mouth. She was probably in her late thirties. But still a stunner. Definitely a stunner. Although the sun had almost disappeared, she continued to wear sunglasses, so I had no idea what her eyes looked like. But her full lips were smiling. The body I had first stared at was now safely hidden under a yellow wrap.

'Is that book yours?' She nodded towards my beaten-up copy of *War and Peace*, which I had inappropriately brought with me down to the pool.

'Yes.'

'Boring.'

'It's not that bad, once you get into it,' I said.

'Boff. I thought it was boring. I prefer *Anna Karenina*, don't you? Now there is a woman I can spend a thousand pages with.'

'I haven't read it,' I said, surprised.

'Oh, but you must.' She laughed, a hoarse, throaty laugh. 'You look shocked. Why shouldn't I read *Anna Karenina*?'

'Er, I don't know.'

'You thought I was just a dumb model?'

Yes, I thought. 'No,' I said.

She laughed again. 'Yes you did. Well, I studied philosophy at the University of Avignon. The modelling was supposed to be a, how do you call it . . . sideline. But then my studies became the sideline.'

'That's a shame,' I said, without thinking.

'Why?'

'Er . . . I don't know,' I stammered, fearing I had been rude.

She laughed. 'I could at this moment be in an insurance office or something, putting little bits of paper into files. Is that what you mean?'

'No,' I said. 'But don't you regret it a little bit?'

'Sometimes. Not often. I have had some fun. A lot of fun. Do you have fun, David?'

'Well, um, I suppose so.'

'Oh, yes?'

I gulped at the wine, and then came to my senses. 'You're winding me up, aren't you?'

She laughed. 'I am. I love to corrupt the Englishmen. Unfortunately, when I had found Tony he had been corrupted already. It seems as if his son follows in his father's footsteps.'

At the other end of the table Mel's coolness was visibly melting as it was exposed to the combined charm of the father-and-son team, and Ingrid was smiling broadly, her eyes shining.

'He does have quite a reputation at school. I'd say he's a natural.'

'I can see he is. Abdulatif certainly seemed to appreciate him.'

'Is Abdulatif the gardener?'

'Yes. Delicious, isn't he? I love the way he walks around without his shirt.'

'But he likes men?'

'I think Abdulatif likes anything beautiful.'

I wasn't quite sure how to respond to that.

'And you?' she said. 'Are you a natural with the women?'

'I thought you'd stopped winding me up?'

'That is just. But you and Guy, you seem very different.'

'We are. We share a room at school, so I suppose we know each other pretty well. I was only the second choice to come out here, though.'

'Yes. Tony said that Guy was bringing Helmut Schollenberger's son with him.'

'That's right. Torsten.'

She shuddered. 'I detest that man. And before you ask, I have appeared in his magazines. Wearing less than perhaps I should. After my first marriage they discovered some old pictures.' She laughed. 'Actually, I didn't mind. But Henri? Ooh!'

'Who's Henri?'

'He's a politician. And he's so boring. I fell in love with his eyes. He had bedroom eyes, or he had them until we got married. Then they changed.'

'So you got rid of him?'

She shrugged. 'We got rid of each other.'

'And you met Tony?'

'I met Tony.' She smiled a slow smile. Not a smile of pleasure, more a smile of sadness, even pain, I thought.

'How long have you known him?'

'Aha. That, I cannot tell you.'

'Why not?'

'The divorce. Guy's mother would love to know.'

'Oh, I'm sorry. I didn't mean to pry.'

She laughed. 'But of course you did.'

Just then Owen, who had said nothing to anyone all evening, pushed his plate to one side, stood up, and made his way inside the house.

'Owen! Are you sure you don't want to stay?' his father called after him.

Owen paused and turned. 'No,' he said without a smile.

'All right. Well, good night, then.'

Owen grunted and turned away.

'Good night, *chéri*,' called Dominique to the back of Owen's hulking shoulders. Owen didn't break his stride to acknowledge her.

'He is strange, that one,' said Dominique. 'He has been here for two days and has said scarcely a word. He talks to me like I do not exist. Tony tries to speak to him, but he never says more than two words back. I think Tony has given up.'

'They haven't seen much of their father, have they, Guy and Owen?'

'No,' said Dominique. 'Tony's life does not mix with the kids. And Robyn, their mother, hates them to see him. She would not even let them come to our wedding. I had never met Guy until just now. But I think Tony was feeling guilty, so he persuaded Robyn to let them come here for a couple of weeks. Also, Guy is older. I suspect Tony and he have more in common these days.'

The servant cleared our plates, and Dominique poured another glass of wine. '*Mon Dieu*, my husband is enjoying himself, isn't he?' Mel and Ingrid were laughing uncontrollably at something he had just said. So too was Guy for that matter. Tony put his hand on Mel's arm to steady her, and left it there. She didn't draw away. Guy didn't seem to notice.

I didn't reply.

'To have two beautiful young girls hanging on your every

word. What more can a forty-six-year-old man want, eh, David?'

'I don't know,' I said neutrally.

'Huh.' She tossed back her hair. 'Miguel! Another bottle of wine!'

Eventually the night came to an end. I was pretty drunk. So was everyone else, with the possible exception of Ingrid. Guy and I lurched our way to the guest cottage, about twenty yards from the main house.

As I sat on my bed, the room spun. I concentrated on trying to force the window to stay in one place. Miraculously, I succeeded.

'I think I'm going to get lucky this week,' said Guy, as he collapsed on his bed.

'With the gardener? By the way, I heard he's called Abdulatif.'

'Ha bloody ha. No, with Mel, you cretin. Although I quite like Ingrid. I bet she's hot in bed. Maybe with both of them.'

'Guy!'

'OK. With Mel. You know, I'm pretty sure she's still a virgin.'

'That's what they say at school.'

'Yeah, but how would they know? You never really know until, well, you find out.'

'I suppose not.'

'But she's up for it. She's definitely up for it.'

'That's good,' I said without conviction.

Why was it always people like Guy who got the girls? Why didn't girls like Mel and Ingrid laugh at my jokes? Because I didn't have the confidence to make them, was one answer. Because I wasn't good looking, was another. There were no doubt many others. Mel, Guy, Tony, Dominique, Ingrid, even the gardener Abdulatif. All beautiful people. All using their natural gifts in an intricate dance of attraction and temptation, in which the steps consisted of a witty comment, a well-timed glance, a touch. On nights like that night, when sex hung in the air, I felt envious, frustrated and inadequate.

I think I must have fallen asleep, but only for an hour or so. I awoke feeling tense, drunk and hung over all at the same time. I could hear regular breathing from Guy's bed. My stomach didn't feel good, and I needed a pee, but my limbs felt so heavy I wasn't sure I had the strength to get out of bed.

The pain in my bladder worsened until it overcame my feebleness, and I crawled out of bed and staggered through to the bathroom. After I had finished I splashed my face and took a long drink of water. I still felt sick. I thought I would step outside in the hope that the night air would do me good.

It worked. A cool gentle breeze bathed my face. I was surrounded by the urgent communications of a thousand insects. I walked over to the marble railings and looked towards the black silhouette of Cap Ferrat against the shifting grey of the sea. I could make out the ruined watchtower in the gloom next to the lone olive tree, silently guarding the house as it had for centuries. The smell of salt and pine mingled in the air. I leaned over the railings and peered down to the small breakers below, and felt better.

I'm not sure how long I stayed there, slumped against the railings. I may even have fallen asleep. But I slowly became aware of voices in the house behind me. Angry voices. I stood up and strained to listen. It was Tony and Dominique. They were speaking French and I couldn't quite make out what they were saying. Until Dominique's voice rang through the garden towards me. '*Salaud! Une gosse! Tu as baisé une gosse!*' A door slammed and the garden returned to the sounds of the crickets and the wind in the trees and the waves.

'*Salaud! Une gosse! Tu as baisé une gosse!*' My addled brain scraped through my French vocabulary. It was all a bit colloquial for me. What the hell was a *gosse*? A goose, perhaps? Then I remembered *baiser* from a Molière play we had studied at school. Kiss. Tony had been kissing someone he shouldn't have. And somehow I doubted it was a goose. Hm.

I made my way back to my room and crawled into bed, wondering if what I thought had happened really had happened. Perhaps I had got completely the wrong end of the stick, like the time when I had confused the French word for vicar with that for virgin in a French dictation, with disastrous consequences. The words tumbled over and over in my increasingly disjointed mind until I lost consciousness.

5

I had never been sure I could trust Guy in the seventeen years I had known him and I wasn't sure I could trust him now. He was asking me to place my career, my savings, my whole future in his hands and, as so often in the past, he was tempting me.

Guy was like that.

When he had phoned me that afternoon, out of the blue, I had recognized the American-tinged public-school drawl immediately. He suggested we meet for a beer. It was seven years since I had decided I would be better off avoiding him. Seven years is a long time. Besides, I was bored and I was curious. So I agreed to meet him at the Dickens Inn in St Katherine's Dock.

I arrived early; I was eager to escape the office and the walk from Gracechurch Street had taken less time than I had anticipated. I ordered a pint of bitter at the bar and pushed through the heaving mass of bankers, commodity traders and the odd tourist to the door. The evening sun glanced off the smooth water of the dock and slapped against the sleek motor-yachts and sedate wooden sailing boats tethered there. The air was cool, but after a week of rain it felt good to be outside.

'Davo!'

Only one person called me Davo. I turned to see him shouldering his way through the scrum, a lithe figure in black jacket, T-shirt and jeans. 'Davo, how are you?'

'Great,' I said. 'How about you?'

'Large, Davo, large.' The blue eyes twinkled. He glanced inside the crowded pub. 'Jesus, doesn't anybody work any more?'

'I thought seven o'clock was a bit late for you?'

'Not these days.'

'Here, let me get you a beer.'

I fought my way back through the mob and returned with the brand of Czech beer that I knew Guy used to like. I noticed that he had moved a few feet away from the clump of drinkers outside the pub.

'Don't want to be overheard, eh?'

'Since you ask, no,' he said, taking a swig of his beer. 'So, you're a true City boy, now? Leipziger Gurney Kroheim. That's as fancy as they come, isn't it?'

'Not since the merger,' I said. 'A lot of the top people left Gurney Kroheim, and Leipziger is one of the more staid German banks.'

'But it's still a merchant bank, isn't it?'

'We're all called investment bankers now.'

'Are you enjoying it?'

I paused before answering the question. I had been proud to join the ancient and still-powerful institution of Gurney Kroheim four years before. But after it had been swallowed up by Leipziger Bank, one of the largest banks in Germany, it underwent reorganizations every six months or so. And somehow Project Finance, where I had ended up, had turned out to be a bit of a backwater. I usually put an optimistic face on things to people outside the bank. But not to Guy.

'Not really. I seem to do a lot of work and get little credit for it. The story of my life.'

'But they pay you well?'

'I suppose. Most of your pay these days comes from bonuses, and I don't get much of those. Not yet, anyway.'

Guy smiled sympathetically. 'Give it a couple of years.'

'Possibly. I'm not convinced. Leipziger is pretty bad at the moment. How about you? How's the acting? I've been looking out for you on the box but I haven't seen anything yet.'

'Then you obviously don't watch every episode of *The Bill*.'

'I can't imagine you as a cop,' I said, surprised.

'I wasn't even a villain. More a passer-by. But then I got the call from LA.'

I realized now that the trace of American in his accent was stronger than I remembered it.

'Hollywood, eh? I bet Brad Pitt was shaking in his shoes.'

'He coped. There's room in that town for Brad and me. Plenty of room. They wanted me for a movie: *Fool's Paradise*. Have you seen it?'

'No.'

'It got pretty bad reviews. Anyway, they wanted an English actor to speak three lines and snog Sandra Bullock. I was their man.'

'You snogged Sandra Bullock?'

'I did. It turned out it was the pinnacle of my career.'

I had to ask: I couldn't help myself. 'What was it like?'

Guy smiled. 'What can I say? It was a passionate scene. She's a great actress. The bad news was I got killed two minutes later.'

Sandra Bullock. I was impressed.

'I stayed in LA for a couple of years after that, hoping for a big break, but nothing happened. So I came back to London to try my luck.'

'Have you had any?'

'Not much.'

I wasn't completely surprised. Guy had the looks of a certain type of actor and I suspected that his charisma would translate well on to the screen. But I remembered the last time I had seen him, seven years ago, when he had just got out of drama school. His attitude then could hardly have been called professional.

'Still flying?' I asked.

'Sadly, no. Can't afford it these days. Dad isn't quite as understanding as he used to be. You?'

'Yeah, every now and then when the weather's OK. Still from Elstree.' It was Guy who had inspired me to take up flying. An expensive hobby, but one I enjoyed. 'How is your father? Do you see much of him these days?'

'Not much. You could say we've grown apart. Far apart.'

'Too bad,' I said. I didn't mean it. After what had happened in France, it wouldn't bother me if I never saw Tony Jourdan again.

I sipped my beer and waited.

'You and I haven't seen each other since, well, since Mull, have we?' Guy began hesitantly. 'What, six years ago?'

'No,' I said. 'And it was seven.'

Guy touched his nose unconsciously. I noticed a small bump, the only blemish in the symmetry of his face. A reminder of that day every time he looked in the mirror.

'I'd just like to say . . .' he paused and looked straight into my eyes. 'Well, I'm sorry. About what happened.'

'So am I,' I said. 'It's a long time ago now.'

Guy smiled with relief. 'A long time. Yeah, a long time.'

Guy hadn't changed. I knew I was being warmed up. 'You want something from me, don't you?'

'You cynic,' Guy said. Then he smiled sheepishly. 'But you're right, I do. I expect you're wondering why I rang you out of nowhere like that?'

'I was, actually.'

'There's something I want to talk to you about.'

I leaned back. 'I see. Talk.'

48

'I want to start an internet company.'

'You and a thousand other people.'

'It's where the money is.'

'Funny money. It's not real money. No one's made any real money out of the Internet yet.'

'I will,' said Guy, a quiet smile on his face.

'Oh, yes?' I smiled myself, at the idea of Guy as a thrusting entrepreneur.

'Yes. You can too, if you like.'

'Me?' Then the penny dropped. 'Guy, I might work for a merchant bank, but I don't have much money. And what I do have, I'm not going to throw into cyberspace.'

'No, I don't mean that. I mean I'd like you to join me.'

'Join you?' I laughed. But I saw he was serious. 'Guy, starting a business, even an internet business, is a big deal. You need financing, you need to employ people, you have to work. You have to get up before noon.'

'I can get up before noon,' said Guy. 'In fact, I've been working on this during every waking moment for the last month. I'm going to do it. And I'm going to make it work.'

I felt a little guilty. Perhaps I had been a touch patronizing. There was no way in hell I was going to work with Guy, but I thought it polite to let him have his say.

'OK. Tell me about it.'

'I'll give you the elevator pitch.'

'The elevator pitch?'

'Yeah. You have to be able to tell your story in the time it takes to ride an elevator with a venture capitalist. You don't have more than thirty seconds to catch these guys' attention.'

'Fine. Give me the elevator pitch,' I said, unable to keep the sarcasm out of my voice.

Guy ignored it, if he even noticed. 'The company is called ninetyminutes.com. It will be *the* brand for soccer on the web. We'll start out with the best football website on the Internet.

As we become well known, we'll sell sports clothing off the site, including our own brand. Football is big business and sports clothing is a thirty-billion-dollar market worldwide. We'll be to soccer what amazon.com is to books.'

He watched me, a smile of supreme confidence spreading across his face.

'*The* brand. You mean the number-one brand?'

'The only brand.'

I composed myself, pretending to take him seriously. 'That will make it quite a big company.'

'A very big company. An awesome company.'

'I see,' I said, maintaining my composure. 'That will also take some money.'

'Fifty million bucks to start. More later.'

'Hmm.'

'That's why I need you,' said Guy.

That was too much. I burst out laughing. 'You'd be lucky to get five hundred quid out of me.'

'No, stupid. I want you to help me raise the money.'

'You're the one with the rich friends.'

Guy's enthusiasm dropped a notch. 'I'll try them, of course,' he said. 'But I'm not sure how many of them I can count on. Most of them have already financed me in one way or another.'

'Oh, I see. And they didn't get much of a return?'

'Not much.'

We both knew what Guy meant. He had led an expensive lifestyle for quite a while with dwindling support from his father and little from his own earnings. He had borrowed from everyone he knew. The lenders had never really expected their money back. You spent money on Guy, you didn't invest in him.

'So why me?'

'I want someone who understands finance. Someone

who's solid. Someone I trust. Someone I've known for a long time and who knows me. You.'

I watched him. He was sincere. And I was flattered. I couldn't help it, I was flattered. Ever since school I had wanted Guy to count me as one of his friends and I had never been sure that he did. Now he said he needed me. Only me.

Then I pulled myself together. 'You want me to give up a secure job in one of the City's foremost banks for this? You've got to be crazy.'

Guy smiled. 'You hate your job, you told me so yourself. And it's not secure. Everyone gets fired these days. How do you know it won't be you next time they reorganize everything?'

I didn't answer, but shifted in my chair. He had hit a nerve. I glanced at him. He knew it.

'So who else is involved? You know sod all about computers.'

'I know a bit now. But Owen's over here with me. He'll help.'

'Owen?' I remembered Guy's brother. Whatever his faults, I couldn't deny his proficiency with computers.

'Yeah. He's spent the last six years in Silicon Valley. He joined a start-up that went bust, and then became a freelance programmer. He's worked on half a dozen different internet ventures. He knows his stuff.'

'All right. But what about the soccer angle? I know you're a Chelsea fan, but you're hardly an expert. And marketing? And you mentioned your own brand of clothing. Who's going to design it? Where will it be manufactured?'

'I'll get the people. That's my role. I'll get the people. Good people.'

'Who?'

'I'll find them. Don't forget, I'm starting with you.'

Flattery again. I had to admit Guy's confidence was impressive. But my mind had been trained to spot the holes in the most thorough of plans and this idea was full of them. 'What about the competition? There have to be some soccer websites out there already. And what about the TV companies? The cable companies?'

'We'll be faster than they are. While they're still drawing up their marketing budgets or whatever, we'll be up and running and grabbing eyeballs.'

I laughed. '"Grabbing eyeballs"? Sounds painful. What is this, gouge.com?'

'Sorry. I've been reading too many e-business books.'

'You have. And the fifty million bucks? Where will you get that? Do you even need fifty million?'

'Fifty million was just a guess. That's why I need you. To tell me how much we need and where we can get it from.'

'I'm not sure I can do that,' I said.

'Sure you can.'

He looked at me steadily. He meant it. Guy really thought that I could find him the money to put this thing together.

'You know what's really good about this idea?' he said.

'What?'

'The Americans can't do it. It's soccer. The Americans are incapable of understanding soccer. They can dominate everything else on the Internet, but they can't dominate this. If there is ever going to be a global soccer brand on the Internet, it's got to come from Europe.'

'That's true, I suppose.'

'Admit it. It's a good idea, isn't it?'

'I suppose it is,' I agreed. And it was. I couldn't deny the Internet was growing exponentially. And football was a huge source of entertainment for people throughout the world. But I couldn't quite see Guy as the man to take advantage of that.

'Look, you're dead right,' Guy went on. 'For this to work, someone is going to have to persuade a lot of talented people to take big risks for no guaranteed return. And I'm not just talking about employees. We'll need all kinds of partners: technology, marketing, content, merchandising, financial. *That's* where I come in. I can persuade people to do things they don't really want to do.'

'Can you?' I asked.

'Can't I?'

I drained my pint. I could feel myself getting sucked in, and I wanted to escape before it was too late. 'I've got to go.'

'Look at it this way, if it works, we'll make millions. If it fails, we'll have a lot of fun.'

'Goodbye, Guy.'

He pulled a brown A4 envelope out of a shoulder bag and thrust it into my hands. 'I'll call you tomorrow.'

I left him at the table and fought my way through the crowd of drinkers towards Tower Hill station. I looked for a litter-bin to toss the envelope into, but there weren't any around, so I stuffed it into my briefcase.

Me work for Guy? No chance.

6

I flopped into the only empty seat in the carriage. A miracle. Normally I didn't mind standing, but that morning I felt as if the world owed me a little something. Not much. Perhaps one journey a month sitting down for the price of my tube card. Travelling to work was always a nightmare. Travelling back wasn't so bad: I didn't usually leave the office until well after the crush had thinned.

I opened my briefcase to take out the *Financial Times* and saw the brown envelope Guy had stuffed into my hands the night before. I hesitated. I had planned to throw it away, but I was curious. Curious to see what had Guy so worked up, and curious to see what he was planning to do about it. Guy was certainly no businessman, so I wasn't expecting much. I pulled out the envelope and opened it. Inside was a neatly bound business plan of about twenty pages or so. I started to read.

It began with the two-page Executive Summary, which was much the same as Guy had described in his 'elevator pitch'. Then there were discussions of the potential market, revenue-generating models, competition, technology, implementation, and some very sketchy sections on management and financial analysis. With the exception of the last two sections, it was good. Very good. Every time a question popped into my mind, the answer appeared on the next page. Like a good novel, it drew me in. It was carefully researched and, apart from a couple of grandiose claims on the first page, it was understated, which made it more powerful. I was surprised by the quality of the work and a little ashamed at my earlier underestimation of its author.

I was three-quarters of the way through when my train pulled into Bank. I fought my way through London's most labyrinthine underground station to the surface and headed for my usual coffee shop. Rather than taking the cappuccino away, I decided to drink it at a stool by the window and finish the report.

Most start-ups failed. I knew that. The Internet was all hype, I knew that too. I was a banker, good at my job, known for my high standards of work. I could enumerate the risks, spot the downside. This wasn't the kind of business that a bank like Gurney Kroheim, sorry, *Leipziger* Gurney Kroheim, should get involved in. My considered opinion should be to politely turn the proposal down.

I put the report to one side and sipped my coffee, watching thickening crowds rushing along the pavements outside. The trouble was, at that moment, I didn't want to be a banker. Guy was talking about a dream. About a spark of an idea that could become a vision, then a small group of dedicated people, then a real company, and then . . . who knew?

There was definitely a market opportunity. During the 1990s English football had transformed itself into a money-spinning machine with the conversion of the First Division into the Premier League, the flotation of a number of clubs on the stock market and above all the heavy investment in TV rights by satellite companies. Everyone knew the Internet was going to change everything, even if they didn't know exactly how. Guy's plan to capitalize on this opportunity made a lot of sense. Would I, as a diligent Gurney Kroheim banker, have backed Bill Gates? Or Richard Branson? Or any of the billionaires that were springing up all over Silicon Valley? No. Because David Lane, Vice-President, Project Finance, didn't have that kind of vision or imagination.

At Broadhill I had caught a glimpse of a wide variety of exciting lives. The children of actors, sports stars, millionaire entrepreneurs all suggested that there was much more to be done in life than get a job, a wife and a mortgage. Then at university the world had narrowed. I graduated during a recession, when the best and the brightest competed hard to become chartered accountants. I had competed too, succeeded, qualified as a Fellow of the Institute of Chartered Accountants, and then joined a merchant bank. The City had its glamour, I knew, but it was not to be found in the Project Finance Department of Gurney Kroheim. Sure there was travel, and that was interesting, and I found much of the work intellectually challenging, but where was it leading? To a wife, as yet unidentified, and mortgage in Wandsworth? Was that so bad? Isn't that what I had worked for since leaving school?

Guy was right, it would be fun to work with him. I had admired him at school. We had had difficult times together in France, and then again in London when he was a struggling actor and I a soon-to-be-qualified accountant. More than difficult. But despite these the idea of spending the next few years with him tempted me. Of course he had let me down in the past. And he came from a world totally different from mine. But that was the point. I could give him the stability he needed and he could give me, well, excitement. Although in theory my career was steadily moving upwards, it didn't feel like that. It felt like it was going nowhere. With Guy, something would happen. Something that would shake up my life. Whether it would be good, or bad, or both, I did not know. But I wanted to find out.

There is a premise that underlies almost all financial theory and it is this: a rational investor will avoid uncertainty. At that moment, I didn't feel like a rational investor.

I finished my coffee and sauntered towards the office, brushed on either side by workers more eager than me to reach their desks.

When it had built its Gracechurch Street offices in the 1960s, Gurney Kroheim had been a major power in the City. Since then it had become a minnow. As I walked through the lobby, I instinctively searched out Frank, the commissionaire who had guarded this entrance since my first day in the bank and for a few decades before then. His memory for names and faces was legendary and outdid any database in Human Resources or Marketing. But he had been pensioned off the week before to be replaced by a tattooed operative with an earring from an outside security firm who looked as if his previous assignment had been in Wormwood Scrubs rather than Threadneedle Street.

The third floor, my floor, had also changed in the last year. The Project Finance Department was now four desks tacked on to the end of a larger entity known as Specialized Finance. Teams of specialists in the funding of ships, aircraft, films, local government, and oil and gas were grouped together in an uneasy alliance. There had been a time when Gurney Kroheim had excelled in all these fields. But since the merger most of the best people had left to be replaced not by Germans, but by either outside hires or people from the second-tier US investment bank that Leipziger had swallowed a few months after Gurney Kroheim. My own group, Project Finance, had consisted of ten people. The best six had gone, leaving my nice but ineffective boss, Giles, in charge of a rump of three of us. We hadn't closed a deal in six months.

I powered up my computer and, with my cup of coffee already drunk, got down to work. Work was a huge spreadsheet, a computer model of all the flows of gas, steam, electricity and money in and out of a proposed electric cogeneration plant in Colombia. It was a gigantic beast, literally thousands of numbers all linked together that attempted to recreate all the variables involved in building, financing and operating the plant. I had started the model on my laptop computer six months before when Giles and I had visited the Swiss offices of the firm that was bidding to construct the plant. The thing had grown since then; grown, but still remained under my control. If you wanted to change the dollar–peso exchange rate in 2002, I could do it. Oil prices falling in 2005? No problem. Borrowing in fixed-rate Swiss francs rather than floating-rate dollars? Give me a minute and I'll print off six pages analysing the results.

Working on a computer model like that for as long as I had, I had developed a good feel for the key variables of the project: those risks that mattered and those that didn't. Giles and I had come up with what we thought was an ingenious financial structure that would allow our client to put in the lowest bid for the contract.

Giles came in, pink shirt, loud tie and sharp pinstriped suit beneath a dull brain.

'Morning,' I said.

'Oh, morning, David,' he said nervously.

I looked up sharply. Bosses shouldn't be nervous, certainly not at eight-thirty in the morning.

His eyes dodged mine and moved to his own computer.

'Giles?'

'Yes?'

'What's up?'

Giles looked at me, looked backed at his computer, real-ized there was no refuge there, and let his shoulders sag.

'Giles?'

'They've pulled their bid.'

'What do you mean?'

'I mean the Swiss have pulled their bid. They are convinced they won't win. Apparently the Americans have the best local partners, and our boys have lost confidence in their own people. You know what Colombia's like.'

'No! I don't believe it.' I glanced at my spreadsheet. At the box-files stacked three feet high and two feet wide beside my desk. 'So we just drop it?'

'I'm afraid so, David. You know how it is. We only get paid if we back a winner.'

'So I was right. Remember when we first saw them in Basel? I told you they were flaky then. They never were serious about making a bid.'

'We don't know that. Look, I know you've done a lot of work on this, but you have to get used to these things not coming off.'

'Oh, I'm getting used to it all right. This is, what, the fifth in a row?'

Giles winced. 'It will give us a chance to look at that sewage project in Malaysia. We can go to Dusseldorf on Friday and pin the deal down.'

'Pin the deal down! Face it, Giles, you've never pinned a deal down.'

I had gone too far. I was right, of course, but because I was right I shouldn't have said it. Giles appeared more hurt than angry.

'Sorry,' I said.

Giles closed his eyes for a couple of seconds, wincing under the strain. Then he opened them. 'Get Michelle to book those flights, will you?'

We sat there staring at each other. We'd never get the Malaysian deal. I knew it and Giles knew it. Suddenly everything became very clear.

'Giles.'

'Yes?'

'I resign.'

7

July 1987, Côte D'Azur, France

I awoke about nine, with the worst hangover I had ever experienced in my short drinking career. Guy was still asleep and I tried to stay in bed, but once I had woken up there was no going back. Besides, I needed to do something about my head. I wasn't sure what – water, coffee, food, pills – but I had to do something.

I pulled on a T-shirt and some shorts and staggered out of the guest cottage. The morning sunshine was absurdly bright, and I stood still for a full minute with my eyes shut, gently swaying. Delicately I opened them, and saw that the table we had eaten at the night before was now laid for breakfast. Ingrid was sitting there, with some coffee and croissants. I stumbled over to her.

'Morning,' she said.

' . . .' I opened my mouth and no sound came out. I tried again. 'Morning.' It was a hideous croak.

Ingrid tried to suppress a smile. 'Are you always this sprightly in the morning?'

'God,' I said. 'I'm never going to drink Pimm's again. How come you look so good?'

And she did. She was wearing a light denim dress. Her skin shone golden in the morning sunlight, and her pale-blue eyes smiled at me. 'Practice.'

'Really?'

'Actually, not really. I think I must have a good head for

it. I got myself in quite a lot of trouble last year over drinking so I try to stay clear of it.'

'Trouble? What kind of trouble?'

'Big trouble. I got thrown out of Cheltenham Ladies' College.'

'You did?' That explained why she had arrived at Broadhill in the middle of the A-level syllabus. I squinted at her in the strong morning sunlight. 'You don't look much like a Cheltenham Lady to me.'

'I beg your pardon? You haven't seen me in my uniform.'

'That's true.' Broadhill didn't have a uniform. Or rather it did, but it was imposed by the pupils and was far too complicated to be written down. I wasn't even sure I understood it. Guy did, of course. So did Mel. 'I bet your parents were proud of you.'

'I think my mother thought it was quite funny. My father was furious, though. And since my mother doesn't talk to my father her support didn't help much. It was a bit unfair. It was a first offence and it was my birthday.'

'And Broadhill didn't mind?'

'You know they have an appeal going for a new library?'

'Yes.'

'They got quite a large anonymous donation.'

'Ah.'

The young North African gardener appeared on the other side of the pool and began weeding. Shirtless. Ingrid happily watched him, but I closed my eyes. The sun shone pink through my lids. A grasshopper started up somewhere very close. I winced. 'Is anyone else up?'

'Mel's awake, but she's still getting herself ready. She's in a pretty bad way too. I haven't seen Tony or Dominique. Or Owen. What about Guy?'

'Asleep. Where did these come from?' I asked, glancing at the croissants.

'Miguel. Here he is.'

And he was. 'Orange juice, monsieur?' he said, bearing a large jug of the stuff.

'Yes, please.'

He poured me a glass and I drained it, realizing that it was orange juice I craved. The cold sweet liquid made me feel very slightly better. Miguel understood and refilled the glass.

He noticed Ingrid's glass was almost empty. '*A senhorita aceita um pouco mais?*'

'*Sim, por favor.*' He filled it. '*É o suficiente. Obrigada.*'

'*De nada.*'

'What the hell was that?' I asked, as he withdrew.

'Miguel's Portuguese,' she said.

'Of course. Silly me.' I sipped some more juice. 'I can't get over this place, can you? I mean having someone bringing you your breakfast in the morning.' Then I paused. I really had no idea what Ingrid's background was. 'Sorry. Perhaps you're used to it. You probably have a dozen places like this.'

She saw my hesitation and laughed. 'You're right. This is a nice place.'

'Where do you live?'

'That's quite difficult to answer. And you?'

'Easy. Northamptonshire. England. How can it be difficult to answer?'

'It assumes that you have a family. I have several families. And each one has several houses.'

'Sounds very grand.'

'Actually, it's a pain in the arse.'

'Oh. What kind of name is Ingrid Da Cunha anyway? It sounds like an island off the coast of Sweden.'

Ingrid laughed. A little too loudly for my head. 'I feel like an island off the coast of Sweden. Perhaps that's a good description of me. It's actually Ingrid Carlson Da Cunha. My mother is Swedish, my father's Brazilian. I was born in London so I actually have a British passport. I've lived in Tokyo, Hong Kong, Frankfurt, Paris, São Paulo and New York. Broadhill is my ninth, and I hope last, school. Believe me, I would love to be able to say that I'd lived in one place for the last eighteen years.'

I didn't believe her. Her background sounded impossibly glamorous to me. I rubbed my temples. 'How long does it take for a hangover to go away?'

'A week, I think,' said Ingrid.

'That's not funny. A week of this and I'll be dead.'

Ingrid smiled with amusement, tinged with just a little sympathy.

Then I remembered what I had overheard last night. 'I suppose you speak a lot of languages?'

'A few.'

'Is one of them French?'

'It's supposed to be. I've just done my French A level.'

'Do you know what "*gosse*" means?'

'Yes. It's slang. For a child. Or a kid.'

'Oh. And just to make sure I haven't got something wrong, "*baiser*" means "to kiss", doesn't it?'

Ingrid laughed. 'It used to. But not any more.'

'Not any more?' Suddenly I remembered the giggling that followed Madame Renard's explanation of the meaning during that French lesson a couple of years before. 'Oh, God. It means *fuck*, doesn't it?'

Ingrid nodded.

'Ah.' This was more serious than I had feared.

The smile had disappeared from Ingrid's face. 'Why do you ask?'

'I heard it last night.' Ingrid was looking at me oddly. 'Did you hear anything?'

'No,' she said. 'But I think some people were doing more than just saying it.'

'Yes.'

We sat in silence for a moment.

'So where did you hear it?' Ingrid asked.

'It was the middle of the night. As you can tell, I'd had a bit too much to drink, so I went out into the garden for some air. I heard shouting. It was Dominique. She was screaming at Tony: "*Salaud! Une gosse! Tu as baisé une gosse!*"' I hesitated. There was really only one conclusion.

I glanced at Ingrid, afraid to voice my thoughts. Did she know? It was hard to tell. Her face was impassive. But she was watching me, too.

'Tony slept with Mel last night, didn't he?' I ventured.

Ingrid nodded slowly.

'I can't believe it. What a perv!' Teenage boys like to think that there is nothing about sex that can shock them. But Tony was somebody's father, a parent. It seemed unnatural. It seemed wrong. 'But his wife was right there in the house!'

'I know,' said Ingrid. 'And it sounds like she's guessed what he was up to. Hold on,' she whispered. 'Here's Mel.'

Mel crept out on to the terrace from the house. She looked dreadful. Her face was a grey shade of off-white and her eyes were red and puffy. She had applied lipstick and some black eye shadow, but that just made her look worse.

'Hi,' I said.

'Hi.' She sat down and dived for the coffee. I didn't know what to say. She didn't say anything. So the three of us sat in silence.

Feeling a little better for my breakfast, I went for a swim in the pool. The cold water felt wonderful. There was life after alcohol after all. I was joined by an energetic Tony, who did thirty lengths at a disgusting speed. After a few minutes,

Guy appeared. He dived in, keeping up with his father stroke for stroke. It seemed obscene to me to see them both striving to outdo each other in the water after what Tony had done with his son's girlfriend the night before. It was almost as if the night's activities had given Tony a shot of unnatural energy. Unlike the dazed and bleary-eyed Mel, who was still nursing a cup of coffee on the terrace.

I left them to get on with it, pulled myself on to a chair by the pool and closed my eyes, letting the sun do its stuff.

Around midday Guy roused me. 'Come on! Get your clothes. We're going to a restaurant in Monte Carlo. Then we're off to the beach in the afternoon.'

I grunted and did as I was told, not quite sure whether I was up to a big lunch and the alcohol that would probably go with it. Everyone was milling around in the large hallway. Dominique had appeared, wearing her sunglasses and acting as though nothing had happened the night before. The only person not present was Owen. Guy said he was plugged in to his portable computer and didn't want to join us. That bothered nobody.

'OK, let's go,' said Tony. 'We can all squeeze into the Jeep.'

'I'll take my car,' said Dominique.

'If you like.'

'I can take someone with me,' she turned to me. 'David?'

I was a little surprised that she had picked me. I would have preferred to go with the others and slump in silence in the back; I wasn't sure I was up to making conversation with Dominique that morning. But I didn't want to be impolite. 'OK,' I said.

We all trooped outside, Tony pulled up in the Jeep and everyone but me piled in. Dominique had gone back inside for something. Tony waited a few seconds, muttering to himself, and then started the engine.

'Sorry, David, she's always late for everything. We should go on ahead. Do you want to come with us?'

I hesitated a moment. 'No, I'd better wait for her,' I said eventually, deciding that that was the least rude thing to do.

'OK. Tell her we've gone to the usual place. See you there!' and the Jeep shot off up the driveway.

I waited a couple of minutes and then went inside myself. 'David!'

I heard Dominique's voice calling from the living room. I went in. She was drinking from a large crystal tumbler of clear liquid.

'Do you want some?'

'What is it?'

'Vodka. It's cold.'

I shook my head. 'Not after last night.'

She laughed. 'Do you have a headache?'

I nodded.

'Well, have some, then. It will do you good. I promise you'll feel much better.'

'I don't believe you.'

She poured a large amount of vodka into a tumbler and handed it to me. 'Here. Try it.'

I looked at her doubtfully. What the hell, I thought, and took a big slug. The ice-cold liquid turned to fire as it hit the back of my throat, and I scowled.

'Wait a moment,' she said, smiling. 'It won't take long.' She watched me, as I held the tumbler awkwardly. 'Well?'

It was true, I did feel slightly better as the vodka entered my bloodstream.

'Have some more. *Salut!*' She drained her glass and refilled it. Under her watchful eyes, I drank more from mine.

'Shouldn't we be going?'

'There is no hurry. This is France. In any case, Tony always complains I'm late for everything.'

'OK,' I said, not quite knowing what to do. We were standing a couple of feet apart. She was wearing a loose white dress, and her blonde hair was tied back behind her neck. She had taken off her sunglasses. Her eyes rested on me as she drank. I wasn't sure what to do or where to look. I could feel the warmth in my face; I didn't know if it was from the vodka or the embarrassment or both. I gulped some more of my drink nervously. In the end, my eyes ran out of other places to look and I met hers. They were blue. There was something odd about them, but I didn't have time to work out what.

She moved towards me.

I let her come. She brushed my lips with hers. Then she put her arms around my neck and pulled me down to her. Her tongue was coarse and she smelled of perfume and tobacco; to me at that moment a heady, adult smell. Eventually, she broke away.

'Come,' she said.

She led me up the stairs by the hand, like a child. We passed through her enormous bedroom, dominated by a large unmade bed, and out on to a balcony. The blue of sea and sky surrounded us. My heart beat fast. My throat was dry.

She kept her eyes on me, those strange eyes. She reached behind her back, undid something and wriggled. Her dress fell to the ground showing her body, naked apart from some tiny panties. I had never seen a real, breathing, three-dimensional woman's body before, and certainly never one like this. I could scarcely breathe. I stretched out a hand towards her. She placed it on her breast. I felt the nipple spring hard under my fingers.

'Come here, David.'

8

I paused at the top of the steps and glanced at the traditional red-and-white striped pole. I was in a narrow alley behind the Bank of England. In front of me, crammed into a basement, was the barber's shop I had visited every six weeks or so for the previous three years. Except that it was only a fortnight since I had been there last.

I took a deep breath, descended the steps and pushed open the door.

Within five minutes I was in the chair, examining my hair in the mirror. Short. Slightly curly. Not fashionable, but not unfashionable either.

'The usual, sir?'

'No, George. I'll have a number two all over.'

I had been mumbling the phrase to myself all morning. I had rejected a number one as just being a little too final.

The Greek Cypriot barber raised his heavy eyebrows, but said nothing and reached for his electric clippers. He fiddled with attachments and switched it on. The buzz made my heart rate soar. In the mirror I saw him hold the vibrating clippers just above my head. He caught my eye and smiled. Sweat poured from my armpits. Get a grip, I thought. This is only hair. It will regrow. I smiled back.

He lunged. I closed my eyes. The noise increased. I braced myself for the pain of hair being ripped from my scalp, but the sensation was more like a brief, intense massage. I opened my eyes again. A swathe of stubbled skin bisected my hair where my parting used to be. It was like an inverted Mohican. George's smile widened.

There was no going back now.

Wapping High Street wasn't much of a high street. More a lane between converted warehouses, or modern apartment blocks made to look like converted warehouses. There was little traffic, no pedestrians, but plenty of grinding and chugging from the construction equipment hidden behind hoardings.

I found Malacca Wharf and took the lift to the second floor.

'Nice haircut,' Guy said as he opened the door.

'I knew you'd like it.' I pushed past him into the flat. Half of the small living room was taken up with a pine table, groaning under the weight of computers and piles of paper. Owen's bulk was hunched over a keyboard, tapping away. He looked little different from when I had last seen him several years before, except that the hair peeking out beneath his baseball cap was dyed an unlikely shade of white-blond.

'Hello, Owen.'

He glanced up at me for a moment. 'Hi,' he responded in his high-pitched voice.

'What do you think?' Guy said. 'This is ninetyminutes.com's global HQ.'

'Impressive. And where's my office?'

'Just here.' Guy indicated a chair at the table, opposite a pile of paper.

'Very nice.'

'Good view, though, don't you think?'

I walked over to the French windows that opened on to a small balcony. The Thames rushed past brown and turbulent, and on the opposite side of the river more converted warehouses stared back at us.

'Why do you live here? Not much going on, is there?'

'It's Dad's place. An investment he bought a while ago. He's trying to kick me out, but I won't go.'

'You said you two weren't getting on.'

'We're not. We have as little to do with each other as possible.'

'Ah.'

I realized that that meant more than just Guy having to curtail his spending habits. It meant that the most obvious source of finance for ninetyminutes.com had already dried up. I'd find out more about that later.

Guy went through to the tiny kitchen and began making coffee. 'How did they take it at Gurney Kroheim?'

'My boss didn't like it at all,' I said. 'I was quite touched, actually. He tried to plead with me at first, but he gave up after a few minutes. He said I was better off out of it. Poor guy. I don't give him long.' Giles was history and he knew it. The next reorganization would see him whited out of the Specialized Finance organogram. I hoped he would find another job.

'Much better job security here,' said Guy.

'Of course,' I replied with a wry grin. I took off my jacket and hung it on the back of my chair. 'So. What do we do?'

Guy started talking. And talking. It was like a dam bursting. He had obviously been thinking of nothing else for weeks and he was desperate for someone to share those thoughts with. Owen wasn't exactly right for the job, but I was. Guy was clearly glad to have me around. It made me feel needed and totally involved right from the outset.

The first thing to do was to get the ninetyminutes.com website up and running. Guy had a pretty good idea of what he wanted to put on it. There was the basic stuff: match reports, news, photos, player profiles, statistics, different sections for each club, the kind of things every soccer website needed. Then there were the things that Guy hoped would make Ninetyminutes different: gossip, chat, humour, cartoons to start with. And later betting, a fantasy football game, video clips, and the ultimate prize: e-commerce. Once we had attracted visitors to the site, we would begin selling merchandise: clothing, mugs, posters, anything and everything the football fan could want. Stage three would be to design our own range of clothing and other products to push through the site.

It was amazing how much of all this could be done by outsiders. Owen was working on the technical specifications of the site, making sure that it was 'scalable', in other words it could grow as the traffic and complexity increased. But outside companies would provide us with the software and hardware we needed, and a design consultancy would help us with the all-important look and feel of the website itself. News, photos and statistics could be downloaded in digital form from press agencies and then manipulated however we wanted.

This left the all-important question.

'Who's going to write all this?' I asked. 'The opinions, the humour, the chat? Are we going to leave it all to Owen?'

'Ha ha,' said Owen, his only contribution to the conversation so far.

Guy smiled. 'Come and look.'

He hit some keys on his computer and a sheet of bright purple flashed on his screen. The words 'Sick As A Parrot' in a shaky font were emblazoned on it in green.

'Nice title,' I said. 'And lovely graphics.'

'I know, I know. But take a look.'

I looked, clicking on stories about the latest England manager, a volatile Arsenal striker, the rumoured transfer of a French international to Liverpool. There were articles about grounds, commentators, notorious supporters, the businessmen behind the clubs, what had happened to the star players in the previous year's World Cup in France. There was a whole section comparing the tactics of the Premier League teams in terms that even I could understand. It was brilliantly written. Witty in places, opinionated in others, every piece was concise, clear and interesting.

'This guy knows his stuff,' I said. 'That is, assuming it is all one guy.'

'Oh, it is.'

'What's his name? Gaz?' I said, peering at the screen.

'His full name is Gary Morris and he lives in Hemel Hempstead.'

'But who's behind it?'

'No one. Just him. It's an unofficial site. He probably has a day job, but spends the rest of his waking life watching football and reading and writing about it.'

'So what do we do?'

'It's our first corporate acquisition, Mr Bigshot. We're going to buy Sick As A Parrot.'

'For how much?'

'I don't know. A pint of lager and a packet of peanuts? We won't find out until we meet Gaz.'

'And when are we going to do that?'

Guy looked at his watch. 'In about two hours.'

Number 26 Paget Close was a white pebbledashed terraced house in a row of white pebbledashed terraced houses. We opened the low wooden gate and stepped carefully through a tiny, immaculately kept front garden. A plastic ginger cat guarded the door. Guy rang the bell. It chimed sweetly.

A small but stout woman with tight grey curls appeared.

Guy hesitated for a moment, but he recovered quickly. 'Mrs Morris?' he asked with his best smile, which was generally recognized as a pretty good smile.

The woman glowed. 'Yes.'

'Is your son in?'

'You're the people from the internet company, aren't you?'

'That's right,' said Guy. 'I'm Guy Jourdan, Chief Executive, and this is my Finance Director, David Lane.'

'Come in, come in. Make yourselves at home. Gary's still at work, but he should be back any minute now.' She led us through to a small living room. 'Can I get you a drink?' And then hastily, to make sure we hadn't misunderstood her: 'A cup of tea, perhaps?'

Guy and I sank into a deep chintz-covered sofa while Mrs Morris busied herself in the kitchen. Then we heard the front door open and close and a male voice call 'Hi, Mum!'

'Those internet people are here to see you, dear.'

Gaz appeared. He was a thin man in his early twenties, dressed in light blue shirt and blue trousers with red piping. A postman. Guy was wearing black jeans and a lightweight black polo-necked jersey. I was in an old denim shirt and crumpled green trousers. We all sat down on the three-piece suite and the takeover battle began.

He was no fool, Gaz. Guy started on some spiel about how ninetyminutes.com was a leading European internet holding company, when Gaz stopped him.

'You're just two blokes with some bullshit, aren't you? I know all the footie websites, and ninetyminutes.com isn't one of them.' He had a prominent Adam's apple that wobbled up and down as he talked, and he spoke with a sub-cockney accent. But he was right. 'So how much will you pay me for Sick As A Parrot? Cash on the table.'

Guy smiled. 'I discussed this with my finance man this morning, and we've got an opening offer.' He looked across to me. We had discussed a price on the way, but I thought it was far too early to put it on the table. I decided to give Guy the benefit of the doubt and nodded sagely.

'A pint of lager and a packet of peanuts,' Guy said, with a smile. 'That's just a down payment, of course. There's more to follow.'

Gaz frowned, then returned the smile. 'That'll get you to the table. Let's go and discuss this properly.' He stood up and called down the hallway. 'We're just going out, Mum!'

Mrs Morris rushed to the door to hold it open for us, and fluttered her eyelashes at Guy.

'Nice cat, Mrs Morris,' said Guy as he passed the plastic mog.

'Oh, thank you. I do like cats. We'd have a real one, but Gary's allergic.'

'Bye, Mum,' said Gaz, escaping through the wooden gate.

We continued the discussion in the pub around the corner. Guy bought Gaz his promised pint of lager, and he got one for himself and his Finance Director as well.

'Sorry about the bullshit, Gaz,' he said. 'It's what I do. I'll give you the real scoop in a moment. But before that, tell me about the site.'

Gaz was happy to talk. He was proud of his work, as well he should have been. 'I started it two years ago. At first it was nothing more than a home page. Then it sort of developed a following all by itself. I adapted it into a proper-looking site, people told other people about it, pretty soon it had more or less taken me over.'

'How many visitors do you get?'

'About a hundred thousand a month, last time I checked.'

'Wow. It must take a lot of time to keep it up.'

'It does. I spend almost all my free time on it. I don't get much sleep. But I enjoy it.'

'It's very good,' said Guy.

'I know,' said Gaz.

'I can tell you're an Arsenal fan. Why didn't you just do an Arsenal site?'

'There are two types of people who like football,' Gaz replied. 'The tribal type, who are looking for a grouping to give them some kind of identity, and those who just love the game. I'm not writing for the tribal type. Sure, it makes it much more interesting if you support one team or another, but I'm just as happy watching and writing about teams other than Arsenal. More happy: it's easier to be objective.'

'And do you design the website yourself?'

'Yeah. That's no problem. I studied physics and philosophy at uni, so I can get my head around a computer. At first I did the whole thing from scratch in HTML, but these days you get packages like Dreamweaver that make it all pretty easy anyway. Don't get me wrong,' Gaz said. 'I'm not a geek. It's football I love. It's just that I understand computers and that's how I tell people about football.'

'So if you've got a degree in physics and philosophy, how come you're a postman?' I asked.

'I like being a postman,' Gaz replied defensively. 'It gives me time to do what I like to do. And funnily enough knowing about Wittgenstein and the theory of matter didn't seem to impress the recruitment people.'

'It should have done,' I said.

'OK, OK. But where did you learn to write like that?' Guy asked.

'I've always written, ever since I was a kid. It comes naturally, especially when I'm writing about football. It's like I'm compulsive. I just have to get it down.' He sipped his beer. 'What about you? Tell me what your real story is.'

Guy talked about his plans for ninetyminutes.com and for its growth. He admitted Ninetyminutes would need a lot of money to get off the ground, and that we hadn't raised any of it yet.

Gaz listened hard.

'What do you think?' Guy asked him.

'You've read my site?'

'Yes.'

'Then you know my views on the commercialization of football.'

'Yes.'

'Well?'

'Do you like living at home?' Guy asked.

'It's all right, I suppose.'

'Wouldn't you like your own place within walking distance of Highbury? Wouldn't you like to write this stuff during the working day instead of at night or at weekends?'

'Yes. But I don't want to sell out. All the commercial sites are crap. They're all pushing this TV station, or that football shirt. You can't say the chairman is a wanker if he's the one paying your salary. Or if his best mate is.'

'That's the point,' said Guy. 'The commercial sites are all crap. But so are the unofficial ones too. Even yours.'

Gaz raised his eyebrows. He wasn't expecting this.

'The design's crap. Sorry, but it is.'

The colour rose in Gaz's thin cheeks. He slammed his pint down on the pub table. 'What's wrong with the design?'

'Gaz, we're not here because of your eye for colour, or your sense of perspective. We're here because you write the best stuff on the net and off it. But you need more. You need a good site design, you need a PR and marketing campaign so millions of people will hear about it, you need hardware that can deal with the traffic, you need people working for you who can write the stories you want in the way you want. You need someone to pay those people, you need someone to pay you, you need an office, a computer, time to think, time to watch football.

'This site is going to be what you make it, Gaz. And it's going to be big. And I'm sorry, but you're going to make a shit-load of money out of it too.'

Gaz was listening. I watched his face. I could see Guy's magic working on it. 'OK. So, what's the deal?'

'Twenty thousand quid up front and five per cent of the shares of the company.'

Gaz looked from Guy to me. We let him think.

'Thirty.'

'Twenty-five.'

'Done.' Gaz held out his hand. Guy shook it. 'And another pint of lager.'

'So, what do you think, Davo? Six hours in the job, and we've already done our first deal.' We were zipping down the outside lane of the M1 in Guy's electric-blue ten-year-old Porsche, roof down, stereo and wind loud in our ears.

'I tell you, that's more than I did at Gurney Kroheim in the last year,' I said. 'But I couldn't believe that bullshit you gave him at first! People aren't going to fall for that, Guy.'

Guy smiled. 'Precisely. He was expecting bullshit, so I gave it to him. Then he had a chance to see through it and I could make the real story more credible.'

'Wasn't that a bit risky?' I said. 'Don't we want him to think he can trust us?'

'Oh, he'll trust us now. But remember what he's looking to us for. He wants us to talk the talk. He can't do that. I wanted to show him that we can do his bullshit for him. And it worked, didn't it?'

'It did. Not bad.'

'There are some advantages to an actor's training.'

'So I see.' It was clear that Guy's finely honed skills in manipulating people were going to come in handy in the months ahead.

Guy slowed as he spied a police car on the inside lane.

'You know,' I said, 'at some point soon we've got to talk about money.'

'Money?'

I leaned forward and turned the Gallagher brothers down. 'Yes. Like, how much of it do we have?'

'I've got zip in my account. I think Owen's got about thirty k left in his.'

I winced. 'Which he's willing to give to Gaz?'

'Absolutely. Owen's willing to put everything he's got into this. We both are. In fact we both have. Owen's already put over twenty thousand in.'

'And you?'

'Well, as you can guess, I had less. But that's all gone too. What about you?'

'I think I can put in forty thousand.'

Guy slowed a fraction, and turned to me. 'Forty? Is that all? Come on, Davo, if you're in, you're in. You can't keep nest eggs on one side.'

'Forty thousand is all of my savings. Or nearly all. It will leave me with a few thousand to get through the next few months. I told you I wasn't seeing any of the big bonuses at Gurney Kroheim. And my place in Notting Hill is mortgaged up to the hilt.'

'OK, Davo, I believe you,' said Guy. 'And the forty is good. Very good.'

'But we need more money.'

'Right.' Guy slowed as he entered the slip road off the motorway. The traffic thickened.

'What about your father?'

Guy shook his head. 'No.'

'You mean "no you won't ask him", or "no he'd say no"?'

'I mean both.'

'You've got to try.'

'I can't, Davo. I've asked him for money so many times in the past. At first he used to give it to me. I think he liked the idea of me having a good time. Plus he felt guilty about what happened in France. Neither of us really got over that, as you know.'

Guy drove on in silence, embroiled in his own thoughts. I didn't interrupt him; France was a topic I wanted to stay well clear of.

Then he came back to the present. 'Dad paid for my flat in London, he paid for drama school, he paid for me to go to Hollywood. Remember the Cessna I used to fly? Golf Juliet? He paid for that. And there's all kinds of other stuff.'

'But this is different.'

'That's the point. This *is* different. This time I'll use that money properly. But I've fed him so many stories over the years, I don't want this to be another one. If I tell him I'm going to start an internet company, he'll laugh in my face. Worse than that, he won't even laugh. He'll just look disappointed.

'And I wouldn't blame him. I know I've pissed away the last few years. Sure I've had a good time, but I've never actually achieved anything at all. I used to think Dad was cool because he knew how to have fun. But at least he'd earned the money to spend. He'd done something. I haven't. Until now. But it's all going to change, you'll see. No drink. No women. I know I can make something out of Ninety-minutes, Davo. But I'm going to have to do it without my father.'

'OK,' I said. 'If you're sure?'

'I'm sure.'

'Have you tried anyone else? Friends? Contacts? Relations? Your mother?'

'I have. Lots of them. It's humiliating. The truth is, they all think I'm a loser. Just like you did when I first told you about it in the Dickens Inn. At least you listened in the end. Most people don't. Anyway, any of them that would be willing to give me money without much chance of ever seeing it again have already done it.'

'What about Torsten Schollenberger?'

'Torsten's worth a try. I haven't seen him for a while, but he's always up for a night on the town. And his father's loaded. I'll go to Hamburg and give it a whirl.'

'Can't do any harm.'

'But what about venture capitalists?' Guy said. 'Won't they be falling over themselves to get into this deal?'

'I doubt it. At least not yet. I think they'll think the same as Gaz did at first. Two bullshitters with nothing.'

'But you said the plan was good?'

'The plan is good. And as soon as we get back to your flat I'll make it better. But it's too early to go to them yet. They'll want to see a website with real people visiting it. Lots of real people.'

'We're going to need some money from somewhere,' said Guy. 'Once we go to the next stage with the web consultants, we're going to have to pay out real cash. And when we hire people we'll need an office. And we'll need money for the marketing campaign. TV advertising, that sort of thing.'

'I think we're probably going to have to start slower than that, Guy,' I said.

Guy slammed his hand down on the steering wheel. 'No! We have to move fast. If we start slow, we'll end up nowhere. We have to start in the lead and move ahead quickly enough to stay there.'

I frowned. 'Let's see what we can do.'

9

I had never worked so hard in my life. My social life ended, I had no time for flying, I scarcely watched any TV. Every morning I arrived at Guy's flat before eight. I walked from the tube station opposite the Tower of London, alongside Tower Bridge and St Katherine's Dock to Wapping High Street, passing the grim faces of suited bankers on their way in to the City sweatshops. Guy was already at work when I arrived, but Owen didn't emerge from his bedroom until about eleven.

For the first couple of days I found his hulking silent presence intimidating, but I soon got used to him. He preferred to communicate by e-mail rather than speech. Sometimes Guy and I would discuss something for half an hour, only to get back to work and find an e-mail waiting for us from Owen giving his views on the matter. Very strange. But it was quite possible to work a few feet away from Owen all day and ignore him completely, and he liked it that way.

He was making good progress on the architecture of the website. But, as Guy tacitly recognized, Owen had a people problem, so normally either Guy or I would accompany him to meetings. I quickly began to gain a basic understanding of the various components that would make up our website: the host servers lodged in fireproof, bombproof, high-security premises, the internet connections, the routers, the proxy servers, the firewalls, the databases. At this stage, it was all fairly straightforward, but once we started selling stuff over the web it would become much more complicated fast. Owen was wise to look ahead.

I spent a lot of time on the finances. One moment I would be worrying about whether the revenue in year five should be £120 million or £180 million. The next I would be figuring out how to save a few quid on printer toner. Guy had picked up a lot about internet businesses in a short time, but the money side had passed him by. I bought a bookkeeping software package and laboriously typed strings of figures into it. I set up files and simple procedures. I opened a company bank account. And I put a lot of thought into company structure, who owned what proportion of how many shares, how much to keep back for future key employees and how to value the company now and in the future.

I was concerned about the shareholders' agreement. I wasn't a lawyer, but it seemed to me that there were holes in it. As the number of shareholders grew, this agreement would become more important. Guy had used a law firm who specialized in film and TV contracts. They were difficult to pin down and when I did get hold of them, they waffled at my objections. We considered using some of the City firms I knew, but they would be far too expensive at this stage so we decided we would have to put up with Guy's lawyers until we had proper funding.

Ninetyminutes wasn't exactly going to be a 'virtual' company but it was going to be pretty close. Especially in the early stages. We didn't have the time or the money to employ our own experts on everything: we were going to have to use consultants. The most important of these was the web designer. Guy had selected a firm called Mandrill, and they called us to say they were ready with our design.

Mandrill's office was a large loft above a garment trader in one of the small streets just north of Oxford Street. Brick, pipes, skylights, precious little furniture, no internal walls. A folded-up micro-scooter rested against a cappuccino machine by the door. There were three islands of people working their computers around large curved black tables. We were met by two men and a woman. They intimidated the hell out of me. The men had tightly cropped goatee beards, carefully arranged combat trousers and T-shirts, hair cut just so. I had suddenly become an aficionado of shaven heads, but neither of the two men had had a simple 'all over' job. The woman, whose black hair was at least an inch longer than the men's, sported an eyebrow stud and at least six rings in each ear. Against this, Guy's all-black kit and inch-long blond hair looked so 1998. Owen and I weren't even contenders.

We crowded round a small table bearing a projector. The leader, one of the goatees called Tommy, asked for the lights to be dimmed and switched on the machine. It flashed a search-engine page on to the screen. We watched as Tommy typed the letters www.ninetyminutes.com. A click and up it came, our new logo on a light blue background. Another click and we were into the site. It didn't look anything like the other soccer sites on the web. Most of these resembled the contents pages of magazines transferred to the Internet. Mandrill's site, or rather *our* site, consisted of a series of dark blue bubbles floating on a light blue background. There was something about it that invited you to click to see what was in the bubbles. We clicked. And clicked. And clicked.

'Nice,' said Guy. 'What do you think, Gaz?'

'Cool. Yeah, cool.'

'Let's take a closer look at the logo.'

Tommy clicked on the opening screen. The woman with the multiple earrings handed round a T-shirt with the new logo printed on it.

'Obviously the real clothing will be better quality than this,' she said. 'But it should give you an idea.'

The T-shirt bore the figures nine and zero, with a few

strokes suggesting a stopwatch within the zero. Next to it was a tiny football, and the word 'com' in forward-sloping lower-case letters. It looked good.

'It's like a kind of mixture between Ralph Lauren and Adidas,' Guy said.

Tommy changed the screen. An image of a whiteboard splattered with scribblings appeared. I recognized Guy's writing. Tommy zoomed in on the words 'Adidas' and 'Ralph Lauren'.

Guy laughed. 'You're just giving my ideas back to me!'

'Dead right,' said Tommy. The lights came up. 'Well? What do you think?'

Guy glanced at me.

Mandrill were charging thirty thousand pounds plus one per cent of our equity. At this stage in Ninetyminutes' life thirty thousand was a lot of money. But a well-designed website was vital. I nodded to Guy. 'OK with me.'

'What do you think, Owen?'

'Cotton candy. It's, like, pink fluffy cotton candy.'

'But do you think they understand the technical stuff?'

'It's like I always say. No one understands the technical stuff in this country.'

'Well, thanks for not calling them morons, Owen,' Guy said, flashing a reassuring smile at Tommy and his team.

'No problem.'

'Gaz?'

'I like it. I think it's cool.'

Guy smiled. 'So do I. Tommy, we've got a deal.'

Saturday came. We all worked in the morning, but Guy told me I had a mystery meeting in the afternoon. We took the tube to Sloane Square and then grabbed a cab.

'Stamford Bridge,' said Guy, as we climbed in.

I smiled. 'I didn't realize you still went.'

'Every home game, when I'm in London,' said Guy. 'And I intend to keep going. It is the point, after all.'

'That's true.'

As a small boy my loyalties had fixed on Derby County, and I had stuck with them until university, making the trip up from Northamptonshire a couple of times a year to see a game. But once I started working, there never seemed to be the time. My interest in the game, both as a player and a spectator, had quietly slipped out of my life, unnoticed. The last time I had been to a football match was seven years before, with Guy.

Then Stamford Bridge had been undergoing major improvements. There was still some work in progress, but I was amazed by the transformation. The ground was reached through the glitzy 'Chelsea Village' full of shops and bars. There were some families in the horde of people thronging the ground, but there were also some pretty frightening individuals. Thugs perhaps, but thugs with cash. Money was changing hands everywhere. I looked at my ticket. Twenty-five pounds. Extortionate. As we filed into the all-seater stadium and sat down in the warm spring sunshine with thirty-four thousand other people, all of whom were shelling out at least that much for their Saturday afternoon entertainment, I began to see that there really was a lot of money in football.

The Blues were playing Leicester City. Within ten minutes of the kick-off I had forgotten all about websites and money, and was urging them on with the rest of the crowd. I cheered after half an hour when Gianfranco Zola calmly lobbed the ball over the Leicester goalkeeper. I cheered some more when an own goal from a Leicester defender put Chelsea two up. And then I felt the agitation and frustration boil up inside me as Leicester pulled back first one and then two goals in the last ten minutes.

The draw at home had put paid to Chelsea's hopes of winning the Premier League that season, and Guy was fuming. But it had been a great game to watch and, as I fought my way home on London's creaking transport system, I couldn't help smiling to myself. This was going to be fun.

IO

July 1987, Côte D'Azur, France

I leaned against the car door as the Alfa Romeo Spider took the hairpin bend fast. Too fast. Dominique was an aggressive driver. She had told me not to worry, she knew the road well, and it was some comfort to know that she had torn along this stretch many times before without killing herself.

It was impossible to believe. Here I was, sitting in the passenger seat of a sports car, a beautiful blonde beside me, the Mediterranean below, the sun above, the air rushing past as we careered down the Corniche. It was one of those moments I wanted to freeze into my memory so that back in my grey life in grey England it would always be within reach, ready for me to take out and enjoy.

And I had made love for the first time.

I felt like punching the air and letting out a whoop of victory. But with Dominique beside me I had to keep cool. Even so, I couldn't prevent a grin creeping across my face.

Dominique saw. '*Ça va?*'

'*Ça va bien.*'

Actually, making love wasn't quite the right description of what had happened. It was more like an explosion of adolescent lust. It couldn't have lasted much more than two minutes. Dominique hadn't seemed to mind. In fact she seemed to find the whole thing amusing, which didn't bother me in the slightest. Afterwards, she had gone to get a cigarette. She had sat opposite me, naked, her legs crossed, and lit up. She offered it to me. I had never smoked, to be honest

I didn't know how, but I accepted the cigarette and took a long drag. She thought the paroxysm of coughing that resulted very funny. She kissed me. I stirred.

She noticed and raised her eyebrows. 'So soon?' she said.

I shrugged and smiled. 'It looks like you get two for the price of one.'

She giggled. 'What a deal.'

The second time took longer and produced much more sweat. I lay in a crumpled heap on the balcony as she took a quick shower.

'Come on,' she said. 'I know we're going to be very late, but we should at least try to get there before they leave. It's only polite.'

The gradient was levelling off and we turned onto a busier road with houses and apartment buildings on either side. We were nearing Monte Carlo. Nearing lunch with Guy and his father. Nearing the enquiring glances, the questions, the excuses. Since the moment when Dominique had led me up the stairs by the hand I had blanked out all thought of the consequences of what was about to happen. But those consequences were only five minutes away.

I had slept with another man's wife. I had slept with my friend's stepmother. It was wrong. I knew it was wrong. There were all kinds of justifications to myself that I could use, probably would use. Her husband had been unfaithful to her the night before. She knew entirely what she was doing. I hadn't encouraged her in any way, I had been an accomplice rather than an instigator. This was France; married people in France had lovers, everyone knew that.

But after I had argued it all through with myself, I knew the answer would still be that I had done wrong.

I wouldn't have changed the decision, though. I couldn't have done anything else. For a moment I was being offered a small taste of life from another world, a life of money, sun, sex, beautiful women. I had seen glimpses of this life reflected through some of the other pupils at Broadhill, but I had never experienced it myself. Perhaps I wouldn't experience it again. Carpe diem.

How the hell would I deal with Guy and his father? There was no need to lie, just mumble. They would never find out. Dominique wouldn't tell them. Just stay quiet and I'd get away with it.

Dominique hustled the Alfa through the cramped streets of Monte Carlo, orange and yellow high-rise apartment buildings rising above us on all sides, and parked illegally by the port, blocking in a yellow Rolls. The restaurant was just over the road, and Guy, Tony, Ingrid and Mel were sitting at a table outside. A large man was sitting with them.

'Darling, I'm sorry we're so late,' Dominique said, approaching Tony with a broad smile. He stood up and accepted her energetic kisses. The debris of a finished meal littered the table. 'And Patrick! *Comment vas-tu?*'

The stranger stood up with difficulty, almost upsetting the unsteady table with his stomach, and kissed Dominique on both cheeks.

'David, this is Patrick Hoyle,' Dominique said. 'He is Tony's lawyer. He is a very clever man. He lives here in Monte Carlo and saves himself millions of francs in taxes. Patrick, this is David Lane, a friend of Guy's from school. A *charming* friend.'

I shook Hoyle's hand, which was damp. 'Pleased to meet you, David,' he boomed. He had a large, round head edged with black tufts of hair. He wore pink-tinted glasses and his skin was pasty for someone who lived in such a sunny place. He was also fat. Really, really fat.

I mumbled something in return. I thought the *'charming'* was a bit unnecessary and I tried not to go red.

'We'll just order a salad,' Dominique said.

The others seemed awkward, uneasy about something. Mel looked miserable, Ingrid cool, Guy mildly irritated and Tony pensive. Only Hoyle seemed comfortable as he poured himself another glass of red wine.

Dominique gazed out over the multi-million-dollar motor-yachts that were crammed into the harbour in tight rows. 'Ah, Tony, it's such a lovely day, don't you think?' she said, giving him a dazzling smile.

Tony was caught off guard. I knew they had been screaming at each other the previous night, and I'd seen them ignore each other before lunch. He looked at Dominique questioningly, and then turned his eyes to me. They met mine for a fraction of a second before I had time to look down at my menu in panic. But that fraction of a second was enough.

He knew.

I wanted a hole to open under my chair and swallow me up.

He knew.

And what's more, I realized that the whole thing had been done by Dominique for just this delicious moment of revenge against her husband. He could fuck a child; well, so could she.

I glanced over to her. She was chattering away, smoking a cigarette and smiling a smile of triumph. I couldn't hear what she said. It was all meaningless anyway, and only Guy seemed to be responding half-heartedly to any of it. I didn't hear anything at all. I was buried deep in my menu, wishing to God I was somewhere else.

I felt used. Used and dirty. But I knew I didn't deserve sympathy. Because most of all I felt stupid. I should have realized what Dominique was after, that all she wanted was to hurt her husband, that I had nothing to do with it. My self-esteem could cope with the idea that it was all just a laugh on her part, but not that I was an inept instrument in a piece of petty malice.

What an idiot.

Lunch was a nightmare of awkwardness. Afterwards, we set off for the beach, thankfully leaving Hoyle to return to his office. This time I made sure I was in the Jeep. Ingrid went with Dominique.

The beach was just a small stretch of sand in a rocky cove beneath the cliffs upon which Les Sarrasins perched. It was difficult to get to: we had to scramble down a rocky path, and the waves rushed in with more vigour than at the sedate beaches of Beaulieu. It was flanked on one side by nudists and on the other by gays. There were very few other people there and in a better mood I would have thought it beautiful. It did at least give me the chance to lie down, shut my eyes and ignore everyone else.

I spread my towel over a smooth rock next to Ingrid, lowered myself face down upon it and closed my eyes. I could hear activity around me. Guy and Tony had brought a cooler of beer and were getting stuck into it. It sounded like they were having some kind of father-and-son bonding session, but nobody else was interested.

It made me sick. Tony had just screwed his son's girlfriend and yet he was quite happy to drink and joke with him. Guy didn't have a clue. The girlfriend in question was keeping very quiet, despite Guy's efforts to bring her into the conversation.

I felt a gentle tickle on my thigh. I turned and opened one eye. Dominique was lying next to me, leaning on one elbow, her uncovered breasts hanging down towards the smooth rock. A smudge on the inside of her forearm caught my eye, as though there were a patch of make-up that had picked up the sand. Odd.

'Ça va?' she said with a smile that could have been seductive, or could have been mocking, or could have been both.

I turned the other way. It was rude, perhaps, but it was the only way to make my point I could think of.

The other way was Ingrid. She too was topless, as was every woman on the beach apart from Mel. Although her skin was a lovely warm golden colour, her breasts were nothing like as full as Dominique's, and she didn't have Dominique's curves. She was quite ordinary looking, really. But suddenly a girl my own age seemed so much more attractive than the supposed sophistication of Dominique.

I realized that Ingrid was watching me through her dark glasses. She grinned.

'Sorry,' I said and closed my eyes, too wretched to feel embarrassed. The sun beat down on my back and I think I fell asleep.

Some time later, I heard the hiss of a beer can being opened next to me. Then the shock of cold aluminium on my overheated back. My head jerked upwards. Tony was sitting where Dominique had been. I looked round. The others had gone. I scanned the waves and saw them splashing in the sea.

'Want one?' asked Tony.

'No thanks,' I said.

He took a swig of his. He was sitting a foot away from me, staring out to sea.

'If you touch my wife again, I'll kill you,' he said matter-of-factly.

My throat went dry. I swallowed. 'I understand.'

'Good. Now tomorrow morning you are going to ring your parents in England. They are going to tell you that there is a family emergency and you have to fly home immediately. What the family emergency is, is entirely up to you. I will drive you to the airport and you will catch the four o'clock flight to Heathrow. Don't worry, I'll pay for the ticket.'

'All right,' I said. That was fine with me.

'Good. And let me make it absolutely clear. I don't want to see you ever again.' His eyes glinted. 'If Guy invites you here or to any of my other properties you will say no. Do you understand?'

'Perfectly.'

'Excellent. Now, I think I'll join them.'

Without looking, he poured the remains of the beer over my stomach. I flinched as the cool liquid touched my skin, but I let him do it. I watched him climb down towards the waves: a rich, powerful man who wanted to prove to himself that he was still as young and good-looking as his son. Which, of course, he could never do. However much power he had, however much money he spent, however many young girls he seduced, he would always be twenty-eight years older than Guy. It was sad to see someone otherwise so successful in life fail to grasp this inescapable truth. But I wasn't going to argue about leaving so soon. The prospect of six more days had been weighing heavily on me and now Tony Jourdan had given me the perfect way out. I wouldn't miss him.

As soon as we arrived back at the house I excused myself, saying I wanted to go and lie down. Guy walked with me back to the guest cottage.

'What's up with everybody, Davo?'

'I've no idea,' I said.

'Everyone's acting weird. Mel's gone ice-cold on me. Something's up.'

I didn't answer.

'At least Dad seems in good form. You should talk to him more. He's a great guy. It's cool when you can talk to your parents like normal people, don't you think? It's hard to believe he's forty-six. I just wish I'd had a chance to see more of him these last few years.'

'Uh huh.'

'What he's doing with that French tart, I don't know. Sure,

93

she looks hot, but I think Dad can do better than that. What do you think? You've spoken to her more than I have.'

'I don't know,' I mumbled.

'Jesus, Davo, you as well! Cheer up, will you? What's wrong with you? And why were you and Dominique so late for lunch?'

I was going to have to lie. I answered Guy speaking to my feet.

'She realized I had a bit of a hangover, so she decided to give me some neat vodka. I took it. It worked for a little bit, but I feel even worse now.'

'Stupid sod. I thought you said you'd never drink again?'

'I won't,' I said, looking him in the eye for the first time. 'Believe me, not for a long time. Now I've got to hit the sack.'

Guy left me to curl up in a little ball of my own misery.

I couldn't hide in bed for ever, so I emerged at supper-time. Wine and beer were on offer on the terrace, but I didn't take anything. Neither did Ingrid, nor Owen, who had appeared after a whole day spent on his portable computer. Guy and Tony were drinking more beer, Guy with determination.

'How are you feeling?' I asked Mel, who was holding an almost empty glass of wine.

She glanced up at me, as though surprised by the sympathy in my voice. 'A bit shaky,' she said.

'Me too.'

'Cheer up, Mel,' said Guy, putting his arm round her and refilling her glass. 'This place isn't so bad, is it?'

'Oh, no,' she said, summoning a smile. 'No, it's lovely.'

'We'll go over to Monte again tomorrow. Check out a casino.'

'Sounds great,' said Mel, unenthusiastically.

I drifted away from them, leaving Guy working hard. I

wandered over to the marble railings and stared down at the sea far below. As I watched closely, I realized that it was so far below that the sound of the waves breaking on the rocks was out of synch with the rhythm of the waves themselves. A long way down.

A voice spoke beside me. 'This is awful, isn't it?'

It was Ingrid.

'Mel looks bad,' I said. 'Has she spoken to you about it?'

'A little.'

'How did it happen?' I'd seen Mel laughing at Tony's jokes all evening, but I had never suspected anything would come of it.

'Everyone was drifting off to bed. Dominique had already gone. Apparently Tony started talking to Mel about the Romans and the watchtower. He took her over to look at it in the moonlight. Then he kissed her. Then . . .'

I shuddered.

'Why did she do it? He's in his forties, for God's sake!'

'He's a charming man. He may be in his forties, but he's sexy, and he knows it. Men like that have a pull for some women. Mel's a romantic and Tony had engineered the most romantic of situations. He's a pro. She's an amateur. She never really stood a chance.'

'But it wasn't rape or anything?'

'No. Mel was willing. At least at the time.'

'Do you think she regrets it?' Throughout the day I had seen no sign of Mel showing any interest in her lover of the night before.

'Oh, yes. She definitely regrets it.'

'What's she going to do?'

'Brave it out, I think. What else can she do?'

'Go home?'

'Maybe.'

'She doesn't look too happy now.'

'Neither do you,' said Ingrid.

I didn't answer.

'Hey, what are you two doing here? Won't you come and join us?' It was Dominique, now dressed in tight white jeans and black top under a white jacket. She smiled broadly. 'Come on, David. Come talk to me.'

'I think I'll stay here for a bit, thanks. It's a beautiful spot.'

'As you like,' Dominique replied, touching her lip with her tongue.

'What was that?' said Ingrid, watching Dominique swing her hips back to the terrace.

'Don't ask,' I said. 'Please.'

Ingrid gave me a look. 'Curiouser and curiouser.'

The evening was flat. I avoided talking to anyone much, especially Dominique. No one was having a good time and Tony still looked angry. At about ten the gathering broke up, and I went back to the guest cottage with Guy, who was still bemused by everyone's lack of sparkle.

I lay in bed for a long time in a kind of crazed semi-consciousness. Images of Dominique naked spun around my brain in a tumult of excitement and shame, until my eyes burned and my loins ached. There was a strange sickness in my stomach and a tightening in my throat. My heart beat fast. I would open my eyes and try to calm myself down. Then it would all begin again. I had no idea what to expect of sex for the first time, but it certainly wasn't this. Eventually, somewhere in the middle of the night, the images left me and I fell into a deep sleep.

I was woken by a loud rap at our bedroom door. A moment later the ceiling light was turned on. I sat up to see Tony standing in the doorway, his face haggard in the artificial light.

'What time is it?' croaked Guy.

'Four o'clock.'

Guy and I just blinked. What the hell was Tony doing waking us up at four o'clock in the morning?

'I have some bad news,' Tony said. 'Very bad news. It's Dominique. She's dead.'

April 1999, The City, London

You have to get to Sweetings early to get a table. It is a crowded little fish restaurant near the Mansion House presided over by an Italian with a full moustache who harries his customers mercilessly. Quickly in, quickly out, and a huge bill to settle at the till as you leave. The place has a kind of institutional feel to it, like a school dining room with alcohol. And excellent fish. But I think it is the jam roly-poly and the spotted dick with custard that keep pulling in the punters. My father loved it.

Every few months since I had started work at Gurney Kroheim he would meet me there for lunch while on one of his trips up to London for business. He was never specific and I never quite understood quite what business the manager of a small building-society branch had to do in London, but I never questioned him. I suspected he just wanted to get out of our little town, see an old crony or two, wander around the metropolis for a couple of hours and have lunch with me. I enjoyed those lunches and so did he.

I was five minutes late, but he had grabbed a couple of stools by one of the bars set for lunch, behind which hovered a spotty teenage waiter. He was nursing a half-pint of Guinness in a pewter tankard, and had one ready for me. His face lit up when he saw me, and he pumped my hand enthusiastically.

He was a large, kind man with a balding head and glasses perched half way down his nose. It was a minor miracle that he had managed to survive into his sixties as the manager of the branch. The reason was his shrewdness, which he always kept well hidden, and his refusal to accept promotion to the political minefield of the higher regional offices. He was very good at his job. He was well known throughout the small market town where we lived, and trusted. Competitors might try new marketing campaigns, higher deposit rates and thrusting customer-service managers, but none of that made a dent in his following. The building society he worked for had not yet been shaken up by demutualization, and his bosses realized that there was nothing to be gained from moving him and a lot to be lost. There had been a rocky moment during the recession of the early nineties when he had been criticized by head office for not taking a tougher line with some of his clients who were in arrears on their mortgage payments, but he had weathered it. Two more years and he would make it through to retirement.

'Sit down, David. I got you a Guinness. Thanks for coming here. I suppose I could have gone to Wapping . . .'

'Oh no, Dad. Don't worry. This is fine.'

'I've been looking forward to my pudding all week. Your mother doesn't cook that kind of thing any more.' He rubbed his comfortable stomach. 'It's not as though she'd notice another pound.'

We ordered potted shrimps and sole and a bottle of Sancerre.

'I like the haircut,' said my father. 'Reminds me of my National Service days. It certainly makes you look different.'

I smiled. 'I feel different, I suppose.'

'What? Colder?'

'No. This thing I'm doing with Guy Jourdan. It's nothing like anything I've ever done before.'

I was slightly nervous as I said this. I knew that my father had been pleased when I had become a chartered accountant and very proud that I had joined a prestigious merchant bank. I had made my decision to join Guy without referring to him, but I found I wanted his approval none the less.

'It was a big step to leave Gurney Kroheim,' he said.

'It was. But it's changed so much since Leipziger took over.'

'Don't like working for the krauts, eh? I can understand that.'

'No, it's not that. There aren't many Germans around in any case, and those that I dealt with are perfectly fine. It's just the whole industry. The hire-and-fire culture, mergers, reorganizations, politics, it just doesn't seem any fun any more.'

'And this thing with Guy Jourdan is fun?'

'Oh, yes. At least so far. In fact, I've never had so much fun in my career before. I mean, there are just the three of us working out of Guy's flat. We have nothing but a blank sheet of paper. We're building something from the ground up entirely ourselves. It feels totally different from working for a huge organization.'

'How's it going to work?'

I told him. Through the first course, the fish and most of the bottle of wine. He listened. He was a good listener.

The waiter whipped away our plates and thrust menus into our hands. My father agonized over his decision before going for the jam roly-poly with custard. I had the bread and butter pudding.

'What about Guy?' he asked.

'He's fine. He's very good, actually.'

'Do you trust him?'

I hesitated. 'Yes,' I said.

My father raised his eyebrows.

'Yes,' I repeated, more firmly this time.

'I thought you and he fell out a few years ago. Something to do with a girl?'

'That and other things.' I hadn't told my father much about that.

'And there was that business in France.'

'Yes.' I hadn't told him much about that either.

'Tony Jourdan was a bit of a sharp operator, I seem to remember. Successful, but a sharp operator.'

'That's true.'

'Well?'

'I think Guy's changed,' I said.

'You think?'

'I'm pretty sure.'

My father watched my face closely. 'Good,' he said at last. Then he beamed as the pudding arrived. 'Ah. Tuck in.' He took a mouthful. 'Delicious. Well, I think it's an excellent move.'

'You do, Dad?'

'Yes, I do. There's a time in everyone's life when they should take a risk. I missed mine somewhere along the line. But it sounds as if this is yours. I'm glad you've got the guts to go for it.'

'Thanks,' I said, trying to suppress my smile. I wanted to pretend that I was adult enough not to care what my father thought. But actually I was pleased that my act of rebellion had received the parental seal of approval.

We talked about my mother and sister. My sister had recently moved into a flat in Peterborough with her boyfriend. My mother was having difficulties with this. My father disapproved too, but more of the boyfriend, whom he thought dull, than of the cohabitation. A few moments after the last trace of custard was scraped off my father's dish it was whipped away and we were out on the street.

'Tell you what, David. Send me the business plan, will you? I'd love to have a look at it.'

'Will do, Dad. And thanks for lunch again. Give my love to Mum.'

I left him outside the restaurant and disappeared underground to take the three stops to Tower Hill, the wine and my father's blessing leaving a warm glow inside me.

I posted the business plan off to him as soon as I returned to Wapping. Four days later I found a letter waiting for me back at my flat addressed to me in my father's handwriting. I opened the envelope and a cheque fell out. I picked it up and read it. *Pay ninetyminutes.com fifty thousand pounds.* Jesus! I had no idea my father had that much money lying around. With trepidation, I read the letter.

Dear David
I very much enjoyed having lunch with you at our old haunt yesterday.
I was fascinated by what you had to say about ninetyminutes.com and by what I read in the plan you sent me. It sounds like a terrific opportunity. So terrific, in fact, that I'd like to make an investment in the firm myself. Is this possible? I enclose a cheque for £50,000.
I have the greatest confidence in you, David, and I am very proud of what you are doing.
Love
Dad.
PS. Don't tell your mother about this, will you?

I stared at the letter. I couldn't suppress a smile. There was the evidence that he believed in me. Incontrovertible. Fifty thousand quid.

I realized immediately that I couldn't accept it. I didn't know what my father's savings amounted to, but there had never been very much money around the house and I was pretty confident that the cheque I was holding accounted for a large proportion of them. He would need the money for his retirement. Sure, I believed in ninetyminutes.com, but I knew it was risky. Not the place to put your retirement nest egg.

The injunction not to tell my mother was another problem. If I went ahead and cashed the cheque, that would be a disaster just waiting to happen. I picked up the phone and punched out my parents' number. After some small talk with my mother, she put him on.

'Dad, I don't believe what came in the post today! Are you crazy?'

'Not at all,' he said. I could hear the smile in his voice, which was low, presumably so my mother wouldn't hear. 'I'm sure it will be an excellent investment.'

'But, Dad. It's a start-up! It could go bust within a year. It's an enormous risk.'

'That's the point, David. We talked about it at lunch. I feel it's about time I took a risk and what better way to take it? The Internet is going to change the way we live, even I realize that. And I have confidence in you. I can't think of anyone else I would trust to do what you're doing. At my age I can't give up everything and start a company myself. But I can invest in one.'

'I'm sorry, Dad. I can't accept it.'

'What do you mean, you can't accept it? Is fifty thousand too little? What's the problem?' He was beginning to sound angry. My father rarely sounded angry.

'It's not that. It's just if I lose your money I'll feel terrible.'

'And what if ninetyminutes.com is a runaway success? What if I could have earned ten times my money and you hadn't let me invest? How would you feel then?'

'Oh, Dad, come on . . .'

'No. You come on. You have to admit there's a good chance that this is going to work, don't you?'

'Yes, I do.'

'Well then?'

'I can't let you do this, Dad.'

'David. I don't believe this.' My father's voice was still low to prevent my mother hearing, but he sounded genuinely angry now. 'I am capable of making up my own mind about investments, you know. I know this is high risk. I want to take a risk, just like you. And in the same way I won't stop you from risking your career, you shouldn't stop me from risking what is, after all, only money.'

I took a deep breath. 'OK, Dad, I'll think about it.'

'David –'

'I said, I'll think about it. Bye.' I hung up. I rarely fought with my father, if ever, and I felt bad. I knew the right decision was not to accept his money.

But we needed money from somewhere. Guy was finding it difficult to pin down a meeting with Torsten in Hamburg and he was still adamant he didn't want to ask his father. Which left us with the venture capitalists.

Venture-capital firms invest in new or growing companies. Until the late 1990s they were cautious and careful. It was not unheard of for them to spend months investigating a start-up company before deciding that they did not want to invest. I knew what they were looking for: experienced management, proprietary technology and a proven method of making money. None of which Guy and I had. Which was why I had been reluctant to approach them until we had at least a website to show that we meant business.

But Guy couldn't wait that long. And in the increasing heat of the last year of the century, neither could they. Stories were emerging of venture capitalists falling over themselves to back young entrepreneurs barely out of business school. Boo.com, an internet fashion retailer that was nothing but an idea and two hip Swedish founders who had started and sold an internet bookshop, had just raised forty million pounds. We only needed three million to get us going. Guy saw no reason why we shouldn't get it.

So, despite my doubts, I polished up our plan. Now all I needed was people to send it to.

12

The place was heaving. It was Tuesday, the first Tuesday of May, and I was at First Tuesday, *the* event for anyone in the internet world. It had all started six months before when a group of entrepreneurs had agreed to meet in a pub once a month to share war stories, and it had grown and grown. It was now the place to network, to find employees, office space, clients, suppliers, and that most precious commodity of all, money. I was there to make contact with venture capitalists, to give them the thirty-second 'elevator pitch', to collect their cards and send them our plan. Pretty straightforward, really. I was wearing a green badge, showing I was an entrepreneur. The venture capitalists were wearing red badges.

The venue was the converted warehouse of an internet consultancy company near Oxford Street, quite close to Mandrill's offices. There must have been two hundred people there, all talking frantically. Most were my age or younger, most were dressed in T-shirts or fleeces, nearly all were men, and nearly all had green badges.

I took a deep breath and dived in. I was searching for the red badges. They were few and far between, but I soon realized how to spot them: they were the ones in the middle of tight groups of men and women all talking at once. Be forceful, I thought, pushing my way through to one such group. At its centre was a young-looking man in a suit being harangued by a voluble American who had an idea for selling wedding gifts over the net. It was clear he wasn't going to go away until the VC had given him his card and told him to send him a plan. There was an unruly crush of green badges in front of me vying to give their own pitches. Most of them were selling something mundane over the Internet, from babyloves.com selling gifts for babies to lastrest.com selling prepaid funeral services. I wondered who lastrest.com's target customers were – perhaps people who woke up in the middle of the night with chest pains and nipped off to their computer to make sure their funeral was sorted before it was too late. Some of the ideas were highly technical and incomprehensible. One or two made some kind of sense. But the venture capitalist had no chance of distinguishing one from the other.

I tried to get the attention of the red badges, I really did. I managed to exchange cards with one harassed woman before being elbowed out of the way by the wedding-gift American. But otherwise, nothing. You had to be very pushy to get attention. Most of the green badges were expert attention-seekers. They left me way behind.

I retired to the gents. Standing next to me was a man in a suit. I didn't look up at the face, but I saw the lapel. A red badge. Now, if I were a true entrepreneur I would have no compunction about foisting myself and my elevator pitch on a man while he was urinating. It was then that I discovered something about myself. I wasn't a true entrepreneur. I kept my eyes down.

The suit next to me moved. 'David? David Lane?'

I looked up at his face. 'Henry, how are you?'

It turned out I knew the owner of the badge. Henry Broughton-Jones had trained with me as an accountant. He was a tall man with thinning fair hair brushed back above a high forehead. His father was a gentleman farmer in Here-fordshire, and you would have thought Henry would have been happier in an agricultural college than a big firm of accountants, but in the end he had done rather well. When I had left the firm he had been one of the rising stars groomed for eventual partnership.

'Hassled,' he said. 'Severely hassled. I've never been to one of these before. I thought it would be a good place to look for deals, but I can barely fight them off. Here, let's get a drink.'

We left the gents and grabbed a couple of glasses of wine. Within thirty seconds they'd spotted the red badge and were circling. Henry glowered at them. 'Do you mind?' he growled. 'This is a confidential conversation here.'

'So you're a venture capitalist, now?' I said.

'Yes. Orchestra Ventures. I've been doing it for three years now. Left soon after you. It's quite jolly. Crazy days, though. And you? I see you've gone over to the ranks of lunatic entrepreneurs.'

'A soccer website,' I said. 'It's called ninetyminutes.com.' A hunted look appeared in Henry's eyes. I made a quick decision. I didn't want to spook my only venture-capitalist friend. 'Don't worry, we don't need any money at the moment. I'm just here to "network", whatever that means.'

'Thank God,' said Henry, relaxing.

We talked for several more minutes. He told me he was married and had two small children. They were just about to buy a cottage in Gloucestershire. I told him Gurney Kroheim was miserable and I was well off out of it. We exchanged news about mutual acquaintances and then he couldn't fend off the green badges any longer. Just as he was being dragged away, he thrust his card into my hand. 'Look, if you do need any money, give me a call.'

'Will do, Henry. Good to see you.'

I fingered his card, smiling to myself, and fetched another glass of wine.

After half an hour or so, a Chinese-American in a checked shirt and neat chinos climbed up on to a table and gave a gung-ho speech about how we were in the middle of something big. The most significant technological change to hit the world in the millennium. Right here. Right now. Tomorrow's movers and shakers were here in this very room. Then the scrum continued as the crowd moved and shook.

I circled, looking for that rarest of species, an unattended red badge. I couldn't see one, but I did see another face I thought I recognized. I moved closer.

She looked about thirty-five and she was wearing a blue suit with her hair scraped severely back. Downward-sloping lines edged her mouth, but her lips wore a familiar pout.

'Mel?'

She turned to me and blinked for a second before she placed me. 'David!' She smiled and proffered her cheek for a kiss. 'What on earth are you doing here?'

'I'm working for a start-up. An internet company. Soccer website.'

'You're not? Not you? The chartered accountant!'

'I am,' I said, grinning. 'With Guy.'

'No! I don't believe it.'

'It's true. And it's going well. Although we need some investors pretty badly.'

'Doesn't everyone?' said Mel, surveying the crowd. 'I'm amazed you're working with Guy. You know, after what happened in Mull and everything.'

'That was seven years ago.'

'Yes, but still.'

'He's changed.'

'Oh, yeah?' Mel looked doubtful.

'He has. Have you seen him recently?'

'Not since then. In fact, I've more or less forgotten about him.'

'Probably not a bad thing,' I said. 'Anyway, what are you up to? Still a lawyer?'

'Yes. The only people wearing suits here are lawyers. Still at Howles Marriott. It's going quite well, actually. I'm not a partner yet, but perhaps soon.'

'I never had you pegged as a corporate lawyer.'

'Well, I wouldn't have imagined you as a dot-commer. It's a miracle I recognized you with that hairstyle.'

'You haven't changed much,' I said. It was a lie. Mel had aged more than seven years, but that's not the kind of thing you say to an acquaintance. It was the kind of thing I would tell Guy, though.

'Rubbish,' she said. 'I've even got the odd grey hair now.'

It was true, she had. I remembered her hair as it used to be when she was eighteen, dark, with a streak of blonde. Now the streaks were grey.

'Have you seen Ingrid?' I asked.

'No. Not since then,' she replied, the enthusiasm leaving her voice.

'Oh.'

We were silent. Both of us remembering.

Mel breathed in and sighed. She still had a fine chest, I couldn't help noticing. Something else to tell Guy.

'Have you any clients here?' I asked.

'Two or three.'

'Can they pay their bills?'

Mel grinned. 'So far. I'm betting the Internet will be the next hot market for lawyers. I've got about half a dozen internet clients at the moment. I reckon at least one of them will make it. And that could mean lots of legal work in the future.'

'Sounds like a good strategy,' I said. We sipped our wine. 'Um. I wonder . . .'

'Yes?'

'This may sound a bit cheeky. But would you mind having a quick look at our shareholders' agreement? The firm who drew it up are entertainment lawyers Guy knows from his acting days. I'm not sure it's quite right.'

'No problem,' said Mel. 'Fax it to me tomorrow. I'll tell you what I think. And no charge. Here's my card.' She handed me one.

I gave her mine. 'One of Qwickprint's finest,' I said. 'It's funny I bumped into you. You're the second person here tonight I know.'

'That's not so strange,' said Mel. 'Everyone our age is doing this now. There are probably two or three more people you know here you just haven't spotted. As the man said just now, this is the place to be.'

'He did say that, didn't he?'

Mel stood on her toes in an effort to see over the heads. 'Oops. Just spotted one of my clients. Speak to you to-morrow.' With that she disappeared into the throng.

I tried to work the crowd again, but I didn't get very far. Half an hour and only one venture capitalist's card later I decided to call it quits.

I emerged into the cool night air feeling low. There were an awful lot of people doing the same kind of thing as Ninetyminutes, and all of them seemed pushier than me. I had read about the internet revolution in the press, but I had never seen it, felt it. And it didn't feel right. The cautious Gurney Kroheim banker in me didn't like it. There were a couple of people with good ideas, such as an articulate blonde woman I had spoken to who had started a company that sold cheap last-minute tickets. But most of it was rubbish. And the rubbish was getting funded.

For the last few weeks I had felt like a true entrepreneur, on the cutting edge of a new wave of technology. Now I just felt like a chartered accountant with delusions. Unlike the Chinese guy who had made the speech, I feared I was in the wrong place at the wrong time.

13

July 1987, Côte D'Azur, France

Guy stared uncomprehendingly at his father standing in the doorway of our bedroom. 'Dead? Dominique's dead?'

'That's what I said.'

'How?'

Tony sighed and rubbed his eyes. 'A drug overdose.'

'Drug . . . Jesus!'

'The police are here. They want to talk to everyone. You'd better get up.'

We staggered out of bed and I struggled to gain some control of the random thoughts colliding around my brain. Dead? Suicide? Police? Drugs? Dominique? Me? Sex? Investigation? Guy? Tony?

As I followed Guy into the garden illuminated by the first chilly fingers of dawn I had a horrible feeling that everything was going to come out. Everything.

We crossed the garden and I looked up at Dominique's bedroom and the balcony where we had made love the previous afternoon. There were lights, shadows moving around, the intermittent flash of a photographer. There was the murmur of footsteps, voices, instructions, and the sound of a vehicle sweeping into the front courtyard.

We followed Tony into the living room. Ingrid, Mel, Owen, Miguel and a couple of maids were sitting there in silence, all looking stunned. Mel had been crying. Two gendarmes in uniform stood a few feet distant, watching us idly. It was a large room, with tile floors covered in chic rugs, abstract sculptures dotted about the place and large canvases with bright splashes of colour daubing the walls. It was a room for the elegant and the sophisticated to relax in, not for a bunch of eighteen-year-olds just out of school to wait for interrogation. Not for the first time I found myself thinking, what am I doing here?

'The police will want to ask you questions individually,' Tony said in a monotone. 'It should be just a formality. Nothing to worry about.' He looked exhausted, numb. I could still smell the alcohol of the previous night on him.

'What happened, Dad?' said Guy.

Tony turned to his son. 'I found her an hour or so ago. She was in bed. There was a needle on her bedside table. Heroin.'

'Are you sure?'

Tony nodded, all his vitality gone.

He knew she took heroin, I thought. In fact, that probably explained the strangeness in her eyes. And the make-up on the inside of her forearm hiding the injection marks.

I stared up at the ceiling, at the motionless fan. A drug addict. I had had sex with a drug addict. Who was now dead. The urgent question was, what should I tell the police?

My first instinct, of course, was to lie. Or at least not to mention what had happened that afternoon. But a moment's thought persuaded me that was a bad idea. I had done nothing wrong; or rather nothing illegal. Once I started lying to the police I would be breaking the law. And there were all sorts of ways they might find out. The post-mortem, Tony, perhaps even Ingrid. Besides, I wasn't a good liar at the best of times, and this was the worst of times. A competent policeman would find me out in no time.

The door opened and two detectives entered. One of them signalled to Tony. They spoke in heated whispers. Whatever it was the policeman said, it shocked Tony. He looked anxiously over towards us. The detective broke away from him and approached us.

He was a tall, burly man in a baggy double-breasted suit who managed to look both tired and alert at the same time.

'My name is Sauville. Inspector Sauville,' he said, in good but strongly accented English. We were listening. 'I must inform you that we believe we are investigating a murder. In a few minutes I will begin questioning each of you in turn. It is imperative that you stay here at the house today. And keep well clear from the scene of the crime. Do you understand?'

We nodded. A murder. No wonder Tony looked so shocked. I glanced at Guy. He seemed stunned.

Sauville spoke to his detectives and disappeared into the dining room. In a moment he called in Tony. One of the other detectives began to interview Ingrid. They were splitting up the work.

The interviews took a long time, especially Tony's. When he came out he looked dazed. He spoke to Guy quickly and then disappeared.

'What did he say?' I asked Guy.

'They think Dominique was suffocated with a pillow. She had taken heroin, but the police have no reason to think it was an overdose. They'll know for sure when they've done the post-mortem. Dad said they think he might have done it. He's gone to call Patrick Hoyle.'

Guy looked stricken. Both by the idea that his stepmother had been murdered and that his father might be suspected of doing it.

More police were arriving. I could see them outside, picking their way methodically through the garden. We heard movement on the stairs and we went outside into the hallway to watch as Dominique's body was carried down and out of the house. She was covered, of course, but we could easily make out her shape beneath the sheet. A chill ran through me. I glanced at Guy, whose face was drained of all colour. Ingrid let out a tiny gasp and Mel began to weep. I put my arm round her; of all of us, she had had a particularly hard couple of days.

Then Sauville called her into the dining room. She wiped her eyes and tried to pull herself together. But she looked scared. I realized she must be agonizing over whether to tell them about Tony seducing her. Like me, she had no choice; I hoped she understood that. Meanwhile the other detective was cracking through the witnesses. I was anxious for my turn. I wanted it to be over. We talked little, but drank many cups of coffee. Ingrid stayed close to Mel, and took her up to her room after she had finished her interview. Guy looked agitated and anxious. Owen sat impassively, as if he were in a doctor's surgery, waiting for a routine check-up. My turn came eventually, after Guy.

I got Inspector Sauville. He sat at the head of the table, a lackey by his side taking notes. He gestured for me to sit down.

'Your name is David Lane?'

'Yes,' I whispered.

'*Comment?*'

'Yes,' I said more strongly. He had only asked my name, but already I could feel my palms sweating. This was not going to be fun.

'How old are you?'

'Eighteen.'

'And you are a friend of Guy Jourdan's?' He pronounced 'Guy' to rhyme with 'key', just as Dominique had.

'That's right. We go to the same school in England.'

'When did you arrive here in France?'

'Two days ago.'

'I see.' He paused and leaned back in the dining chair. It

creaked. For a moment I was worried he would break it. 'David?'

'Yes?'

He swung forward. 'What were you doing at about one o'clock yesterday afternoon?'

He knew. The bastard knew. I'd have to tell him now. My mouth was dry and I hesitated.

'*Hein?*' He was a big man, and leaning forward he seemed even bigger.

'I was, er . . . with Mrs Jourdan.'

The policeman exchanged glances and a twitch of the lips with his sidekick. 'And what were you doing with her, David?'

I was, that is, we were, well . . .' I squirmed.

'Yes?'

'We were having sex.'

'Ah.' A smug smile of triumph crossed the policeman's face. He thought this was funny. 'Tell me more.'

So I told him the whole sordid story, and it did seem sordid that early in the morning when told to a policeman in slow English. I told him about overhearing Dominique shout at Tony the night before, and my suspicions about Tony and Mel, and Dominique's motivation for seducing me.

'Did you see or hear anything last night?'

'No. I went to bed pretty early. About ten. It took me a while to get to sleep, maybe an hour or two. Then I slept until Mr Jourdan woke me up this morning.'

'And Guy?'

'He went to bed the same time as me.'

'Did you hear him get up in the night?'

'No.'

'No other noises outside?'

'Nothing woke me till this morning.'

'I see.' Sauville paused, studying me. He was probably just thinking of his next question, but I found the silence unnerving. At last he spoke. 'When you were with Madame Jourdan yesterday, did she seem suicidal?'

I thought before answering. 'No. Quite the contrary. She seemed animated, excited. I think she was enjoying her revenge on her husband.'

'And you? How did you feel about being manipulated in that way?'

'Actually, it made me quite angry,' I said. Then I hesitated, worried I had put my foot in it. 'Of course, not angry enough to murder her or anything.'

The inspector dismissed my comment with a contemptuous wave of his hand. 'What about Guy Jourdan? What was his opinion of his stepmother?'

I paused. I was still a schoolboy. I didn't want to get my friend into trouble with the authorities. I tried to think through the angles.

'Just answer the question honestly,' Sauville commanded.

I did as I was told. 'I don't think he had ever met Dominique before this week. I think he didn't like the idea of her. He called her a bimbo and a tart.'

'I see. Not nice things to say about your stepmother?'

'No,' I said. 'But as I said, it wasn't her he didn't like. It was the idea of her.'

'Very philosophical. And the younger brother? Owen?'

'I have no idea what Owen thinks about anything. I doubt if anyone has.'

The large policeman raised his eyebrows. Then he leaned back once again in his chair. '*Bon*. Thank you for your cooperation, David. But I must ask you to remain here until we have concluded our investigation.'

My heart sank. I wanted to get out. Quick. I was looking forward to the family crisis Tony had ordered me to invent, now more than ever. 'Do you have any idea how long that will be?'

'A few days,' replied the inspector. 'Perhaps more.'

'You won't tell Mr Jourdan what I said about his wife, will you?' I asked.

'Oh, we will have to. But I think you'll find he knows already.' Sauville winked and smiled gratuitously. '*Au revoir.*'

I left the room to be met by Patrick Hoyle, who was demanding to see the inspector urgently in fluent French. He pushed past me, almost crushing me against the door-frame with his great stomach, and began to harangue Sauville. I left them to it and went to look for Guy.

I found him in the garden, sitting against the trunk of the olive tree beside the old watchtower. He was looking down between his knees, ignoring the morning sun throwing golden sparkles across the sea in front of him. Bees were murmuring in the lavender behind. I winced as I remembered this was the spot where his father had seduced Mel.

'Guy!' He ignored me. I ran over to the watchtower. 'Guy!' He turned to face me. I had never before seen Guy as he looked then. The muscles in his face were clenched tight, his blue eyes were cold and hard and his skin pale.

'Yes, Lane?'

'Look, I'm er, sorry . . .'

'Sorry? Sorry! For what?'

'Well, about Dominique.'

'What about Dominique? About shagging her? Do you want to apologize for screwing my father's wife? Is that it? Because if it is, then your apology isn't accepted.'

'Yeah. I'm sorry about that. I wish I'd never done it.'

'Bullshit. You loved every second of it. You probably thought you were a real stud, didn't you? I bet it beat fondling some slag's tits at the school disco. If you could find one desperate enough to let you, which I sincerely doubt.'

I tried to ignore the venom in his voice. 'Who told you? The police?'

'They asked me about it. But I've just spoken to my father. He told me a lot of things. About you and her. And about him and Mel.' He watched my face for a reaction. 'You knew about that, didn't you?'

'I guessed.'

'You guessed! What the fuck is going on here? My father screws my girlfriend, my friend screws my stepmother, and I don't have a fucking clue. And you know where my faithful father was when his wife was being smothered with a pillow?'

'No.'

'In some club in Nice. And for club read bordello, by the way. That's why he didn't discover her till three o'clock this morning.'

'Guy, I am sorry. If there's anything I can do . . .'

'There is. I should never have asked you out here. This isn't your world, Lane. You're way out of your depth. Go back to the sad little semi-detached stone that you crawled out from under and leave me alone. OK?'

He was glaring at me with something close to hatred in his eyes.

'OK,' I said. I left him alone.

I hid in my room and tried to make sense of the previous couple of days. I couldn't. I had never known anyone who had been murdered before. And I wasn't sure I had ever really known Dominique. The body I had thrilled to touch was now lifeless, the skin cold, the muscles stiff and rigid. But the person? Who was she? The very proximity of death made me shiver, the callous nature of my relationship with the victim made me cringe with guilt. Then there was my friendship with Guy ruined, probably permanently. He had shown me the kind of anger that would take years to die away, if it ever did. He hated me now, and I had so badly wanted him to like and respect me. I even felt guilty about

Guy's father, although I knew his sins were greater than mine. I had done something very wrong, and someone had died, and I would have to live with it.

I picked up my book. For the first time since I had started to read it, *War and Peace* came into its own. I wanted to lose myself in Napoleonic Russia, which seemed at that moment much less threatening than twentieth-century France.

But after two or three hours, hunger began to gnaw at my stomach. I hadn't eaten anything since a croissant very early that morning and the anxiety was releasing its own juices. I was eighteen. Eighteen-year-old boys get hungry regularly. I decided to brave the possibility of bumping into Guy or Tony for the chance of food.

I walked through the garden. It was another bright, cloudless day outside. It was hot, but the edge was taken off the heat by the sea breeze. There was no one on the terrace, but I could detect movement and plates of food inside.

I walked into the main house, and through the dining-room door I spied a table laden with bread, cold meats, cheese and salad. Mel was standing outside the room, listening. I stopped just behind her. I could hear Guy talking to Patrick Hoyle in an urgent whisper. I couldn't make out what he was saying, but I heard Hoyle's response.

'Abdulatif? The man's name is Abdulatif?'

Guy murmured in confirmation. Then Mel suddenly became aware of me standing at her shoulder. She reddened and walked into the room. I followed her. Guy turned and glowered. Hoyle coughed and nodded at me. I made straight for the lunch, to be joined a moment later by Mel.

In the awkward silence, the two of us helped ourselves, a large pile of food for me, a couple of spoonfuls for Mel. As Guy and Hoyle left the room I turned to her. 'What was that about?'

She glanced at me quickly and just shook her head. She

clearly didn't want to talk. I knew she must be feeling fragile, and I didn't want to intrude. So I sat down and began to eat.

Ingrid appeared at the door. 'There you are,' she said. 'I'm famished.'

'I know what you mean,' I said. 'Help yourself.'

Ingrid did just that.

'Are the police still here?' I asked her, glad to have someone to talk to. 'I didn't see any in the garden.'

'They've been combing it all morning,' she said. 'Perhaps they've finished, or maybe it's just a lunch break.'

'Have you seen Tony?'

'He's with some French guy in a suit. I think Patrick Hoyle got him a lawyer.'

'I thought Hoyle was a lawyer.'

'He may be. But this guy's probably a criminal lawyer. I imagine they're different.'

'Do you think Tony killed her?'

'Your guess is as good as mine. The French cops seem to think he did, though. Hang on, here comes one of them.'

I looked up. Sauville was marching towards us. My heart sank as I realized his eyes were focused on me. 'Monsieur Lane. When you have finished your lunch, I would like you to assist us, please.'

'What do you want me to do?' I asked doubtfully.

'We need to search your room. And we would like to take samples from the clothes you were wearing yesterday afternoon. Also we need your fingerprints. And afterwards I invite you to the police station.'

'The police station?' I didn't like the sound of that. 'Why do you want me to go to the police station?'

Sauville glanced at Ingrid and Mel. He coughed. 'Er . . . We need some samples.'

'What kind of samples?' I said, my suspicions aroused by his hesitation.

Sauville glanced at the girls again. 'You will find out at the station.'

He left the three of us alone at the table. Mel remained sullen and withdrawn. But Ingrid looked as if she was trying to control a giggle.

'What is it?' I asked.

'I think I know what they're after,' said Ingrid.

'What?'

'They want your sperm,' she said.

I grimaced. 'Oh, God.'

Sauville returned to hurry me along with my meal.

'Have fun,' said Ingrid as I left the room with him.

A policeman drove me down the switchbacks to the prosperous little town of Beaulieu-sur-Mer. We passed through streets lined with bright awnings, under which parfumeries, boutiques, galeries and salons de beauté enticed wealthy tourists in off the pavements. There were flowering trees everywhere. Above and behind the town stretched a curtain of high grey cliffs. Les Sarrasins and its watchtower were clearly distinguishable up there, silhouetted against the brilliant blue sky.

The Gendarmerie Nationale was a scruffy building near the railway station. It was scruffy inside too: linoleum floors, dog-eared posters, functional metal and chipboard furniture. Thankfully, Ingrid was wrong about the precise nature of the samples they wanted, but I was sure she was right about their purpose. A doctor took a swab of saliva from my cheek, a syringe full of blood from my arm and hairs both from my head and, humiliatingly, from my pubic region. Afterwards I hung around in a waiting room until the policeman who had brought me down the hill came by to drive me back.

We were just leaving the building when a police car pulled up outside. Sauville stepped out, followed by another detective and two other figures, Tony and Patrick Hoyle. Tony looked tired and grim. He caught my eye as he entered the station. The hostility of that brief glare made me flinch.

It looked as if he was going to have some difficult questions to answer.

14

As soon as I arrived back at Les Sarrasins I headed for my room and opened up *War and Peace* again. This time I couldn't lose myself in its pages. I just kept thinking about Tony.

Had he murdered his wife? He must have. He had the motive: I had provided that. He had discovered the body in the middle of the night. And I had seen him being led into the police station for questioning. Did he look to me like a murderer? I had no idea what a murderer looked like. He was certainly charming. Just as certainly I would never trust him. But I couldn't envisage him actually killing Dominique.

Despite my last bruising meeting with Guy, I couldn't help feeling sorry for him. I knew how much he admired his father, and now he had to face the possibility that he was a murderer. It would be tough on him.

Tough on Owen too, but I didn't care about that.

There was a gentle knock on the bedroom door. Ingrid put her head round. 'How was your trip to the police station?'

'Horrible.'

'Look. I'm sorry I teased you about it earlier. That was hardly fair. Mel and I are having a drink. Would you like to join us?'

I dropped my book with a thud on to the floor by my bed. 'Yes,' I said, 'I would.'

I followed Ingrid out on to the terrace, where Mel was sitting alone at a table under the shade of a pine tree. Two glasses half-full of bubbly clear liquid and ice were standing in front of her. I went to fetch a beer for myself. I couldn't face a vodka and tonic: vodka reminded me of things I would rather forget.

'I saw Tony at the police station,' I said, taking the first sip.

'Yeah. They said they wanted to ask him some more questions,' Ingrid said. 'He didn't seem anxious to go.'

'What did Guy say?'

'Nothing. But he looked worried.'

'I bet he did.'

Despite all that had happened, the sun was shining brightly. Too brightly. Mel was cowering behind dark glasses. I couldn't blame her. She was drinking determinedly.

'Are you OK?' I asked her gently. I knew it was a stupid question, but I wanted to show her I cared about how she felt.

She sniffed and rubbed her nose. She had been crying. 'Not really. And you?'

'Not really.'

Mel looked at me awkwardly. 'Was it your first time?'

I nodded. 'And you?'

'Yes.'

'Pretty bad way to start, isn't it?' I said.

Mel laughed. 'Yes. After all those years of saying no, all that saving myself for the right man, and I go and do it with a fifty-year-old pervert.'

'Quite a good-looking fifty-year-old pervert, isn't he?'

'That's not the point. He's old enough to be my father. And that's what really scares me. Maybe I'm going to be one of those sad girls who chase after men twice their age because they're trying to get their fathers back.'

'Are your parents divorced?'

Mel nodded. 'My dad ran off with his secretary two years ago.'

'Sorry.'

'And yours?'

'No. They seem quite happy. But then, Dominique is nothing like my mother.'

'Or anyone's mother.'

'It's strange,' I said. 'She didn't seem like a real person at the time, and she seems even less like one now that she's dead.'

'Yes,' said Mel. 'It's easy to forget that someone has died.' She shook her head. 'What if Tony *did* kill her? I was with him just twenty-four hours before.' Her face filled with disgust, for herself as much as for Tony, I imagined.

'Don't beat yourselves up,' said Ingrid. 'You were both taken advantage of by two very manipulative people. Tony was trying to prove to himself he can pull girls better than his son. Dominique was having her piece of petty revenge. It wasn't either of your faults.'

'Of course it was my fault,' said Mel. 'I let him do it. In fact, I was a willing accomplice. It seemed so glamorous, so grown-up. I thought I was in control.' A tear ran down her cheek. 'You know the worst thing, David?'

'What?'

'I really like Guy. I had just about decided that he was the one that, you know . . . What's happened has just made me realize how much I like him. And of course now he won't talk to me. He won't ever talk to me again.' She fought back a sob.

Once again I marvelled at the effect Guy could have on girls. And on this one it was clearly deeper than superficial physical attraction. Did he know? Did he care?

'I'm pretty sure I've lost him as a friend,' I said. 'If he ever was my friend. He was furious with all of us when I saw him this morning: you, me, his father.'

'I'll tell you what I think,' said Ingrid. 'You've both had a bad time. But we're all young. We can learn from it. You can't feel guilty about it for ever. Those two, Tony and Dominique, were fucked up. You can't let them fuck you up too.'

She was right, of course, but Mel and I had plenty of guilt to wallow in.

The police came to see us once more that day. They wanted to check the shoes we had been wearing the previous evening. They had found a footprint, I supposed. Not much good that would do them, we had all been tramping around everywhere from what I remembered. But I gave them mine, again.

There was no sign of Tony. Presumably he was still at the police station, answering questions. Guy managed to avoid us that afternoon and evening and Owen was tucked away in his room playing with his portable computer. But we did see Hoyle. He spent most of the time ensconced with Guy somewhere upstairs, but he dropped in on Ingrid, Mel and me in the living room before he left.

He was wearing a baggy tan suit and a tie, and beads of sweat sparkled on his broad forehead with the exertion of running up and down the stairs. 'I trust Miguel is taking good care of you?'

'He certainly is,' Ingrid answered. She had used her Portuguese to charm the servant and he had responded by looking after us very well.

'Good, good. Let me know if you have any problems. But I'm sure Tony will be back tonight.'

'Mr Hoyle?' Ingrid said as he tried to leave.

'Yes?' He frowned. He had things to do.

'Can you tell us how the investigation is going? We've been left in the dark up here.'

'Of course,' Hoyle said reluctantly, lowering himself on to the edge of an armchair. 'As you know, they're interviewing Tony at the moment. But they haven't arrested him yet, and

I don't think they're going to. He's innocent, and I'm quite sure we can prove it.'

'How?' I asked. 'Does he have an alibi?'

'Yes. But not a reputable one.' A companion from the Nice bordello Guy had mentioned, I thought. 'No, we're, um . . .' Hoyle hesitated, 'working on something else.'

'So who did kill Dominique?' Ingrid asked.

'It must have been a thief. Someone broke in in the middle of the night, stole some jewellery and disturbed her. When she saw him, he suffocated her with the pillow. She had taken heroin, so she was probably disoriented.'

'So there's some jewellery missing?' I asked.

'Yes. Just her day-to-day stuff. But still worth a few hundred thousand francs.'

'And the police are certain she was suffocated?'

'They've done the post-mortem. She had some heroin in her bloodstream, but it wasn't an overdose. She died of asphyxiation. And the pillowcase was missing.'

'What does that mean?'

'It means the murderer got rid of it to avoid leaving any traces for the police to find. After he'd used the pillow to smother her.'

'Do you have any idea why they wanted to examine our shoes?'

'Not specifically. But it's good to hear they're checking other leads. They probably realize they've got the wrong man.' He shook his head. 'I still can't believe Dominique has been murdered. It just doesn't seem real. Tony and I have been in some scrapes together, but nothing like this.'

I nodded in agreement. It all seemed totally unreal to me.

Hoyle checked his watch. 'I need to get back to Beaulieu. I've got Tony a good criminal lawyer, the best in Nice. But I want to make sure they don't try to keep him in the station overnight.'

With that he heaved himself up out of the armchair and left us.

Sure enough, he returned an hour later with an exhausted-looking Tony. They ignored us and shut themselves in the study. Tony clearly wasn't off the hook yet.

I went to bed but stayed awake reading my book. Guy came in at about eleven. He ignored my greeting, quickly stripped off his clothes and jumped into bed.

I carried on reading.

After a minute or so, Guy leaned on his elbow and glared at me. 'Turn the fucking light off, Lane.'

I turned the light off. It took me a long time to get to sleep that night.

I was woken by a violent banging. I opened my eyes to see the door flung open. It was Sauville and two uniformed gendarmes. Morning sunlight streamed in behind them.

'What the . . . ?' Guy began.

Sauville's eyes scanned the floor and found a pair of trainers. He picked one up and glanced at the sole.

'Is this yours?' he demanded of Guy.

'Er . . . Yes.'

'Put on your clothes and come with me down to the police station. You are under arrest.'

Guy sat up in bed. 'I'm what?'

'You heard me.'

'That's stupid!' Guy protested. 'You've got no reason to arrest me. I didn't kill anybody!'

Sauville picked up some of the clothes at the end of Guy's bed and flung them at him. 'Get dressed!'

Guy swung himself out of bed and put them on, glaring at Sauville the whole time.

Sauville muttered something in French to one of the police-men behind him. The man produced a pair of handcuffs, gesturing for Guy to hold up his arms. Guy stared at the cuffs, as if he was only just realizing what was happening to him, and slowly did as he was told. They closed around his wrists with a snap.

'Good luck,' I said.

Guy turned towards me. For a moment I thought he was going to ignore me again. But then he spoke. 'This is all bullshit. They have nothing on me.'

'We will see,' said Sauville, as the policeman grabbed Guy by the elbow and shoved him roughly out of the room.

15

May 1999, Wapping, London

'So, how did you do last night?' Guy asked. The two of us plus Owen were getting down to work in the cramped Wapping flat. It was the Wednesday after the Tuesday before.

'Not too well. It was a zoo. I couldn't get a word in.'

'How many cards did you get?'

'Only three.'

'Three! That's pathetic. You've got to hustle, Davo. You can't get trampled by the herd.'

'I did come across one V.C I knew from my accounting days. I talked to him for a bit.'

'Did he like the idea?'

'I didn't ask him. It didn't seem appropriate.'

'Didn't seem appropriate! Why do you think you were there? Why do you think he was there?' Guy shook his head. 'I knew I should have gone myself,' he muttered.

I felt a flash of anger, but bit my tongue and put my head down. I was angry because I knew Guy was right. I felt guilty and inadequate. I was not good at this. Guy had hired me to help him raise money. He relied on me. I didn't want to let him down, especially at this early stage.

Guy and I worked on in angry silence. Of course, Owen was working in silence too, but there was nothing new in that. The tension crowded in on us in the small flat, hovering over the dining table we all shared as a desk.

Determined to make up for the previous evening's failure, I sent our plan to the three venture capitalists I had met, including Henry. I took some time over his covering letter. I toyed with elaborate excuses as to why I had suddenly discovered a need for funding the day after I had told him I didn't have one, before settling on the truth, which sounded better anyway. He just hadn't looked as if he wanted to hear yet another elevator pitch.

I looked up the British Venture Capital Association website, found three more likely names and sent the plan off to each of them.

Now all I could do was wait and see.

'Coffee?' asked Guy, after an hour or so of silence.

'Please,' I said.

He returned a couple of minutes later with a mug. 'I'm sorry I jumped on you like that,' he said. 'I know you tried your best.' He smiled a smile that said 'friends again?' and was impossible to resist.

'No, you're right. You probably should have gone. You'd have done better than me.'

'Next time.' He sipped his coffee. I was pleased that the tension had eased a little. We just didn't have the room for it.

'Bet you can't guess who else I saw last night?' I said.

'Who?'

'Mel.'

'Mel Dean?'

'That's the only Mel I know.'

'Well, well,' Guy said. 'There's a memory. What does she look like? Has she changed much?'

'She's aged a bit.'

'Don't they all? What about those lovely breasts?'

'They're in great shape.'

'That's good to know. They always were fine specimens.'

'She's still a lawyer,' I said. 'Apparently she does a lot of work with internet start-ups. I've just faxed her our shareholders' agreement. Remember I was unhappy with it?'

'You faxed it to Mel?'

'She said she'd take a quick look and come back to me.'

'Waste of time.'

'We'll see,' I said, feeling the irritation rising again and successfully controlling it.

It wasn't a waste of time. Mel called back late that afternoon. 'You were right,' she said. 'I think there are some real problems with that document. It would do fine for a small business with only a couple of shareholders. But for something that's going to grow into a venture-funded company, it's a disaster.'

'Oh. You mean it's not scalable,' I said, remembering some Owenspeak.

She laughed. 'Precisely,' she said. 'I see you've learned the lingo.'

'Some of it. Is it something we can change later on, when we get a bit more money?'

'You could, but it would be messy. Much better to start off with a proper structure.'

'Could you draw up a better one?'

'Certainly. I'd have to see the other company documents. And I'd probably have to charge you.'

'What do you think about working with Guy?' I asked as quietly as I could.

There was silence for quite a time. In the end she spoke. 'You are,' she said.

'That's true.'

'And are you happy with it?'

'Yes,' I said.

'OK. If it's good enough for you, it's good enough for me.'

'All right. Let me talk to him. I'll call you back in a couple of minutes.'

'Now that's what I call a short decision time,' Mel said.

I hung up and turned to Guy.

'I heard most of that,' he said.

'Our shareholders' agreement stinks.'

'Says Mel?'

'Says Mel.'

'Do you believe her?'

'Yes.'

'What do you think we should do?'

'I think we should get rid of the other lot and hire her.'

Guy snorted. 'But it's Mel, for God's sake! She's an airhead. Everybody knows that.'

'She was pretty bright at school, I seem to remember. She just acted like an airhead.'

'Well, she fooled me.'

'Obviously.'

Guy sighed. 'Are you sure about this?'

I nodded.

We were a team. Shareholders' agreements were more my thing than his thing. Suddenly it was very important to me that he showed he understood that.

He paused. Thought. Then smiled.

'Call her.'

Guy finally pinned Torsten down. He flew to Hamburg for a late-afternoon meeting that would slip into a night out. All part of the plan.

I met him at City Airport the next morning. I spotted him coming through Arrivals. He looked tired after the previous evening's excesses, but he was grinning.

'He said yes?'

'Not quite, but close enough.'

'What do you mean "not quite"? Did he say yes or didn't he?'

'Calm down, Davo. Everything's cool. He likes the deal. He likes it a lot. But he'd be investing money from the family trusts. And that means his father has to agree.'

'How likely is that?'

'Torsten says he'll have no trouble.'

'I hope Torsten is right. How much are we talking about?'

'Five million Deutschmarks.'

'That'll do.' Five million marks was just under two million quid. Not quite as much as we had hoped for, but enough to get us going. 'That'll do very well.'

Guy's smile broadened. 'Shall we see if we can get a bottle of champagne somewhere in this airport?'

Now it looked like the money was on the way, Guy was anxious to gear up. I wasn't so sure. I remembered Torsten from school. He was flaky then and he was probably flaky now. But Guy's view was that that was a risk we would have to take. And if Torsten didn't come through we might still have some luck with the half-dozen venture capitalists who now had our business plan.

Guy persuaded me. I knew I had to change my whole attitude to risk. At this stage in Ninetyminutes' life, we had to take risks, not avoid them.

We started recruiting. We wanted a head of merchandising to set up the on-line retailing. Owen and Gaz each needed help. We were also looking for an office to put everyone in. There wasn't room for Gaz in the flat in Wapping, so he was working from Hemel Hempstead and communicating with us by e-mail. This was asking for trouble, especially once our team grew bigger. So the office search began.

Mel came through with a new shareholders' agreement and some amendments to our articles of association. She decided to deliver them in person to the flat in Wapping. I was surprised when I opened the door for her to see that she had dyed her hair blonde. She also wasn't quite as severely dressed as she had been when I had bumped into her at First Tuesday.

'Very nice,' I said, wondering whether the new look was for Guy's benefit.

'Thank you. I knew I had to do something, but I couldn't quite face going to your lengths.'

'It's due for another trim soon,' I said, running my fingers through my hair, which was now almost half an inch long.

'Hello, Guy,' she said quietly as she entered the living-room-cum-office.

'Mel! Great to see you! Davo says you're just the lawyer we need. And we get a personal delivery service.' He rushed over and kissed both her cheeks. She glowed.

'I make it a point to see my clients face-to-face.'

'Good. I'd show you around the office, but this is it. That's Owen over there. Wave to the nice lady, Owen.'

Owen raised a hand while not moving his eyes from the screen.

'Here you are, David,' Mel said, taking an envelope out of her briefcase. 'I think you'll find these an improvement on the old documents.' I took them.

'Do you want a cup of tea or something?' I asked.

Mel hesitated, glanced at Guy and then looked at her watch. 'No, I've got a meeting in the West End. I'd better be off now.'

'I thought you said she'd gone grey,' Guy said as Mel shut the door.

'That was last week.'

'You were right about her chest.'

'I thought you said you'd given up women?'

'Yeah, but it's only Mel. That was a bit odd. It's a long way to come just to stay for two minutes. She could have sent the papers by courier.'

'Mm,' I said.

'Never mind. As long as she's a good lawyer.'

She was. The new documents all made perfect sense to me. Since Torsten hadn't signed the original papers yet I had the new ones couriered to Hamburg. Guy wasn't concerned by the lack of communication from Torsten, but I nagged him into chasing him up. We needed to know for sure that the cash was there before we moved into a new office and put more people on the payroll. Guy had no success. Torsten was out of town until the following week.

We had some luck with recruitment. The media were beginning to notice the dot-com wave and people wanted to ride it. Gaz brought on board a young sports journalist called Neil from a regional newspaper in the Midlands. Owen somehow found someone whom he would deign to work with, Sanjay, a football-mad programmer. We signed up Amy Kessler to be Head of Merchandising. She was a friend of a friend of Guy's, an American MBA who had worked for Adidas in Germany for a couple of years. She seemed frighteningly competent.

Guy and I realized we had too many chiefs and no Indians, and so I gave my old secretary at Gurney Kroheim a call. Actually, she wasn't exactly my secretary, she was more of a general dogsbody for about eight people. She was an Australian woman called Michelle. I had been impressed with her attention to detail and her cheerfulness. Although we weren't friends, I had always been careful to treat her with respect, something that most of my colleagues in the new Leipziger Gurney Kroheim hadn't done. When I told her what we were looking for at ninetyminutes.com she jumped at the chance, even though it meant a significant cut in salary.

We found an office. It was in Britton Street in Clerkenwell. Plenty of other dot-com companies were springing up in the neighbourhood; there were four other start-ups in our building alone. Importantly for us, the internet access was excellent. But the best part was that we could move in immediately. Which was good, because we needed somewhere to put our new recruits.

My father phoned me.

'You haven't cashed my cheque.'

'No, Dad.'

'Why not?'

I took a deep breath. 'I don't think ninetyminutes.com is a good investment for you.'

He was not impressed. 'I should be the judge of that.'

'I know, but . . . Look, how much have you got saved beyond this fifty thousand?'

'That's none of your business. Now please cash my cheque. I've always trusted you, David; now it's time for you to trust me.'

I hesitated, weighing it up. I was right; this was a bad place to put his retirement nest egg. But he was right; I should trust him. And things were really rolling. Of course, I couldn't guarantee ninetyminutes.com would succeed, I wasn't even certain we would get our initial funding, but I did feel good about it. And my father wasn't looking for guarantees.

I sighed. 'OK, Dad, if you're positive about this. I'll cash the cheque this afternoon. Thank you.'

'Thank *you*,' he said. 'And good luck. I'm counting on you.'

'I know.'

I put down the phone with the nagging feeling that I had just made a big mistake.

16

July 1987, Côte D'Azur, France

I stood at the front door as the police car carrying Guy drove out of the courtyard, followed by Tony in his Jeep. I heard rapid footsteps on the stairs. A moment later Mel and Ingrid joined me, wearing the T-shirts they had been sleeping in.

'What's happened?' Mel asked.

'They've arrested him.'

'Guy?'

I nodded.

'Oh, my God!' She put her hand to her mouth, her eyes wide. Another shock. I wasn't sure how many more she could bear.

I described Guy's arrest.

'I can't believe they've taken him,' she said. 'David, you must tell them they've made a mistake.'

'I can try. I'm sure he is innocent. But I doubt Inspector Sauville will take my word for it.'

'But what possible reason could they have for suspecting him?'

'They must have found a footprint somewhere,' Ingrid said, 'Guy's footprint.'

'If they have, I'm sure there's an explanation,' I said. 'After all, why would he kill Dominique?'

'There's no reason why he'd kill her,' said Mel fiercely. 'It's that scumbag Tony. It must be.' She collapsed into a chair and began to weep, gently at first and then in earnest, huge sobs wracking her shoulders.

Ingrid shot me an anguished glance and put an arm round her. Mel was cracking up. I couldn't blame her, but there was little I could do to help. Ingrid led her outside to the terrace. Miguel had heard the commotion, and a couple of minutes later he materialized with breakfast.

Then Owen appeared, bleary eyed. 'What's the fuss?' he asked, picking up a croissant and stuffing it into his mouth.

I told him.

He stopped chewing in mid-mouthful and stared at me, as though unable to comprehend what I had just said. 'Shit,' he whispered at last.

'I'm sure they'll let him go soon,' I said. After all, Owen was Guy's younger brother and I thought he deserved some words of comfort.

Owen ignored them. 'Why did they arrest him?'

'I think it might have something to do with a footprint.' I described again Sauville's visit.

'Shit,' Owen repeated. He looked anxious, almost panicked. His reaction was nothing like the sullen indifference he had displayed when his father had been interviewed at the police station. But then I knew how strongly he cared about his brother.

'They'll let him go,' Mel said, her face damp with tears. 'They've got to let him go.'

Owen glared at her. 'What do you care, you slut?'

She just looked at him. Stricken with shame and self-loathing, she couldn't answer.

'Owen!' I snapped. 'There's no need for that!'

Owen scowled and disappeared back indoors.

It was a long morning. I sat on the terrace and took refuge in *War and Peace*: past page 900 and going strong. Ingrid read her own book next to me and Mel withdrew to her room to lie down. And cry, no doubt.

It was eerily peaceful in the garden, with the quiet

disturbed only by the competing hums of the bees in the lavender and the distant traffic a long way beneath us. No sign of Guy. Or Tony. Or the police. The action was all going on down there, in that scruffy police station in Beaulieu.

Then, just before lunch, we heard a car draw up to the front of the house. Ingrid and I rushed round to see who it was. To our disappointment, it wasn't Guy. It was Tony.

He led us into the house and to the drinks cabinet in the living room, and poured himself a large gin and tonic. 'God, that tastes good,' he said, taking a long swig. 'The room service in that police station was lousy.'

There was the sound of rapid footsteps down the stairs as Mel appeared.

'Any news?' Ingrid asked.

'No,' said Tony. 'They're still holding him.'

'Have they charged him?' I asked.

'Not yet. Patrick says they can hold him for up to four days before an arraignment in front of an examining magistrate. Don't worry. We'll get him out before then.'

'But they've arrested him, haven't they?' Mel protested. 'They must have some evidence against him.'

'Some mix-up about a footprint. Patrick will get him off.'

Mel didn't seem convinced. 'What about you?' she said.

'Me? Looks like I'm in the clear.' Tony smiled. Which was fair enough, I supposed. But I couldn't help thinking that his exoneration had been won at the expense of Guy's guilt. Not that I believed for a moment that Guy was guilty, myself. I just didn't trust the French police to uncover the truth when they could nail the easy suspect.

Tony looked at the three of us. None of us appeared in the slightest bit pleased to see him. He sighed and poured himself another drink. 'I'll be in the study if anybody wants me,' he said, and left us.

'I wish they had let Guy go instead of him,' Mel said.

'I'm sure Hoyle will swing something,' I said, with as much confidence I could muster. But I wasn't sure at all.

At around two o'clock a detective came to fetch me. Sauville wanted to talk to me again. I wasn't surprised.

I thought hard during the car journey down the hillside. Thought about what I had done. Where my loyalties lay.

I was led into a small interview room. Sauville was there with his sidekick. He looked even more tired and irritated. He lit up a cigarette and offered me one.

I shook my head.

'Thank you for coming here, Monsieur Lane.'

'Not at all.' I hadn't been aware that I'd had a choice.

'I am glad to say that your version of your liaison with Madame Jourdan accords with the forensic evidence. You have been honest with me. This is good. Good for you, good for me. Now . . .' He took a long drag on his cigarette. 'I want you to continue to be honest with me.'

'Of course.'

'*Bon.* You remember Tuesday evening? The evening that Madame Jourdan was killed.'

'I do.' I was alert now.

'This is very important. When you went to bed, did you go alone?'

'No. I went with Guy.'

'OK. Tell me what happened.'

'I wasn't in a good mood that evening. No one was, really, apart from Dominique. At about ten o'clock I said good night and went off to bed.'

'And Guy came with you?'

'Yes.'

'Did you go straight to your bedroom.'

'Yes.'

'Are you sure? You didn't delay on the way?'

'Um . . .'

'Monsieur Lane?'

'Let me think. It was a couple of days ago.'

And I thought. Rapidly. I knew the answer, of course. Guy and I had gone straight to the little guest cottage together. I could remember that clearly. But what should I tell the policeman?

My first instinct was to say just that. That Guy had been with me the whole time. That he couldn't possibly have slipped away to murder Dominique.

But . . .

But they had found a footprint, that was clear. Guy's footprint. I suddenly realized that that was what Sauville wanted an explanation for. I had to give him one, or at least the possibility of one.

'I don't think so. Or, at least, I didn't. But, actually, I think I went first, and Guy followed me a couple of minutes later.'

'A couple of minutes?'

'I'm not a hundred per cent sure. But I can remember that he was brushing his teeth when I was getting into bed. So he can't have been more than a couple of minutes longer than me.' I wanted to give Guy enough time to leave a footprint but not enough time to murder Dominique.

'Did you see where he went?'

'No.'

'Could he perhaps have gone into the bushes to er . . .' Sauville was searching for the right word. 'To piss?'

'Possibly.'

'That seems strange, don't you think? To piss in the bushes when there is a toilet in the guest cottage?'

'Not so strange,' I said. 'A bit drunk. A lovely night. The stars are out. It's the kind of thing Guy might do.'

'We found his footprint outside Madame Jourdan's window. The soil there was watered during the afternoon, so we know it must have been put there that evening. Or perhaps later that night.'

'Oh, I see. That explains it, then.' So I was right. Fortunately I had managed to back up the story Guy had told.

'Perhaps,' Sauville said, considering the point. 'Just one last question. Do you know the young gardener who works here? A North African?'

'Yes. Abdulatif.'

Sauville frowned, as though surprised that I knew his name. 'That is correct. When did you last see him?'

'Hmm.' I thought. 'It was the morning before Mrs Jourdan was killed.'

'And not since then?'

'No. No, not since then.'

'Did you see him doing anything suspicious?'

I remembered the smile he had given Guy, but didn't mention it. It almost certainly didn't mean anything, and even if it did, it was hardly suspicious. 'No,' I said. 'He was just gardening.'

'We are trying to locate him. It seems he has disappeared. He hasn't been seen since the morning after Madame Jourdan was killed.' Sauville stood up. The interview was over. 'Thank you once again for your cooperation, Mr Lane. Now my colleague will take you back to the house.'

As the police car climbed up the hill, I watched the sun lowering itself towards the western horizon and for the first time since Dominique had died I felt good about myself. I had let Guy down by sleeping with Dominique. His contempt for me had been painful because it had been justified. And now I had helped him.

I had no idea how Guy's footprint had turned up wherever the police had found it, but I knew it wasn't because he had gone for a pee in the bushes on the way to bed. They didn't know that, though. I looked honest and I looked scared and I was sure Sauville had believed me.

At that point I was only concerned with covering for my friend, making amends for my betrayal. The possibility that Guy might have been involved in some way in Dominique's death didn't occur to me. I wasn't at all worried about how or when Guy's footprint had been placed outside Dominique's window, if that was indeed where the police had found it.

Perhaps I should have been.

It was strange staying at Les Sarrasins without Guy. None of us felt we should be there, we were like guests who had long overstayed their welcome, but there was no chance that Sauville would let us leave. Guy's plea for me to crawl back under my semi-detached stone rang in my ears. He was right, of course. I had no business being there; I should be in the caravan in Devon with my parents. I should never have come.

We all gathered for an awkward supper. There was little conversation; we were all wrapped up in our own thoughts. Tony made a half-hearted attempt at small talk, which received little response from any of us. But he did have some news. The search for Abdulatif had turned into a full-scale manhunt. Miguel had heard from the Arab gardener of a nearby property that the police had turned over Abdulatif's house, and had been asking about him in all the Arab hang-outs in the area, with no success.

For the first time in three days there was the glimmer of hope in Mel's eyes.

I was doing lengths in the pool the next morning when I became aware of laughter on the terrace. Familiar laughter. I stopped swimming and looked up. There were Tony, Guy and Hoyle, broad grins on their faces. Miguel was opening a bottle of champagne.

I pulled myself out of the water and grabbed a towel. Ingrid and Mel emerged from the house.

The cork popped. Tony poured.

'I told you Patrick would get him off,' Tony said, slapping Hoyle on the back. 'Hey, where's Owen? Guy, get him, will you? I won't have him missing this.'

Guy went off to look for his brother.

'Of course, it helps that they know who did kill her,' Hoyle said.

'Who's that?' I asked.

'The gardener,' he replied. 'The police have been looking for him everywhere. But it's hard to find one Arab boy on the Riviera, there are so many places he can disappear.'

'How do they know it was him?' I asked.

'He ran away, didn't he?' Tony said. 'And they found Dominique's empty jewellery case in his room. I hope they catch the bastard.'

'But they don't have any conclusive proof?' I persisted.

Tony frowned, unamused by my quibbling. 'That's conclusive enough for me. Ah, here he is!' he said as he saw Owen approaching behind his brother. There was almost a spring in his step. He was as pleased as the rest of us to have Guy back. 'Champagne, Owen?'

'I'll take a Coke.'

'You'll have champagne,' his father said, thrusting the glass into his hands. 'Here's to liberty.'

We all drank. All of us but Dominique, I thought. She wouldn't be joining in the celebration of her stepson's new-found freedom.

Mel, Ingrid and I left as soon as we possibly could. Neither Guy nor his father was sad to see us go, although Tony was polite and charming to us, even to me. But he called a taxi this time to take us to the airport.

I packed my stuff and went to look for Guy. I found him beneath the watchtower staring out at the sea. I sat next to him.

'I know this was a horrible week, but thank you for inviting me,' I said.

He didn't answer. I waited. He wasn't going to answer.

'OK,' I said, getting to my feet. 'Goodbye, Guy.'

I turned to go. 'Davo?' he said.

'Yes?'

'Thank you. For what you said to Sauville.'

'No problem.' I considered trying to say more, but Guy was still looking away into the distance, his hunched back towards me. I was dismissed. I should leave.

Ingrid, Mel and I climbed into the taxi for the airport.

'Thank God that's over,' Ingrid said as the car pulled out of the courtyard, through the electrically driven iron gates and on to the road down to the Corniche.

'Yeah. And thank God Guy's out of jail.'

'That was all very convenient, wasn't it?' Ingrid said.

'What do you mean?'

'You know what I mean.' She was looking at me closely.

I thought through Ingrid's suggestion. It was indeed fortunate that the gardener had disappeared. I remembered hearing Hoyle repeat his name to Guy. I remembered the mysterious footprint from Guy's shoe. And Owen's reaction when he heard that his brother had been arrested, almost as if he knew something.

Then I stopped thinking.

'You know what?' I said. 'I don't care. I'm just glad to be out of here.'

'Hear, hear,' said Mel, her voice stronger than it had been for the last four days.

Tony hadn't come through with his earlier promise of the fare home and my meagre funds wouldn't stretch to a one-way plane ticket, but Ingrid lent me two hundred francs which gave me enough for a bus fare. The taxi dropped me off at the bus station and I was sorry to say goodbye to her and Mel, but very pleased to get on the coach for the long trip back to England.

As the bus powered up the autoroute towards the lowering cloud of northern France, I pondered the one lesson I had learned from the previous week. I had finally glimpsed what the glamorous lives of people such as Guy were really like and I had discovered something.

They weren't nearly as desirable as they seemed.

17

May 1999, Clerkenwell, London

It was Monday morning and we had the keys to the new office. The whole team showed up: Guy, myself, Owen, Gaz, Neil, Sanjay, Amy and Michelle. For most of them it was their first day in the job. Everyone was wearing jeans and ready for hard physical labour.

Britton Street was picturesque in its way, a narrow lane of modest Georgian houses and converted metalworking shops like ours, with the white spire and golden weathervane of St James's Church, Clerkenwell, peeking out above the rooftops. There were signs of the dot-com invasion everywhere: young thin men in fleeces with wispy facial hair, flashier men and women in black on mobile phones, convenience shops full of convenience snacks, 'Offices To Let' signs where old jewellers' or watchmakers' premises were being refurbished. But our own office was nothing special: one side of the fourth floor of a brick building with white walls, blue-painted pipework, a light grey carpet and no furniture.

Workmen brought up second-hand desks, chairs, partitions and computer equipment, which everyone shifted around enthusiastically. We had thought of most things in advance, like the photocopier and the computer network, but we needed a coffee machine, a water cooler and a fridge. Michelle was despatched to find them. Gaz had arrived with his uncle's van, in the back of which was a table-football table and a pinball machine. He said it was pointless keeping them at home if he was going to be at the office all the time.

He and Neil played a couple of games of table football; they were both astoundingly good.

Owen had planned the phone system and the computer network meticulously, but it was Sanjay, rather than he, who directed the engineers who came to install things. The characters of the new members soon became clear. Amy was an adept organizer with leanings towards bossiness, who spent most of the day wandering round with a cloth and a bucket of hot water wiping things. Neil was willing but useless, but Gaz turned out to be surprisingly practical, especially with wires. Owen could lift anything. Miraculously, by four o'clock, the office was functional.

Guy disappeared for ten minutes and came back with three bottles of champagne and some glasses.

'To ninetyminutes.com,' he said.

We all raised our glasses and drank. I looked around at the odd assortment of twentysomethings, dirty, sweaty but smiling, and thought how much happier I was to be there rather than surrounded by the humourless bankers of Gurney Kroheim.

We were aiming to launch in August in time for the coming football season, only three months away. This meant that we needed to finish the site by mid-July to give us time to test it and to iron out any bugs. It was a tight deadline, but we were confident we could meet it. Owen had finalized the architecture of the system, and we had signed contracts with the firm that would house and maintain our server. Mandrill's design was coming on well and Gaz was putting together some excellent content.

But I was becoming increasingly worried about Torsten and the venture capitalists. Suddenly cash was flying out of the door. Unsurprisingly, none of our suppliers was willing to advance credit to an internet start-up; it was all cash up front. It was fortunate we had my father's funds, otherwise we would have been caught short. Alarmed by the dwindling balance of the company account, I checked my cash forecasts. We would run out in ten days unless we received Torsten's two million pounds.

Three of the venture capitalists had turned us down cold. Henry Broughton-Jones at Orchestra Ventures had agreed to see us, but not for another week. And we were still waiting for replies from the two others. Even if Orchestra or one of the others did show interest, it was extremely unlikely that they would be willing to invest within our ten-day deadline.

We needed Torsten.

I pestered Guy. He called Torsten repeatedly at the office with no response, or rather a string of implausible excuses from his assistant. I could see Guy's confidence in his friend evaporating before my eyes. I suggested we wait until eight o'clock, nine o'clock his time, and call him on his mobile. Torsten might hide at work but, knowing him, he would want to make himself available during his leisure hours for his friends. He wouldn't risk any parties taking place without him.

Guy dialled Torsten's mobile number and I leaned forward to try to catch what was going on. We had arranged our desks so that they faced each other, and I could see the tension on Guy's face as he waited for an answer. It was five to eight, but everyone was still in the office working, even Michelle, whose hours officially ended at five-thirty.

'*Ja?*' I could just hear through the receiver in Guy's hand.

'Torsten? It's Guy.'

I could only hear one side of the conversation. But from Guy's face I could tell it was bad news. Very bad news. It was quick, too. Torsten couldn't wait to get rid of his friend.

Guy slammed down the phone. 'Shit!'

I closed my eyes for a couple of seconds, then opened them. 'Did he say why?'

'Not exactly, but I can guess.'

'What?'

'Daddy. Herr Schollenberger doesn't want his little blue-eyed boy investing money in me.'

'Are you sure?'

'Yes. I know Torsten. He tried to make out it was his decision, but it wasn't. Torsten knows where his bread and butter come from. His father says "jump", he jumps. His father says "no" and . . .' Guy held up his hands in a gesture of hopelessness.

'Any chance of him changing his mind?'

'None. Absolutely none.'

I exhaled. Suddenly I became aware of all those people beavering away around us. People who had given up well-paid, promising careers to join us. And within a couple of weeks we were going to tell them, sorry, it had all been a big mistake. You know that two million quid we said we were getting in soon? Well, that was just a joke. Game over.

And what about my father? I had known all along he might lose his money, but never had I assumed he could lose it in less than a month. What kind of idiot would he take me for? And my mother? He had kept the investment from her. At some point he would have to tell her that he had given it to sonny-boy David, who had pissed it away in three weeks. Boy, would she be angry. And with some justification.

I looked across the desk at Guy. 'What are we going to do?'

'I have no idea.' He met my eyes. 'I have absolutely no idea.'

We decided to tell them straight away. They had all put their trust in us, and we couldn't let them think we were hiding anything from them.

Guy walked out into the middle of the office. 'Listen up, everybody.'

Everybody listened. I watched their faces as Guy told them the news. Shock. Bewilderment.

'How much cash do we have?' Amy asked.

Guy glanced at me.

'Twelve thousand, six hundred and thirty-four pounds,' I answered. 'That will only keep us going for the next ten days. We have no chance of meeting the salary payments at the end of the month.'

'What if we put in some of our own money?' said Michelle. 'I've got two thousand saved. I was going to use it for a trip, but that will wait. I'd like to see this through.'

Guy gave Michelle his broadest smile. 'Thanks, Michelle. But we'll need more than two thousand.'

'I reckon I can get my brother to put in a few thousand,' said Neil. 'He fancies himself as a savvy businessman.'

'I can put in another ten,' I said, to my surprise. I had been careful to leave a portion of my savings on one side in case Ninetyminutes hadn't worked out. And now Ninety-minutes wasn't working out, here I was committing it. Sod it. It was only money.

'And perhaps we can take a minimum salary this month?' said Amy. 'Just enough to live on.'

Guy looked round the group. The enthusiasm had returned. 'Excellent. That should buy us enough time to get some serious money from somewhere. David will talk to all of you about how much you can put in, and he and I will work on a plan to raise more finance. And I promise we will keep you informed all the way.'

We broke up.

Over the next few days and the weekend everyone became fund-raisers. They were good at it. On Monday morning I had cheques totalling sixty-seven thousand pounds. Amazingly,

Neil had come up with twenty, most of it from his brother in Birmingham whose pest-control business was doing very well. Then there was my ten, seven more from Owen, which just about cleaned him out, two from Michelle, three from Gaz, ten from Amy, five from Sanjay and even ten from Mel. I did a series of complicated calculations to ensure that each person got a slice of equity commensurate with their investment. It was difficult, but they all seemed happy with the result.

We had to slash costs. We followed Amy's suggestion; everyone agreed to take only five hundred pounds pay that month. The site had to be up and running for the start of the new football season in August. That would still be possible on our reduced budget, but the advertising and PR we had been planning would have to be cut way back. Too far back. If we wanted ninetyminutes.com to be anything more than just a revamp of Gaz's Sick As A Parrot site we would need more cash. Very soon.

Two more rejections came in from the venture capitalists. Five down, one left.

The day came for our meeting with Henry Broughton-Jones. Orchestra Ventures was a relatively new fund, set up by three partners who had left a more established venture-capital firm three years previously. Henry had been one of their first recruits and had recently been elevated to the position of partner. He had his own glass-encased box, complete with armchairs and conference table. He welcomed us genially and encouraged Guy to talk.

Guy gave the twenty-minute pitch and he gave it well. He had me convinced yet again, and I was hopeful that he would convince Henry. Afterwards Henry asked the right questions, which Guy answered confidently. Henry touched on management, and Guy admitted his own lack of experience, but pointed out that Amy, Owen and I all had relevant backgrounds.

When our hour was up Henry showed us out, promising to call us with his initial reaction.

He did. The next day.

It was a no.

I cursed to myself, counted to three and asked him why.

'It's got a lot going for it. The idea makes a lot of sense to me. Especially if you really can sell clothing over the web. The way the Internet is developing, on-line retailers will need good content to sell their products and good content will need some way of making money out of visitors, so this is a neat combination. The real problem is the management.'

'The management?'

'You know how venture capital is supposed to be about management, management, management? Well it's all true. Especially at our shop. Guy Jourdan talks a good story, but he's never managed anything remotely like this before. Neither have any of the rest of you, although you all have good technical experience. I'd like to help, but I know if I took this further my partners would shoot me down in flames.'

'You're sure about that?'

'Quite sure. Sorry, old chap.'

I sighed. 'OK, Henry. Thanks for looking.'

'No problem. And good luck.'

I turned towards Guy, who had just finished his own phone conversation. He saw the look on my face. 'Oh, no.'

'I'm afraid so,' I said.

'Why? I thought he got it. Why did he say no?'

'Management.'

'Management? Meaning me, I suppose.'

I nodded.

'Bloody hell! What do these people expect? It's like *Catch 22*. They won't give you any money unless you've been a big success before, but you can't be a really big success unless they give you money. It makes no sense! I'll tell him.' Guy reached for his phone.

'Whoa! Wait a moment. He's not going to change his mind just because you shout at him. He gave us a good hearing, we can't ask for any more than that.'

Guy withdrew his hand. 'All right. So where does that leave us?'

'Nowhere.'

'Oh, come on. There are plenty more VCs out there. Let's have another look at the BVCA website.' He began tapping at his keyboard.

'No, Guy.'

'Davo! We need the money!'

I nodded. 'But we're not going to get it from venture capitalists. At least, not yet.'

Guy could see the way I was looking at him. He knew what I was thinking. 'No, Davo. No way.'

'You've got to try. He's our last chance.'

'I've told you, I want to succeed without him or not at all.'

'That was OK when we talked about this a month ago,' I said. 'But now things have changed. Everyone out there has put most of what they own into this. So have I. Ninety-minutes isn't about just you any more. It's about all of us.'

'He'll say no.'

'We'll never know that until we try.'

Guy closed his eyes and raised his face towards the ceiling. I let him struggle with himself. Finally, he spoke. 'OK,' he said. 'We'll go and see him. You have to come with me, though.'

'But he hates me more than he hates you.'

'I know. But I'm not doing this alone.'

This time, Tony Jourdan didn't pick us up from Nice airport. We took a taxi. We barrelled along a highway through the centre of the city and climbed the steep Corniche. As I saw the sea, the trees and the rocky cliffs, that week twelve years before came back to me. I shuddered. And I remembered Tony's threat to me. Did I really think he would talk to me, even twelve years on?

The door was answered by Miguel, who looked even smaller than I remembered him. He greeted Guy politely and led us through the house to the terrace. Once again, the view took my breath away. Cap Ferrat reached out into the Mediterranean, green and rich and lush, with its fabulous mansions and flotilla of super-expensive white craft buzzing around its shoreline. This early in the summer the sky was an even clearer blue. I couldn't help taking a quick look for Corsica, and I thought I caught a grey smudge on the horizon.

Tony rose from a chair to meet us. The wrinkles around his eyes had deepened and his sandy hair was fading to grey at the edges, but he still looked slim and active. At least he wasn't openly hostile. He smiled politely and introduced me to the dark-haired woman who was sitting with him. She stood up, and towered over him by at least three inches. A beautiful woman, I was not surprised to see, but in a more subtle way than Dominique.

'Sabina, this is David Lane, an old school friend of Guy's.'

'Hello,' she said, with a friendly smile. She held out her hand for me to shake, and then kissed Guy on both cheeks. A baby started crying inside. The noise shocked me, it seemed so out of place in these surroundings.

'I must go and check on Andreas,' said Sabina in a Germanic accent. 'Make sure you see your brother before you go, Guy.'

'I will.'

We sat down. I looked around. Up at the house and Dominique's bedroom, which was presumably Tony and

Sabina's bedroom now, the place where I had lost my virginity and she had lost her life. At the guest cottage where I had skulked during the French police's inquisition, at the old Roman watchtower where Tony had seduced Mel and where his son had declared his hatred of me.

Tony was watching. 'I thought I told you I never wanted to see you again,' he said. But he said it without hostility, as though he wanted to note our past enmity for the record, before putting it to one side.

'I know,' I said. 'And I'm sorry. But this isn't a social call.'

'Of course not. You want some more money, don't you, Guy?'

'Yes,' said Guy.

'And why should I give it to you?'

'I don't know why you should,' he answered. 'Which is why I haven't asked you before. In fact, I didn't want to ask you even now, but David insisted.'

'Oh, yes?' said Tony, glancing inquiringly at me.

'Guy didn't want to ask you for money because he didn't want to rely on you to bail him out of a hole yet again,' I said. 'But I'm not asking you to bail Guy out. I'm asking you to invest in something because you can make a good profit out of it.'

'Hm.' Tony lifted up the newspaper on the table to reveal the business plan we had couriered to him the day before. He picked it up and began leafing through it. 'Did you write this?' he asked me.

'Some of it. Guy wrote most of it, though.' Tony glanced at his son. It was a good document, and Tony knew it.

Then he started asking questions. They came thick and fast. Henry Broughton-Jones had asked some pretty good general questions, but they were nothing like this inquisition. Although Tony had only had the plan a day, he had virtually memorized it. He asked me to justify the assumptions behind the financial projections, an uncomfortable process. He had looked at several other soccer sites already on the web, and he wanted to know what we thought of them. He asked us about Champion Starsat, the big satellite TV company, and what their strategy for the web would be.

After an hour and a half, Miguel brought lunch and the questions continued. We did well. Guy in particular held his own. He knew his stuff, Tony couldn't deny it.

'So, Dad,' said Guy eventually. 'What do you think?'

Tony looked from Guy to me and back again to his son. He grinned. 'It's a good idea. I'll do it.'

Guy could hardly believe it. His jaw dropped open.

'I need to make some real money again,' said Tony. 'All this has to be maintained.' He gestured to the house and gardens around him, seeming to take in his wife and son indoors. 'The life went out of the property market years ago. The Internet is the place to be. The challenge will be good for me. But,' he said, glancing at me, 'David is right. I'm going to do this on a purely commercial basis. Which means I'm going to want a stake for my two million quid. A big stake.'

Guy and I exchanged glances. 'Fair enough.'

Tony held out his hand for his son to shake.

'Thanks, Dad,' Guy said.

'Good. I'll come to England next week and we can finalize things with your lawyers.' Guy winced. Tony noticed it. 'You do have lawyers, don't you?'

'Yes,' said Guy. 'We have a very good lawyer.'

'Well, I look forward to negotiating with him.'

I wasn't quite sure how much Mel would look forward to negotiating with Tony. Neither was Guy, judging by his expression.

We ordered a taxi to take us back to the airport, and after a quick look at Guy's six-month-old half-brother, we left.

Neither of us wanted to stay in that house a moment longer than we had to.

Guy shook his head. 'I still can't believe it.'

'I told you it was worth a try,' I said. 'Cheer up. We've just saved the company yet again and you're looking worried.'

'It doesn't feel right,' said Guy.

'Oh, come on. What do you want to do? Turn down his money?'

'No.'

'Well, then? This can only be good news.'

'We'll see,' said Guy. 'I don't trust him.'

18

June 1992, The City, London

The long hot afternoon was beginning, and I was going to spend the whole of it in Nostro Reconciliations, reconciling nostros. The very thought of it made my limbs feel heavy and my brain tired, so tired. Computer printouts to go through, boxes to tick, mindless tedium. I was a junior member of the audit team for United Arab International Bank. My current task was to make sure that the balances at the bank's main accounts in each currency, known as nostro accounts, reconciled with the bank's own accounting system. In theory I might uncover a multi-million-dollar money-laundering fraud at any moment. In practice they added up, with mind-numbing regularity. I glanced across at the manager in charge of the department. He was a small, rather scruffy man who seemed to have a permanent itch just below his collar. He was too nervous to talk to me. I fantasized that this was because he was a master criminal, afraid I would unmask him at any moment. Of course I knew he was actually worried that my boss might criticize his department. But there wasn't even much chance of that, I thought, as I ticked another box.

I had tried to get myself on the audit teams for as many banks as possible, on the theory that it would make it easier to escape accountancy for banking once I qualified. A fine theory, but boring, boring, boring.

I had one thought to sustain me, like the glimpse of an oasis across the desert sands. That evening I was attending a reunion for the old pupils of Broadhill School. It would be held at a hotel near Marble Arch, the headmaster would make a speech pleading for cash and there would be lots to drink. Lots and lots. I was looking forward to it.

I was also looking forward to meeting the people there. I hadn't kept in touch with anyone from school; my life at university and as an accountant had taken me away from them. I had read about one or two of them in the papers: a quiet girl in my economics class who had won a swimming medal at the Seoul Olympics and a boy who had rescued his fellow explorers after two weeks lost in the Borneo jungle. I had also read about their fathers: Torsten Schollenberger's had been accused of bribing a senior German minister and Troy Barton's had won an Oscar. No mention of Guy's, though. Nor of Guy. The thought of them both made me shudder. Even five years after the event I couldn't think of Guy without the guilt flooding back. I hoped he wouldn't be there that evening.

He was. He was the first person I saw as I walked into the already crowded hotel function room.

He was standing holding a glass of wine, talking to two people I vaguely recognized. He hadn't changed much: his blond hair was now brushed back off his forehead and he had filled out a bit. I hesitated, flustered, unable to decide how to enter the room without him seeing me.

He looked up and his eyes met mine. His face broke into a wide smile, and he strode over to me. 'Davo! How the devil are you!' He held out his hand and pumped mine. 'Let's get you a drink.' He peered at his full glass, downed it all, and dragged me over to a waitress with a tray. He swapped his empty glass for a full one, and handed me my first. 'Cheers,' he said.

An extraordinary wave of relief swept over me, as though a ball of tension that had been screwed up tightly somewhere inside me for the last five years had been released. I had assumed Guy would never want to talk to me again and I had told myself that this didn't matter. I now realized it did. I also realized Guy was drunk. That was fine with me, but it did mean I had some catching up to do.

'Thank God you've come,' said Guy. 'Do you remember those two? I don't. But they seem to think we were best mates at school. Tedious as hell.'

My immediate thought was that they couldn't possibly have more boring lives than mine.

'So, what are you up to, Davo?'

'Working undercover.'

'Working undercover! Who for?'

'I can't tell you. Well, I could tell you, but I'd have to kill you. And that would be messy. I've been specially trained, you know. You wouldn't stand a chance. What about you?'

'I'm a famous actor.'

'Famous actor, eh? How come I've never heard of you, then?'

'I don't use my real name. I've been in a lot of big movies recently. *The Division*, *Morty's Fall*.'

'I saw *Morty's Fall*,' I said. 'I didn't recognize you in that.'

'That's because I'm such a good actor.'

Just then, a big man with square shoulders and a rugby-player's neck clapped his hands for attention. He was the new headmaster, and he talked about the school and how it needed money for a new theatre. He was inspiring in a down-to-earth way. But my attention was distracted by Guy. He seemed to have come to some kind of silent arrangement with a pretty black waitress who kept bringing us new glasses of wine.

We drank them.

'Hey, isn't that Mel Dean over there?' Guy whispered.

I followed his glance. It was Mel. Dressed in a smart navy blue suit. And with her was Ingrid Da Cunha.

'You're right.'

'Shall we go and talk to them?'

'Yeah. If you like.' I was surprised Guy actually wanted to talk to Mel, but I welcomed the chance to see Ingrid again.

Just then the headmaster stopped talking, there was clapping and the crowd, which had been becoming increasingly restless, began to move again. Guy and I weaved our way through to the two women. Guy gently placed his hand on Mel's behind. She swung round, ready to say something sharp. When she saw who it was she froze, stunned.

'Hi, Mel,' Guy said. 'You look amazed to see me. I did go to Broadhill, you know. They have to let me in, although I'm sure they don't want to. You remember Davo.'

He kissed Mel and Ingrid on both cheeks. Neither of them had changed very much since school. Mel wore significantly less make-up, and the blonde streak in her dark hair had disappeared. But she still had the pouting softness that I was sure had first attracted Guy. Ingrid looked relaxed and tanned, as though she had just come back from a holiday. She gave us both a warm wide smile.

Mel recovered. 'Have you been groping every woman in the room, or am I specially privileged?'

'Only you, Mel. Although I could include Ingrid if she asked nicely.'

'Little chance of that,' said Ingrid.

Within a minute, we were all four talking like old friends; old friends who hadn't seen each other for a couple of months, perhaps, but who had no trouble catching up. Guy, abetted by his pet waitress, kept everyone topped up and knocked back huge quantities of wine himself. He seemed to be able to take it well enough: practice, I assumed. Meanwhile I was getting pleasantly drunk.

Time passed and suddenly we were some of the last people left in the room. Guy looked at his watch. 'Anyone want some dinner?' he asked. 'I know a good place near here.'

Mel glanced at Ingrid, who nodded her agreement, and soon we were out on the street and heading towards Bayswater. Guy led us into a Greek restaurant, ordered some retsina, and we were away. The group seemed to split into two, with Guy concentrating on Mel, who was quite drunk by now and giggling ecstatically at everything he was saying.

'You're not really working undercover for the CIA, are you?' asked Ingrid.

I shook my head. 'No, it's much worse than that.'

'Really?'

'Look, I'll tell you, but you have to promise not to leave the table immediately.'

'OK.'

'I'm training to be a chartered accountant.'

'Oh, my God,' said Ingrid. 'Are you sure I can't leave?'

'You promised.'

'I've heard about people like you, but I didn't know they really existed.'

'We do. But we're not let out much, so we're not a threat to society.'

'It can't be that bad.'

'Oh, it can,' I said, thinking of my fun-filled afternoon in Nostro Reconciliations.

'Mel's doing her articles to be a solicitor. That must be almost as dull.'

We looked over at Mel, who had just exploded in a shriek of laughter, eyes shining and hair all over the place.

'I'm sure she'll make a perfect lawyer. Sober, serious, reliable.'

'We're all grown-ups now,' Ingrid said.

'So what do you do when you're not editing *Vogue*?'

'Actually I'm a sub-editor on *Patio World*. It's a new title. You may not have heard of it.'

'Not yet. But I'll be sure to subscribe.'

'Well hurry, because I think they're going to close it down soon. It's only been going six months, but it's been a bit of a disaster.'

'Oh dear.'

'Don't worry. They won't blame me. They'll find something else for me to do.'

'I'm surprised you're still in England. I'd have imagined you somewhere far more exotic.'

'But London is exotic. The sky with all those fascinating tinges of grey. The people with their low-key warmth and friendliness. Very low key. And I find those dark wet winters so romantic.'

'A real aficionado.'

'Actually, it's nice just to be in one place for once. My mother's moved to New York with a new man and I'm so grateful I don't have to follow her around the world any more. There is something pleasantly stable about London. And it's a good place for my career.'

'No better place for patios.'

'When I'm running my own publishing empire, I'll know where I can find someone to add up cab fares.'

'I'd be more than happy to help,' I said. 'Just don't forget to keep the receipts.'

'I'll start a special collection for you today.'

I poured us both another glass of wine. 'It's nice to see you again,' I said. 'You were kind to me in France. And I don't know what I'd have done without that two hundred francs you lent me.'

'I was so pleased to get out of there,' said Ingrid with a shudder. 'That was one of the more unpleasant experiences of my life.'

We were both silent, watching Guy and Mel.

Guy noticed us and seemed to sober up. 'What are you two thinking about?'

Ingrid didn't answer. 'Nothing,' I said.

Guy leaned forward. 'It was France, wasn't it?'

I nodded. Mel was suddenly still.

Guy poured out the dregs from the second bottle of retsina. 'Well, let me tell you something. That was five years ago, when we were all still kids. I've forgotten about France. Totally and completely. And I hope you all will too. Is that a deal?'

'Deal,' I said, raising my glass. Ingrid and Mel raised theirs too, and we all drank to obliterated memories.

I was seriously drunk by the time we spilled out of the restaurant. Ingrid took the first taxi and I took the next, leaving Guy with his arm around Mel waiting for two more.

Who was I kidding? I didn't know whose flat they were going to, but I could tell they were going there together.

I saw quite a lot of Guy after that evening. He seemed happy to count me as a friend, and he certainly made my life more interesting. It turned out he really was an actor, of the struggling kind. After three years at university, where he had only just escaped being thrown out, he had somehow managed to get into a reputable drama school, where he said he had done quite well. Since then, things had been difficult. He had had a few bit parts in repertory theatres and a small number of tiny roles in TV. He had been an extra in *Morty's Fall*. He had an agent, who ignored him. He attributed his lack of success to the oversupply of young actors and an invisible network of contacts and friends of contacts that excluded him. That may have been partially true. A greater reason, I suspected, was that he just didn't try hard enough. He went to the gym and watched *Countdown* on the telly when he should have been writing letters and knocking on doors. Young actors are supposed to be hungry. Guy was thirsty. And slaked his thirst every evening and many lunchtimes.

I was happy to join him in this. It made the afternoons much easier to get through if I knew I was going to meet Guy for a pint or five after work. Of course, it made the mornings quite painful and it played havoc with studying for my professional exams, but at least it shook things up a bit. Guy had a small flat off Gloucester Road and we frequented several pubs and bars in that area. We were occasionally joined by other friends of his, including Torsten Schollenberger when he was visiting London.

What did we talk about? I have no idea. Probably meaningless drivel. For our different reasons we needed to find friendship and escape the tedium of the daylight hours. Often, as the evening progressed, Guy would begin to chase women. He was usually successful at this. He was good-looking, of course, but he also seemed able to transmit an aura of danger and excitement that hooked them. I tried, unsuccessfully, to work out what kind of women went for him. Then I realized that almost any woman would, provided she was in the right kind of mood. The curious, those looking for excitement or searching for a quick escape were drawn to him. Guy offered sex, fun, danger and absolutely no chance of commitment. He provided an opportunity for good girls to be bad for a night.

Many of them took it.

Mel was different. He treated her like a backstop, someone to go to when he felt like sex and the evening had failed to provide him with any. He rarely seemed to make any arrangements to meet her, but often at ten or eleven o'clock he would slip off to her flat in Earls Court. From what I could tell, she was always there waiting for him.

Just occasionally she would come out with us. She was always lively and amusing and often ignored by Guy. He was never rude to her, but he was often indifferent, which was worse. I could see what was going on: Mel was in love with Guy and Guy was using her. Mel was too scared of losing him to complain and so she put up with him. If I had thought about this, I would have realized that this showed a deep self-centredness in Guy's character. So I didn't think about it.

Guy took me flying with him. His father had bought him his own plane, an expensive Cessna 182 with the registration GOGJ, which he kept at Elstree aerodrome, just to the north of London. We went for lunch to Le Touquet and Deauville in France and to a pretty grass airfield on a hill opposite Shaftesbury in Dorset. Guy was a skilful flyer, and enjoyed skimming along at fifty feet above the waves, or a few hundred feet above the English countryside.

Inspired by Guy, I decided to learn to fly myself. I trained in an AA-5, an old banger compared to Guy's BMW. I was taught that it was safer not to fly much below two thousand feet, that it was important to check the aircraft thoroughly before every flight and that drinking any alcohol before flying was strictly banned. I wasn't at all surprised that somehow different rules applied to me than to Guy but, as I learned more, I became increasingly nervous sitting next to him in an aeroplane.

On the surface, Guy seemed to be leading a great life. And I was very happy to deal with him on the surface. But it is hard being a struggling actor, even a struggling actor with a wealthy father.

One evening I left work on the dot of five to meet him at a pub near Leicester Square. He had an audition near by, and he had suggested a drink afterwards. He was already there when I arrived, staring at his bottle of Beck's.

'I take it you didn't get the part?'

'Don't know,' he said. 'They promised they'd call. They only call you if you get the part, you know. So I probably won't hear anything.'

'Cheer up, you might get it.'

'It's just a crappy part in a dumb commercial. That's not it, Davo. It's just so humiliating.'

'You've got to start somewhere.'

'I know. But it's not what I expected. I loved drama school. I mean really loved it. Standing in the middle of the stage, being someone else, taking the audience along with the fiction that *I* was creating, manipulating their emotions. It was great. A real power kick. And I was good at it too. Chekhov, Ibsen, Steinbeck, even bloody Shakespeare, I could do them really well. At the end of the year we had a graduation performance and I was one of only four people to get a call from an agent asking me to go on her books.'

'Sounds promising.'

'And now what happens? I go along to meet Diane from Casting, who takes a Polaroid of me, gives me a few lines of truly horrible dialogue to speak at a camera and then it's "goodbye, we'll call you."'

'One day they will.'

'Yeah, but most days they won't. And to be rejected by Diane from Casting makes you feel like the tiniest speck of shit. I mean, it's me they're rejecting, isn't it? What don't they like about me? My voice? My face? Maybe I can't act after all. Maybe this whole thing is one huge mistake.'

'Come on, Guy. You'll make it. You always do.'

'Yeah, precisely. I've always been a success. I did well at school, didn't I? Tennis, soccer, head of house. And I thought I'd do well at acting. I thought I'd do something that even my father would notice. But at this rate I'll never get the chance. Diane from Casting will see to that.'

'You need another drink, quick,' I said. I went to the bar and bought him one. As usual, the alcohol did its work. Half an hour later we were chatting up two Italian girls. Guy got the pretty one and I passed on the ugly one. But it turned into a good evening.

I was in a newsagent's looking for a copy of *Private Eye* when I caught sight of the cover of *Patio World*. I bought it, leafed through the pages with a total lack of interest and spotted a phone number printed inside the front cover. As soon as I was back at my desk I dialled the number, got through to Ingrid and suggested a film. We went to *Dances with Wolves* and afterwards to a Thai restaurant in Soho for dinner.

The evening didn't seem like a 'date' but rather like two old friends meeting up after a long absence. Which was nice, especially since in reality we hardly knew each other. I liked Ingrid. She was refreshingly straightforward, but also perceptive. She seemed to understand what made me tick without me explaining it to her. She was a good listener, tempting me to tell her more about myself than I intended. Not that I had anything shocking to tell, rather the opposite. But that, too, she seemed to understand.

Our conversation turned to Guy. 'Have you seen him since that Broadhill do?' she asked.

'Yeah. I see him quite a lot, actually. It's fun.'

'He sees Mel as well, doesn't he?'

'From time to time.'

'Oh. That doesn't sound good.'

'It probably isn't for Mel. It's fine for Guy.'

'Selfish pig.' Her comment surprised me. Ingrid noticed. 'Well, he is, isn't he?'

'I suppose so,' I conceded.

'I mean, Mel is totally gone over him. Always has been.'

'Even after what Tony did to her in France?'

'Yeah. Especially after that. You know how much she regretted it. I think since then she's been desperate to show Guy that she made a mistake.'

I shook my head. 'I don't know what they all see in him.'

'Oh, I think I do,' said Ingrid with a twinkle in her pale-blue eyes.

'Not you as well?'

'Don't get me wrong. The last thing in the world I would want is to be his girlfriend. I assure you I don't envy Mel. But one can't help wondering . . .'

'I'll tell him.'

'Don't you dare!'

I paused to chase a piece of curried fish around my bowl with my chopsticks. Not great technique, but I was hungry. I noticed Ingrid whipping the food into her mouth like a pro.

'How do you do that?' I asked. 'It's unnatural.'

'I learned as a child. When I was little and we lived in São Paulo, we used to go to Japanese restaurants a lot. Did you know there's a massive Japanese community there? And then we lived in Hong Kong for a bit, so I've had plenty of practice.'

'Well I'm afraid I haven't,' I said, finally spearing the fish.

'Mel's had a rough time,' Ingrid said. 'She doesn't need Guy making her life any more miserable.'

'I'm sure she doesn't.'

'She used to talk to me a lot about her family when we were at school. It sounded like her parents hated each other and used her as a weapon. Especially her father.'

'Didn't he run away with a secretary?'

'That's right. I think Mel has been pretty uptight about sex ever since.'

'Tony Jourdan can't have helped.'

'No. Yuk.' Ingrid shuddered. 'I visited her a couple of

times when she was at university in Manchester. For someone who used to look like such a good-time girl at school I think she led a pretty celibate life at university. And afterwards probably.'

'Until Guy.'

'Until Guy.' She helped herself to some more rice. 'What about you?' she asked.

'What about me? Are you asking me about my sex life?'

'Is it a secret? Like the accountancy? Surely it's not as embarrassing as that?'

'Not quite,' I sighed. 'It hasn't been as successful as I would have liked, but it's not a total disaster. No one really serious, though. And you?'

'Hey, I'm Brazilian. But actually I only ever seem to sleep with the wrong men. That's something I've decided I'm going to change.'

'Oh,' I said. Ingrid went very slightly red. I noticed, but pretended not to. 'This green curry stuff looks horrible but it's really tasty. You should try some.'

We went out again, a week later. It was another good evening, but marred for me by some disappointing news. Ingrid's fears over the future of *Patio World* proved well founded. It was closing, slipping away from the specialist magazine shelves, leaving only a tiny band of readers with unfinished patios to mourn it. But her firm wanted her to go to Paris for a few weeks to work on a couple of titles that were proving successful there and might translate well to England. Ingrid was excited. It was a good career move, she spoke French and she loved Paris. I made encouraging noises, but I didn't mean them.

I found myself looking forward to her return.

19

I saw Owen only once that summer. I hadn't known he was coming; one evening I went to meet Guy in one of our usual watering holes and there he was.

Guy bought the beer and chatted away as though Owen wasn't there. But it was hard to ignore his presence. He had filled out. He was now about twenty and he had transformed from overgrown kid to muscular adult. He hardly drank his lager, despite Guy's attempts to ply him with more. I tried conversation.

'What are you up to these days, Owen?'

'UCLA. Studying computer science.'

'Do you like it?'

'College sucks. The course is OK.'

'I know what Californian colleges are like,' I said. 'I've seen the films. Beaches, babes, parties.'

Owen peered at me suspiciously. It was true I was mocking him, but in what was supposed to be a good-humoured, English kind of way. He didn't get it.

'I'm not into that kind of stuff.'

'Er, no. I suppose not.' I drank my beer. 'How long are you here for?' I asked, hoping the answer was not long.

'Four days. I've just been to see my father in France.'

'How is he?' I asked politely.

But Owen had had enough of my small talk. He ignored my question and spoke directly to his brother. 'Abdulatif's dead.'

That got Guy's attention. And mine. He glanced rapidly at me and then spoke. 'Abdulatif?'

'Yeah. Abdulatif. The gardener. He's dead.'

'Oh. They found him, then?'

'They found him all right. In, like, a trash can in Marseilles. It took them a week to figure out who he was. Matched his fingerprints.'

'Do they know who killed him?' Guy asked.

'No. He was some kind of rent-boy. The local cops say they get killed all the time.'

Guy drank his beer carefully. 'Well, I can't say I'm sad to hear that.'

'No.' Owen turned to me and gave me a mocking smile. 'Did Guy tell you, I saw him humping Dominique?'

'No,' I said, my blood suddenly running cold.

'Yeah. It was the day before you and Guy arrived. Dad was out somewhere. I think she thought I was on the computer. But I wasn't. I was walking around. Looking.' He caught my eye and grinned.

'Oh,' I said. What else had he seen, I wondered.

'Of course that would have been a couple of days before you had it off with her. I bet you didn't realize you were having the gardener's leftovers?'

I felt the anger boil inside me. Of course I hadn't realized! Damn Owen.

'I told the cops of course. That was why they were so sure he'd killed her.' Owen saw my discomfort and laughed. 'I've been wanting to tell you that for years.'

Guy noticed my unease and tried to change the subject slightly. 'What did Dad say when he heard about the body being found?'

'He was pretty damn happy.'

'I bet he was.'

'He's coming over next week,' he said. 'He'd like to see you.'

'Great,' said Guy. 'But you'll be back in the States by then, won't you?'

'Yeah. He won't care, though. He wasn't real pleased to see me in France.'

'I'm glad you went.'

Owen snorted into his beer.

For the rest of the evening Guy steered the conversation away from France and his father. Eventually we left the pub and headed back to his place to play some music and drink some more. We had just crossed a road when a scrawny red-haired man with a ravaged face and ragged clothes lurched in front of us.

'Have you got change for a cuppa tea?' he said to me. He was obviously drunk. But then so was I. I ignored him.

'Wharrabout you?' he said to Guy, standing in his way.

'I'm sorry,' said Guy politely.

'Come on. Gi' us ten p. You can spare ten p, can't yer?' He pushed his face close to Guy with an unsteady leer.

Guy tried to step around him.

The man wasn't having it. 'Yuppy bastard!' he shouted.

Owen moved fast. He grabbed the man by the collar, whipped him off his feet and pinned him against a wall. 'You leave him alone,' he hissed.

The man's intoxicated eyes looked confused. Then they seemed to focus. He spat, spraying Owen full in the face.

Owen dropped one hand and hit the man in the stomach. Hard. Very hard. The man slumped to the ground retching.

Guy grabbed hold of Owen and pulled him back. Owen stared at the man on the pavement, his black eyes gleaming.

'Get him away!' I shouted to Guy.

I bent down next to the man, who was gasping for breath. I sat him up against the wall. As the breathing came back the swearing started.

'How are your ribs?' I tried to feel the man's chest but he pushed my hand away. 'Shall I get an ambulance?'

A stream of abuse. I sat there with him swearing at me for

a couple of minutes. He seemed to be recovering. I pulled out a ten-pound note, stuffed it in his pocket and left him. He didn't thank me. I didn't expect him to.

I waited until I was quite sure Owen was in California before I saw Guy again. We went to see a friendly international at Wembley. England were playing Brazil and amazingly managed to hold them to a one–one draw. After the game he gave me a lift in his electric-blue Porsche. As we sat in the car park with U2 loud on the stereo, waiting for several thousand vehicles in front of us to move, I mentioned Owen's visit.

'It was interesting what your brother said about the gardener being found murdered.'

'Yes,' said Guy, sounding uninterested.

'Were they sure it was him who killed Dominique?'

'Absolutely sure.'

'I see.'

I listened to Bono for a minute, summoning up the courage for my next question.

'Guy?'

'Yes.'

'Do you remember the police found one of your footprints outside Dominique's window?'

'Yes.'

'How did it get there?'

Guy paused to let in the clutch as the car in front moved forward six feet.

'I went for a pee on the way to bed.'

'No you didn't.'

'Of course I did,' said Guy, avoiding my eye, focusing on the car in front.

'I was there, remember? You came straight back to the guest cottage with me.'

'No. You've got that wrong. You're thinking about some other night. That night I stopped off for a slash in the bushes. The police checked it all out. It's five years ago. You must be confused.'

I opened my mouth to protest and then closed it again. History had been rewritten as far as Guy was concerned, and the rewriting had received the official police stamp of approval. It was his version of what happened and he would use the force of his personality to make sure it was the only version. The trouble was, I knew it was a lie.

'I'm seeing Dad tomorrow night. Do you want to come?' Guy asked.

'No thanks.'

'Why not? It'll be fun. We'll go out to dinner and then maybe on to a club later. Don't worry, he'll pay.'

'No, really. I'd rather not see him. I suspect he'd rather not see me.'

'After France?'

'After France.'

The line of cars in front of us began to move. Guy kept the Porsche within a foot of the Vauxhall in front to make sure no one else barged in.

'I try, but it's hard to forget France,' he said. 'I still blame my father for what he did to Mel.'

'I'm not surprised. But you still see him?'

'Oh, yes. He's a player, you know what I mean?'

'Not exactly.'

'He knows how to live. How to have a good time. He doesn't take himself too seriously, or other people. Sure, sometimes other people get hurt, like I did and Mel did. But they forget.'

'You can't go through life thinking about yourself all the time.'

'Why not?' Guy said. 'It's not as if anyone else is going to look out for you, is it? I don't mean you should actively harm other people. But you have to go out and grab what you want.'

'And that's what you've learned from your father?' I said, unable to hide the distaste in my voice.

'Oh, come on, it's not that bad. Live and let live is all it is.'

'So what does Owen think?'

'Owen and Dad are on different planets. The only reason he talks to Dad at all is to keep me happy.'

'It seems strange to me you two are so close. I mean, you seem so different from each other.'

'We are. But we've always helped each other out. Right from when Owen was born.'

I felt like pointing out the obvious contradiction with Guy's earlier musings, but I decided not to. Emotions have their own logic, as do families.

'Mom and Dad have occasionally shown some interest in me,' Guy went on, 'but none at all in Owen. Basically, I've been the only person looking out for him. And he looks out for me.'

He laughed. 'I remember when I was eight. Mom and Dad were still together and we were living in LA. We were by the swimming pool. I had committed some minor crime, taking a glass down to the poolside or something, and my father was tearing strips off me. He used to get really angry then, probably because he was pissed off with Mom. Anyway, he was taking it out on me. It went on for ten minutes or so.

'Owen was watching it all. He was only five, but he was a big five-year-old, as you can imagine. Suddenly he let out this horrible scream and charged my father. The two of them went flying into the pool. Dad was wearing a suit. He was not amused. Owen went to bed early for a week. But he didn't care. He was just pleased he'd helped me. It's good when you've got a brother like that.'

'It must be,' I said, but I was thinking how lucky I was to have a normal sister whom I quite liked but scarcely saw rather than a brother like Owen.

'Are you sure you don't want to come tomorrow night?' Guy said.

'Quite sure. But I hope you have a good time together.'

I saw him a couple of days later in the pub after work. Or after my work. I guessed he had spent the afternoon watching television.

'So, how did it go with your dad?'

Guy scowled. 'Nightmare.'

'Late night, was it?'

'No. Not that kind of nightmare. A real nightmare. He wants me to get a job.'

'Outrageous.'

'Don't be so bloody sarcastic. I told him acting was my job. It can be damned hard work. But he doesn't seem to think that counts. He says I'm pissing away my life. He said he's going to cut off my money.'

'Harsh,' I said. I had always been curious where Guy got his funds from.

'Yeah. I've got a couple of trusts set up by Patrick Hoyle and I get the income from them. I said he couldn't do anything about them, they were mine. He assured me he could. And I'm sure he can. Hoyle would do anything for him, including stopping me getting my hands on my own cash.'

'The rest of us have to work,' I said.

'Don't come over all proletarian with me, Davo. I know lots of people have to work. But not my father. It's the hypocrisy that gets me. If it's OK for him to spend his life lying around by pools on the French Riviera or skiing in Villars, why can't I go to the pub every now and then?'

'But he made his money,' I said.

'That's exactly what he said,' Guy muttered crossly. 'It still pisses me off. And he's going to sell my plane.'

'Sounds like you're in trouble.'

'Yeah.' Guy finished his beer and stood up to fetch a refill. 'But I'm not going to give in. I know I can act. In a couple of years, I'll show him.'

He returned with a bottle of beer for him and a pint of bitter for me. 'Anyway, how are you?'

'Good,' I said. 'Ingrid's coming back to London next week.'

'Really? Are you going to make a move?'

It was a question I had been asking myself ever since I had last seen her. The truth was, I wasn't sure. There was no doubt I liked her, and I thought she liked me. But I didn't want to screw up our friendship.

'I don't know.'

'Go for it,' said Guy, the master strategist. 'I can get Mel to put in a good word.'

'I don't think that will be necessary.'

'Hey! I've got an idea. Why don't we go for a trip together for a long weekend in Golf Juliet? You, me, Mel and Ingrid. We could go to France. Or how about Scotland? I've always wanted to fly around the Hebrides. If my father's serious about selling the plane I want to get the most use out of it I can this summer. What do you think?'

'Sounds good.'

'At the very least, you'll get to know Ingrid better. At best . . .'

'Are you trying to set me up?'

'Of course I am. What's the matter? Don't you want to do it?'

I was slightly embarrassed at Guy trying to direct my love life, and I wasn't even sure what my plans were for Ingrid if I even had any. Also, I had a big accounting exam the following week, for which I had done precious little work. I had performed very badly in the last exam after a heavy night out with Guy, and I had been warned by my boss to 'pull my socks up' this time. But a trip to Scotland would be fun. I'd worry about my socks later.

'Yeah, I do,' I said. 'It's a good idea.'

20

We all met at seven thirty on a wet, cloudy Friday morning at Elstree aerodrome. Guy and I whipped the covers off the plane and walked round to make sure everything was as it should be.

'Are you sure this is a good idea?' asked Ingrid doubtfully, looking up at the sky, a roof of thick grey only a few hundred feet above us.

'It'll be fine,' said Guy. 'My rating lets me fly through this. I've checked the weather and the sun's shining in Scotland. All we have to do is get there.'

I sat in the front next to Guy, with Ingrid and Mel in the rear seats. The Cessna 182 was one of the few single-engined planes powerful enough to carry four people and enough fuel to go any distance. We took off, and within a few seconds we were in cloud. A minute later, and we were above it.

We skimmed along on autopilot up the backbone of England a couple of hundred feet above the clouds, being passed from RAF controller to controller. We didn't need it: ours was the only aircraft in the sky that early in the morning. I had only a few hours' training under my belt, I hadn't even done my first solo flight, but I was fascinated to watch Guy. He had already told me a lot about how the Cessna worked, and now he told me more.

As we reached the Clyde the cloud began to break and Guy lowered the aircraft beneath it. We crept along the Firth of Clyde through the gloom, passing low over a nuclear submarine and its attendant helicopter, skipped through a gap in the hills by the Crinan Canal, and emerged into glorious sunshine. Suddenly the sea changed from murky grey to brilliant blue, with patches of turquoise and cyan. Everywhere we looked there was sea, coastline, rocks, inlets and mountains. It was very difficult to tell what was the mainland and what was island. In the back, the women stopped talking and started looking. It was unbelievably beautiful.

We reached the south coast of Mull and followed it along until we passed over the monastery at Iona, a cluster of white and stone buildings clinging to the edge of the world. Guy descended to a hundred feet and we sped across the water towards the island of Staffa and Fingal's Cave. At that height we could see right into the cave, with its black basalt columns. A couple of sightseeing boats rocked as we flew over and a flock of birds rose into the air in protest. We followed the north coast of Mull, passed low over an impossibly romantic castle and climbed for the approach to Oban, where we had planned to land for fuel and food. Guy dodged the mountain that blocked the approach path and landed the Cessna expertly, with the barest whisper from the wheels as we touched down.

We had lunch at a hotel close to the airfield. The girls, who had been showing signs of advanced boredom as we had droned over the English cloud, had come alive. We sat in the garden of the hotel, the heat of the sun tempered by a pleasant sea breeze, congratulating ourselves on not being in London. In the afternoon Guy planned to take us up between the Inner Hebrides and the mainland to Broadford, a small airfield on the Isle of Skye. We would spend the following day walking, before nipping over to Barra in the Outer Hebrides in the evening and then home the day after that.

I noticed that Guy drank a couple of pints and it made me uneasy. I also felt foolish. I knew Guy was an experienced pilot and I knew he could handle his drink, but I also knew that he was breaking the rules. Of course, that was the difference between him and me. He broke the rules and I didn't. Although as a student pilot I wasn't allowed to handle the controls without a qualified instructor, I restricted myself to a Coke, as if reducing the average intake of alcohol in the cockpit would help.

We returned to the airfield and refuelled. I checked the weather fax. I had just completed the meteorology paper in my pilot's course and found the subject fascinating. What I read worried me. I went out to the apron and found Guy.

'Here, come in and look at this,' I said quietly.

He followed me into the caravan, which doubled as a control tower, and looked at the fax. Under Inverness it had the words 'PROB 30 TEMPO TSRA BKN0010CB'.

'So?' said Guy.

'So doesn't that mean thunderstorms?'

'No, Davo, it means that in Inverness there's a thirty per cent probability that for a temporary period there might be a thunderstorm. Inverness is on the east coast and we're on the west.'

'But isn't Inverness the nearest place on the fax to Skye?'

Guy hesitated. 'Maybe. But look outside. Where are the clouds? It's a great day.' He saw the doubtful look in my eyes. 'They always say there's a chance of thunder in the summer. It's just the Met Office covering its arse. We see a thunderstorm, we fly around it, OK?'

'OK,' I nodded, reflecting how much happier I had been flying with Guy when I knew nothing about the subject myself.

We took off into clear skies and headed north along the craggy coastline, passing lighthouses, lochs, birds, crofts and castles. We nosed up the Sound of Sleat, past Mallaig towards the Kyle of Lochalsh. To our left were the dark mountains of Skye and to our right the Highlands. I looked over my right shoulder for Ben Nevis, which should have been about thirty miles behind us. I couldn't see it. An enormous black cloud had suddenly appeared, rearing up over the mountains. It rose thousands of feet up into the sky, tapering into a tower that formed a flat white top. An 'anvil'. It was a massive cumulonimbus. A thundercloud.

I had read about thunderclouds in my meteorology texts. They are a pilot's worst enemy. Wind can make landing difficult, rain can make visibility tricky, but a thundercloud can shake an aeroplane to bits. In a big, mature thundercloud, warm air is dragged into the centre of the thunderstorm and thrust thousands of feet upwards, where it cools and rushes back towards the ground in a vicious downdraught. The resulting turbulence produces sudden shocks that an airframe is not designed to withstand.

I tapped Guy on the shoulder and pointed.

'That's OK,' he said. 'You often get cloud over mountains. We'll be all right down here.'

We were approaching the shoulder of a hill that plunged down to the sound. We passed it and turned northwards. Right in front of us was a wall of black. The aeroplane shuddered a little, as if in nervous anticipation.

Another one.

Mountains rose above us on either side. It was impossible to fly around this as Guy had promised.

'What now?'

'We go under it,' said Guy. 'There might be a bit of turbulence, but we're nearly there.'

'Shouldn't we turn back?'

'No, we'll be fine. It's just forming. It's not even producing any rain yet.'

'Are you sure?'

'Of course I'm sure,' Guy said, irritation flaring in his voice. 'Hold on back there, this might be a little bumpy.'

Guy descended to about four hundred feet, at which point it was possible to see underneath the cloud to the shoreline behind.

We approached the grey wall at a hundred and thirty knots. I was nervous. In front of us was what was increasingly looking to my inexperienced eye like a huge beast of a cumulonimbus, below was water, on either side mountains. Only behind us was safety. But glancing at Guy's determined face, I could see there was no chance of us going that way.

He was an experienced pilot. I would have to trust him.

The air became bumpy, with jolts and lurches that prompted a cry of 'Whoa' from Mel. A bit uncomfortable, but easy to put up with, if that was all we were going to suffer.

Perhaps we would be OK.

We weren't.

Suddenly the aircraft was slammed downwards as if a giant hand had slapped the roof. The water shot up towards us. Guy cursed, put on full throttle and tried to climb. The water was dark and choppy and only a few feet below us. Despite Guy's efforts we weren't going up. Another downdraught like that and we'd get very wet. Worse than that, the force would shatter the aeroplane against the surface of the water. But it didn't happen. One moment the engine was straining to gain a few feet in altitude, and the next that great hand reached down and dragged us upwards. The water disappeared far below and after a few seconds we were enveloped in the cloud. Everything became very dark.

'Jesus Christ!' swore Guy as he wrestled with the controls. I didn't know what he was trying to do. There was nothing he could do, the forces all around us totally overwhelmed any instructions Guy was giving to the airframe. I looked at the altimeter. We were being pulled up past one thousand and two thousand feet. Debris was flying all over the cabin:

the map, a kneeboard, a flight guide. I felt a whack in the back of my head, and Ingrid's bag flew upwards and hit the ceiling. I was totally disoriented as my insides were pulled and pushed in every direction. Outside, a sheet of water fell on us, flooding over the windshield. It didn't matter. There was nothing to see but black cloud out there.

Mel started to scream. I turned. She was terrified.

'Tell her to shut up,' muttered Guy beside me. He was pale and sweating, straining hard at the controls.

'Mel!' I shouted. 'Mel!'

It was no use. I couldn't get the poor girl to stop screaming, but I could turn off the intercom to the rear seats. That helped.

There was a sudden flash of brilliant white light and then an explosion. It was as if we were actually inside a thunderclap. I looked out to check the wings. Unbelievably they were still attached to the plane.

'What about the mountains?' I shouted. There were mountains on either side of us. We couldn't see anything. We could easily charge into the side of one at any moment.

'I know,' said Guy. 'But look at the altimeter. We're nearly at three thousand feet. We should clear most of them.'

I looked, and as I did so the altimeter started spinning the other way. We were going down. Two thousand. One thousand. There were plenty of hills that height within a couple of miles of our track. I peered through the rain into the darkness. They could be right in front of us, there was no way of telling.

Then the blackness ripped apart and we were out. Below us was water. Straight ahead was the brown flank of a mountain. The water split, one arm going to the left, one to the right. Guy had only seconds to decide. He took the right.

'Thank God,' I said.

'Where's the map?' screamed Guy.

It was wedged on the coaming above the instrument panel. I handed it to him. He glanced around him and down at the map. We were entering a glen a couple of miles wide. Ahead of us and a little above was what looked like a saddle, a narrow pass between two mountains. Behind us was the storm.

'We're over Skye now,' said Guy. 'The airfield's just over this saddle.'

He put on full power and began to climb. The Cessna 182 has a powerful engine and can usually climb at a thousand feet a minute, but we were achieving much less than that. We'd be lucky if we made it up to the saddle at that rate. We were climbing against a wind blowing down the mountain.

Mel had stopped screaming.

I looked down. We were passing over a small crescent-shaped loch. I grabbed the map and searched for it. I saw where Guy thought we were, just to the south of Broadford on the Isle of Skye. There was no crescent-shaped loch there. My eyes scanned the map, until I found one. There it was! On the mainland. Half way up a long valley that had a three-thousand-foot mountain at its head.

'Guy, I don't think we're over Skye.'

'Of course we are,' said Guy.

'But that loch down there. It's on the mainland. We should turn back or we'll hit this mountain.' I tried to show him the map, but he brushed it away.

'No way am I going back into that storm,' said Guy. 'And the airfield's just a few miles ahead.'

'It isn't. Look at the compass. We're flying north-east, not north.'

'The compass is screwed up by the storm. Look. I'm the pilot-in-command. I'm the one with the licence. Will you just shut the fuck up!'

I shut up. Beyond the saddle was cloud. It might be hiding a mountain or it might not. The valley was narrowing. Soon it would be impossible to turn back without hitting the hills on either side. We were making some progress upwards and it looked like our rate of climb would just get us over the saddle. But after that? If I was right and there was a mountain there and not an airfield, we would have nowhere to fly but into it.

I looked down again. Another tiny loch with a clump of trees around it. I checked the map. Sure enough, a couple of miles up the glen from the crescent loch was a blue dot next to a green splodge.

'Guy, turn around! I'm one hundred per cent sure there's a mountain ahead.'

'No! Now will you keep quiet!'

Guy wanted to believe that there was sanctuary over that saddle. He wanted to believe it so badly that he would ignore any evidence to the contrary. The saddle was close now. So were the sides of the valley. We might just be able to turn now, but if we waited ten more seconds . . .

I did what I had to do. I snatched the control column in front of me and yanked it to the right. Guy tried to regain control by pulling on his column but I was stronger than he was. The aircraft was sharply banked and we were turning. Turning right into a cliff.

'Leave it, Guy, or we'll hit it!' I shouted. If Guy had succeeded in pulling us out of the turn we would fly straight into the mountain. He let go.

I saw rock, trees, bracken, a waterfall. Close, closer. We were only a few yards from the rock. Despite the steepness of the turn, we seemed to be moving round so slowly. Come on. Then the nose pulled away from the cliff and we were facing back the way we came. The throttle was still all the way in and I pointed the aeroplane upwards.

'What are you doing!' screamed Guy. 'Are you crazy? You nearly got us killed!'

I looked back over his shoulder. There was a break in the cloud above the saddle. And through the break was a mountain.

If I hadn't turned the aircraft round we would have ploughed straight into it. For sure.

Guy gasped. 'Oh, my God.' He went pale and his lips began to tremble. 'Oh, my God.'

We were still climbing. The air was bumpy but I could see clear sky between the storm and the mountains. I pointed the aircraft towards it. I wasn't sure I had the engine settings completely right, but the aeroplane was moving steadily and powerfully upwards and that was all that mattered.

The Isle of Skye was engulfed in cloud, but I was able to follow the coastline back to Mallaig in clear skies.

'God,' said Guy. 'I'm sorry, Davo. Christ, I can't believe it.'

I glanced at him. He was pale, in shock. I realized I would have to fly the aeroplane. I only had twelve hours in my logbook, and I had never flown anything as powerful as the Cessna before, but I could steer it and the throttle seemed to work in more or less the same way as the AA-5. I could have called up Scottish Information on the radio, but I wasn't sure my radio-telephony skills were up to it. Fly to Oban and get Guy to land it was all I intended to do.

I turned the rear intercom on again and heard Mel sobbing. Ingrid was trying to comfort her.

'Is it over?' she asked.

'I think so,' I said.

But it wasn't quite. I kept the coast on my left until I reached the white Ardnamurchan lighthouse, and then I followed the Sound of Mull towards where I hoped Oban would be. But what I saw was another towering thundercloud. There was no way we were going anywhere near one of those again. I remembered we had passed a grass airstrip on the north coast of Mull on our way up and I soon found it, just a couple of miles ahead.

I turned to Guy. He was hunched up, staring out of the window.

'Can you land it now, Guy?' I asked.

'You do it,' Guy said.

'But I've never landed this aeroplane before. And I don't know how to land on grass. You have to do it.'

'OK,' said Guy weakly. He took the controls and began to fiddle with the throttle and the propeller settings. Then he pushed them away. 'No,' he said. 'I can't do it. You do it.'

'Guy!'

He didn't answer and just looked away.

So I pointed the aeroplane towards the tiny grass strip. It was right by the sea with a bloody great hill in the direction I was supposed to land from. I had done a few landings, some of them without even bouncing, but each time on a familiar tarmac runway with an instructor next to me for when I cocked it up, which at that stage was quite often.

This time, if I cocked it up there might not be another chance.

I pulled out the throttle and let down two stages of flap. The aircraft began to slow and lose height. I flew towards the hill and at the last minute turned to face the runway. In the Cessna the perspective was totally different from what I was used to and everything was happening very quickly. I was too high and too fast. Desperately I pulled the throttle all the way out, pushed the nose down and lowered the last stage of flap. Still too high, still too fast. The runway seemed to rush up at us, and before I had time to raise the nose, we had hit the ground hard. The aircraft reared back into the air in an enormous bounce. I hung on, and two bounces later we were on firm ground, speeding towards a hedge at the far end of the runway. I braked as hard as I could and waited. We shot past the runway threshold into long grass. That slowed us down more effectively than my braking and we came to rest a couple of yards from the hedge.

I killed the engine and the four of us sat there in the silence, unable to believe that we were actually on the ground.

21

August 1999, Clerkenwell, London

'So, how are we doing, Guy?'

'We're live, we're on the web and we're getting forty thousand hits a week.' Guy grinned at his father, brimming with the excitement of the previous few days.

It was ninetyminutes.com's first formal board meeting, although of the four directors only Patrick Hoyle was wearing a suit, a huge baggy thing that flapped around his enormous body. Our new chairman was dressed all in black, the same as his son. He was in a great mood: he clearly liked the internet lifestyle.

Tony had invested two million pounds of capital for eighty per cent of Ninetyminutes, leaving the rest of us to split the remaining twenty per cent amongst us, with Guy rightly receiving the lion's share. It was a bad deal for us, but we had had no choice. Mel had helped us in the negotiations, behaving totally professionally towards Tony throughout. But it made little difference. Tony had us by the balls and he squeezed. The worst thing was, he seemed to enjoy it. All in all a very different experience from my own father's investment.

'No problems at all?' he asked.

'Oh, there were problems. But we fixed them. The site hasn't fallen over once since we launched ten days ago. Which is more than I can say for some of the staff. We pushed them pretty hard.'

'So, if I type www.ninetyminutes.com into my computer, what happens?'

'I didn't know you could type, Dad.'

'Of course I can bloody type!' But Tony allowed himself a quick smile, caught up in Guy's enthusiasm.

'Sorry. Try it,' said Guy, pushing his own laptop towards his father. Tony laboriously pecked out the letters and the by-now familiar Ninetyminutes logo floated to the surface. Guy guided Tony around the site, while Hoyle watched over their shoulders.

'You know, this is really good,' Tony said.

'I know,' said Guy. 'And it's going to get better.'

'Has anyone out there noticed us?' he asked, still clicking away at the laptop.

'There's been some excellent press coverage.' Guy handed round a sheaf of articles for everyone to look at. 'And we've had some outstanding reviews of our site on-line. We expect more of those over the next few weeks.'

Tony scanned the reviews. '"The best soccer site on the web by miles." That's not bad for your first week.'

'There's still a lot to do,' Guy said. 'We're talking to one of the offshore bookmakers for on-line betting. That should be a money-spinner. And we're recruiting. New writers, a couple of programmers to help Owen and Sanjay, and some admin people. We've also had interest from our advertising agency about selling space on the site. Remember, that's something we wanted to hold off doing until we could show people what we've got.'

'It would be nice to see some revenues,' said Tony.

'Absolutely. And we're making progress on the retailing side.'

Tony pushed the reviews and Guy's laptop away and picked up the financial attachments to the board papers. He frowned.

'Amy has a team of designers working on a range of sports-casual clothing,' Guy went on. 'She's lined up suppliers in the UK and Portugal.'

'Wouldn't the Far East be cheaper?'

'We need the flexibility of rapid turnaround times for orders and new designs. Whatever happens when we start selling our own-label stuff, it's going to happen quickly, and we'll need to respond quickly. She's also negotiating deals with the suppliers of club and national strips and memorabilia.'

'It's a bit early for that, isn't it?'

'There are long lead-times. We need to be ready.'

'It all sounds exciting,' Tony said. 'Tell us how we're going to pay for it, David.'

I ran through the numbers, which were set out amongst the board papers. I'd worked hard on them, and I was pleased with the result.

When I finished, there was silence. Tony was staring at me, absent-mindedly tapping a pen against his chin. I tried to catch his eye and smile. His expression remained stony. Hoyle was watching his client closely. He knew him better than me, and he knew something was up.

I tried to remain calm, but inside alarm bells were ringing. What had I said wrong? What had I missed? Why was Tony so warm to his son and so cold to me? Did this still have something to do with Dominique?

Eventually Guy cut in. 'Thank you, David. As you can see, we are being prudent with our cash, and we're keeping within budget.'

'We might be within budget, but we're not making any money. Are we, David?' There was an edge to Tony's voice.

'Not yet, no,' I admitted. 'But at this stage in Ninety-minutes' life we should be investing in the business.'

'We're making losses, with no prospect of that changing. I don't call that "investing in the business". I call that spending more than we earn.'

Anger flashed inside me. My professional pride was hurt. I was the accountant, what did he mean by lecturing me? 'This is a start-up,' I snapped. 'What do you expect?'

Tony raised his eyebrows. He slowly moved his gaze to Guy and then back to me.

'Very well, then,' he said. 'Till next month. I'm glad the site is going so well. Congratulations.' This was aimed more towards Guy than me. 'Perhaps at our next meeting we can go a little bit further into our financial strategy.'

That sounded ominous, but I wasn't as concerned as perhaps I should have been. It had been an uncomfortable meeting, and I had let Tony get to me for a brief moment, but I had survived. I had received a cooling rather than a roasting. That I could learn to handle, I thought. It was just a question of attitude.

We soon forgot about our chairman. Ninetyminutes was buzzing, and the loudest buzzing came from Guy. He was everywhere. If he didn't have the ideas himself he encouraged the other people in the team to have them. He truly was inspirational. Decisions were made in a matter of seconds, all by Guy. His yardstick was, would a certain idea get us closer to being the number-one site in Europe? If it did, we went ahead with it. If it didn't, we forgot it and moved on to the next thing.

Despite the site's initial success, Guy was unhappy with it. Gaz's ideas were good, his stories were brilliant and Mandrill's design was better than anything else out there. But in Guy's view the site lacked something, although it was difficult to get him to pin down exactly what. After long discussions into the night we decided that what we needed was someone to pull all these elements together and organize them. But what kind of person? And where could we find them?

We didn't have the time to advertise and we didn't have the money for a headhunter. Then I thought of Ingrid. Neither of us had seen her for seven years, but she had been working in magazine publishing then. If she didn't know anyone herself, she might at least help us identify the kind of person we should be looking for and suggest where we might find them. If she'd talk to us.

I dug out her number from an old address book and called her up. She was surprised to hear from me, but she agreed to have lunch with us the next day.

We met at a small pizza place near her office on the South Bank. She was cool, composed and confident. She looked a little older, lines were beginning to show around her mouth and pale-blue eyes, smile lines. Her chestnut-brown hair was cut shorter, and she wore an elegant but informal trouser suit. Jade earrings dangled from her ears. She looked poised and in control. And amused.

'I can't believe it,' she said. 'You two joining up to become dot-commers. A dissolute actor and a buttoned-up chartered accountant.'

'Killer combination,' said Guy with a smile. 'And unique.'

I wasn't sure I quite liked the description of myself as a 'buttoned-up accountant', but I didn't quibble. Suave merchant banker, perhaps? But of course one of the reasons I was doing this was to lose the accountant label.

'I almost didn't recognize you. Guy has no signs of a hangover and you seem to have lost your suit, David. And your hair.'

'Well, we recognized you,' said Guy.

'It's lucky you had the same phone number,' I said. 'Seven years on.'

'Same number. Same flat. Same job, I'm afraid.'

'That dull, huh?' said Guy. And then, in response to Ingrid's sharp look, 'Just getting my own back.'

She smiled.

We ordered our pizzas, and caught up on what we each had been doing. Then Guy asked the question. 'What do you think?'

'Of your site?'

'Yes.'

Ingrid put down her knife and fork, pondering the question for a few moments. 'It's good. I'm impressed. The design is excellent. I know nothing about football, but you've got some very good writers. Easy to load. No bugs that I could find. Not bad at all.'

Guy looked disappointed. 'Nothing wrong with it, then?'

'No. For an amateur site, it's really first class.'

'But it's not an amateur site!' Guy said, with too much vehemence.

'Oops,' Ingrid said. 'I didn't mean amateur. But you can tell it hasn't been done by a professional media company.'

'Why? The design's OK, isn't it?'

'Yes. As I said, it's very good. But the whole thing doesn't quite hang together properly. It lacks coherence. It's inconsistent in places, some things are a little difficult to find, everything is given equal weight.'

'What do you mean, equal weight?'

'Well, in a magazine it's up to the editor to tell the reader what the really interesting stories are and make them easy to see. You can do that on the web, too, although most people don't. But if you look at some of the good newspaper sites, they are carefully edited. If you know what you want, you can find it. If you just want to browse, the interesting stuff will be there for you.'

'That's it!' said Guy, glancing at me in triumph. 'That's exactly what I was saying! So what can we do about it?'

'You need someone to coordinate everything. Editor, publisher, call it what you like.'

'Well? Is there anyone you know who might be able to help us? Or who would want to help us?'

Ingrid paused, as though flicking through a Rolodex in her head. 'Maybe.'

'Oh, yes?'

But Ingrid didn't give us a name. At least not yet. 'I still can't get over you two teaming up. Despite my crack about chartered accountants, I'm not really surprised about David. But you, Guy? What about the late nights? The women? The drink?'

Guy took a sip of the sparkling water in front of him. 'All in the past,' he said with a grin. 'Just ask Davo.'

Ingrid glanced at me. I nodded.

'Seriously,' Guy said. 'I've changed since the last time you saw me. I've come to that point in my life where I want to prove that I'm not a loser, that I can create something worthwhile. I've worked hard at this. Fourteen-hour days, weekends, I haven't had a holiday since I started this thing. And this is just the beginning. But I'm prepared to do whatever it takes. I really badly want this to work, Ingrid. And when I want something, I generally get it.'

Ingrid raised her eyebrows.

'So who are you thinking of?' I asked. 'And do you think they'd do it?'

'I think I do know the right person,' said Ingrid. 'But I'm not sure whether they'd do it or not.'

'Tell them to spend a day with us,' said Guy. 'If they can't get away from their job, there's always Saturday. We'll be in the office all day: Chelsea are playing away.'

'All right.'

'So who is it?' Guy asked.

Ingrid smiled. 'Me.'

Guy returned her smile. 'In that case we'll see you on Saturday.'

*

Ingrid came in that weekend. She clicked. Gaz liked her. Neil liked her. Even Owen liked her. At midday, Guy and I talked it over. After our lunch with her we'd both taken a look at the on-line magazine she had developed. It was aimed at professional women in their thirties, not exactly our target market. But it was smooth, sophisticated, interesting, seamless. It worked.

We offered her a job that Saturday lunch-time. She accepted it on Sunday. She took Monday to go into work to resign and she was in our office on Tuesday morning.

She turned out to be the final ingredient that made ninety-minutes.com really come alive. She listened to Gaz, encouraged him, and coaxed him into getting his ideas into some kind of priority. She talked to Owen about streamlining links and upload times, agreeing with all his concerns about scalability. And she told Mandrill what to do. It turned out that you can tell enigmatic men with goatees what to do, if you do it in the right way.

Under Ingrid's guidance, our site was looking better and better. It was certainly an improvement on the other glitzy but clunky sites which inhabited the soccer space on the web. It looked professional. It looked a winner.

22

'We need to move faster.'

I choked in my pint. Guy's eyes were shining in that messianic way I was beginning to recognize whenever he was talking about Ninetyminutes' future. 'Move faster? You're crazy. We can hardly keep up with things as they are now.'

We were in the Jerusalem Tavern, the pub just across the road from the office. It was half past nine, the end of another long day. But Guy had plenty of energy left.

'Doesn't matter. We've got forward momentum. Ninetyminutes will go as far as we push it.'

'What do you mean?'

'You know all that stuff we were going to do in our second year? Open European offices, the on-line retailing, our own-brand merchandising?'

'Yes.'

'We should start on it now.'

'But we've only just got the site going!'

'I know. But it's like this. There's a land grab going on at the moment. It's like the Californian gold rush. Amazon have got books in the US and in Europe. Tesco are going for grocery sales. Egg for on-line banking. We have to get soccer. We're going to overtake the others in the UK, and we've got to overtake them in Europe too.'

'But how can we manage all that?'

'We'll manage it. All we have to do is think big and think fast.'

He was mad. But probably right. It had to be worth going for. 'We're going to need more money. Now.'

Guy nodded.

'I think it's still a bit early to go to the venture capitalists.'

'We have to do it.'

'Your father won't like it.'

'I know,' said Guy. 'But I'm not going to worry about that now. Look. Think through how much we need and then let's work out how to get it.'

It was stupid. The whole thing was stupid. I smiled. 'OK,' I said. 'I'll work on it.'

I had only just started to get down to the numbers when the phone rang. It was Henry Broughton-Jones.

'I took a look at your site the other day,' he said. 'Very impressive.'

'I'm glad you like it. Although I never had you down as much of a football fan, Henry.'

'I prefer the horses. Just to watch, you understand. Look, do you fancy a spot of lunch?'

If you are the finance director of a start-up and a venture capitalist asks you out to lunch, then you say yes. Especially when he seems pleased that you can fit it in the next day.

He chose a smart restaurant just off Berkeley Square, the like of which I hadn't lunched in since my Gurney Kroheim days. I noticed he wasn't wearing a suit, but green cords, checked shirt and a blazer, with ox-blood brogues. Sort of Wall Street dress-down casual meets Cirencester Agricultural College. It didn't quite work.

'So what's this, Henry?' I said. 'Dress-down Friday on a Wednesday?'

'It's subtly chosen to impress thrusting entrepreneurs, David. You are impressed?'

'Definitely.'

'Actually, it's a bloody nightmare,' he said, running his hand through his thinning hair. 'I much preferred pinstriped suit, blue shirt and a blue tie. This way my wife laughs at me every morning. She says blue and green don't go together. Is that true?'

'Couldn't tell you, I'm afraid. It's not the kind of thing we have to worry about on our side of the fence.'

'No, I suppose it isn't.' He examined the menu. 'Shall we get a bottle of wine? I won't tell anyone if you don't.'

'Sure.'

Henry ordered an expensive Montrachet to go with our fish.

'OK, Henry, what's going on?' I asked.

Henry laughed. 'I'm being proactive. I want you to humour me.'

'Proactive?'

'Yes. We had a big strategy conference at Gleneagles a couple of weeks ago. We talked about the Internet. As you can't help but have noticed, things are hotting up. In the States websites are going public at astronomical valuations. The VCs over there are making bucket loads of dosh. It's going to happen here and we don't want to be left behind.'

'Of course not.'

'As we see it we have two choices. We can either give the next twenty-five-year-old management consultant who comes through the door with a plan to sell bagels on-line a couple of million quid, or we can work out the sectors that look interesting, find the promising firms that operate in those spaces and see if they want our money. Make sure we get to them before someone else does. I thought you were a good place to start.'

'You're not serious?'

'I certainly am.'

'So you're going to give us money just like that?'

'Certainly not,' said Henry. 'We'll beg you to let us consider your business, string you along and then turn you down. We are venture capitalists after all.'

'Henry?' I said.

'Yes?'

'You aren't doing a very good job of marketing me.'

'Aren't I?' He had a sly smile on his face. Henry was no fool. He knew he was hooking me with candour where bullshit would fail.

'What about the management issues?' I asked.

'The rules are changing. You've started up. The site looks great. And you've got Tony Jourdan on board. Now he has made money before. Also, I know you: you're a safe pair of hands.'

I winced. It might be true, but I didn't want to be known as 'a safe pair of hands' any more. I wanted to be a successful, imaginative moneymaker. Give it time and I'd show Henry.

'By the way,' he said. 'I never realized that Guy was Jourdan's son.'

'Sorry. We discussed telling you earlier, but Guy was dead against the idea. He wanted to raise money as his own man.'

'Admirable, I'm sure.' Henry sipped his wine appreciatively. 'So. How's Ninetyminutes getting on?'

I told him. I incorporated all Guy's ideas for an accelerated roll-out into Europe and an early start on merchandising. I told him the visitor numbers and extrapolated them wildly.

'Golly, David,' he said eventually. 'I've never seen you that excited about anything before.'

I smiled. 'Really?' I thought about it. 'I suppose you're right.'

'How much do you need?'

'To do all that we need ten million pounds now, and maybe another twenty in six months.'

'So Orchestra does this round and then we float the company in the spring?'

'That will work. We should have a great story by then.'

'Sounds good. Will you give us an exclusive to look at the deal?'

I couldn't help laughing. Here was a venture capitalist asking me for the business.

'Hey, that's not fair!' Henry protested.

'No, you're right,' I said. 'I'll have to discuss it with Guy.'

'You'll let me know?'

'I'll let you know, Henry.'

Guy went for it. The following Monday, Henry arrived in our offices with his associate, Clare Douglas, a small, slim, no-nonsense Scottish woman with wispy blonde hair and enquiring grey eyes. They crawled all over us, asking everyone about everything. I was impressed by Henry's thoroughness, but Clare was particularly well prepared. She must have spent the weekend scouring the web for everything she could find on football. She was a tenacious interrogator, picking up on any hesitation or waffle from any of us and pinning us down until she had the details right.

Henry asked Guy, myself, Ingrid, Gaz and Owen for references, several each. We were all happy to oblige, apart from Guy. I overheard his conversation on the subject with Henry. He refused, saying that since his previous career was acting there was no one who would have anything relevant to say about him. Henry didn't back down: in fact he became more persistent. In the end Guy got away with giving him the phone numbers of his agents in London and Hollywood. Henry left him alone, but he didn't look satisfied.

Neither was I.

After Henry had gone, leaving Clare to her interrogation of Sanjay, I voiced my fears to Guy. 'Henry thinks you're hiding something.'

Guy nodded.

'Are you?'

Guy looked me in the eye. 'Fancy a walk?'

We strolled out into the small street, bathed in the gentle sunlight of an Indian summer, and made our way north towards Clerkenwell Green.

'Well?' I said.

'I had a bad time in LA,' Guy said.

'So I can imagine.'

'No, it was worse than London. I totally lost it. Not just drink. Drugs. Lots of them. Very little work. I became low, very low. Clinical depression, they called it. I went to see a shrink.'

'What did he say?'

'She had lots to say. I have issues, Davo. Issues with my father. Issues with my mother. Issues with Dominique. She almost wet herself when I told her what had happened in France. To hear her talk about it, I'm lucky I'm not a psychopath.'

'I can't imagine you depressed,' I said.

'Can't you?' Guy replied quickly, his eyes searching mine.

He was asking me to think about it, so I did. Guy the charmer, Guy with the capability to make everyone around him smile, Guy the centre of attention, the natural leader. But I did remember those moments of inexplicable melancholy at school, when he brooded over the failure of a particular girl to fall for him, or just brooded over nothing at all. I had dismissed them at the time as just silly. Guy had the perfect life, everybody knew that.

But perhaps he didn't.

'One day I woke up fully clothed on the floor of some guy's apartment in Westwood feeling like shit. Worse than shit. It took me twenty minutes to realize it was Monday morning and another ten to figure out I was supposed to be at an audition for a part in a TV pilot. It could have been my big break. There was no way I was going to make it.

'The guy whose apartment it was came in. He was only a few years older than me, but he looked closer to forty. "What's up, John," he said. He didn't even know my name! I'd gone there on Saturday night. Sunday had just disappeared.

'I had an appointment to see the therapist that afternoon. She wanted me to talk about my mother and my feelings about her. Which I did. My brain felt like mush.

'Then she began talking. About how I was angry with my father, how my mother hadn't met my expectations, I don't know, some psychobabble. I was sitting there, and suddenly my brain cleared. She was talking bullshit. It was all bullshit. I was the one who had got myself on to that floor. I was the one who was screwing up my life. And I was the one who could stop it.'

'So what did you do?'

'I walked out of her office there and then. Drove up into the hills. Thought about it. Came back to England. Started Ninetyminutes.'

We walked on in silence until we came to Clerkenwell Green, where we sat on one of the benches. Of course it wasn't green any more, but it was a relatively quiet oasis away from the traffic of Farringdon and Clerkenwell Roads. 'You never told me this,' I said.

'No.'

'You should have done.'

'I didn't think it was relevant.'

'Guy!'

'I still don't. The point is, I couldn't admit to myself that it was relevant, let alone to you. All that stuff is in the past. Really. You've seen me every day for the last five months. You can see I've changed.' He turned to me, begging for my agreement.

'Yes, you have,' I said. 'Do you think Henry will find out?'

'I don't think so,' Guy said. 'The only number in LA I

208

would give him was Lew, my agent. He knows the story, or most of it, but I know Lew. His first instinct will be to lie. He'll cover for me without really knowing why.'

'You hope.'

'I hope.'

He probably would. People did that kind of thing for Guy, as I knew very well.

We sat looking up at the dour façade of the Old Sessions House, the Masonic Centre for London, which seemed to frown down on the trendy bars and restaurants springing up around it. A latex-clad cyclist chained his bike to the pale-green railings of the public lavatories that decorated the centre of the green and sauntered into the one remaining caff in the area.

'Should I tell Henry?' Guy asked.

I thought about it. My strategy with Orchestra was to tell them everything. We would be working together through tough times and we needed to trust each other. But Henry thought Guy was flaky already: this would just make it worse. Also, I was inclined to accept Guy's point of view. He had changed, I knew that. The past just wasn't relevant.

'No,' I said. 'We'll leave it to him to find out, if he can.'

Henry still harboured doubts about Guy, but he definitely liked the business. Guy, Ingrid, Gaz and I made a presentation to Henry's partners later on that week that seemed to go well. Guy and I went back to Orchestra's offices the following day to thrash out a deal.

It took time. Essentially, we were arguing about what proportion of Ninetyminutes Orchestra's ten million pounds would buy. After several hours we were still some way apart when Henry raised the question of Tony's stake.

'I'm not happy with how little of the company management will have after this round,' he said. 'Whatever price we agree, it's going to be less than ten per cent. I don't like that. Not enough incentive.'

'I wouldn't argue with that,' I said. 'Perhaps you should pay more?'

'That's not what I mean, and you know it,' said Henry. 'It's Guy's father. He must be diluted.'

'That's going to be difficult,' said Guy.

'How did he end up with so much of the company in the first place?' asked Henry.

'We were desperate,' I replied.

'Well, I don't mind giving him some uplift on the value of his shares, but we need to figure out a way of getting you chaps a bigger stake.'

'I'm not sure he'll agree to that,' said Guy.

'I'll make it easier for him,' said Henry. 'He'd better agree to it, or there will be no deal.'

'We have our board meeting on Monday. We'll discuss it then,' said Guy.

So Guy and I went away to plan our approach to Tony. Guy had told Henry it would be a difficult discussion. Neither he nor I had any idea just how difficult.

23

July 1992, Mull

The airfield was nothing but a strip of mown grass with an unmanned caravan beside it, which contained a cash box for landing fees. But only a few yards away was a hotel with a Scandinavian-style conservatory giving an excellent view of my landing. None of us had any desire to fly any further that day, so we checked in. Half an hour later we were in the bar. A couple of hours after that we were all well on the way to getting plastered.

You couldn't blame us. Guy's nerve had been seriously shaken and alcohol was his natural refuge. I had kept mine, but had a felt a surge of relief when we had finally landed. Mel had been terrified. Even Ingrid, who had seemed to stay cool, was knocking them back. For all of us at that age and in those circumstances drink was the natural response.

None of us mentioned what had happened. Far from admitting his error, Guy indulged in alcoholic bravado. I let him. Deep down I knew that I had trusted Guy for too long and that as a result of that trust he had almost killed us. It was a truth that I was unwilling to face, or at least not yet. I was unsure whether the girls had realized exactly what had happened. I wasn't about to tell them. I was quite happy to share in the excitement of being alive.

The nearest we got to touching on the subject was when Mel put down her rum and Coke and said: 'Tomorrow.'

'What about tomorrow?' said Ingrid.

'Sod tomorrow,' said Guy.

'Tomorrow I'm going to take the train home.'

'Won't work,' said Guy. 'We're on an island.'

'Good point. I'll take a ferry and then a train.'

Guy looked at her for a moment, as though considering argument. There was no point. 'OK,' he said.

'I'll go with you,' said Ingrid.

'Davo?' After all the bravado, Guy suddenly looked small, deflated. He needed my support.

'We'll make sure the girls get away OK and then I'll come with you,' I said. 'But I think we should fly straight back to Elstree. Provided the weather's OK.'

'That makes sense,' said Guy, relieved. He stood up and reached for our glasses. 'My round.'

We drank on into the evening, nourishing ourselves on crisps and peanuts. Ingrid's eyes began to close. 'I'm sleepy,' she said, with a small smile on her face, and slipped over against Guy's shoulder. He moved her upright. She slipped over again. He lifted her up. She waited a few seconds and then fell back. This time he let her head rest there.

It was innocent drunken fun, but there was something about it that sparked a surge of irritation in me. The purpose of this trip had been for me to get closer to Ingrid. How was I supposed to do that when she was slumped against Guy? In fact, how was I supposed to do that when she was so drunk? A little tipsy was fine, but I didn't want the start of a relationship to be a drunken bonk that she wouldn't remember and couldn't prevent.

I felt Mel tense next to me. 'Guy?' she said.

'Yes?'

'Where were you on Tuesday?'

'Tuesday? I don't know. Why?'

'Because you said you'd come round to my place on Tuesday.'

'Did I? I don't remember that.' Guy was the picture of

innocence. Hammy, unconvincing innocence. You would never have known he was an actor.

'So where were you?'

'I was with Davo. Wasn't I, Davo?'

I remembered Tuesday. We had gone to a bar in Chelsea. Guy had picked up an American redhead. I had left early. Guy knew he could rely on me to cover for him in these situations.

But not this time.

'Only at the beginning of the evening. I left at half past eight.'

Guy looked at me askance. 'That's not right. That can't be right.'

'I got home for the nine o'clock news. I can remember it.'

Mel was watching this. She wasn't dumb. She could see that there was a little wedge between me and Guy. She hammered at it.

'So what did you do when David left you?'

Guy shrugged. 'Went home, I suppose. Watched the nine o'clock news myself.'

Tears sprang into Mel's eyes. 'You were with a girl, weren't you?'

'Of course not,' said Guy. 'I wasn't with a girl, Mel.' He spoke slowly and steadily and looked her straight in the eye. I watched him. He was convincing. Totally convincing. I found myself wondering whether I had really seen him with the redhead that night. Maybe he was an actor after all.

Mel hesitated, her certainty shaken for a moment. Then she renewed her attack. 'I called you. You weren't in. You were with a girl.' She turned to me. 'Wasn't he, David?'

I shrugged.

Guy shot me a look of the 'Cheers, mate' variety. But he wasn't too worried. He knew Mel knew. She must have known for a while. But she still stayed with him. He was toying with her.

'And what about the Friday before?'

'Let me see . . .' said Guy.

'Was it the same girl?'

It had been a different girl. It was always a different girl. But I couldn't tell Mel that.

'I don't know what you're talking about,' said Guy.

'Do you think I'm stupid? Do you? Do you!'

Mel stared at Guy. Ingrid was upright now, watching her.

Guy was just a little too drunk. The corner of his mouth twitched up. Just a smidgeon. Just enough to send Mel over the edge.

She slammed her glass down on the table. 'You sit there laughing at me! Treat me like some stupid tart who'll keep a bed warm for you when you can't find anything better. Do you ever wonder how I feel? Do you know what it's like to sit at home, waiting for you to come, never knowing whether you will or whether you'll have picked up some schoolgirl at the local Burger King?'

'Schoolgirl?' said Guy, as though insulted that he had been accused of underage sex.

'You're just as bad as your father!' said Mel. 'Worse!'

'I guess you'd know,' said Guy, quietly. Dangerously.

'What's that supposed to mean?'

'You'd know how I compared to my father.'

'How can you say that?'

'How can I say that?' Guy said, his anger finally rising. 'You say you don't like the way *I* treat you. I didn't seduce your mother. You want respect, but how do you expect me to respect you after what you did with my father?'

'That's unfair,' Mel said. 'I've told you how much I regretted that.'

Guy shrugged and reached for his glass.

'And anyway, what about what *you* did in France? Your little secret deals? Your cover-ups.'

Guy looked at her sharply, his glass an inch from his lips.

'Don't act all innocent, Guy. I know.'

Guy didn't look at all innocent. He looked shaken. And worried. He put his glass down without taking a drink.

'Like I said. You're worse than your father.' There was a note of cruel triumph in Mel's voice. She knew she had hit home.

'Mel,' said Ingrid, reaching a hand unsteadily towards her.

'You keep out of this. I saw you falling all over him!'

'We were only mucking around,' said Ingrid.

'You've had your eyes on him the whole time, you slut!' Mel sneered.

Ingrid withdrew her hand. She looked genuinely hurt.

'That wasn't fair,' I said to Mel.

'I don't give a shit.' She stood up. 'I'm getting my stuff and I'm going to stay somewhere else tonight. And I'll make my own way back to London tomorrow.'

She stormed out of the bar and up the stairs to her room.

We exchanged glances, stunned. Ingrid swayed unsteadily and looked as if she was going to cry. Guy grinned weakly. I got up to follow Mel.

Guy and Mel were sharing a room. I found the door open and Mel zipping up her bag.

'Where are you going to go?' I asked.

'I don't know. Anywhere.'

'But we're in the middle of nowhere!'

'I don't care. I'll walk all night if I have to. I just have to get away from those two.'

'You're imagining things,' I said. 'There's nothing between Guy and Ingrid.'

'You show me a woman that isn't after Guy and I'll show you a lesbian,' muttered Mel.

'That's not true.'

She stood upright, a tear trickling unrestrained down her cheek. 'I was right about him though, wasn't I? About last Friday?'

Her eyes were burning, looking straight into mine. I couldn't lie to her. I nodded.

'And other times?'

I shrugged. There was no need to nod.

She grabbed her bag and pushed past me down the stairs. She was marching past the front desk when I called after her. 'Hang on a minute, Mel.'

She paused.

'They'll need your key.'

She handed it to me. I asked the manager behind the desk whether there was a bed and breakfast nearby that Mel could go to. I told him she had had an argument with her boyfriend and her room at the hotel would still be paid for. He understood, reached for his telephone, and had a brief conversation with a Mrs Campbell. He directed me to a place half a mile down the road.

'I'll walk with you,' I said to Mel.

I handed the key to the manager, picked up her bag and walked out with her into the dusk. Although it was late, it wasn't dark yet at this latitude. The birds were noisily preparing for their brief sleep. There was no traffic on the road. On one side was the sea, with the Scottish mainland clearly visible over the sound, on the other a mountain. We trudged along in silence, silence apart from intermittent sniffs from Mel.

She mumbled something.

'What?'

'I said, I probably deserve it.'

'No you don't,' I said.

'After France. And his bloody father. I probably deserve it.'

I put my arm around her and squeezed. She needed comfort. She deserved comfort. 'Not because of that,' I said. 'Never because of that. That's best forgotten.'

'I try to push it out of my mind. And I can for a while. But only for a while.'

'I know,' I said. Remembering Dominique. Her body. Making love to her. The ridiculous euphoria afterwards. And then learning about her death. And the guilt. The guilt.

That week had left its scars on all of us: Mel, me. And Guy.

'Back there you said something about Guy,' I said. 'About his secret deals. His cover-ups.'

'That was nothing.'

'It must have been something,' I said. 'It seemed to worry the hell out of him.'

'You're right, it was something.' We walked on as Mel gathered her thoughts. Then she spoke. 'You know why the gardener ran away?'

'Yeah. He'd killed Dominique. He didn't want to hang around and get caught.'

'No.'

'No?'

'No. He was paid to run away. By Hoyle and Guy.'

'What do you mean?'

'I overheard them talking. They were in the dining room and I was just outside.'

'I remember,' I said. 'I found you there.'

'Did you? I don't remember that. But I do remember what they were saying.'

'What?'

'They were talking about how they would pay the gardener five hundred thousand francs to disappear. Apparently Owen had spied on him having sex with Dominique, and the idea – Guy's idea – was to tell the police this. Then once he had gone they would be bound to suspect him of killing her. Especially since the jewellery was missing.'

'Bloody hell.'

'Sure enough, that afternoon the gardener disappeared. And the police never found him.'

'Until this year.'

'What?'

'Yeah. Didn't you know? Actually, I'm not surprised Guy didn't tell you. They found him a few weeks ago in a dustbin in Marseilles.'

'How tidy.'

'So the gardener was the fall-guy to deflect suspicion from the real killer?'

'To deflect suspicion from someone, certainly.'

'What about the jewellery case that was found in his room?'

'Must have been planted.'

'By Hoyle?'

'Presumably. Or maybe he arranged for somebody else to plant it.'

'Jesus.'

The road was empty. It was getting dark now, the gloom was pressing down on the water a few yards away from us. I thought through what Mel had just told me. It all hung together. I had heard Hoyle repeating the gardener's name; it was quite possible that Mel could have overheard the rest. I remembered Ingrid's comment as we were leaving Les Sarrasins: the disappearance was too convenient. According to Mel it was Guy's idea and Hoyle fixed it. Very possible.

'So they were trying to cover for Tony? Divert the police's attention away from him and on to the gardener?'

'That's what I've assumed,' said Mel. 'Most of the time.'

'Most of the time?'

'Sometimes, just occasionally, at times like now, I wonder.'

'What do you mean?'

'Sometimes I wonder if Tony didn't kill his wife. If Guy was trying to cover for someone else.'

'Himself?'

'As I said. Sometimes I wonder.'

'That can't be right,' I said. I could believe Tony had killed Dominique. But not Guy. Surely not Guy. 'You're just angry with him.'

'I'm certainly that,' said Mel.

'You didn't tell the police any of this?'

'No. If Guy was covering for his father, I didn't want to spoil it.'

'What about Guy? Have you ever told him?'

'He doesn't know I know. Bastard.'

We approached a row of cottages, one of which bore a discreet B&B sign. Mrs Campbell must have been briefed by the manager because she was very welcoming to Mel, even though it was so late. I left her at the door and wandered back to the hotel in the gathering dark, thinking about what Mel had said.

Could Guy really have killed Dominique?

I was confident that Mel was telling the truth about what she had overheard. But not about her conclusions. She was just being vindictive, surely. It was ridiculous to think that Guy had killed his stepmother. Wasn't it?

I thought about Guy. I had known him for many years. I counted him as a friend. He wasn't a cold-hearted murderer.

Or had I just fallen under his spell like Mel and so many other women before her? Like Torsten, for that matter. Like all his other friends.

I thought about the flight that afternoon. About the blind determination with which he had flown the aeroplane up that glen, ignoring me, leading us on to a certain collision with the mountain.

Did I really know Guy?

Then I remembered something. The footprint outside Dominique's window. Guy's footprint. Unlike Mel, unlike the French police, probably unlike Patrick Hoyle, I knew it hadn't been put there by Guy on his way to bed. So how the hell had it got there?

The police had had a theory. That's why they had arrested Guy. What if their theory was correct?

I stopped and looked out over the sound. It was dark now. I could hear the wavelets lapping against the shore a few yards in front of me. A solitary car drove past, its headlights briefly illuminating the ruffled surface of the sea before plunging it into an even greater darkness. I could hear the engine for a full minute after it had passed me.

I had fallen under Guy's spell. I had known it was happening: more than that, I'd been happy to let it happen. I had had more fun in the last couple of months than any time since I started work. The drinking, the late nights, the chasing women. We were only young once, so we may as well enjoy it: that was Guy's motto, and I was embracing it. His life seemed so much more colourful than mine. I coveted it.

Or did I? I remembered the bus journey back from France when I had realized that the lives of people like Guy weren't all they were cracked up to be. I had forgotten that lesson. Guy's father was a bastard, I knew that. Was Guy turning into a bastard as well? He might ignore the way he was treating Mel, or claim that she deserved it, but that didn't mean I should too. His acting career was going nowhere. His life was going nowhere. Did I really want to join him on that journey?

When I reached the hotel I looked into the bar, but it was empty, apart from the manager. I thanked him for finding Mel somewhere to stay and went up to bed.

I checked my key. Room 210. Deep in thought, I walked down the landing, put the key in the door and opened it.

Three things hit me.

First, room 210 wasn't my room.

Second, Guy was lying on the bed in room 210 locked in a deep embrace with a girl.

Third, the girl was Ingrid.

I stood there stupidly. For some reason the question that most puzzled me was why wasn't I in my own room. I looked at the key in my hand. I must somehow have mixed up the keys: passed my own to the manager when I had left the hotel with Mel and kept hers.

Then I looked at the two figures on the bed. They were both still mostly clothed. Ingrid sat up, dishevelled, bleary eyed. Guy looked stricken.

'Davo. It was just a bit of fun. We weren't doing anything.'

I looked at Ingrid.

'Why?' I said.

Without waiting for an answer I turned and left the room, shutting the door behind me. I ran downstairs and grabbed my own key from behind the desk in the hallway. I remembered the number clearly now: room 214. I climbed the stairs two at a time and opened the door, although my hands were shaking so much with anger I could barely hold the key steady enough to insert it into the lock.

'Davo! Davo, wait!'

I turned to see Guy approaching me down the landing.

'Davo. I'm sorry, OK?' he said, following me into my room.

'Piss off, Guy.'

'It was nothing. It means nothing.'

'I'm quite sure it meant nothing to you.'

'Or to Ingrid,' Guy said.

'Yeah. Well, it means something to me.'

'Oh, come on. It's not like you were going out with her or anything. You told me you weren't even sure you wanted to try.'

'So that makes it OK, does it?'

'No, no it doesn't. I'm sorry. I said I'm sorry.'

He smiled that Guy smile. Just for a second I felt like saying everything was all right. He could forget it. But only for a second. Then the anger returned. I wasn't going to let him charm his way out of trouble again. Suddenly I wanted to pin him down.

'What happened in France, Guy?'

Guy scowled. 'Not again. It really would be best to forget all about France, Davo.'

'I can't. Mel told me about the cover-up. She says she overheard you and Patrick Hoyle talking about paying the gardener Abdulatif to disappear.'

'That woman has a serious problem with her imagination,' Guy said dismissively.

'I know she overheard you two talking about him because I caught her at it. Until tonight I didn't know what you said. Now I do.'

Guy closed his eyes and sighed. 'You're not going to let this go, are you?'

'No,' I said firmly.

'OK. You're right. We did discuss it. Owen told me he had seen Dominique with the gardener and we talked about telling the police. It seemed a good idea because it would put the gardener under suspicion. Then I thought it would be an even better idea if he scarpered. So Hoyle paid him off. And he did an excellent disappearing job.'

'Until last month.'

'Until last month.'

'Do you know how he was killed?'

'You heard Owen. He was found in some slum in Marseilles in a garbage can. That's all I know about it. I don't want to know any more.'

'Why did you do it?'

'To help Dad,' Guy said. 'He was under a lot of pressure from the police. It was clear they were about to pin the murder on him. Hoyle and I thought this idea would take the pressure off. It worked.'

'Did you think he had killed Dominique?'

'No.' Guy shook his head emphatically. 'Of course not.'

'Why not?'

'He's my dad. He's not a murderer. Do you think your father's a murderer?'

'No. But then my stepmother hasn't been murdered.'

Guy glared at me. 'I knew Dad didn't do it,' he said with contempt. 'He was with a hooker at the time. The police established that.'

'All right. But if your father didn't kill Dominique, and Abdulatif didn't, who did?'

'I have absolutely no idea. Perhaps it was a thief who came in off the street. Or perhaps it really was Abdulatif after all.'

'Hm.' I considered Guy's response. It sounded honest, but could I trust him? 'What about the jewellery case found in Abdulatif's room?'

'We grabbed the case from Dominique's bedroom and gave it to Abdulatif. He left it in his room.'

'What happened to the jewellery?'

'He kept it.'

It all made sense. But I had one more question. An important question. 'And the footprint they found outside Dominique's window?'

'My footprint? I told you before, I was having a pee in the bushes.'

'That's a lie, Guy. I know it's a lie. I was there, remember?'

Guy tried his smile on me again. This time a bit more sheepish. 'Come on, Davo. We're both too strung out for all these questions. Let's find the manager and get him to rustle up a couple of whiskies.'

'It just washes over you, doesn't it?' I said.

'What do you mean?'

'I mean France. I mean being so cruel to Mel. I mean trying to sleep with Ingrid when you know I like her.'

'Look, I said I was sorry about that.'

'You don't get it, do you? You nearly killed us all today. You would have done if I hadn't pulled the control column away from you.'

'Yeah, thanks for that. You reacted quickly. But we were unlucky to be hit by such a big storm. I've never seen one like that before.'

'We weren't unlucky! You flew into it, Guy. You were deliberately flying us to our deaths and then you expect everyone to just forget about it afterwards. As usual.'

As I thought about that flight, the anger boiled over. The tension and fear of those minutes had been bottled up inside me, the pressure rising, and now it all came out.

'Face it, Guy. You're a loser. A rich loser. You say you're an actor, but you never actually get off your arse and get a job. You don't have to. Daddy will bail you out, again. He'll buy you a plane. A car. A flat. And you'll get pissed again and whine that you might have to do a job like everyone else.'

'So you want me to be like everyone else,' Guy sneered, no trace of charm left now. 'The thing is, I'm not like everyone else. You might lead a sad little life, but there's no need to expect me to.'

'There's nothing sad about getting a job.'

'Give me a break! You'll become a chartered accountant and then you'll get a wife and two point two kiddies and a mortgage and a nice family saloon, just like your parents did.' Guy's words were laden with contempt. 'It's your destiny, Davo. Sure you can come out for a few beers with me now and again but you can't escape it. I'm not going to live like that. I don't want any of that.'

Something inside me clicked. I was angry, I was drunk and I had nearly died only a few hours before. And Guy was pressing on a very sensitive spot. Hard.

I swung. Fast. My fist connected with Guy's nose with a light crunching sound. Guy swore. Suddenly there was blood everywhere.

Guy bent down and held his nose. Blood poured out on to the carpet. He straightened. I prepared to hit him again.

'What the hell's going on here!' bellowed a strong Scottish voice. It was the manager, closely followed by Ingrid.

I pushed Guy out of my room, shut and locked the door, and ignored the banging and angry shouts from outside.

I got up early the next morning, paid for my room and walked the half-mile to Mrs Campbell's. I woke Mel up, organized a taxi and began the long journey with her back to London. We stopped off in Glasgow for an hour so that I could buy a couple of accountancy books for the rest of the trip. The last two months had taken its toll on my work. I did want to qualify as a chartered accountant. I did want to get a decent job in a bank.

Above all, I didn't want to piss away my twenties in a pub with Guy.

PART THREE

24

September 1999, Notting Hill, London

It was very late by the time I got home. I was far too wound up to go to bed. I looked for some whisky, couldn't find any, and so I opened a bottle of wine. I slumped on to the sofa and thought about Tony.

He had been a horrible sight. He must have died instantly, but if his death was quick, it was also messy. The shock had been numbing, but as it wore off it was replaced by a feeling of great unease, which it took me a while to realize was guilt. I didn't like Tony. Seconds before he had died I was very angry with him. Angry about what he had done to Guy, angry about what he was doing to Ninetyminutes, angry about what he was doing to me. And then, in an instant, he was dead. I knew I hadn't killed him. I hadn't even wished for his death. But the source of my present problems had been removed, as if by a miracle of the devil.

I drank three-quarters of a bottle of wine and went to bed. Some time in the small hours of the morning I went to sleep.

I managed to get into work early the next morning. I told the team. There was shock but also relief. Although Ninetyminutes' future was uncertain, things looked better than they had twenty-four hours earlier.

Ingrid didn't come in. Neither did Owen or Guy. I tried their home numbers but without success. But in the middle of the morning the police arrived in the form of Detective Sergeant Spedding.

'Is there anywhere we can talk?' he asked.

I showed him into the boardroom, the room that had been the scene of that acrimonious meeting only three days before. He sat opposite me and pulled out a notebook. He was about my age, with red hair, scattered freckles and an open, friendly face.

'So this is one of those dot-com companies I've been reading about?' he said, looking through the glass wall of the boardroom at the jumble of computers and young men and women.

'Doesn't look like much, does it?'

'A mate of mine at the station said he's had a look at your website. Says it's very good.'

'Thank you. Do you follow football?'

'Bristol Rovers.' I thought I'd detected a slight West Country burr. 'I've been thinking about hooking up to the Internet at home, now you can sign up for free. Do you cover Rovers?'

'Not yet. We just do the Premier League at the moment. But we hope to get on to the other divisions by the end of this season.'

'Well, when I do sign up I'll take a look myself.' He glanced out at the office again. There was some bustle, but it was more lethargic than usual. 'Must be a difficult day for you.'

With the Chairman killed and the Chief Executive gone missing he could say that again. 'Do you think Tony Jourdan was run down deliberately?' I asked.

'It's a possibility we have to consider. I know you gave a statement to my colleagues last night, but I'd like to ask you some more questions.'

'Fire away.'

'I understand that there was some conflict between Tony Jourdan and his son relating to this company?'

'Yes. Although Guy founded Ninetyminutes, Tony was

the biggest shareholder. There was a board meeting on Monday and they had a major disagreement over strategy. Tony wanted us to go into the pornography business and Guy refused. So Guy resigned.'

The policeman asked me plenty more questions about Guy, his father and Ninetyminutes, all of which I answered as honestly as possible. Then he asked me to go over my conversation with Tony at his flat the night before. He took careful notes.

'In your statement last night you mentioned seeing a car waiting outside Mr Jourdan's flat,' he said. 'Can you tell me a bit more about it?'

'I don't know. I'll try.'

'Do you remember what model it was?'

'No,' I replied immediately.

'Are you quite sure? Think.'

Spedding was sitting back in his chair calmly, confident that I would be able to come up with something. So I closed my eyes, trying to picture the street sign and the vehicle in front of it.

'Wait a minute. Yeah. It was some kind of hatchback. Oldish. A Golf. Something like that.'

'Colour?'

'Don't know. Darkish. Black? Blue, maybe. No, it was black.'

'I know you said you couldn't remember the number plate. But can you remember part of the registration? The year prefix, perhaps?'

'Yes. Yes, I can. N. It was N.'

'Well done. What about the driver? Can you give even a vague description?'

'I don't know. I couldn't see him clearly and I really wasn't focusing on him.'

'But he was male? White? Black? Young? Old?'

'I see. Yeah, he was male. White. Wearing some kind of jacket. But no tie. Dark hair thinning a bit. Over thirty. Under fifty. That's about the best I can do.'

'Would you recognize him again if you saw him?'

'Maybe. Maybe not.'

'Could it have been anyone you know?'

'No. Definitely not. At least, not anyone I know well.'

'Are you quite sure you can't remember anything more about him?'

The policeman's friendly face encouraged me to be helpful. But there was not much more I could say. 'I'm sorry. I know this is important and I wish I'd been more observant, but I had other things on my mind. Frankly, if the car hadn't been obscuring the street name I wouldn't have seen the man at all.'

Spedding nodded. He pulled out a sheet of paper, which was a diagram of the street. 'Can you show me where the vehicle was parked?'

I placed an 'X' on the spot.

'You say you heard the car start up. When was that?'

'It was when Ingrid and I were walking round this corner *here*,' I pointed to the diagram. 'And Tony was coming out of his house *here*.'

'Did you see it pull off?'

'No. But once we were round the corner, I heard the engine rev up and then the thud and the scream. But by the time I'd run back to the street the car had gone.'

'Well, we're looking for it now. Our best hope is if we can find another witness.'

'So you think it was intentional?'

'I suppose there's a chance it could have been an accident and the driver drove off – a hit and run. But on such a quiet narrow street it seems unlikely. I have one more thing to ask you. Do you mind if we examine your own vehicle?'

'What for? It was outside my flat in Notting Hill at the time. Ingrid and I went by tube straight from work.'

'Of course. But it will be useful to eliminate it from our enquiries. I'm sure you understand.' I handed him the keys, told him where it was parked, and he left.

Very little work was done by anyone that day. Ingrid arrived about lunch-time, looking pale. And in the afternoon Mel rang.

'Have you heard what's happened?' I asked her.

'Guy called me an hour ago. He's in Savile Row police station. He asked me to get him a lawyer.'

'Christ! Do the police think he killed Tony?'

'It's not clear yet. But he's obviously a suspect. He decided to do the smart thing and not talk to them without a lawyer. I've got hold of a good one who should be with him now.'

'A detective came round here this morning. He was asking about Guy's relationship with Tony. I'm afraid I told him.'

'Don't worry,' Mel said. 'They'd have found out soon enough. That's not the kind of thing you can hide. If you had tried it would just have made them suspicious.'

'Will he be OK?'

'I'm sure he will. Unless they've got convincing evidence against him they'll have to release him.'

'Isn't it terrible?' I said. 'About Tony.'

'Yes,' said Mel. 'Although quite frankly I never really liked that man, as you well know.'

There was an awkward silence as I searched for a response to Mel's honesty. I couldn't quite admit out loud that I agreed with her. 'Well, let me know if I can be of any help,' I said eventually. 'And tell Guy to call me when he gets out.'

'All right.'

He did get out. He came straight to the office. It was eight o'clock and most people had gone home. He looked a wreck. Pale face, dark circles around his unsteady eyes.

'So they let you go?' I said.

'Yes. Mel got me a good lawyer. The police were getting quite aggressive with me about my relationship with Dad. I just thought it made sense to ask for one. They don't have any evidence against me, but they sure as hell are suspicious.'

'Did you put them off?'

'Yeah. They asked me where I was last night. Fortunately I was out drinking with Owen in a pub in Camden. I think they'll be able to check up on that, so I should be OK.'

'Did they tell you I saw a man in a car outside Tony's flat? Right before he was run down?'

'No. No, they didn't. Have they found him?'

'I couldn't give them much of a description. But there was definitely someone there.'

'I wonder who that was.' Guy paused for a moment, but didn't come up with any ideas. 'They should leave me alone then. But the timing's awful. Just after my row with Dad. I can see it must look really bad.'

'How do you feel about it?'

Guy took a while to answer. 'Numb. I feel numb. I mean, I've spent the last few days thinking how much I hate him. And then he goes and gets himself killed. It makes me . . . It makes me so bloody angry.'

'I'm sorry.'

'Angry at him. Angry at myself. Angry at the police for being so bloody stupid. But I know it hasn't really sunk in yet. I still can't quite believe I won't see him again.' He bit his lip.

Seeing Guy like this put my own feelings into perspective. My own guilt was nothing to his. I was in a much better position to cope.

'Davo?' Guy squinted at me.

'Yes?'

'Can you keep things together at Ninetyminutes for the

next few days? Someone's going to have to figure out what we're going to do and I'm in no shape to do it.'

'No problem. You take a few days off. Sort out your father's affairs. Think about him. Spend time with Owen if it will help. I'll mind the shop.'

Guy smiled. I was touched by the gratitude in that smile.

25

I did what Guy had asked me. I held Ninetyminutes together.

The staff were easy. This was a crisis and they performed well in a crisis. After the initial shock, they put their heads down and got on with the job. They knew Guy needed time, but they trusted me to sort things out.

I called Henry and told him the story. The whole story. About how Tony had been against Orchestra's investment, about how Guy had threatened to resign and about Tony's accident. Henry was still keen. Orchestra Ventures hadn't made an investment for three months and they were worried they were missing the internet bus.

It turned out that the key to the whole thing was Hoyle. Tony's shares in ninetyminutes.com weren't held by him directly, but by an offshore trust. In fact, Tony's affairs were a tangle of trusts domiciled in tiny islands around the globe. The ultimate beneficiaries were Guy, Owen, Sabina and her son Andreas, in varying proportions. The estate would be a nightmare to untangle. The only man who knew where everything was and how it related to everything else was Hoyle. He was also the only man left with executive powers over the trusts.

I had dealt with Hoyle before in his capacity as yes-man to Tony. But if Orchestra Ventures were to make their investment in Ninetyminutes, it would have to be with Hoyle's say-so. And with Hoyle acting as an independent-thinking human being.

I managed to fix up a meeting with him a couple of days after Tony's death. It turned out that Hoyle was quite capable of independent thought. It also turned out that he didn't share Tony's enthusiasm for the Internet at all. I sniffed an opportunity. He could either follow his late client's strategy and be a majority shareholder of a small but marginally profitable soccer and pornography site without management of any kind, or he could take cash. Quite a lot of cash.

Hoyle went for the cash.

I didn't have a deal yet, though. I had to persuade Orchestra to put in not only cash for Ninetyminutes to expand, but also enough to buy out Tony Jourdan's trust as well. As a rule venture capitalists hate buying out existing investors, but the deal I suggested had several things going for it: it would allow management to retain enough of a stake to have a meaningful incentive, it would get rid of a potentially awkward shareholder and it would allow Orchestra to invest more money in the internet boom before it was too late. Henry ummed and ahhed and maybed, but then he went for it.

I received one further visit from Detective Sergeant Spedding. He was armed with a couple of photographs. One was of a middle-aged man, with thinning dark hair brushed back.

'Do you recognize him?' Spedding asked.

'That's him,' I said. 'The man in the car.'

'Are you sure?'

'Definitely.'

'He drives a black Golf GL, N registration. This is a photograph of a similar vehicle.' He handed me the other print.

'That's it, I think. Of course I can't be quite as certain about the car as the face, but it was definitely something like that.'

'Excellent.'

'Who is he?' I asked.

'He's a private detective.'

'Really? So he was tailing Tony?'

'We think so. We haven't spoken to him yet. We wanted to get confirmation from you that it was the same man first.'

'I see. Do you know who he was working for?'

Spedding nodded. 'Sabina Jourdan.'

I made my way through the post-modern ironic lobby of Sanderson's Hotel. It was scattered with strange objects, the most noticeable of which was an enormous pair of red lips. I wasn't sure if you were supposed to sit in them or sit on them: I gave them a wide berth. I spotted Guy amongst the other beautiful people in the designer-minimalist bar, nursing a bottle of beer. I asked for a pint of Tetley's, just to see the look of disdain on the barman's face, and settled for an Asahi.

'How was the funeral?' I asked Guy.

'Awful.'

'Who was there?'

'Hardly anyone, thank God. It was just family – we'll have the full-blown memorial service later. There was Owen, Mom, Sabina, Patrick Hoyle, a couple of great aunts and the vicar. Dad was buried in the churchyard in the village where he grew up, and the vicar did a good job in the circumstances. But no one seemed to really care. Apart from Sabina. The aunts hadn't seen Dad for decades. I don't know what my mother was doing there, she just looked bored. And Owen . . . well, you know what Owen's like.'

'What about you?'

'I don't know. During the service I felt nothing. Just cold and angry at all Dad had done. Or rather hadn't done. All the times he ignored me, the times he walked out, what he did with Mel, what he was going to do to Ninetyminutes, they all ran around my head like a never-ending scorecard, with all the points against him. Then, when the coffin went down into that hole, I fell apart. I realized I'd never see him again, that I'd never have the chance to show him I wasn't the loser he thought I was, that we'd never be close again. That we'd never be as close as I always thought we should have been.'

He swigged his beer.

'You know, I used to think he was so cool, Davo. And he was. We're a lot alike, he and I. But somehow we never quite managed to get on with each other, to respect each other like a father and son should. And now we never will.'

'You did your best,' I said. 'It's not your fault.'

'Just a few words every now and then would have done it. A bit of encouragement about how I was doing well, how he was proud of what I'd achieved. But whenever he got involved with anything I was doing he tried to take it over, prove he could do it better than me. Like Ninetyminutes. Or Mel.'

'How's your mother?'

'God, I wish she hadn't come. She's pissed off because her alimony stops now Dad's died. She brought her lawyer with her to talk to Patrick Hoyle, but Hoyle reckons she hasn't a leg to stand on. It won't matter, she'll just get married again.'

'To anyone in particular?'

'Don't know. She'll find someone. And she was horrible to Sabina. As if Sabina didn't have a right to be there. Which was particularly bad since Sabina was the only one who seemed truly upset about what had happened.'

'Did you talk to her?'

'Only briefly. She's a nice woman. And I think she genuinely loved him, not his money. She's probably the best of the three he married.'

'What's she going to do?'

'Go back to Germany. She says she wants me to stay in touch with her and Andreas. I think I will.' He checked his watch. 'Mom will be here in a few minutes. We're going out to Nobu for dinner. Anyone would think she was over here for a couple of days' vacation. Thank God she's going back to LA tomorrow.'

'Are the police still on your case?' I asked.

'I think they're leaving me alone. I've pretty much convinced them I was with Owen when Dad was run over. But they haven't given up on the theory that he was murdered. They've been giving Sabina a hard time, apparently.'

'Did you hear she'd hired a private detective?' I said.

'No.'

'Yeah. The police asked me whether he was the guy in the car outside your father's flat. I said I was pretty sure he was.'

'So she had him tailing Dad?'

'Sounds like it.'

'Huh. No wonder the police are hassling her. And she gets the most out of the will. But I can't imagine her having him killed.'

'The police will get to the bottom of it,' I said.

'I wouldn't be so sure of that. Tossers.' He swigged more beer. 'Anyway. Tell me what's going on at Ninetyminutes.'

I ran through the details of the negotiations with Orchestra and Hoyle. Guy's interest was quickened. Now that his father was buried I could see he was ready to focus on Ninetyminutes again. I was relieved.

'Darling!' We were interrupted by a loud female American voice. I turned to see a well-groomed blonde woman somewhere over forty approach Guy. She had high cheekbones, a polished tan, a well-toned body and bright white teeth. She should have been a good-looking woman, but there was something hard and charmless about her that instantly put me off. She didn't look like anyone's mother.

Guy introduced me. 'Mom, this is my partner, David Lane. He was at school with me.'

'Partner?' she said. 'I didn't know –'

'Business partner, Mom.'

Her interest in me evaporated. 'Nice to meet you,' she said, unconvincingly. 'I'd love to stop for a drink, but our reservation is for eight thirty and we'll be late.'

I let them go.

As she led her son out of the hotel, Guy whispered to me. 'Did you spot the facelift?'

I hadn't.

He smiled. 'See you tomorrow,' he said and was gone.

Guy returned to the office the next day as promised. Everyone was pleased to see him, especially me. There was a lot to do. I had just one or two final details to sort out with Patrick Hoyle, so I went to meet him at Mel's office off Chancery Lane. It didn't take long, and after less than an hour we left the building together.

'You sound as if you're glad to be shot of Ninetyminutes,' I said as we stood on the pavement waiting for taxis.

'I'm not convinced by the Internet,' Hoyle muttered. 'And it was a very bad idea for Tony to get involved with his son.'

'It wasn't a good idea for Guy, either.'

Hoyle snorted. 'At least he's still alive.'

Something in the way Hoyle said those words caught my attention. I looked at him closely. He was an intelligent man. He suspected something. 'Do you have any idea who killed Tony? Or why he died?'

'No,' he said. 'But it was awfully convenient for some people.'

'Like Guy?'

'Like Guy.'

'You don't think he killed his father, do you? There's no proof.'

Hoyle shrugged, as though he didn't want to be drawn

any further into the conversation. But his use of the word 'convenient' reminded me of something. Something Ingrid had said more than ten years before.

'I know what happened to the gardener in France,' I said. 'Abdulatif.'

'Do you?' said Hoyle, neutrally.

'Yes. I know that you paid him to disappear after Dominique's death. To protect Tony.'

'And who told you that?'

'Guy.'

Hoyle wasn't even looking at me, but at the occupied taxis driving past us. 'Can't get a bloody taxi anywhere these days,' he muttered. 'What we need is another recession.'

'I know Abdulatif was murdered a few years ago.'

'So I understand.' Still a neutral voice.

'That was convenient too, wasn't it?'

Hoyle finally turned his attention away from the traffic and on to me. 'Yes, it was.'

'Did you organize it?' I asked.

Hoyle looked at me. 'Let's get a cup of coffee,' he said, indicating a café just up the street.

Neither of us said anything until we were sitting down with two cups at an isolated table.

'I like you, David,' Hoyle said.

I didn't answer. I wasn't entirely sure I wanted to be liked by Hoyle.

'You're a good negotiator and you're loyal to your friend. Loyalty is a quality I admire. But you should be careful.'

'Of Guy?'

'Let me tell you about Abdulatif. I suspect you know only half the story.'

'I'm *sure* I only know half the story,' I said. 'Go on.'

'You're correct that Guy told me Owen had seen Abdulatif with Dominique. And he suggested paying him to disappear.

It sounded like a good idea. It would deflect enquiries away from Tony. At that time I wasn't entirely sure of his innocence. Tony had said he was with a prostitute when Dominique was killed, but prostitutes can, by definition, be bought. So I arranged things. I gave Abdulatif half a million francs and told him to make himself scarce. Guy had got hold of some of Dominique's jewellery and we gave that to him as well.'

'Why did he take the money?' I asked. 'Surely he ran the risk of getting caught and prosecuted for murder.'

'I thought that at the time. There's quite an extensive North African community in the South of France: it's hard for the police to find a young man who wants to go underground. But I was soon to learn there was another reason.'

'Which was?'

'Blackmail. I'd assumed Abdulatif would leave the country. But he didn't. He went to Marseilles, and after a year he got in touch with me again. He wanted two hundred thousand francs to stay quiet. So I paid him. Another year, another demand. A little higher this time. And so it went on.

'I wanted to get the cash from Tony, but Guy was anxious that his father shouldn't find out what we'd done. So I insisted Guy pay. The years went by and the demands got higher. It became more difficult for Guy to find the money: Tony was becoming less generous with him. It got to the point where I thought we should call Abdulatif's bluff. By that time I was convinced of Tony's innocence. And, of course, if Abdulatif went to the authorities he would be getting himself into just as much trouble as us. But it was an uncomfortable situation for me and for Guy. Paying off a key witness in a murder investigation is a serious crime.'

'And then Abdulatif was found in the dustbin?'

'Precisely. As we said. Very convenient.'

'You have no idea how he got there?'

'You mean, did I arrange it?' Hoyle sipped his coffee. 'I can't blame you for asking. But no. I didn't. That's not the kind of thing I do, even for my best client.'

'Do you think Guy arranged it?'

Hoyle shrugged. 'What do you think?'

I paused. Was my friend a murderer? Of course not. 'You said initially you thought Tony might have killed Dominique, but then you changed your mind?'

'Yes. They weren't getting on well. Neither of them was particularly faithful, as of course you know.'

I sighed, angry rather than embarrassed. Hoyle noticed.

'Sorry. You were young, she was beautiful, and she was using you. Tony knew that. But I'm sure he didn't murder her. I've spoken to him many times over the years about her death and, while I wouldn't expect him to admit it to me, I'm sure I'd be able to tell if he had killed her.'

Hoyle sipped his coffee thoughtfully. 'Tony Jourdan was much more than a client. He was my friend. We met when we were students together. He was one of the reasons I moved out to Monte Carlo. We've been through a lot together over the years, ups and downs. I was very sorry when he died. Very sorry.'

He put down his cup. 'Now, I really must find a taxi.' With a heave, he pulled himself to his feet and left me hunched over my cooling cup of coffee.

We closed a deal with Orchestra Ventures in record time. Orchestra bought out Tony Jourdan's trust for four million pounds, twice his initial investment, and put in a further ten million. They ended up with seventy per cent of the company, leaving plenty for the management and employees. The board changed, of course. Orchestra found us a new chairman, Derek Silverman. He was a trim grey-haired business-man of about fifty. He had already made several million pounds from a management buyout of a marketing business that had been funded by one of Orchestra's partners. More importantly, he was chairman of a Premier League club. Henry also joined the board as Orchestra's representative and Patrick Hoyle was booted off.

Guy suggested Ingrid as a third executive director. She had made herself an indispensable member of the team and both Guy and I valued her judgement more by the day. Henry liked her, so she was in. Her only difficulty was with Mel. They were cool towards each other, but professional, and they did their best to keep out of each other's way.

With the deal done and the ten million in the bank, we hit the ground running. There was plenty to spend it on. More office space: we took over the floor below. More staff, especially more journalists. Advertising. Gearing up the on-line retailing. Henry didn't mind this profligacy. In the upside-down world of internet valuations, the more you spent on getting a website established, the more it was worth. So spend, spend, spend.

It worked. Visitor numbers to the website rose strongly as the season got under way. In the month of September we logged over four hundred thousand visitors and nearly three million page impressions. There were other soccer websites out there, but we were eating into their market share. Gaz's stuff was just better. The site looked more attractive. It was quick, easy and fun to use. Guy began to sign up a network of partnerships with everyone from the leading search engines, to internet service providers, to on-line newspapers, to special-interest sites like ours. We signed a deal with Westbourne, one of the largest bookmakers in the country, for on-line soccer betting. It became popular immediately, and even generated a revenue stream.

We needed to generate dozens of stories a day for the site: transfer and injury news, gossip, opinion, and, of course, match reports. This required an ever-growing band of journalists, each controlling a network of freelances and contacts within the club system. We put television screens on the walls and, more importantly, installed software that allowed the journalists to watch video or listen to radio commentary live on their computers.

Gaz came up with a high-profile scoop: the signing of one of Brazil's top strikers by a major Premier League club for twenty-five million pounds. The club denied it and for two days it looked as if we had got things badly wrong. The tabloids ridiculed us, but Gaz was confident. Sure enough, the story was confirmed. Later, Gaz told me his source was the fourteen-year-old son of one of the club's directors, who was an enthusiastic fan of our site.

With all this activity, there was scarcely time to think. And when there was time, I thought about Ninetyminutes. I didn't hear any more from the police, nor did I discuss Tony's death with Guy. But Patrick Hoyle's words rankled. I tried to push them out of my mind, but they kept returning.

It *was* too convenient.

One morning I phoned the office to say I wouldn't be coming in until the afternoon. Guy sounded a little surprised, especially when I told him I was going flying. He knew I hadn't been since I had started working at Ninetyminutes nearly six months before.

It was a sunny day in early October, with a fresh breeze to blow away any autumnal mist or London smog. It felt good to be at the controls of an aeroplane again, alone, a couple of thousand feet above the ground, with England stretching out like a carpet of green, gold and brown beneath me. I flew over the Hampshire downs to one of my favourite airfields, Bembridge on the Isle of Wight, and walked the mile or so up the steep hill to the cliff tops above Whitecliff Bay.

It was cool up there in the breeze, but it was quiet and it was a long way from Ninetyminutes. I was hoping the distance would give me some perspective.

It did.

For the first time I faced up to the question I had been avoiding. Had Guy killed his father?

On the face of it, it was possible. Ninetyminutes had meant everything to Guy and his father had threatened to take it away. Tony had a hold over Guy that was difficult for me to understand, but it was powerful and I knew Guy wanted to break free from it. The police had certainly thought of Guy as a suspect. Owen had stood by him, provided him with an alibi, but then Owen had always stood by Guy.

But I had spoken to Guy on the day of the funeral. He had seemed genuinely upset about his father's death. That was the thing with Guy. We were close. He could lay open his emotions to me. Over the last few months I had seen him in the good times and the bad. He trusted me with his feelings.

But he had also been a professional actor once. Could I really trust him?

I remembered when these same thoughts had invaded my mind, on Mull, when Mel had told me about Guy arranging to pay off Abdulatif. Both Patrick and Mel had seemed to suggest that Guy had done this to protect himself. That he had killed Dominique.

There was one other loose end. The footprint Guy had left outside Dominique's window the night she died. I had never received a satisfactory answer from him on that. I knew he hadn't put it there when the two of us had gone to bed. So how had it got there?

And then Abdulatif had himself been murdered. By Guy?

Had Guy really killed three people over the last thirteen years? That went against everything I knew about him, against the trust and friendship we had built up over the previous six months, and against everything I had put into Ninetyminutes. Unless I was able to put my doubts about Guy behind me, they would undermine everything.

I stared out over the sea. A fat ferryboat inbound from France was charging towards a sleek warship. It looked from my vantage point as if they were going to collide, but they passed each other without noise or fuss: it was only as they overlapped that I realized the warship was a couple of miles further away.

The trouble was, the doubts weren't going away.

Until I knew for sure whether Guy was involved in these deaths, I wouldn't be able to trust him. If I didn't trust him, we couldn't work together. If we couldn't work together, ninetyminutes.com would fall apart.

But this wasn't just about Ninetyminutes. Guy's friendship was vital to me. If I was ever to do something interesting or unconventional with my life, to become more than just a bean-counting accountant, it would be because of Guy.

I had to convince myself that he was innocent.

26

I arrived in the office mid-afternoon to confront the usual pandemonium, the mixture of the very important and the entirely inconsequential, all of which had to be dealt with. Guy didn't mention my morning off, although I could tell he was curious. He went off to a meeting at four, and never came back to the office.

I left work early, which was still about seven thirty, and took the tube to Tower Hill. I followed my familiar path past the Tower of London, looming murderously in the darkness, and the bright lights of St Katherine's Dock, to Guy's building in Wapping High Street.

He was in, working on a presentation.

'What's up, Davo?' he said, seeing the expression on my face.

'I want to talk to you. I need to talk to you.'

'OK. Come in. Beer?'

I nodded. He pulled two out of the fridge, handed one to me and opened his own. 'What is it?'

I hesitated, searching for the words. I wanted to know the truth. But I didn't want to make it seem that I didn't trust Guy. In fact, it was because I wanted to trust him that I was here at all.

In the end, I looked him in the eye. 'Did you kill your father?'

Guy was about to protest. Then he thought better of it. He returned my gaze.

'No.'

We stayed like that for a few moments, his brilliant blue

eyes looking steadily into mine. He used to be an actor. He was a professional at hiding his real self. Yet he was my friend. We had been through so much together.

'Good,' I said at last. 'But do you mind if I ask you a few questions? Difficult questions.'

'Do you feel you have to?'

'Yes,' I said firmly.

Guy sighed. 'OK. Ask.'

'Where were you on the night he died?' I asked, trying to make the question sound as dispassionate as possible.

'I went out for a drink with Owen.'

'Where did you go?'

'The Elephant's Head in Camden,' he muttered, his impatience showing. 'Near his place.'

'What time did you leave?'

'What is this?' Guy protested. 'I told the police all this. They checked out my story. Don't you trust me?'

'I want to trust you. But I can't get Tony's death out of my mind. I need to know who was responsible.'

'Don't you think *I* want to know too? He was my father.'

'If I can start off by eliminating you it'll make me feel much better.'

Guy scowled. 'All right. I'll tell you what I told the police. And what they checked out. Owen and I went to the pub about seven o'clock. We left about nine. I was already half-pissed, but Owen hadn't had much. He went back to his flat. I went on to Hydra, you know, that bar in Hatton Garden? I came home about eleven.'

'And your father was killed at nine twenty-five, wasn't he?' I said, remembering my interviews with Sergeant Spedding.

'Something like that.'

Owen and Guy had left the pub at about nine. Just time to get to Knightsbridge if one of them hurried. It was such an obvious point, I didn't need to make it.

'Before you say anything,' Guy said, 'the police checked out the Elephant's Head and Hydra.'

'What about Owen?'

'He stopped off at a Europa to buy some food on the way home. The CCTV got him. Timed at nine twenty-one. Can't get better than that.'

You couldn't.

'Anyway,' Guy went on. 'What about the man you saw in the car? The private detective. He has to be a better suspect than me, doesn't he?'

I nodded. 'That's true.'

'Any more questions?' Guy asked.

I had gone this far. I may as well go the whole way. 'Yes. I was thinking about what happened to Dominique and the gardener.'

Guy looked angry again. 'Why? What's that got to do with anything? That was years ago, for God's sake!'

'I was talking to Patrick Hoyle about it. He's convinced your father didn't kill Dominique. And he told me how Abdulatif tried to blackmail you about paying him off.'

'I don't know who killed Dominique! Nor do I care. It was twelve years ago. And as for that bloody gardener, it's true he tried to blackmail us. But I've already told you we paid him off.'

'You didn't tell me about the blackmail.'

'No. Because it wasn't important. Anyway, he was black-mailing Hoyle, not me. So what are you saying here, Davo?' Guy's voice was laced with scorn. 'I killed all three of them? Because if you are, you can just sod off out of here.'

'No, no,' I said. 'I was just wondering whether there was any connection between what happened in France and what happened to Tony. Perhaps I should mention it to the police.'

'For God's sake, don't do that. It'll open up a whole can of worms. This thing is bad enough as it is.' Guy got a grip on his anger. 'Look, I'm sorry, Davo. It's hard not to get worked up when a friend doubts you. You're a mate. A good mate. You were with me in France. You've been with me this last six months. You should know I don't wander around killing people.'

'I know I should,' I said. 'But . . .'

'But what?'

The truth was, I didn't know what. There was circumstantial evidence against him, so some suspicion was natural. But he was my friend. He did have a comprehensive alibi that the police had investigated thoroughly. It was Patrick Hoyle's doubts against Guy's word.

I considered asking him about the footprint, but I knew that he would only say what he had always said: that he had gone to relieve himself in the bushes. More than ten years on I wouldn't be able to get him to change that story, even though I knew it was wrong.

I shook my head. 'I'm sorry. You're absolutely right. But I had to ask those questions just to clear things up in my head. And you've answered them. I ought to go.'

'No. Have another beer,' Guy said. He dug a couple out of the fridge and handed one to me with a smile of friendship. My suspicions were forgiven. 'Now, how are we going to get a Munich office off the ground in three months?'

We chatted amicably about Ninetyminutes for an hour or so. But as I sat in a taxi making its way west towards my flat, I realized that although Guy had made me feel better, I still wasn't one hundred per cent sure of his innocence. The question was whether I could live with ninety per cent.

The following afternoon I had a meeting with the people who were going to administer the credit-card payments once customers started buying from us on-line. We had chosen this particular company because they had assured us that the process would be straightforward. It wasn't. It was one of those meetings where more problems emerged than were solved. Frustrated, I returned to the office. I turned on my computer and checked my e-mails. There was one from Owen. I opened it, preparing myself for an obscure techie rant.

You've been asking questions about Guy, haven't you? About Dominique and our father.

I looked up sharply to where he was hunched over his machine only a few feet away. Jerk. I hit Reply.

So? If you have a problem with that, come over and talk to me. Better still, tell me what really happened.

I glanced up. Owen's fingers were flying over the keyboard. Whether he had read my response or not, I couldn't tell.

Forget it. Forget Dominique. Forget our father. See attached.

I opened the file attached to the e-mail. My computer whirred and ground, then an animation appeared of a man about to take a swing at a golf ball. Except the golf ball was a head. The image zoomed in on the face. It was mine, taken from a photograph on the corporate section of the website.

The club was a driver, a wood. It swung back, then sliced down, making contact with my head, exploding it in a mess of blood and brains, to the amplified sound of cracking eggs. Despite myself, I flinched. It was only an animation, but it made me feel sick. I glowered over at Owen, who refused to meet my eye.

I looked back at the screen that was now displaying the message:

```
A Fatal Error has occurred. Press
CTRL+ALT+DEL to restart your computer. You
will lose any unsaved information in all
applications.
```

I swore, did as I was bid and drummed my fingers for a full minute while my machine ground and beeped itself to life again. I opened my e-mail program and typed furiously.

That wasn't funny.

The reply came back in a moment.

It wasn't meant to be.

I closed down my e-mail in disgust. What a sicko. What a twisted deviant.

When I left the office that evening, Owen was still working. I stopped at his desk. He ignored me. Sanjay, sitting next to him, gave me a nervous smile.

I bent down. 'I'll ask as many questions as I like,' I whispered.

Owen paused for a moment. His screen was full of code. Then he began fiddling with his mouse.

'No more threats,' I said. 'No more funny little e-mails. Let's just stay away from each other.'

Owen looked up at me. His black eyes seemed to pierce right into me. Then he turned back to his screen.

I stretched my foot under his desk and flicked a switch with my toe. His screen went blank. All his work lost.

'What the fuck?' he muttered.

'Whoops,' I said and left him to it.

Owen's threats just made me more determined to ask questions. The next day Mel and I were at my desk working on how we could secure the Ninetyminutes domain name in Spain and Italy. Guy was in Munich, talking to someone we might hire to start a German office. There was no one else within earshot. Mel was gathering her papers together to leave when I stopped her.

'Have you got a minute?'

She noticed the seriousness of my tone. 'What is it?'

'I want to ask you something about France.'

Mel frowned. 'Surely it's best to forget all that, isn't it?'

'I know. I'd like to. It's just, I can't. I only have one question. That night on Mull when we were walking to the bed and breakfast, you told me you thought Guy might have killed Dominique. Did you mean that?'

'You're not serious?' said Mel.

'I am,' I said. 'I haven't been able to get the question out of my mind. Partly because of what you told me that night. Which was confirmed by Patrick Hoyle, by the way.'

'Well, you should. I was angry with Guy and that whole France episode left me feeling guilty. Blaming him was a way of sharing the guilt with him. I certainly didn't mean it. I can't even remember exactly what I told you.'

I could. 'So you don't think Guy was covering for himself when he got Hoyle to pay Abdulatif to disappear?'

'No.'

'I see.' That was clear enough.

Mel hesitated. 'I have a question for you. Just as awkward.'

'What's that?'

Mel swallowed. 'Do you think there's anything going on between Guy and Ingrid?'

I looked at her. 'Now *you're* not serious.'

'They seem to spend a lot of time together.'

'We all spend a lot of time together. If you work fifteen hours a day in the same office, you're quite likely to.'

'So you're sure there's nothing going on?'

'Quite sure.'

Mel looked at me doubtfully. 'I don't trust that woman,' she said, and walked off.

I stared after her. Although I had meant what I had said, Mel's suspicions about Guy and Ingrid echoed around my brain long after she had gone.

I wanted to find out more about the private detective. Guy was right, he did seem the most likely person to have run Tony down. Although if he had, he was being paid by someone. Sabina, according to the police. But perhaps it was someone else? I called Sergeant Spedding. He sounded pleased to hear from me.

'I wondered what progress you're making in your investigation?' I asked.

'We still have some leads,' Spedding said, 'but nothing solid. Why? Have you got something for me?'

I felt uncomfortable. The last thing I wanted to do was tell him my suspicions about Guy. Nor did I want to mention France.

'No, not really. It's just, we're curious here.'

Spedding's tone changed, became more formal. 'If we have anything concrete to report, we'll inform the family.'

'Yes. I see. I just wondered whether you'd arrested the private detective. Since I might have to identify him in court you can probably understand my curiosity.'

'We've ruled him out as a suspect, although he might be a useful witness.' A pause. 'Is there anything else?' I could tell from Spedding's voice that he suspected there was something other than curiosity behind my questions.

'No, no, nothing,' I said. 'Thank you.'

I put the phone down. I hadn't even got the private detective's name.

I needed to talk to Sabina Jourdan. I knew she had gone back to Germany, but I couldn't really ask Guy for her address, so I rang Patrick Hoyle at his office in Monte Carlo. He took a little persuading, but he gave me an address in Stuttgart.

Our plans to open an office in Munich were gathering pace, which meant that Guy and I were making frequent trips there. On my next one of these I engineered a gap in my schedule. I finished a meeting at three in the afternoon and drove my hired car west out of the city along the autobahn.

It was only an hour and a half's drive from Munich to Stuttgart. It was a grey October day with a fine drizzle obscuring the German countryside. I fought through the industrial outskirts of the town, wondering why anyone would want to give up the clear blue sea and sky of Les Sarrasins for this. But then the stern factories gave way to suburban streets lined with trees dressed in autumnal golds and browns and neat, large houses with high-gabled Germanic roofs. Prosperity, order, tranquillity, security. Perhaps this was a good place for Sabina after all.

I found the address Hoyle had given me and rang the bell. The door was answered by a tall middle-aged woman with grey hair and finely sculpted features. For an instant I panicked that I had got the wrong house. Then I knew who she was. Sabina's mother.

'*Ist Frau Jourdan hier?*' I asked slowly, in what I hoped was German.

'Yes,' the woman replied in English. 'Who is it?'

'David Lane. I'm a friend of Guy Jourdan's. Tony's son.'

'*Ein Moment.*'

The woman was suspicious, not surprisingly, so she left me at the doorstep while she disappeared inside. A moment later Sabina appeared wearing a sweatshirt, dark hair hanging loosely over her shoulders, long legs in faded jeans, bare feet. She was beautiful.

She frowned for a moment and then recognized me. 'I remember you. You're Guy's partner at Ninetyminutes. You were with him when he came to see us at Les Sarrasins?'

'That's right. I wonder if I could have a quick word?'

'Of course. Come in.'

She led me through to a large spotless kitchen. A baby was playing with a plastic contraption on the floor. 'Do you remember Andreas?' she asked.

'Hi, Andreas,' I said.

'He doesn't speak English,' Sabina said firmly.

'No, of course not.' He didn't look to me as though he could speak any language quite yet, but I didn't want to argue the point with Sabina.

'Would you like some tea? We have some Earl Grey. Tony always liked Earl Grey.'

'Yes. Yes, that would be lovely.'

She put the kettle on, and her mother said something rapidly to her in German, scooped up the baby and left us alone.

'You haven't flown all the way from England just to see me, I hope?'

'No. We're opening an office in Munich and since it isn't too far away, I thought I'd come and see you.'

'If you want to talk to me about the estate's investments I'm afraid I can't help you. Patrick Hoyle deals with all that.'

'No. It's not that. I want to talk to you about your husband's death.'

'Oh.' Sabina sat down at the kitchen table. She clearly wasn't excited about the subject, but she seemed willing to talk, for the moment at least.

'I was the one who saw Tony just before he died. And I also saw the private detective who was waiting outside his flat. I understand from the police that he hasn't been charged. I wondered what he was doing there?'

'I hired him,' she said.

'Why?'

'I was worried about Tony's safety.'

'Really?' My eyebrows rose. 'So he was a sort of bodyguard?'

'That's right.' Sabina fiddled with a spoon on the table. 'A bodyguard.'

I didn't believe her. If Tony needed a bodyguard he would have organized one for himself. It was obvious that Sabina had hired a private investigator to spy on her husband for the reason that wives always hire private investigators to spy on their husbands. She just didn't want to admit it to me. Which was understandable.

The kettle boiled. Sabina busied herself with the tea.

'How long were you married to Tony?' I asked as she handed me a mug.

'Three years last April. We met five years ago at a party in Cannes. I was working for a film company. There was instant chemistry between us. I've never known anything like it. After the festival he flew over to Germany to see me: I was working in Munich at the time. We fell in love.'

'I'm very sorry about what happened to him, by the way. Sorry for you.'

'Thank you,' she said, biting her lip.

'I only saw you for a few minutes this summer. But you seemed to be very fond of each other.'

'We were,' she said. 'Then.' She looked at me doubtfully.

She wasn't much older than me and at that moment she seemed young and vulnerable. She wanted to talk.

'Then?' I said quietly.

'Yes.' She took a deep breath. 'Until I found out he was having an affair. That's why I hired Leonard Donnelly. I overheard Tony talking to a woman on his mobile. I checked the last-numbers-called on his phone later when he wasn't looking and got the number. It was British. London. So I contacted a private detective agency and asked Mr Donnelly to watch Tony next time he went there. It was a terrible thing to do, but I couldn't stand the thought of him seeing another woman. I mean, what did he find wrong with me?'

A very good question, I thought.

'After Andreas was born I was convinced he didn't think I was attractive any more. I wanted to know who this other woman was.'

'Did you find out?'

'Yes.' Sabina looked crushed. 'It was the wife of a friend of his. Mr Donnelly thinks she is forty-eight. I was humiliated. And very angry.

'And then . . . Then he was killed. Can you imagine how bad I felt then? I hadn't stopped loving him. In fact, it was because I loved him that I was so angry with him. It almost destroyed me. And now, whenever I think of him, I think of him and her. I wish I'd never heard that phone call. I wish I'd never hired Mr Donnelly.'

'Do you have any idea who might have killed him?'

'No. None.'

'What about business enemies? I remember reading many years ago that he forced out his partner.'

'That was *many* years ago. In fact, the man died last year. Cancer, I think. No, it's a long time since Tony's property days. He hardly ever spoke about them, and I never met anyone from then.'

'What about in France? Had he made any enemies there?'

'Oh, no. Or none that I'm aware of. No, I don't think so.'

'So what was this man Donnelly up to?'

'Well, as you can imagine, the police had lots of questions about him. They thought I might have paid him to do it. But he's not that kind of man, and they know that. Anyway, I was the one who first told them about him.'

'He must have seen who did run Tony over?'

'Apparently not.'

'But I don't see how he can have missed it?'

'I don't know the details. I don't want to know the details.' Sabina shuddered, her face pinched. 'Why are you asking all these questions?'

'Tony's death was very close to home. I don't know whether it had anything to do with Ninetyminutes. The police haven't got anywhere. So I thought I would check, myself.'

'I'm sure the police will find who killed him in the end.'

'I hope so. What are you going to do now?'

'I'm not sure. I'm not living in Les Sarrasins, that's for certain. I'll stay here with my parents until I decide what I want to do. According to Patrick, Tony left me quite well off. And, of course, he left me Andreas.'

Her eyes began to fill with tears. I decided it was time to leave.

27

I caught the first flight to London the next morning, and was in the office by ten. Guy didn't know and didn't care that I had spent the night in a Munich airport hotel. I did some research on the Internet and soon located Leonard Donnelly. I phoned his number and spoke to a man who informed me he was Donnelly's partner. I made an appointment to see Donnelly that afternoon.

His office wasn't far from Hammersmith tube station. There was a doorway right next to a bookmaker's with a steel plate proclaiming AA Abacus Detective Agency. Not very imaginative, but it had snared Sabina. I pressed the bell and climbed the dingy stairs in front of me. AA Abacus was on the second floor, and I was greeted by Mr Donnelly himself. I recognized him, as much from the photograph Spedding had shown me as from when I had seen him in his car that night. He was thin, with small bright eyes that quickly moved over me. He was wondering whether he recognized me too.

He led me into a small office with two desks, two computers and lots of filing cabinets. Both desks were empty. His partner was out on the streets. There was a funny smell in the place. Damp or drains or both.

'Take a seat, Mr Lane,' he said. 'What can I do for you?' He spoke rapidly in a clipped Irish accent.

'We've met before,' I said, sitting down. 'Or, if we didn't actually meet, we saw each other.'

Donnelly nodded, and smiled a thin smile. In doing so he displayed protruding front teeth with a clear gap between them. I wished I'd seen them when I was describing him to Sergeant Spedding.

'I saw you waiting in a car the night Tony Jourdan died,' I began.

'I know.'

'I was wondering if you could tell me what happened. What you saw.'

'I told the police.'

'I know. Now perhaps you would tell me.'

Another smile. Those teeth again. 'Doing a little detective work, are you, Mr Lane?'

'Possibly.'

'Now, why would it be in my interest to help you?'

I had anticipated his question. I pulled out five twenties. 'I believe you make your living by providing information for a fee. There's the fee.'

Donnelly glanced at me. I had no idea what the right amount to offer him was. He could see that. He could also see that I was keen to get the information.

'That's quite true,' he said. 'But I charge more than that.'

'How much?'

'Two-fifty. Including VAT.'

I counted out another five notes. 'Two hundred. That's all.'

Donnelly pocketed the notes.

'What do you want to know? I warn you I can't divulge any private information relating to my client. That would be unethical.'

'Of course not,' I said. 'Just tell me what you saw that evening.'

Donnelly took a well-worn notebook out of a desk drawer and thumbed through it until he found the right day. The smell seemed to me to be getting worse. I glanced at the window. Shut.

Donnelly noticed. 'Got to keep it closed, I'm afraid. Street noise is pretty bad here. Can't hear yourself think.' He smoothed open the pages. 'This is it. I had been following Jourdan on and off for two days, since he arrived at Heathrow on Sunday morning.'

'Did you see him with a woman?'

'That's confidential to my client.'

'Fair enough,' I said. I didn't think it was important.

'At eight fifty-eight I saw you and Ms Da Cunha enter Jourdan's flat. At nine twenty-one you left. A couple of minutes later, Jourdan left the flat as well. He started walking south, towards Old Brompton Road. This was a bit of a problem for me because of the one-way system round there.'

'What do you mean?'

'It means that I couldn't follow him by car if he walked south. The one-way pattern is north. So I had to drive north, go around the block and pick him up as he came out on to Old Brompton Road looking for a cab. I'd already done that a few times before, so I thought it would work this time.'

'But it didn't.'

'It didn't. I went around the block and waited on the main road. No sign of him. Then I heard the sirens. I drove back towards his street and as soon as I saw it was filled with police cars I drove on.'

'Why didn't you stop and talk to them?'

Donnelly smiled. 'Usually my clients don't like me to do that sort of thing. I find things work more smoothly if I avoid the police. Although in this case that was a mistake. My client told them all about me. They weren't impressed with my discretion.'

'I imagine not. So you told them what you saw?'

'I didn't see anything. Apart from you.'

'You must have!'

'I didn't. It's true someone else must have been parked on

that street watching Jourdan's flat, but I didn't see them. It was dark, I couldn't tell whether any of the parked cars were occupied or not. It looks as though the second I'd driven out of sight round the corner, the other car started up and ran Jourdan down.'

'Is that what the police think?' I asked.

'It is now. For a while they seemed to think I'd squashed him. They took my car apart, took me apart. But they didn't find anything.'

'So they let you go?'

'Yes. They know I didn't do it. Mrs Jourdan had picked me at random through the Yellow Pages. They know I'm not a professional hit man. I mean, look at this dump. I tell you, if I were a pro I'd be able to afford a better place than this. Also running someone down is about as hit and miss as you can get. A shot is much cleaner and quicker. They know I didn't do it.'

And so should you, he didn't need to add.

As I studied the weasel of a man in front of me, I couldn't help but agree. He didn't look like my idea of an underworld thug.

'Have you ever met Guy Jourdan, Tony's son?'

'No. I did catch sight of him when I followed Jourdan to your offices in Clerkenwell. But I've never spoken to him.'

'Do you have any theories as to who did kill Tony Jourdan?'

'I'm sure I could find some if you retained me.'

'No chance of that.'

'No? Well I'll give you my opinion for free. This was no professional hit. It was personal. Personal usually means family. And not my client. I've seen jealous wives before and frankly they come a hell of a lot more jealous than Mrs Jourdan.'

'The sons, then?'

Donnelly shrugged. 'My fees are thirty-five pounds an hour plus expenses. I could find out for you.'

'No thank you, Mr Donnelly. And thanks for the information.'

'Thirty? And there wouldn't be much in the way of expenses.'

'Goodbye, Mr Donnelly.' It was a relief to get out on to the pavement and taste the fresh Hammersmith air.

Guy grabbed me as soon as I got back to the office.

'There you are, Davo. I've been looking all over for you. You've got your mobile switched off.'

'Have I? Sorry.'

'Where were you?'

'Howles Marriott. With Mel,' I said too quickly.

Guy looked at me sharply. 'No you weren't. I phoned her there half an hour ago.'

I didn't tell him where I had been. And beyond looking at me strangely, he didn't ask. We trusted each other not to skive off. Which made me feel guilty: I had abused that trust.

'Never mind,' he said. 'I want to go over the stuff I was planning to talk to Westbourne about. I won't be able to see them tomorrow, you'll have to do it.'

I pushed my conversation with Donnelly out of my mind and focused on Ninetyminutes.

Things were coming together. Ninetyminutes now had a profile as one of the up-and-coming internet companies everyone had heard of. This was partly to do with the efforts of our PR firm and partly to do with Tony's death, which had provided an unlooked for and unwanted hook for the press. But it was mostly to do with Guy. He was excellent with journalists. He had a good story to tell, which he told well. His vision of what the Internet was all about sounded original and made sense. He had an interesting background and he looked very good in a photograph. The November issue of one of the leading business magazines carried a picture of him on the cover, and inside a write-up of ninety-minutes.com as one of the top-ten internet businesses to watch out for in Europe. As a result of all this we were now better known than many of our longer-established rivals. This wasn't just good for the ego: it was vital if Ninetyminutes was going to overtake the other soccer sites.

Derek Silverman was a real asset. He knew many of the top club chairmen and, more importantly, he seemed to be well respected by them. Guy and he developed deals with a number of clubs where they would pass on visitors to us who were interested in the football world beyond their official club site, and we would integrate our club zone with theirs. It was difficult to do: the areas of overlap had to be carefully dealt with, but for us it was very powerful. Die-hard club supporters would always look at their own club's site first. This was a way of capturing at least part of their attention.

More work.

Owen was a problem. Not because of his understanding of the technology. That had worked brilliantly: the architecture of the site had proved totally scalable, as he had insisted it should be. It was his inability to communicate. He insisted on using e-mail. His messages were terse, often insulting and frequently meaningless. As the company grew, this mattered. He angered the consultants we had hired to put in place the e-commerce system so badly that they quit. That set us back three weeks. Guy was furious, Amy apoplectic. But Owen was untouchable. He was Guy's brother.

We were planning to launch the on-line retailing site at the beginning of December. It was a tight deadline. Too tight. After the fracas with the consultants, Guy agreed to move it back another week, but that was all. We were all nervous we wouldn't hit it and Owen wasn't inspiring us with confidence.

Ingrid, though, was doing a brilliant job. For someone who knew very little about football, she picked it up fast. Not that she ever interfered with Gaz's views on the substance of what was written. But she was constantly asking herself and anyone who would listen why a visitor would spend time on different parts of the site and what each visitor wanted. She didn't believe we had a 'typical' visitor. Each was different, each wanted different things. Ingrid wanted to provide as much as possible for everyone as seamlessly as possible. We didn't want to be a niche player, we wanted to be *the* soccer site for everyone. Not easy.

I spent a lot of time with her and I enjoyed it. She was fun to work with. She never became too uptight and in the whirlwind that was everyday life at Ninetyminutes, she was a voice of sanity. Although I knew she took Ninetyminutes desperately seriously, she never showed it, and she was always ready with a joke to defuse tense situations. We all trusted her to have the right answer to difficult problems and she nearly always did.

I found my relationship with her slowly changing. I began to miss her when she was out of the office. I would go and talk to her about issues that I should have been able to deal with by myself. I would watch her in meetings. And when I was alone at the end of the day, or when I was travelling, I would think about her.

This all crept up on me. When I did finally realize what was happening, it unsettled me. I wasn't sure what to do about it, if anything.

I had hoped talking to Mel about Guy would clarify things, but it had just made them more opaque. I wasn't sure what Mel's real views on Guy and Dominique were. And although I had been firm in my opinion that there was nothing going on between Guy and Ingrid, Mel's suspicions had stayed with me. They nagged at me and raised another question I had wanted answered for a long time.

Ingrid and I were sharing a taxi to our ad agency in Soho. Except we weren't going anywhere. They were digging up High Holborn and the only thing moving was the meter. Ingrid was staring out of the window at the pedestrians overtaking our cab at a stroll. She checked her watch. 'We should have taken the tube.'

'Too late now. You said we didn't have time.'

'See that man there? The one in the Barbour? I bet you five quid he gets to those next traffic lights before we do.'

'You're on.'

Three minutes later I handed her five pounds. The taxi moved forward ten feet.

We were locked together in the back of the cab. The driver's window was shut. A wall of noise from pneumatic drills seemed to shield us from the street outside.

'Ingrid?'

'Yes?'

'About Mull?'

'Mull?' she said in surprise.

'Yes, Mull.'

She tensed. 'What about Mull?'

I swallowed. Afraid to ask the question, but knowing I had to ask it some time and now was as good a time as any.

'Why?'

Ingrid looked at me. 'You asked me that then. I never answered you, did I?'

'No.'

'You deserve an answer.' She sighed. 'I could say I was drunk and Guy seduced me. And that would be true. I'm sure that if I'd been sober I'd never have gone into his room.

But I wanted him to seduce me. And I didn't want to say no.'

'Why not? Especially given what he'd done to Mel?'

'I guess I just wanted to see what it was like. I admit it, I was attracted to him. And the fact that I knew nothing would come of it made it more exciting. I could sin for a night and forget it. I'm not proud of it, not proud of it at all. I was stupid. I lost Mel as a friend. And you.'

So now I knew. But knowing made me disappointed in Ingrid. I had assumed she was different, but she was just like all the rest of them, queuing up for Guy's favours.

'If it makes any difference,' Ingrid said, 'it didn't go any further. He flew back on his own the next day and I took a ferry to the mainland and a later train to make sure I missed you and Mel. I felt pretty small.'

I looked away from her. But it did make a difference.

It was ten o'clock and I was tired. Time to go home. I was shuffling the papers around on my desk ready for the next day, when I noticed a legal document. Damn! Guy was going to Paris first thing in the morning to finalize discussions with the man we had found to set up an office there. And I had forgotten to give him the contract.

I dialled Guy's home number. No answer. Tried his mobile. Switched off. Damn, damn, damn. I stuffed the contract into an envelope, grabbed my briefcase and walked up to Clerkenwell Road, where I hailed a cab for Wapping.

The driver dropped me outside Guy's building with his meter running. I told him I would only be a minute. I followed a woman into the building and took the lift up to the second floor. I rang the bell.

No answer. Bloody hell. What was plan B? Should I wait here, or try to meet him at Heathrow the next morning? Or was he flying from City Airport? I range the bell again.

This time I heard muttering. 'All right, all right.' A few seconds later Guy opened the door in his dressing gown. He seemed surprised to see me.

'Sorry to get you up,' I said. 'I forgot to give you the contract when you left this evening. You couldn't really go to Paris without it, so I took a taxi here. It's waiting outside.'

'OK, OK,' said Guy, with impatience. 'Give it here.'

I was a little put out at this. I had, after all, taken a taxi significantly out of my way to get the bloody document to him. OK, I should have remembered to give him the contract, but then he should have remembered to ask for it –

'Hi, David.'

I looked up. There was Mel. Wearing one of Guy's T-shirts that was barely long enough to cover her. Her blonde hair was tousled. She was smiling.

I glanced at Guy. A spark of irritation flashed in his face. I noticed he had been sweating.

'Hello, Mel,' I said, smiling back at her, as though it was the most natural thing in the world.

'You said your taxi's waiting,' said Guy.

'Yes.' I backed out of the hallway.

'Thank you for this,' he said.

'Bye, David,' Mel called over his shoulder.

'Goodbye.'

'Davo,' Guy whispered as he saw me out of the door. 'You won't tell anyone, will you? Be a mate.'

I didn't answer him. I turned and took the stairs down to my waiting taxi.

It was late morning, not even twelve o'clock, and the Elephant's Head had just opened. While Guy was in Paris I had decided to take the opportunity to check out his story. Somehow, seeing him with Mel the night before had spurred me on. The Elephant's Head was a darkened pub just by

Camden Lock. At this time of day it was very quiet. I ordered a Coke from the woman behind the bar.

'Were you working here in September?' I asked her as she was pouring it. She was a big blonde woman, who looked like she wouldn't take any nonsense from anyone and wanted people to know it.

'I've been here almost a year,' she replied in an Australian accent. 'Why?'

'Do you remember the police asking about two men drinking in here one evening? It would have been Tuesday the twenty-first.'

'Maybe.'

This was not going to be easy.

'What did they ask you? What did you say?'

The Australian woman was suspicious. 'Why should I tell you?'

Why indeed? There could only be one reason. Feeling slightly awkward, I pulled two twenty-pound notes out of my trouser pocket and laid them on the bar in front of her. A couple of early drinkers at a table were immersed in conversation. There was no one else to see us.

'It can't do any harm,' I said. 'You've already told the police. I'm just looking for confirmation.'

The woman considered asking more questions but then thought better of it and reached out to take the money.

'Fair enough,' she said. 'Two detectives came in. They said they were investigating a murder. They showed us pictures of two blokes. One was a big ugly feller with white hair. The other was much smaller. We'd seen them that night. The smaller one was getting pissed. The big one was drinking Red Bull and watching him. They left at about nine.'

'Are you sure about that?'

'It was nine or thereabouts. On his way out the big one

barged into one of our staff coming in to work. He was late. He remembered how late.'

'Thank you,' I said. 'Cheers.' I drank the Coke and left the bar.

I walked out on to Camden High Street. The Europa Owen had visited was about a quarter of a mile away. I found it and wandered up and down the cramped aisles. There were three cameras in there, pointing at the till and various parts of the shop hidden from the view of the shopkeeper.

Fortunately, it was quiet. I picked up a packet of biscuits and took it to the till.

'Hey, I'm on TV,' I said, pointing to one of the cameras.

The man behind the till was a gruff middle-aged Asian who was used to nutters. This was Camden, after all. 'A movie star,' he said to humour me.

'Do those things work?' I asked.

'Of course they do.'

'Have you caught any criminals yet?'

'Someone held up the shop a year ago with a gun. Took three hundred quid. We got his face on the camera. But the police didn't do anything. Never found him. No bloody good, innit?'

'Do the police ever ask you about people that come in here? You know, like people they've spied on?'

'Oh, yes. There was a murder a few weeks ago. One of the suspects said he was here when it was committed. The coppers wanted to look through the tapes to check his story.'

'And was he lying?' I said, with what I hoped looked like innocent curiosity.

'No. The videotape is timed, so they knew exactly when he came in.'

I made a face at the camera, slipping into my harmless nutter role again.

The shopkeeper had had enough. 'Yes, please?' he said to the old woman patiently waiting behind me.

I left the shop and checked my watch. It was half past twelve. So far everything Guy had said he had told the police had stacked up. Was there any point in checking out Hydra? I had piles of stuff to do back at the office. I dithered, but the bar was pretty close to Britton Street, so I decided to stick with my plan.

Hydra was quite crowded at lunchtime, but nowhere near as crowded as it would be at ten o'clock. Bathed in a blue neon glow, it was one of the coolest bars in the area and I had been there a couple of times with Guy. Not often enough to be remembered, though. Was there any chance that the barmen would recognize one solitary drinker a month after the event? I wouldn't know until I asked.

I caught the attention of one of them. 'I wonder if you could help me? I'm trying to find out whether a friend of mine was in this bar one night a couple of months ago. The twenty-first of September?'

'Hold on. I'll get the manager,' the barman said and disappeared through the door. A moment later a purposeful man in a black T-shirt and jacket emerged.

'Can I help you?' he asked, with the strong suggestion that the correct answer to that question was no.

'Yes, I was wondering whether the police have been asking about someone drinking in your bar.'

'If they have, why would I talk to you about it?'

'He's a friend of mine. He's gone missing. We think the last place he was seen was here.' I pulled out a photo of Guy. I had used the same source for the photograph as Owen, the corporate section of our website.

The manager barely glanced at it. 'Have you any idea how busy this place gets in the evenings?'

'I know it's difficult. But I'd be very grateful if you'd try to remember. This would have been about six weeks ago. The twenty-first of September.'

'Sorry, sir. I can't help you.' The manager returned the photo.

'Can you even tell me whether the police have been asking about him?'

'No, I couldn't do that.'

He didn't want to tell me and his look challenged me to try to talk him into it. He was used to defying stroppy customers. I was pretty sure my twenty-pound notes would be wasted on him.

'Thanks for your time,' I said and turned on my heel.

Just as I was reaching the exit, I was stopped by a shout. 'Oi! Hold on a minute!'

I returned to the bar.

'You said the twenty-first of September?'

'That's right.'

'We were closed that week. Refurbishment. So unless your friend is a decorator, I doubt he was seen here.'

Bingo.

I walked back to the office. So Guy had lied to me. I now knew that he hadn't gone to Hydra at nine o'clock that night, as he had told me and, presumably, the police.

So where had he gone?

Had he driven to Knightsbridge and lurked outside his father's flat, waiting for his moment to run him down? Or perhaps it wasn't premeditated. Perhaps he had decided to go and talk to his father about the situation at Ninetyminutes, seen him in the street and put his foot on the accelerator in a flash of half-drunken anger? That was more likely. Uncomfortably likely.

The idea appalled me. My brief euphoria at finally getting

somewhere with my investigation quickly disappeared. My friend had lied to me. Lied to me about something vitally important.

He may even have killed someone.

28

As soon as I got back to the office I phoned Donnelly and asked him whether he had seen an electric-blue Porsche in the street outside Tony's flat. Guy's car was noticeable enough that he might have spotted it.

He prevaricated for a moment, fishing for a further fee, but I refused. Then he answered my question.

No.

Of course, that didn't mean that Guy wasn't there in some other car. And it was possible that Donnelly might have missed a Porsche, even an electric-blue one, in a part of London that was littered with them.

The trouble was, I just didn't know.

I sat at my desk considering what to do. It was difficult. I could confront Guy again, but there didn't seem much point. If he was guilty, he would deny it convincingly. If he was innocent, he would be seriously offended that I had been prowling around checking up on him. He would explode. And an explosion at that moment was the last thing Ninety-minutes needed.

Things were getting tense. The number of site visitors was still growing strongly, but the planned launch of on-line retailing was drawing uncomfortably near. I wasn't sure we were going to make it.

At some point I would have to face up to the problem of Guy's guilt or innocence, I knew, but I decided I would have to put that point off. There was just too much else to do.

Amy had done a phenomenal job of putting together a range of products for us to sell. There were the classic club and national strips and then our own line of clothing, sporting the logo that Mandrill had come up with five months before. She had lined up designers, manufacturers, warehousing and distribution. Everything was ready to go.

The technology was, of course, the biggest worry. Running a website that actually sells things requires much more technology than a site that people only look at. Separate computers, or 'servers', are needed to hold product information and prices, customer and transaction information, financial and accounting records and credit-card verification. Between these and the customer is a web server, which communicates with the customer's computer over the Internet and makes sure that each inquiry is integrated with all the other systems in real time. Firewalls, proxy servers and routers are needed to protect the whole system, provide backup and control the web traffic efficiently.

Originally a company that wanted to sell over the web had to set all this up from scratch. The problem then was getting the different systems to talk to each other. Fortunately, by the time we wanted to install Ninetyminutes' e-commerce system it was possible to buy it all off the shelf. This saved time and was worth the expense, but it did limit some of the features of the site.

This bothered Owen. In California he had been working on on-line catalogues for a big retailer and he had made some interesting breakthroughs in the technology. He showed them to us and we were all impressed. Naturally, he wanted to incorporate these into Ninetyminutes' site. Naturally, they didn't fit.

At first Owen suggested that we delay the launch of the site for a month so he could make them fit. A month was after Christmas. Guy said no. So, without really telling anyone, Owen set out to write an application programming interface to bolt his ideas on to our off-the-shelf system.

Dcomsult, the new firm of consultants we had brought in to implement the system, knew about this, and they didn't like it. But Owen insisted. Guy and I picked up that there were some problems between Owen and Dcomsult, but we assumed this was just another result of Owen's notorious ability to infuriate anyone he worked with. Guy gave him the benefit of the doubt and I wanted to have as little to do with him as possible.

Two days before the site launch we did a dummy run, bombarding the system with fictional requests for clothing. It worked like a dream. And the on-line catalogue looked really good.

The launch day came. We had spent plenty of money announcing it at a time of year when advertising is at its most expensive. The press were warmed up, indeed the fashion editor of one of the biggest middle-market newspapers was planning to make some purchases. Her article would be a terrific way to reach the women who were thinking of Christmas presents for their football-mad boyfriends or husbands.

We went live at ten o'clock in the morning. The hits began immediately. Traffic rose strongly. People started ordering. The system didn't crash. By five o'clock it had been operating without a hitch for seven hours, so we all trooped out to Smiths, a cavernous warehouse-cum-bar opposite the Smithfield meat market that was developing a useful franchise as the watering hole for the internet businesses in the area. Guy ordered champagne. After an hour or so I went home, leaving some of the others to return to the office to check the system.

I came in the next morning slightly late to be met by mayhem. Amy, Owen, Sanjay, Guy and the people from Dcomsult had been there all night. The batch file that was sent to our distributor with all the information on the day's purchases had been corrupted. That meant that the distributor couldn't be confident of what goods to ship to whom. Amy seemed to be having great difficulty getting to the bottom of exactly how it had been corrupted. Owen seemed to know, but said he was too busy to explain and forbade Sanjay from doing anything but try to unravel the problem.

More orders were coming in. We couldn't handle them. At ten o'clock Guy pulled a group of us together. He asked Owen whether he could guarantee that the problem would be solved in the next hour. Owen said he couldn't. So Guy gave the command to shut down the e-commerce section of the site.

Amy called the fashion editor to ask her what she had ordered and to promise her that it would be delivered to her immediately. The fashion editor was unimpressed, although she spotted her opportunity. The next day, ninetyminutes.-com hit the front page for the first time. 'Don't trust the Internet for your Christmas shopping' was the message. Just the kind of publicity we needed. Even worse, we were making the whole industry look bad.

By working all day and long into the following night we managed to piece together manually who had ordered what and to send this information to our distributor's warehouse by motor bike. The goods were shipped. But our credibility had suffered enormous, possibly irreparable, harm.

It wasn't just our credibility. Amy had tried to keep our product line as simple as possible, but we had had to order substantial quantities of clothing from our manufacturers. Clothing that would have to be paid for. If we couldn't sell most of it before Christmas, we would take a big financial hit.

It took Guy to pinpoint what had happened. The fault was in the API Owen had written. There were lots of told-you-sos from Dcomsult. Owen blamed them for not anticipating what he was going to do. Guy tried to put a lid on the recriminations and make everyone concentrate on getting the site on-line again. It was a difficult task. Owen was not prepared to admit he was wrong.

Eventually Dcomsult insisted on a meeting. We were sitting round a table: two of them, Guy, me, Amy, Ingrid and Owen. The leader of the Dcomsult team was a Yorkshireman called Trevor. He was squat, compact, with a permanently intense expression. You could tell he was a techie, because he spoke rapidly, but he was articulate and what he said was clear and understandable.

'We have identified the problem with the system,' he began. 'It's with the API that modifies our product catalogue.'

'The problem's with your e-commerce package, not the API,' interrupted Owen.

Trevor writhed in frustration.

Guy held up his hand. 'Just a moment, Owen. I want to hear what Trevor has to say, then we'll hear from you.'

Owen growled, his small eyes gleaming.

'Don't get me wrong,' said Trevor. 'The API is ingenious. And if we could integrate it with the rest of the solution it could be very powerful. But that's going to take time. And that's basically our choice.'

'Go on,' said Guy.

'We have two options,' Trevor continued. 'One: we can work on the API until we have it reliably integrated into the system.'

'How long will that take?'

'There's no way of knowing,' said Trevor. 'Could be a week. Could be a month. Could be longer.'

'It's trivial,' muttered Owen.

'And the second option?'

'Drop the API. Use the bog-standard catalogue architecture that comes with the package. True, it's not as pretty and it's not as functional. But we will be up and running at the end of the week.'

'And if we follow option two, are you a hundred per cent sure the system will work this time?'

'Nothing's a hundred per cent in this business. But we'll be using a system that has worked dozens of times before.'

'I see.' Guy turned to his brother. 'Owen?'

'It's a second-best solution, man,' he mumbled.

'What do you mean?'

'I mean you talk about having the best soccer site on the Internet. With my API, we'll have it. And we'd get it done in, like, a week if these monkeys would just pull their fingers out.'

Trevor pursed his lips. I was impressed with his self-control.

Guy turned to him. 'Owen says we can do it in a week.'

'And I say we can't.'

It was time for me to intervene. Owen was Guy's weak spot and he could twist himself into knots over this one if I let him.

'I think the answer's clear,' I said.

'Oh, yes?' said Guy.

'Yes. Unless we get the site up in the next week we'll have a total failure over the Christmas season. It'll be hard for us to recover our reputation from that. And financially we'll be strapped. We have to move forward and if that involves making some compromises, we've made them in the past.'

'Amy?' Guy asked.

'I like Owen's application. But I can live without it. And David's right, we have to shift product. We have no choice.'

'Ingrid?'

'We have no choice.'

Guy nodded at the three of us. We were silent. He was dithering. For one usually so decisive, it was obvious he was dithering. Owen's large bulk was slumped in a chair opposite his brother, staring at him.

'Trevor, we'll go with option two,' I said. 'Owen, give the Dcomsult people all the help they need.'

Owen looked at his brother. Guy nodded minutely.

'Let's get to it,' I said.

We returned to our desks, Guy subdued. Ingrid brushed past mine. 'Coffee?' she whispered, so Guy couldn't hear.

I followed her out to a coffee shop round the corner. We collected our cappuccinos and sat down.

'He's got to go,' said Ingrid.

I didn't answer her. I would have loved to get rid of Owen. But it wasn't that easy.

'He's got to go,' she repeated.

'I know, but how?'

'We'll have to tell Guy.'

'But he's Guy's brother!'

'Yeah. And Guy should realize that he's going to cripple the company.'

'He should, but he won't.'

'I don't understand those two,' Ingrid said. 'I mean, I know they're brothers, but I can't imagine two people more different. Their relationship seems much closer than most brothers'. It's weird. It's almost unnatural.'

'It is unnatural,' I said. 'They're both screwed up in their own ways, and the only people they can rely on are each other. It's always been like that. I remember at school when someone started teasing Owen. He was an obvious target. I think they called him "The Incredible Hulk" or something. It was a nasty kid called Wheeler: you know, one of those bullies who maintains power over a group by ganging up on individual members.'

'So Guy beat him up?'

'Worse than that. Wheeler was away one weekend. Guy

went up to the dormitory that night and explained to Wheeler's cronies how Wheeler was manipulating them all, dividing them by bullying each one of them in turn. Guy was cool. People listened to Guy. When Wheeler came back to school, all his stuff was trashed and no one would talk to him. He left Broadhill the following term.'

'So you're saying Guy protects little brother?'

'Always.'

Ingrid drank her coffee thoughtfully. 'That's as may be, but Owen has to go. We can't let him ruin Ninetyminutes. If Guy can't look at the problem objectively, we'll go to Derek Silverman. We have no choice.'

'You're right.' This wasn't to do with my personal problems with Owen. He was threatening the very existence of the company. 'Do we do it together?'

Ingrid nodded. 'Together.'

We wanted to deal with Guy on the Ninetyminutes premises. This wasn't personal, this was business, and we wanted to emphasize that. So as soon as we got back to the office I asked him if we could meet behind the closed doors of the boardroom.

Owen saw us go in.

I told him. As we had expected, Guy protested. 'We can't get rid of Owen! He's one of the founders. He was the one who provided all the cash at the beginning. He came up with the technology for the site. He's worked as hard as any of us. Without him, there wouldn't be any Ninetyminutes now.'

'I know,' I said. 'But with him there won't be any Ninetyminutes in the future.'

'Oh, come on!'

'David's right,' said Ingrid. 'This cock-up was entirely Owen's fault. We may never recover from it. And it's not an

284

isolated incident. There will be more. One of them will finish us off.'

'But he's the most brilliant techie I know! He can run rings round those Dcomsult people.'

'That's exactly right,' said Ingrid. 'He does run rings round them. But the truth is, as we get bigger we're going to have to rely on a team of people for the technology in this company, not just one. Owen doesn't fit.'

'I can tell him to get along better with the others,' Guy said.

'That won't make any difference,' I said. 'You know Owen.'

'What if I say no?'

'We go to Derek Silverman,' said Ingrid.

'Behind my back?'

'No. We're speaking to you first,' I said. 'This isn't just your firm any more, Guy. If it was, then you could keep Owen and that would be your right. But now there are a lot people with stakes in this company. For those people's sake he has to go.'

'Are you ganging up on me?' Guy said. 'You and your old buddy Henry Bufton-Tufton.'

'No,' said Ingrid. 'It's precisely because it's your brother that it's so hard for you to take action. That's why we need to go to the chairman.'

Guy inhaled. 'I'm CEO of this company and I take the decisions. Owen stays. He was here at the beginning and he'll be here at the end. Whenever that is. Now, let's get back to work.'

I went to Ingrid's desk and called Derek Silverman's secretary. I made an appointment to see him in two days' time.

I got back to my flat in Notting Hill late, as usual, carrying a takeaway. I didn't always eat takeaways; sometimes I warmed up something from M&S. Rarely anything more these days. I looked around the flat. It was clean in places; I paid a woman to come round once a week to make sure of that. But overall it was a mess. There was a pile of bills and junk mail to go through. The kitchen needed painting. The tap in the bathroom basin was dripping. The living-room window needed fixing. My taxes were late. I hadn't called my parents for three weeks.

It hadn't always been like this. Until Ninetyminutes I had lived quite an ordered existence. But no longer.

As I flopped down at my kitchen table and unwrapped my doner kebab I decided I'd worry about it all on Sunday. If I didn't spend the whole day at the office.

The doorbell rang. I lived in a purpose-built block, so visitors usually had to announce themselves from the entryphone at the front of the building. Probably a neighbour then. Probably complaining about something I hadn't done.

I opened the door.

It wasn't a neighbour. It was Owen.

He barged past me into the living room, his bulk brushing me aside.

'What are you doing here?' I demanded.

'I want to talk to you,' he said. He was angry. The small dark eyes glimmered dangerously under his brows.

I was too tired to deal with him. 'Can't it wait until tomorrow?'

'No.' He advanced towards me. I stood my ground. I wasn't going to be pushed around in my own flat.

He stopped inches in front of me. 'You tried to get me fired today.' He was so close, I could smell his breath. Mint covering something stale.

'Yes.' I was determined not to be intimidated.

'Why?'

'You're a clever boy, Owen, but you don't talk to people. That matters. It leads to screw-ups we can't afford.'

Owen jabbed a finger into my chest. 'It was that stupid piece-of-shit system that was the problem, not me.'

'Your job was to make the piece-of-shit system work. It didn't. You screwed up.'

'I'm staying,' Owen said.

'We'll see.'

'You plan to go to Silverman about it?'

I didn't flinch. 'That's right.'

'You just changed your plans.'

'I'll do what I think is right.'

Owen backed off a foot or two. 'Has this got anything to do with Dad's death?'

'What do you mean?'

'I mean you keep on asking questions, don't you? About Guy and about Dad.'

'I don't like being threatened.'

'Oh, really?' He grabbed hold of my collar and pinned me against the wall. He was strong enough that my feet barely touched the ground. His large fists clutching my collar squeezed into my neck, making it hard to breathe.

'I'm telling you. No more dumb questions about how Dad died. If Guy really was your friend, you'd let it drop. And you should forget about Dominique too. That was all a long time ago. You understand me?'

I should have placated him, said yes, Owen, no, Owen, and let him go on his way. But I was tired, I'd had a bad day and I really didn't like someone barging into my own flat and pushing me around, even if they were much bigger than me.

So I raised my knee sharply to Owen's groin. His grip on my collar loosened and he bent down, his face contorting in pain. Having started, I had to finish it, so I hit him on the chin. He staggered back, stunned, and I punched him in the stomach. As he reeled, I grabbed hold of his sleeve and dragged him to the door.

'Get out, Owen,' I said. 'And don't come back here again.'

At first he let himself be pulled along. Then as I reached the door and opened it, he straightened up. He was angry. I had a problem.

I tried to hit him again, but my blow bounced off his shoulder and didn't make good contact with his jaw. And then he was on me. He was big and he was strong and he was surprisingly fast. I struggled, but within a few seconds he had me pinned against the wall. He hit me hard in the stomach three times. All the air was knocked out of my diaphragm and somehow I couldn't replace it. I slumped doubled up to the ground, gasping. Then he started kicking. Ribs, head, back. One thump on the skull must have been too hard because everything went dark.

I woke up to find two paramedics leaning over me. Everything hurt. I hadn't been out for long, they said. A neighbour had heard the commotion and called an ambulance. A couple of police uniforms were there as well. They asked me who had attacked me. I was too confused to decide how to answer that and so I just closed my eyes until they left me alone.

I spent a couple of days in the hospital for observation and X-rays. Amazingly, nothing was broken, but plenty was bruised. I had a nasty bout of concussion that didn't just give me a headache, but also made me throw up twice in the most spectacular fashion – 'projectile vomiting' they called it.

A couple of visitors came. First, Guy.

'Jesus, you look a mess,' he said when he saw me.

'Thanks.'

He sat on the chair by my bed. 'I'm sorry about Owen.'

'So am I.'

'He should never have done that to you.'

'It was partly my fault. He barged in and pushed me around, so I hit him. Then he hit me.'

'Are you going to press charges?'

I shook my head. 'The police wanted me to, but I said no. He is your brother. And I did hit him first, after all. But I tell you, Guy, one of us has to go. It's either him or me.'

Guy's eyes searched mine. He saw that I was serious, then he looked down. 'We'll see.'

'We'd better see.'

'Stupid bugger,' he said. 'Look, I really am sorry.'

'I know. Don't worry. I'll mend. I'll be back at work in a couple of days.'

The other visitor was Ingrid. I had been hoping she would come, but I was surprised by how pleased I was to see her. I felt better the moment she walked in. She was shocked by Owen's behaviour. I told her about my ultimatum to Guy and she supported me. The hour she spent by my bedside passed very quickly.

The next day I went home under doctor's orders to stay there. But it was boring and there was so much that needed doing at Ninetyminutes. So that afternoon, despite the continuing headache, I went in to the office.

Everyone was pleased to see me. Everyone was sympathetic. Guy smiled and seemed to be genuinely happy that I was back.

Owen was packing up his stuff.

'So he's going?' I asked Guy.

'Yes,' Guy said. 'It was his decision. I think he realizes his position here is going to be difficult from now on.'

'Well, I'm glad,' I said. 'If he had stayed, I was going to leave.'

'I know.'

I took it slowly. Concentration was difficult with my head,

and I couldn't read for more than a few minutes at a time. After a couple of hours I gave up and left for home.

I passed Owen in the corridor.

'David!'

I stopped. 'Yes?'

He scanned my face and must have seen the still visible signs of our previous meeting. 'It's because of Guy I'm going. You know that, don't you?'

'Yes.'

'It's got nothing to do with you. Ninetyminutes means everything to Guy and I don't want to screw it up for him.'

'OK,' I said neutrally.

'You know I'd do anything for my brother. Anything.' He stepped closer. I tensed. This time if he tried to touch me I'd run. 'If you harm him in any way, or harm Ninetyminutes, I'm coming after you. Understand?'

I nodded. I'd had enough of standing up to Owen.

'Cool.' He stepped past me and returned to his desk.

As I walked to the tube I marvelled at Owen's loyalty to Guy. I also felt a little afraid. Owen meant what he said, that much was clear. And I had no idea to what lengths he was capable of going to protect his brother.

29

I was soon dragged back into the Ninetyminutes maelstrom. Guy and I went to Munich to interview a couple of key people for the operation there, which now consisted of two men, a woman, an office and lots of computers. We had a successful day. Rolf, the man we had hired to set things up, was good. He was efficient, competent and above all quick. Germany would be on-line by March.

I was silent on the plane back, looking down at the lights of nameless German towns flickering through the darkness and wisps of cloud. Guy was in the seat next to me absorbed in some papers on the new French operation.

The time was coming. The time when I would have to satisfy myself once and for all of Guy's innocence. The time was now.

'Guy?'

'Yes?' He put aside his documents.

'What's the connection between France and your father's death?'

'Jesus Christ, Davo! Can't you think about anything else? You've got to focus. There's too much going on at Ninetyminutes. If you keep worrying about all that you'll miss something. We can't afford another screw-up.'

I wasn't going to be put off this time. 'Before Owen kicked the shit out of me he warned me off asking any more questions about your father's death. And about Dominique.'

'So?'

'So, if there's nothing to hide, why should he care?'

'Who knows? Owen's crazy.'

'I checked at Hydra. You weren't there the night your father died.'

'Yes I was. It's a big place. Whoever you spoke to just didn't see me.'

'It was closed that week. For refurbishment.'

Guy didn't answer.

I went on. 'How did that footprint get outside Dominique's window?' Guy was about to protest, but I stopped him. 'Before you say anything, I know it's twelve years ago, and I know what you told the police. But that night is etched in my brain just as it is in yours. I can remember every detail of it. And we went to the guest cottage together. The garden had been watered late that afternoon, which means that your footprint got there between the time we went to bed and the time the police started nosing around the next morning.'

'Can I get you a drink, sir?'

It was the flight attendant with the trolley. Guy was obviously grateful for the interruption. 'Gin and tonic, please. A large one.'

I waited while she prepared his drink. He took a gulp.

'Another thing. When did you take the jewellery box from Dominique's room? The one you gave to Abdulatif. The police cordoned off her bedroom as soon as your father called them. So you must have taken it before then. When?'

Guy drank some more gin.

'I'm waiting,' I said.

He turned to face me. 'I didn't kill Dad. And I didn't kill Dominique.'

'Then who did?'

Guy swallowed. 'I don't know.'

Now he was hiding something. He was hiding it well, but he was hiding it. 'I don't believe you.'

He shrugged.

'Guy. I've been thinking about this long and hard. I don't

want to believe that you killed Dominique. Or your father. I really don't. But there's something going on, something that I think you know about. And until I know what it is, I can't trust you and I can't work with you. When we get to London I will get off this plane and never go into Ninetyminutes again.'

Guy studied my face. I knew he didn't want to tell me. Although my departure from Ninetyminutes would be a blow, it wouldn't be an insurmountable one. But he needed me just like I needed him. At that moment I realized that. And so, I think, did he.

'All right,' he said. 'I will tell you. But only if you give me your word not to tell anyone else. Not Mel, not Ingrid. And not the police.'

I thought before I answered. I had no idea what he was going to admit to, or confess. What if he had murdered his father? I certainly wouldn't work with him any more. And I'd have to tell the police.

Guy saw my doubt. 'If you do tell anyone, I'll deny it. And there's no proof of what I'm about to say one way or the other. Now, do you give me your word?'

He knew that I would take giving my word seriously. He had known me as a well-brought-up public schoolboy and I hadn't changed as much as I would have liked.

'OK,' I said.

Guy breathed in. 'All right. First, let me say I didn't kill my father, and I have no idea who did. No idea whatsoever.'

'What about Hydra? You were never there.'

'No, I wasn't. After I left the Elephant's Head I got a cab to Mel's flat in St John's Wood.'

'Mel's?'

'Yes. You saw her at my place last month, didn't you? Well, I'd been seeing her for a while before that. On and off.'

'I see.'

'The police checked it out. She had a friend staying with her who saw me as well. I didn't want to tell you this when you asked me, because . . . well, you can understand why.'

'I suppose so.'

'So I don't have any idea who killed my father, or why.'

'Might it have something to do with Dominique?'

'Ah, Dominique,' said Guy.

I waited.

'I didn't kill Dominique.' He was definitely telling the truth this time. 'Owen did.'

'Owen did? But he was only fifteen!'

'He was a big guy, even then,' Guy said.

'But why?'

'He hated her. He was seriously messed up when my father walked out on us; you know that. He held Dominique responsible. That whole trip he became obsessed by her, the more he saw her the more he hated her. You remember he said he was always working on his portable computer?'

'Yes.'

'Well, he wasn't. Actually he spent a lot of time watching her.'

'Which is when he saw her with the gardener.'

'And you.'

I took a deep breath. Even after all these years the conse-quences of that half hour reached out to tear at me.

'It tipped him over the edge,' said Guy. 'Not only had she stolen Dad away from us, but then she was cheating on him. He was angry. He watched her. Watched her fight with Dad. Watched Dad leave the house. Watched her shoot up with heroin. Watched her drink. Watched her finally pass out.'

'Then what?'

'He went into her room. He tried to talk to her. Tell her what he thought of her. I don't know what he expected, whether he thought she'd just listen quietly to what he had to say and then let him go. But when she woke up and saw him, she was about to scream, so he put the pillow over her mouth. She tried to struggle. He kept it there. He kept it there a long time.'

'Jesus.'

'Then he left her.'

'God. But it was your footprint, not Owen's, they found.'

'Owen knew he'd done something badly wrong. At the time, I don't think he intended to kill her. I think he barely realized he had. I don't know what was going through his head. But he wanted to talk to me. He woke me up. We went out into the garden and he told me all about what Dominique and you had done, about what a slut she was, about what an evil woman she was. I was shocked about you and her, but I thought Owen was just ranting. Which was strange for him, you know how little he likes to talk.

'Then I realized he'd smothered her with the pillow. I rushed up to her room, climbed in through the balcony. Dad wasn't there. But she was. Lying there, not moving, her face still under the pillow.'

Guy breathed heavily. There was sweat on his upper lip.

'I looked for a pulse, but there wasn't one. I had to take a decision there and then. I could either turn Owen in, or I could help him. I was shocked by what Dominique and you had done. I hated her too. And if Owen was screwed up enough to kill her, it was as a result of her actions. I know now it was all my father's fault, but at the time I blamed her. I knew Owen had done wrong, but he was my brother and no one else was going to stand up for him if I didn't.

'So I crept back outside. Asked Owen exactly what he had touched. Came back and wiped it all down carefully with a cloth. I had to be quick; I had no idea when my father would get back. I took the pillowcase off the pillow. I grabbed the jewellery case to make it look as though a thief had been in there. I left through the balcony and dusted over our foot-prints, although I must have left one of mine. And then I went back to bed.'

'I never noticed,' I said.

'You were out of it. Snoring. Loudly.'

'Christ.'

Guy shrugged.

'I'm amazed the police didn't discover anything.'

'I was careful,' Guy said. 'While they were focusing on Dad, I was safe. I knew they would figure out he was innocent pretty soon, and I needed to give them someone else to worry about. Which is why paying the gardener to disappear was such a good idea. But then I got a real scare when they found my footprint. I'm eternally grateful to you for getting me out of that one. I've never quite known why you did that.'

'I didn't believe you'd killed Dominique,' I said. 'I was still a schoolboy. I was helping my innocent friend against the authorities. Or at least, that was what I thought I was doing.'

'Well, thanks, anyway. Without that explanation they'd have found it harder to blame Abdulatif.'

'Whew.' I thought through what Guy had just told me. Owen had killed Dominique. At the age of fifteen! I shuddered. 'What happened to Abdulatif?'

'He died on the streets of Marseilles. It's a tough place.'

'You don't think Owen killed him?'

'No. I'm sure he didn't.'

'Oh, come on! His death was so convenient. So timely. Just when the blackmail was beginning to really bite.'

Guy shrugged.

'Wait a minute,' I said. 'I remember when Owen told us that Abdulatif had been murdered. It was just before we went to Mull. He'd been to visit your father in France.'

'Hold on, Davo,' Guy said, a note of anger in his voice. 'I

told you the whole truth just now, and I'm telling you the truth when I say Owen didn't kill Abdulatif. Or Dad. I don't think he really meant to kill Dominique. He was young then. And screwed up. He's grown up now. He's less impulsive. He's straightened himself out.'

'Huh.' I wasn't going to enter into an argument with Guy about Owen's psychological well-being.

'I mean it. He's OK now. And I want you to leave him alone.'

'Leave him alone?'

'Yes. Leave him alone.' Guy's voice was firm. It was a command, not a request.

We were silent for a couple of minutes, as I absorbed what Guy had just told me.

'So now you know,' he said.

'Now I know.'

'But you won't tell Ingrid, will you? Or Mel?'

I had given my word. I shook my head.

'Or the police?'

I hesitated.

'It wouldn't matter too much if you did. I'd deny we'd had this conversation. It's a long time ago in a foreign country and the case was closed to everyone's satisfaction. There would be no point. Would there?'

I shook my head. 'There wouldn't.'

'So will I see you at the office tomorrow morning?'

'I don't know.'

I lay in bed that night staring at the bands of light and shadow projected on to the ceiling by the streetlamps outside. I was shaken. Owen was a murderer. He had killed Dominique and I was pretty sure he had killed Abdulatif too. And Guy had helped him cover it up.

Guy had given himself all kinds of justifications at the

time as to why Owen had done what he had done. None of those counted for anything with me. I believed Owen was screwed up, but I also believed he was responsible for his actions. Perhaps it was right for a big brother to cover up for his younger brother, I didn't know. I couldn't even begin to imagine being related to Owen. I was now exceedingly glad that he no longer worked for Ninetyminutes. But what about me? What should I do? Should I just ignore what I knew?

As a good citizen, I should tell someone. But I had also given my word. It was only on that basis that Guy had told me anything.

I thought of the practicalities. Who would I go to? Would anyone in the British police help me with a case that was thirteen years old? Perhaps I should call the police station in Beaulieu. I'd have to go there. I'd have to talk to French officials who might or might not have any interest in what I was saying. I would have to start my own personal crusade for justice.

And what would happen? It would be impossible for me to continue working at Ninetyminutes. It would make it difficult for Guy to run the company properly, especially if the French police decided to investigate further. I might screw the whole thing up. I'd certainly have to find another job, perhaps back in banking, or even worse, accountancy. And I would have lost Guy as a friend. Despite what Owen had done, that mattered.

I decided to keep my word.

Eventually I went to sleep. I was at my desk by eight thirty the next morning, ready for everything that Ninetyminutes could throw at me.

PART FOUR

30

March 2000, three months later, Clerkenwell, London

'A hundred and eighty million! You think Ninetyminutes will be worth a hundred and eighty million?'

The American woman held Guy's incredulous gaze. 'Absolutely.'

'Pounds or dollars?'

'Pounds.'

'Wow.'

I shared Guy's sentiments. We were in the Ninetyminutes boardroom with Henry Broughton-Jones and two representatives from Bloomfield Weiss, a big US investment bank that was hot on technology in the States and was trying to transfer those skills to Europe. We had been besieged by bankers over the previous two months. They all wanted to take Ninetyminutes public through an IPO, or initial public offering. This would involve listing our shares on the London Stock Exchange and the Neuer Markt in Frankfurt and raising money from the investing public and institutions. We had decided to appoint Bloomfield Weiss to guide us through the process.

The two investment bankers were about our age. One, the banker, was a smooth Brit with oiled-back hair and a permanent frown: he acted as the front man. The other, the well-groomed American woman who also wore a permanent frown, was an analyst. She had a record of boosting new-economy shares in the US and was beginning to do the same thing on this side of the Atlantic.

'How do you come up with that number?' I asked. 'Last week you were talking about a hundred and thirty million.'

'This market's hot,' said the analyst. 'The smart US investors who've made a killing on the Internet in the States over the last twelve months have started looking over here for opportunities. Individual investors in the UK have gotten the internet bug, volumes are going through the roof, they're all trading stock tips on electronic bulletin boards. Last-minute.com is coming to market in a couple of weeks with a valuation of three hundred and fifty million. Everyone's clamouring for stock. A hundred and eighty million for you is doable. Very doable. Maybe we'll get more.'

'And how much new money can we raise?'

'I think we can go for forty million. We want to leave some investor demand untapped so the stock goes up on the first day. It's important to get upward momentum. These days investors are buying stocks that are going up simply because they're going up. It becomes a virtuous circle. And one that we want to get started.'

'But none of my forecasts show we'll ever be able to make enough profits to justify those kind of numbers,' I said.

'Doesn't matter,' said the banker. 'We're not allowed to show the investors your forecasts anyway. Don't worry. These guys are smart. They know what they're doing.'

'Are they? It doesn't sound smart to me.'

The banker's frown deepened. 'You've got a great story to tell, David. And you're going to have to tell it many times. You'll have to believe it. You've got to get with the programme or get off the bus.'

'Come on, Davo, get with the programme!' said Guy, poking just a little fun at the mixed American metaphors dropping so pompously from the mouth of the British banker.

'David, we're the sellers here,' Henry said. 'The higher the price we sell at, the more money we make. It's as simple as that.'

'He has a good point,' said the analyst, matching her colleague's frown. 'We need management's commitment to make this thing work. We're going to be taking you to see investors right across Europe in three weeks' time. Investors can smell uncommitted management.'

'Oh, I'm committed to make Ninetyminutes work, all right,' I said, offended. 'I'm just not committed to a valuation of a hundred and eighty million quid.'

'That's fine, Davo,' Guy said. 'Let Bloomfield Weiss worry about the valuation. You and I will worry about the company.'

'All right,' said the banker. 'Our current thinking is that we start off in Amsterdam on the twentieth of March, then Paris on the twenty-first and Frankfurt on the twenty-second. We'll go on to Edinburgh the following day, and then down to London . . .'

Ninetyminutes had recovered from its pre-Christmas wobble. Sanjay had taken Owen's place and, together with Dcomsult, he had retailing up and running again in a matter of days. We shipped a respectable quantity of clothing before Christmas. The millennium came and went without blowing up our computer systems and we hit the New Year running. The German site was on-line by the beginning of March with the French site due to join them by the end of April. We bought a small company based in Helsinki that specialized in Wireless Application Protocol or WAP technology. Eventually this would allow people to check our website from their mobile phones for the latest football scores and news. And the visitor numbers kept on going up and up. Advertisers loved this, and we had no trouble signing them up.

This wasn't enough for Guy: the more we achieved, the more he wanted. He had plans for even more rapid expansion. More advertising, more marketing, opening up several more European offices, a big ramp-up of the retailing operations. All this would need money. But now that didn't seem to be a problem.

The IPO got everyone excited. Orchestra Ventures was enthusiastic about the idea: although they wouldn't be able to sell any of their own shares immediately, they would be able to mark them up to show a huge profit on their books. Bloomfield Weiss liked it because of the fees they could charge everyone. Guy liked it because it would give him as much cash as he could spend.

And I liked it because it would make me a multi-millionaire.

It was a very strange feeling. Of course, I had gone into all this with the vague idea of making a lot of money. And, in theory, when Orchestra Ventures had committed their initial investment the value of my stake had increased considerably. But at that stage survival was all I was worried about. In a few weeks my shares would be worth silly money. Of course, it would all be paper profits, but at some time in the future I should get my hands on real cash. What would I do with it? Buy my own Cessna 182? Buy a house on the Corniche? Send my children to Broadhill? It would change my life. I would be a wealthy man, just like Tony Jourdan. Somehow, despite my ambition, I couldn't imagine that.

I realized that the money had little meaning for me in what it could buy. But it would mean a lot to me to know that I had made it.

Not just me. There was a smile on everyone's face. Everyone had some kind of stake in the firm, everyone was going to make money. There was a huge amount of work to be done and no time to celebrate, but the place hummed with suppressed excitement. People put in sixteen-hour days and never seemed to get tired.

To my relief, there was no sign of Owen.

The IPO required a massive amount of preparation, especially on the accounting systems and the legal documentation. There was a prospectus to be written and checked and rechecked. Much of this work fell on me. Mel was a great help, and we spent long evenings together going over obscure points.

My father called, proposing lunch at Sweetings. I had blown him off the last two times he had suggested it, so this time I agreed. Besides, I had good news for him.

They had heard of dot-com fever in deepest Northamptonshire. Even the *Daily Telegraph* was reporting it excitedly. So my father could hardly wait to ask me how Ninetyminutes was doing.

'It looks like we're going to float at the end of the month,' I said.

'No! You haven't been going a year yet.'

'I know. Absurd, isn't it?'

'I didn't even realize you were making profits.'

'We're not.'

My father shook his head. 'The markets have gone mad,' he said as he tucked into his dressed crab. But he couldn't keep the smile off his face.

'They have. But I'm not complaining.'

'So, um, how much . . . ?'

'How much will your stake be worth?'

'Er, well, yes. I was wondering that, actually.'

'If the shares come out at anything like the level the bankers suggest, about nine hundred thousand pounds.'

My father choked on his crab. He began to cough, went bright red, and took a desperate swig from his half-pint tankard of Guinness. Eventually he recovered. 'Did I hear you right?'

'I think you did.'

A broad grin spread across his face. 'Well done, David. Well done.'

I couldn't help smiling back myself. I was proud to have repaid his faith in me so handsomely. I knew what really delighted him wasn't just the money, but the fact that it was his son who had made it for him. What I hadn't told him was that my own stake would be worth just under ten million pounds.

'Don't count the cash until you've sold your shares,' I cautioned. 'And certainly don't spend any of it.'

'Of course not,' said my father. And then, 'Well, well, well. I think the time has come to come clean to your mother.'

'Haven't you told her yet?'

'No,' said my father, looking a little embarrassed. 'She might not have approved. But she'll have to, now, won't she?'

'I suppose she will.'

I returned to the office to find it in full panic. I could tell it was a technology-related panic, because everyone was standing around Sanjay's desk looking anxious, while he was frantically tapping into his computer and trying to communicate with his staff through the bodies around him.

'What's up?' I asked Ingrid.

'Goaldigger has been attacked by a virus.'

The goaldigger.com website was one of our biggest competitors. It had been active a year longer than us and had more visitors, but we were catching them up quickly.

'What kind of virus?'

'Apparently it's been spitting out e-mails to all Goaldigger's registered users. Look.'

She handed me an e-mail. It was addressed to Gaz, who had presumably been keeping tabs on the opposition.

Virus Alert

Please be aware that a virus has been detected in the goaldigger.com system. This virus may be able to access the computers of Goaldigger registered users and might download private information, or even corrupt customers' hard disks. Customers are advised not to log in to the Goaldigger website or open e-mails from Goaldigger. We apologize to those customers who have lost significant personal data as a result of this virus.

The Goaldigger team

'This sounds strange,' I said.

'It is. It's a hoax.'

'You mean there's no virus?'

'There is a virus. But a simpler one. It just sends this e-mail to all Goaldigger's customers scaring them off the site. It'll take Goaldigger weeks to repair the damage to their reputation, if ever.'

'What a shame,' I said with irony. The hard truth was that bad news for Goaldigger was good news for Ninety-minutes.

Ingrid looked at me sternly. 'If someone's done this to Goaldigger, they might do it to us next. Guy wants to be sure that we're not vulnerable.'

'We've got firewalls and anti-virus software and stuff, haven't we?'

'Yeah, but presumably they had all that too.'

Sanjay was pretty sure that we had protection against a similar attack, but he monitored our system constantly over the next few days to make sure. Goaldigger did try to get the message out to its customers that the whole thing was just a hoax, but there was no doubt that the episode did them damage. No one found the perpetrator.

Guy, Ingrid and I decided to take an evening off to attend the March First Tuesday event. They were keen to have us. In the internet world we were already billed as a success story before we had even made our first profit. The event was held in the auditorium of a theatre, specially cleared for the occasion. There were queues to get in and pandemonium once we got there. I felt very different than I had last time: much more secure in who we were and what we were doing. As last time, there were hundreds of eager entrepreneurs with ideas. But even more of these ideas were half-baked. In the case of some of them, no one had even turned on the oven. There was also a new kind of venture capitalist circling the room: the 'incubators'. These were young men or women who had raised money to invest in internet companies at the earliest stage: the equivalent of the Wapping phase in Ninetyminutes' history. They were scarcely less flimsy than the companies in which they were investing, but somehow they had attracted cash and they were throwing it about. They made the thirty-year-old Henry Broughton-Jones look like a dinosaur.

Everyone had a story about one success or another, but the big story on everyone's lips was lastminute.com, run by the woman I had met at my first First Tuesday. This was a website which provided tickets at the last minute for anything ranging from air travel to theatres to sports events. They were in the middle of an IPO, and the investing public were fighting for shares. The flotation price had just been raised again, valuing the company at nearly five hundred million pounds. Everyone in that room wanted to be as successful as lastminute and most of them thought they could be. Even, I'm ashamed to say, me.

After a couple of hours of frantic schmoozing, the three of us met up.

'What a zoo!' Ingrid said.

'Can you believe these people?' said Guy.

'That's where we were nine months ago,' I said. 'I didn't believe it would last then. But it has. It's grown. Lastminute is worth five hundred million. We'll be worth a hundred and eighty. It really is a new economy after all.'

'I told you, didn't I, Davo?' Guy said. 'You should have had faith in me.'

'I did have faith in you!'

'Yes, I suppose you did.' Guy smiled at me. Then he looked out over the throng. 'I wish Dad could have seen this.'

'He would have been proud of you,' I said. Actually, I thought it more likely he would have been envious, but I didn't want to mention that. Nor did I want to ask any more questions about his death. I had asked enough questions and found out as much as I was ever going to on that subject. Although I still didn't know what had happened to Tony, I was convinced of Guy's innocence; Owen was gone and I had told myself to be satisfied with that. Besides, if Guy could feel better about his father, that was a good thing.

We left the throng and went our separate ways. I walked down a side-street looking for a taxi. Guy and Ingrid went the other way. I waited at a corner, and nothing came, so I doubled back, trying to find a better spot for a cab.

I saw them together on the pavement. They were waiting for a taxi too. They were very close together. It looked as if Guy had his arm round Ingrid's waist. I could hear Ingrid's laugh ringing up the side-street towards me.

I stopped still and watched them. They didn't see me.

Suddenly I felt cold. The comfortable glow of internet success left me.

I turned on my heel and walked all the way home.

I slept little that night. The next morning I asked Ingrid to join me for a coffee. She agreed, and we headed for the place round the corner.

'I wonder how many of those people last night will actually get funding,' she said as we stepped out into the street.

'Not many, I hope,' I replied uncharitably.

'I met a guy from QXL, you know, the auction site?'

I grunted. Ingrid went on.

'It's an amazing story. They floated in October with a market cap of two hundred and fifty million, and now they're worth nearly two *billion*. Can you believe that? I knew they were doing well, but I didn't realize it was that well. And all from selling knick-knacks over the Internet.'

I grunted again. We entered the coffee shop and ordered.

'OK, out with it,' she said as we sat down with our cappuccinos. 'Something's bugging you and you want to talk to me about it. By the look of you, it's bugging you pretty badly.'

'Oh, it's nothing really.'

'Come on. What is it?'

I looked her straight in the eye. 'Are you sleeping with Guy?'

Ingrid appeared genuinely shocked. She put her cup down. 'Am I what?'

'You heard me.'

'No. No, I'm not.'

'It's just, I saw you last night.'

'And I saw you,' she said defiantly.

'I mean I saw the two of you. Together. Getting a taxi. Together.'

'So what? I got in one and then he got in another.'

'Oh, I see,' I said.

'Don't you believe me?' It was a challenge. Ingrid did not like having her honour questioned.

'Yes. Yes, of course I do. It's just, he had his arm around you. You were together. I've seen Guy with women. I know what happens.'

'I said we went home in different taxis.' She was getting angry now.

'OK, OK.' I held up my hands to calm her down. 'It's got nothing to do with me, anyway.'

'Too right,' muttered Ingrid. She swallowed the rest of her coffee and checked her watch. 'Well, if that's all it was, we ought to get back to work.'

Our IPO approached. Lastminute.com shares were priced at three hundred and eighty pence. On the first day of trading, desperate investors bid the price up to five hundred and fifty. That meant lastminute was worth over eight hundred million pounds.

I spoke to Bloomfield Weiss. They said they felt a valuation of two hundred million for Ninetyminutes was definitely achievable now, maybe even two hundred and fifty if the stock market's exuberance continued. We'd get a better idea when the roadshow started the following week.

Then Derek Silverman called Guy. He had just received a phone call from Jay Madden, the head of Champion Starsat Sports. Madden wanted to meet Guy the next day. He had a suggestion he wanted him to listen to.

That could mean only one thing.

We met at the Savoy for breakfast. Guy insisted on bringing me along, for which I was grateful. Jay Madden was a forty-year-old South African with an American accent and business manner. He began by discussing Chelsea's performance in the Premier League. A good move. He wanted to show us that although he was South African he knew his English football. He then slid into a quick description of Champion Starsat's sports strategy. Basically, they wanted to own it, especially football. They were a long way towards this as far as TV was concerned, but nowhere when it came to the Internet. This didn't bother Jay: he was sure he had plenty of time. He could either start his own site, or buy one. He liked ours.

I could feel my pulse quickening. This was real. This was going to be big money.

'How much?' asked Guy simply, biting into a croissant.

'A hundred and fifty million pounds,' said Jay.

'Cash or stock?'

'Stock. With a lock-up. We want to keep you people around.'

'Not enough,' said Guy immediately. 'We can get two hundred and fifty million at the float next month.'

'I'm not nickel and diming you this morning,' Jay said. 'We can do that next week. But what do you think about the idea in principle?'

Guy munched his croissant. Then he took another bite. This was a big decision. It might take him a whole croissant to get through this one.

'No,' he said.

No?

'No? Just like that?' Madden looked unhappy.

'Ninetyminutes is doing well as it is. There is a role for an independent soccer website to dominate Europe. That's going to be us. And the stock market will put a value on that. A value much higher than a hundred and fifty million pounds.'

'But we can give you everything you need,' said Madden. 'Cash for expansion, plenty of outlets for promotion, contact with the clubs and the football associations.'

'Oh, I know you'll do well,' said Guy. 'And I'm not looking forward to having you as a competitor. But working for Champion Starsat isn't why I started Ninetyminutes. It's not why any of us work there. And it's not why people come to our site.'

'Are you sure this isn't just about money?' Madden asked.

'Quite sure,' said Guy.

Madden tucked into his sausage. 'You're not going to like us competing with you.'

'I know,' said Guy, staring steadily at Madden. Letting him know he wasn't scared of him.

'We could make you very rich.'

'I intend to be very rich anyway,' said Guy. He poured himself some more coffee. 'Do you think Arsenal will catch United in the League?'

The board was waiting for us back at Ninetyminutes: Derek Silverman, Henry Broughton-Jones and Ingrid. Guy explained to the others Jay Madden's proposal.

'Wow,' said Henry.

'You were just trying to get the price up, right?' I said.

'No,' said Guy. 'I meant what I said. I think we should stay independent.'

'But a hundred and fifty million!' I said. 'That's got to be worth taking now.'

'It's in Champion Starsat stock, remember,' said Silverman.

'Better that than Ninetyminutes stock, quite frankly.'

'The whole ethos of everything we do is based on independence,' said Guy. 'Our relationships with the clubs, our internet partners, our editorial policy. It's how we're going to succeed. Of course Champion Starsat will have a good site that a lot of people will want to see. So will the BBC. But ours will be better.'

'But with their cash we can make our site better,' I said.

'Davo, don't go all chartered accountant on me.'

'That's not fair.'

'I want to make Ninetyminutes the number-one site in Europe. We're almost there. And Henry,' he looked pointedly at the venture capitalist, 'when we are, we'll be worth a lot more than a hundred and fifty million quid.'

'That was just their first shot,' I said. 'They'll go higher.'

'So will the stock market. Tell him what value Bloomfield Weiss thought we might get, Davo.'

'Two hundred million,' I said grudgingly. 'Perhaps two fifty.'

'And it will go up after that,' said Guy with total confidence. 'Hang on in there, Henry, and I'll make you some real money.'

'A hundred and fifty million quid is real money,' I said. I was being outmanoeuvred and I disliked it. I still couldn't believe that Ninetyminutes could be worth anything like twenty million pounds, let alone two hundred, despite all the hype. Guy was right, and that annoyed me: I was a chartered accountant. The numbers didn't add up. This was a great opportunity to get out while the going was good.

'Let's go around the table and see what people think,' said Silverman in his chairman's role. 'Who's in favour of talking to Champion Starsat? Guy, I take it, is a no.'

'Definitely not.'

'And David?'

'Yes.'

'Henry?'

Henry Broughton-Jones paused. He was smiling. You could almost see the greed around his lips. He wanted more, I could tell he wanted more, and Guy was offering it.

'I think we should tell them we mean no,' he said. 'I have a very good feeling about Ninetyminutes. I think we would be selling it just before it takes off.'

'Ingrid?'

I looked at Ingrid hopefully. I knew she had common sense. I could see I was going to lose this one, but it would be nice to have her on my side.

'I agree with Guy,' she said. 'If we stay independent, we could well end up with a higher valuation. Besides, I like this company as it is. I don't want to work for Champion Starsat.'

I was disappointed. Why was Ingrid supporting Guy and not me? Was it because ... No, I'd drive myself crazy thinking like that. But if Ingrid was sleeping with Guy, then should I expect future disagreements to go this way?

'Well,' said Silverman. 'For myself, I think there's a right price for everything, even Ninetyminutes. But if the Chief Executive and the lead financial backer don't want to sell, then that's pretty conclusive to me. I'll tell Jay.'

'If they start up a site, we'll cream them,' said Guy, rubbing his hands.

I left the room in a foul mood.

31

The bubble was bursting.

We didn't realize it immediately. To start with it looked like a temporary correction, a pause for breath while the market regained its strength to climb even higher. Within a few days of launch lastminute's shares slipped under three pounds, well below the issue price. Thousands of individual investors were sitting on a loss. And NASDAQ, the American high-technology stock exchange, fell steadily as the month progressed.

Guy and I didn't notice, and although the people at Bloomfield Weiss must have done, they didn't tell us. At least, not at first. We embarked on our roadshow. Amsterdam went well, as did Paris, and the fund managers almost bit our hands off in Frankfurt. We had practised our presentations to death in front of our PR firm. Guy did an excellent job of extolling Ninetyminutes' prospects, and I swallowed my pride and did my best to come across as a safe pair of hands. Sanjay was there to answer any technical queries. It was clear from the questions that not all the potential investors understood the intricacies of the Internet, but most of them knew something about football. And they understood, or thought they understood, that if you bought shares in markets that just kept on going up and up, you were bound to make money.

We arrived in cold, grey Edinburgh tired but euphoric. We were beginning to believe not only our own story, but Bloomfield Weiss's as well.

Things started to go wrong in Scotland. We had breakfast

at the Caledonian Hotel with some big investors who asked difficult and rather cynical questions about when we would ever make a profit. As the day progressed, the questions became harder. I found them particularly tricky, because I usually agreed with the questioner. How could a company that had been going for less than twelve months and was making no money be worth two hundred million pounds? How indeed.

Our smooth Bloomfield Weiss banker was looking worried. This involved not just a frown, but a stoop of the shoulders and a tendency to scurry off to make a call on his mobile at every pause. I was amazed how he was able to shed this demeanour for the few minutes he was introducing us, when he became transported by excitement over Ninety-minutes and its future.

Even Guy noticed things were going badly after the last afternoon session. He pulled the banker to one side. 'What's going on?'

'Edinburgh fund managers are always awkward. They're notorious for it. They're just trying to live up to their repu-tation as canny Scots.'

'Oh, come on. There's more to it than that. There must be.'

The banker sighed. 'Possibly. The market's a bit shaky. Lastminute was off another twenty p yesterday and the NASDAQ was down again. Have you seen today's *Financial Times*?'

'No.'

The banker handed it over. Articles about investors being let down by lastminute's share price collapse. About fund managers angry with the greed of their investment-banking sponsors. About how companies due to come to market in April were considering waiting to see what happened. And worst of all, an article about us. According to Lex, the

Financial Times's back-page comment piece, we were a promising company but at two hundred million pounds we were wildly overvalued.

The Scots had read the papers. They didn't like us any more.

'Why didn't you show us this earlier?' I demanded, angry that I hadn't picked up the *FT* myself that morning.

'I wanted to wait until you'd done your presentations,' the banker said. 'Didn't want to dent your confidence. These roadshows are all about confidence.'

'So what do we do now?'

The banker frowned more deeply. 'We carry on. We'll win them round, you'll see.'

When we got back to the hotel Guy and I stopped off at the bar for a quick drink. The banker ran off to make calls. The euphoria of the previous few days had worn off: we were tired and we were worried.

The banker returned. 'Bad news, I'm afraid.'

'What?' said Guy, scowling.

'I was just talking to the syndicate desk in London. They don't think they can place the deal.'

'What does that mean?'

'It means we'll have to pull it.'

'You're not serious? We can't do that!'

'If we can't sell the shares, we can't do the deal.'

'But we need the cash! You promised us the cash. You said we could definitely raise forty million pounds.'

'And that was a perfectly fair assessment at the time that we said it. But market conditions have changed. If we go ahead with this deal it'll be a very public flop. That will be bad for all of us.'

'But the Germans loved us!'

'I spoke to Frankfurt. They're getting second thoughts. And the problem with the Germans is they all get second thoughts together.'

'So what do we do?' I asked.

'We wait. This is just a temporary thing. All bull markets pause for breath. In retrospect this will be seen as a great buying opportunity. Things will turn around in April, you'll see.'

'I don't like this,' Guy said. 'I don't like this at all.'

'Believe me, neither do I,' said the banker.

'Do we have any choice?' I asked.

'I'm afraid not.'

Guy looked at me. Then he turned to the barman. 'Two beers,' he said.

The banker left us to it.

We had to put everything on hold until we knew we could get the IPO away. The uncertainty was immensely disruptive for the business, and for Guy's frame of mind. We all watched the stock market closely. Things didn't turn round in April. NASDAQ's slide became a tumble. On the fourteenth of April it fell ten per cent on the day, reaching a level thirty-four per cent below what was now being seen as the all-time high of March. Lastminute's shares were now down below two pounds. More significantly, the founders had been transformed from heroes to hate figures in less than a month. All those speculators who had fallen over themselves to fill their boots with lastminute shares could not be relied upon to do the same with ours.

Suddenly B2C websites were out of fashion; everyone wanted to be in B2B. B2C was business-to-consumer. B2B was business-to-business. Ninetyminutes was B2C.

The following Monday Bloomfield Weiss advised us to delay the IPO for a couple more months until the markets recovered. It was the kind of advice we had no choice but to accept.

That left us with a problem. We had big plans, but not

much cash left to finance them. Guy and Owen could help a little. The winding up of their father's estate had given them a million pounds each they could get their hands on. But that wouldn't keep us going for long: we had been relying on forty. So Guy and I went to see Henry.

He gave us a friendly enough welcome when we met him in his Mayfair office. But despite the smile there was a frown on his high forehead, and he was fidgeting. Not a good sign.

Henry had been involved in the discussions with Bloomfield Weiss to delay the IPO further, and he knew we would need more money from somewhere. Nevertheless I took him in detail through our cash situation and the advice we had received from Bloomfield Weiss. I showed him forecasts for the next six months, which reflected the reduced expenditure levels I had been able to press Guy to accept. We needed ten million to see us through to October, by which time the IPO should have happened.

Henry was listening closely. When we had finished he ran his fingers through his thinning hair. 'I have bad news, I'm afraid,' he said. 'The answer's no.'

'What?' exclaimed Guy.

'I should explain.'

'You certainly should.'

'We had a big meeting here yesterday to discuss the latest market developments. We think there has been a fundamental change. It's at times like this that venture-capital firms are tempted to throw good money after bad. We want to avoid that. So the message to all our investee companies is, conserve cash. You won't get any more from us.'

'But that's absurd! If you don't give us more funds, we'll go under. If you do, you'll make at least a hundred million.'

'And if the stock market doesn't pick up over the summer? What then? We put in yet another ten million?'

Guy calmed himself. 'The business is going just as we said

it would. Better. Our sites in Germany and France have started brilliantly; I wouldn't be surprised if Germany outstrips the UK next year. Visitor numbers are still climbing, we went over four million last month. The retailing is losing money, but our own-brand stuff is doing well. You walk down any street in the country and you'll see people wearing ninetyminutes.com T-shirts and sweatshirts. We're building a brand here, Henry. And good brands, the kind of brands that are worth hundreds of millions, cost money to build.'

'I know. But I can't give it to you. It's the firm's policy.' Henry glanced at me. 'I'm sorry, David. I do understand all this. I've argued your case, believe me. But we're a partnership and I need to abide by the partnership's decision. No more cash.'

'Let me talk to your partners,' said Guy. 'I'll convince them.'

'No point,' said Henry, his voice cooling.

'Let me call them direct.'

I raised my hand to steady Guy. Henry was our ally at Orchestra. Going over his head had no chance of getting us what we wanted. 'So what do you suggest we do now?' I asked him.

Henry raised his hands. 'What can I say? The world's changed. There is no more easy money. Batten down the hatches. Conserve cash. Make profits.'

'But that'll mean we'll screech to a halt just when we're pulling into the lead,' said Guy. 'This is a race. We put on the brakes, we lose.'

We had a real problem, and Guy and I sat down to figure out what to do about it. There really was no choice but to cut back. Stop the advertising campaign in its tracks. Freeze hiring. Hold back on the development of the WAP company in Helsinki. Delay plans for offices in Barcelona, Milan and

Stockholm. And try to slow down the retailing express train that was speeding away, pulling truckfuls of cash with it.

We told the team. They had been through so many tribulations that they took another one in their stride. They all left at seven to have an 'austerity party' at Smiths.

Guy was less resilient. In March, he had been on a high. He had seen what lastminute had done and had genuinely believed he could do better. As far as he was concerned, Ninetyminutes was already the best soccer site on the Internet. Recognition of that fact was going to come in a matter of weeks and bring with it piles of cash. For Guy, that had been a given. He was already thinking how to spend it. Now he had not just to lower his sights, but to change his whole mindset one hundred and eighty degrees from expansion to efficiency, from investing in growth to cutting costs, from shooting for the moon to survival. It was a shock.

Long after the others had all gone to Smiths, he and I went for a pint to the Jerusalem over the road.

'We'll pull through,' I said. 'We always do.'

'I guess so. If we cut back as much as you say we should, we'll struggle on,' Guy said. 'But that's almost the worst thing of all.'

'What do you mean?'

Guy shrugged. 'I always wanted to have either a huge success or a spectacular failure. Struggling along to break even until we eventually fade away is my worst outcome. It will be like death from a thousand cuts.'

'We need to stay in the game.'

'Oh, come on, Davo. You know as well as I do that once we stop growing it's all over. The competition will pull away from us. Champion Starsat will start up its own site and they'll overtake us. We'll just be also-rans.'

Guy's optimism was difficult enough to handle. His pessimism was impossible.

'You never know,' I said. 'Maybe the others will have to cut back too. Maybe the stock market will bounce tomorrow and Bloomfield Weiss will be knocking on our door again. You have to keep going, Guy.'

'Actually, I'm not sure I do have to. You and Ingrid can run things. Maybe I should slip away.'

'That's absurd.'

'This is going the same way as everything else I try. Everything's hunky-dory to start with, but then it just slides through my fingers. At drama school they thought I was a pretty damn talented actor. I looked good. After a couple of years I should have landed some decent roles. It didn't happen. Instead I almost destroyed myself.'

'This is different.'

'Is it?' Guy looked at me witheringly. 'Ninetyminutes was a great idea. I thought I'd done well to get it this far. I thought I was good at this stuff. But then what happens? It runs into a brick wall like everything else.'

'All successful businesses go through rough patches early on,' I said.

'Not this rough.'

'Yes, this rough. Do you think your father never had times as tough as this? Do you think he gave up?'

'Don't compare me to my father.'

'Why not? You do.'

Guy didn't answer.

'He wasn't a superman, you know,' I went on. 'He was just another reasonably successful property speculator. There are many more like him around. Sure, he had flair. But he also had determination. He didn't give up every time property prices crashed, did he? He can't have done, or he'd never have survived.'

'Perhaps he was lucky.'

'Lucky?' I snorted. 'You make your own luck.'

'Well, it looks like I don't make mine.' Guy stared into his beer. I stared at Guy.

Eventually he looked up and met my gaze. His eyes, usually so bright and forceful, were unsteady, hesitant. 'I don't know what I'll do if Ninetyminutes doesn't make it.'

I saw it then; saw the fragile core that was at the heart of Guy. I had caught glimpses of it during the many years we had known each other. Despite the success, the friends, the popularity, the women, the athletic ability and the money, Guy didn't believe in himself. Ninetyminutes was his final attempt to build a solid shield around that core. The attempt had worked for a year or so but now it was all unravelling, leaving Guy soft, vulnerable and unprotected underneath.

Ninetyminutes had to succeed for Guy to survive.

Guy was watching me. He knew I knew.

I opened another beer as soon as I got home, and sank into an armchair. It was very hard not to let Guy's despair rub off on me.

My eyes rested on the telephone. I still had an unpleasant task facing me that evening. It was one of those tasks that doesn't get any easier the longer you leave it, so I decided to face up to it straight away. I called my parents.

Fortunately, my father answered. He was full of expectation.

'Did you tell Mum?' I asked him.

'Yes, I did,' he replied. 'To tell you the truth she was a bit miffed. Can't think why. Seemed to think I had taken a big risk. She said even if it all came out well in the end it might not have done. Still, we'll show her, eh?'

'Perhaps not, Dad.'

'What do you mean?'

'You must have read about our IPO being delayed.'

'Yes. But that was just for a few weeks, wasn't it? The

papers say this is just a correction. The market will be roaring ahead again any moment soon.'

'Well it had better hurry up,' I said. 'Because until it does there will be no IPO.'

'Oh,' said my father, thinking through the consequences. 'So where does that leave Ninetyminutes?'

'Very short of cash,' I said. 'I don't think we're actually going to go bust, at least not for a few months yet, but it means we don't have any funds to invest in the business. It will be all we can do to keep it ticking over.'

'Your mother won't like this.'

'No, she won't. But you'd better tell her, Dad.'

'Perhaps I'll wait a couple of weeks. You never know what might turn up.'

'Tell her, Dad.'

My father sounded deflated. 'OK,' he said. 'And good luck.'

32

I was working late and Guy was out of the office. I didn't know whether he was at a meeting or had sneaked home. I was engrossed in a spreadsheet for calculating Amy's funding requirements for the retailing business over the summer, when I felt as much as saw someone watching me. I looked up. It was Ingrid, sitting in Guy's chair, fiddling with a strand of her chestnut hair.

'Am I disturbing you?' she asked.

'No.' I looked at the papers in front of me representing hours of unfinished work, work that couldn't be done during the hurly-burly of the normal office day. 'That is, you are, but I'm grateful.'

'Stressed?'

I smiled. 'Yeah. I am stressed. And tired. Funny, really, I could handle all the hard work when I thought we were just about to do the IPO, but it's more difficult when we're struggling to survive.'

'What do you think about the IPO?'

'We'll get it away in the summer,' I said. 'It's just a question of getting through the next couple of months. Bloomfield Weiss are confident we've got a good story, and the site's going well.'

Ingrid's pale-blue eyes were watching me steadily. 'Is that what you really think?'

I sighed. 'I don't know what I really think. All that might happen. Or Bloomfield Weiss could be totally wrong and we'll never do an IPO. We might never get another penny of cash from anywhere. Champion Starsat might come back and buy us tomorrow. The site might crash. On-line retailing sales might go through the roof. People might stop using the Internet. The world might stop turning. Doing this job, I've given up trying to forecast even a day ahead. We just have to keep plugging away and hope.'

'I know what you mean,' said Ingrid. 'But Guy seems worried.'

'He is,' I said.

'I think he's losing his nerve.'

'Do you?'

'Don't you?' She looked at me pointedly.

'Yes,' I admitted.

'Unless he pulls himself together, everything will fall apart before we get a chance to do the IPO.'

'Can you talk him out of it?' I asked.

'I don't think so. We don't have that kind of relationship.'

I couldn't help myself raising an eyebrow. Ingrid pretended not to notice.

'What about you?' I asked her. 'Are you worried? You always look so cool about everything.'

'Do I? I don't always feel cool about everything. Yes, I am worried. Of course, everything has always been so uncertain at Ninetyminutes. And I kind of expected that when I joined. It made a change after working for a large corporation with its plans and budgets. But over the last nine months I've really found myself being drawn in. If we'd done the IPO my stake would have been worth three million pounds. That's serious money. It's really why I joined Ninetyminutes. It's so frustrating to have that amount of money so close and then see it whipped away from you. I might never get another chance.'

'Neither might any of us.'

'I don't want to let it go, David. When we're so close.' She must have seen the surprise on my face. 'What is it? You looked shocked.'

'Oh, I'm sorry. I didn't expect you to be so focused on the cash.'

'Aren't you? Isn't Guy?'

'Oh, yes,' I said. 'But I know about Guy. And about me. I suppose I always assumed that this was just a more exciting job for you. I thought you didn't have to worry about money.'

'Oh, because I have wealthy parents, you mean?'

'I suppose so,' I said.

'Rich parents do not solve all your problems. Just ask Guy.'

'I think I'm beginning to understand that.'

'This job is fun, I'll grant you that. And it's true I'm not going to starve. But my father is never going to give me anything much more than pocket money. Nor should he. I don't expect it. I'm going to have to make my own way in the world, and I'm cool with that.

'I've done all right so far. I have a good reputation in the business. I could have walked into any of the top magazine publishers in the UK, or anywhere else for that matter. Good salary, good prospects. A woman can do well in magazine publishing. It's just that a rich woman can do even better.'

'So what will you do if you do make your three million out of Ninetyminutes? Retire to the South of France?'

'No way. I'd stick with Ninetyminutes for as long as was necessary. But then I'd probably start my own magazine. Or maybe website. With my own money instead of somebody else's.'

It made sense, of course. Ingrid had never seemed to me to take life very seriously, but there was no reason why she shouldn't want to make her millions just as much as Guy and I did. And her reasons were more down to earth than ours. For Ingrid, joining Ninetyminutes had been a rational, if risky, career choice, a route to somewhere she wanted to go. She knew who she was. Both Guy and I were still trying to find out.

'Let's hope you get your chance,' I said. 'In the meantime, all we can do is keep our cool and pray.'

'And try to get Guy to do the same thing.'

A week of austerity. Budgets slashed, office heads briefed, Amy placated. I did most of it. Guy's enthusiasm seemed to have left him completely. His energy reached a new low. He showed up every day, but he was of little use. And this sudden lethargy made a big difference. We had all come to rely on his confidence and encouragement, urging us on to do those seemingly impossible tasks. Without it, the hill seemed higher to climb for all of us.

Frankly, this irritated me. Now wasn't the time to give up. I wasn't going to roll over and die, sulking as I did so. I had put a year of my life, fifty thousand pounds and my father's retirement savings into the venture and I wasn't about to give up on all that. I tried to replace Guy's energy with my own. It wasn't quite the same, but the team appreciated it.

And then, the following Tuesday, I got a call from Henry.

'Henry, how are you?' I said. Unlike Guy I didn't hold Orchestra's lack of support against him personally. I believed him when he said he had fought for us against his partners. Plus I still liked the guy.

'I have something to say to you,' he said, his voice cold, colder than I had ever heard it.

'Yes?'

'One. Orchestra Ventures is prepared to invest a further ten million pounds into Ninetyminutes. Terms to be discussed.'

'That's wonderful news,' I said, a little hesitantly. His tone wasn't that of someone bearing wonderful news.

He ignored me. 'Two. As from today, responsibility for the investment in ninetyminutes.com within Orchestra has been passed to Clare Douglas. She will be in touch with you shortly. I will resign from your board and she will take my place.'

'Don't we get any say in this?' I asked. 'We'll miss you.'

'No,' said Henry. 'And three. I and my family are taking a two-week holiday, beginning tomorrow.'

'Oh.' Wishing him a good trip didn't seem to be what he wanted to hear. Why he wanted to tell me at all was a mystery. 'Why the change of heart?'

'You don't know?' said Henry, his voice bitter.

'No,' I said, my suspicions rising. 'No, I don't.'

Henry sighed. 'I hoped as much. Just ask your partner. He'll tell you. Now, if you want to know anything else, talk to Clare.'

I put the phone down. Was this good news? It should have been very good news. It just didn't feel like it, that was all.

I looked across my desk to where Guy was checking the latest news stories on the site. 'That was Henry.'

'Oh yes?'

'Orchestra want to put in ten million quid.'

Guy sat up in his chair, his face suddenly alight. 'You're kidding?'

'I'm not. But he's resigning from the board. Clare Douglas is taking over.'

'I don't care who we've got on the bloody board as long as we've got ten million in the bank.' He let out a whoop. 'Hey, guys, we're back in business.'

They all crowded round. Guy told them the news. As they filtered back to their desks he noticed my expression. 'What's up? Upset that you don't get to cut any more costs?'

'I don't know. It doesn't smell right. Henry seemed very

cold. Eager to get off the phone. And why has he passed us on to Clare Douglas?'

'I don't know,' said Guy. 'He's your friend.'

'He wouldn't tell me why he's changed his mind. He said you'd know.'

'He changed his mind because he's finally realized what a great business this is,' said Guy. 'Not before time, either.'

'It's almost as though someone has been putting pressure on him. Or Orchestra. Do you know anything about that?'

'No, Davo, I have no idea what you're talking about. How could I put any pressure on Orchestra? Cheer up. We've got the cash. We're motoring again.'

But as Guy left his desk to revive the troops, I called Henry back. 'Henry, I don't understand. Something's going on here.'

Henry sighed down the line. 'Did you talk to Guy?'

'Yes. He said he didn't know anything. He told me not to worry about it.'

'He's probably right.'

'Do you want to have a quiet drink somewhere? Just the two of us, so you can tell me what's going on.'

'Listen to Guy. There is nothing going on. And I don't want a drink with you or anyone else from Ninetyminutes. I'm going on holiday tomorrow morning and I hope I will have nothing to do with any of you when I get back.'

We took our foot off the brake and pressed down on the accelerator. Hard. I had some misgivings about this: what if we couldn't get an IPO away in the summer? Then we'd be out of cash again. I voiced these to Guy. His answer was predictable. If we didn't move fast, we wouldn't get to where we wanted to go. If that meant we had to take risks, so be it. I knew he was right.

In an internet start-up, you are always looking ahead. Things are going so fast that there isn't time to look back, consider past mistakes, regret missed opportunities. If you make a mistake you correct it as best you can and move on to the next thing. This was especially true of Ninetyminutes.

But I couldn't help thinking. Thinking how handy it was for us that Tony Jourdan had died exactly when he had. How fortunate we were that Henry had suddenly changed his mind about investing in us. And for that matter, how lucky we were that our biggest rival had mysteriously been struck by a computer virus.

Once again, it was all too convenient.

Someone was going to great lengths to make sure Ninetyminutes survived. There was one obvious candidate. Owen.

True, it was difficult to see how he could possibly have killed Tony. But even after he had left Ninetyminutes I could imagine him still doing all he could to ensure its survival, if not for his own still substantial equity stake, then for his brother.

Henry might not want to talk to me, but I was going to talk to him.

I knew he was on holiday, so I rang his secretary asking for his address, saying I had some urgent documents to courier to him. She was having none of it, insisting that I should send the documents to her for forwarding. It was clear he had told her not to divulge anything.

When I had met Henry at First Tuesday he had told me he was in the process of buying a house in Gloucestershire. Chances were that was where he had gone. But how to find the address?

I called Fiona Hartington, a woman we had both trained with, who was still working for our old firm of accountants. She and Henry had moved in the same social circle. As I had suspected, they still did. I explained that I was going through

Gloucestershire myself that weekend and I thought I might drop by. Did she by any chance have the address?

She did.

Henry's house was on the far side of the Severn, towards Ledbury. It was a dilapidated place on the edge of a quiet village. I drove past slowly and saw a Land Rover Discovery parked outside. Just the kind of car Henry would need to navigate his children through the wilds of South London. I turned around a few yards further along the narrow lane and drove back into the small driveway, feeling like a trespasser. I noticed there was a dent in the back of the Land Rover.

A fair-haired two-year-old boy appeared from nowhere, turned and ran round the side of the house screaming 'Daddy!' A moment later I saw Henry in old checked shirt and jeans. He was sweaty and grimy: he had obviously been working in the garden. He didn't look pleased to see me.

'Hello, Henry,' I said optimistically.

'What the hell do you think you're doing here?'

'I want to talk to you.'

'Well, I don't want to talk to you, so bugger off.' He looked nervously over his shoulder to where his child had disappeared to. I guessed he didn't want to explain my presence to his wife.

'Walk, Henry?'

'No. I said, bugger off.'

'Henry. I've driven a hundred and fifty miles to see you. I'm not just going to turn round and go back. Talk to me and I'll go.'

'I've done what you asked.'

'I haven't asked you to do anything,' I said. 'You know that. Someone has. I want to know who it is and what they asked you to do.'

Henry looked at me, glanced over his shoulder and said, 'OK. But let's make it quick.'

He led me out on to the lane and after a few yards we crossed a stile into a field.

'Someone has scared the hell out of you,' I said. 'Who is it?'

Henry walked in silence for a moment, considering his response. We were making our way diagonally across a field grazed by sheep towards the brow of a low hill. It was mildly strenuous and in the spring sunshine I quickly warmed up. Apart from intermittent birdsong and Henry's heavy breathing as we climbed the hill, there was silence.

'It started a couple of days after I told you and Guy Orchestra wouldn't put any more money into Ninetyminutes. My wife came back from the supermarket with the kids in the car. She let them out first and they ran to the front door. They found my daughter's ginger cat lying dead on the front doorstep. It had been . . . dismembered. The two kids started screaming. My wife had to clear it up and calm them down. She called me at work and I told her to report it to the police, which she did. They came round to take a statement. They didn't seem to know anything about it: there hadn't been any similar attacks in the area.

'As you can imagine, the whole family was pretty upset. The next day, my wife was taking the kids somewhere when her car was rammed from behind by a large van. She had stopped at a T-junction and the impact sent her out into the road in front of on-coming traffic. Fortunately, no one hit her, but it could have been different. They could have been killed. All of them.'

Henry's mouth was locked in a grim line. He was walking faster, it was hard to keep up.

'What happened to the van?'

'It reversed fast and disappeared round a bend.'

'Did your wife see who was driving it?'

'She only saw it in her rear-view mirror. She said it was

driven by a man. Quite a big man. She didn't really see his face.'

'Young? Old? Dark hair? White hair?'

'She didn't see. She was a wreck. I came home from work early and tried to comfort her. Then, the next morning, there was a plain envelope on the mat with my name on it. I opened it and there was a note. All it said was "Give them the money. No police".'

'Was it handwritten?'

'No, it was a standard computer font. I took it to work with me and thought about it. There seemed to be only one option. I was sure it referred to Ninetyminutes. I knew whoever wrote it was serious because they had nearly killed my family the day before. And I remembered what had happened to Tony Jourdan. I also knew I should report it to my partners at Orchestra and to the police, but that would increase the risk to my family and that was something I wasn't prepared to do. After all, it's Orchestra's money, not mine. And it's only a job; a good job, but I can always get another one. Not like my family.'

'Jesus,' I said. 'Henry, I swear I didn't know anything about this.'

He glanced at me. 'I believe you. But I decided I wasn't going to have anything more to do with Ninetyminutes. Or with you. That seemed the safest.'

'How did you swing it within Orchestra?'

'It was difficult. I cashed in every Brownie point I had to get them to agree to the money. And then, once they had, I said I wanted to go off the board. They didn't understand that. But fortunately we've been trying to find a good company for Clare Douglas to look after. She's very ambitious and she's been demanding more responsibility. She worked on the initial investment in Ninetyminutes and I knew she liked the deal, so this kept her quiet. I hated doing it, though.'

'I'm sure.'

'If we lose the money, and I'm pretty sure we will, I'm going to find it hard to live with myself. I owe the guys at Orchestra Ventures a lot. A ten-million hole will make a real dent in their performance. But I didn't have any choice. Did I?'

He was searching my face as we puffed uphill. This wasn't a rhetorical question. He had taken the difficult decision alone, and he needed assurance that it had been the right one.

If I had had a wife and children, what would I have done? I didn't know. But I couldn't tell him that.

'No, Henry. You had no choice.'

We stopped at the brow of the hill and looked over the village towards the Malvern Hills. It was a pretty spot. It seemed miles away from Ninetyminutes and its troubles.

'So now you know,' said Henry, 'what are you going to do?'

'Stop it,' I said, without hesitation.

Henry glanced at me doubtfully. 'Good luck. But please don't tell anyone I told you about this. And whatever you do, don't tell the police. I've given up ten million pounds of other people's money to make sure my family is safe. You'd better not put them in jeopardy now.'

'I won't,' I said, and meant it.

I was angry as I drove back to London. There was no doubt in my mind that it was Owen who was responsible. But I felt guilty by association. The reason Ninetyminutes had survived was because Owen had scared the wits out of a decent man's family. If Ninetyminutes prospered I would know it was because of Owen's brutality, not hard work from the rest of us. I had told Henry I would stop it, and stop it I would.

Of course, what I didn't know was whether Guy had any knowledge of what Owen had done.

I drove straight to Owen's place in Camden. I rang the bell to the first-floor flat with his name on it. No reply. I looked up; the curtains were drawn. Perhaps he was away. I recognized his black Japanese four-wheel drive parked further along the road. Abroad maybe?

I brooded for the rest of the weekend.

On Monday morning, I took the opportunity of a period of relative calm at the office to ask Guy.

'Seen much of Owen lately?'

'Not recently,' said Guy. 'He's gone to France.'

'France?'

'Yeah. He's staying at Les Sarrasins. Since Sabina's gone back to Germany, Owen said he'd look after the place for a bit. We may well sell it, it's not clear.'

'So he's there now?'

'Yes,' said Guy. Then a breath of suspicion brushed his face. 'Why?'

'I never can figure Owen out,' I said, shaking my head as though I had asked for no other reason than curiosity about what made Owen tick.

But Guy was staring at me as I turned my attention back to the pile of papers on my desk. 'Leave him alone, Davo,' he said. 'Leave him alone.'

33

I was supposed to be going to Munich the next day. Instead, I drove to Luton airport and from there caught a cheap flight to Nice. I hired a car at the airport, and drove through the city and along the coast road towards Monte Carlo, passing beneath Les Sarrasins. There was something I needed to find out before I spoke to Owen.

I parked in what seemed to be a burrow in the hill, and climbed up Monte Carlo's cramped streets to the road where Patrick Hoyle had his office. It was in a building filled with lawyers, accountants and investment firms. Hoyle was on the fifth floor. I left the lift to be met by thick carpets, blondwood-panelled walls, and an imperious young secretary with waist-length fine hair and an aquiline nose. I hadn't made an appointment, which drew a pout of disapproval, but once she had announced my presence I was ushered through into Hoyle's office.

It was a large space, flooded with clear Mediterranean light from the windows overlooking the harbour. Hoyle himself was seated in a big leather swivel chair behind a massive desk. As I glanced around the office, I realized that everything was big, as though it had all been made by a tailor to fit its owner.

Hoyle bade me sit by his desk.

'I'm surprised to see you here,' he said. 'I can't imagine what Ninetyminutes might be doing in Monaco. Perhaps you've come to put your cash reserves on the red at the roulette wheel?'

'Not quite,' I said.

'It's been done many times before,' said Hoyle. 'Sometimes it seems like the only solution. But the logic is faulty. It's true that double or quits has a close to fifty-fifty chance of succeeding. But psychology dictates that desperate people play on till they lose.'

'Well, that's not why I'm here. I'm planning to see Owen.'

'Really?' Hoyle raised his eyebrows.

'I understand he's staying at Les Sarrasins at the moment?'

Hoyle didn't confirm this. 'And you thought you'd drop in on me on the way?'

'Yes.'

'Why?'

'Ninetyminutes has had another couple of strokes of good fortune. Like Tony Jourdan's death.'

'What do you mean?'

'Our major competitor was hit by a computer virus. And when our financial backer refused to give us more money, his family was threatened to make him change his mind.'

'I see,' said Hoyle. 'And this is why you're going to see Owen? You think he's responsible?'

'Yes. I don't have proof, but I'm pretty sure he is. But what I still don't know is who killed Tony.'

'Neither do the police.'

'So I understand. They haven't even held the inquest yet. I've checked on Owen and Guy. They both have cast-iron alibis. But I can't help thinking that Owen killed his father somehow.'

I waited for some reaction from Hoyle. I didn't get one.

'What do you think?'

'I think that you are talking about the son of my client.'

'Who may have been your client's murderer.'

Hoyle shrugged his large shoulders. I had hoped for more assistance after our previous chat waiting for a taxi in Chancery Lane. But at least he hadn't thrown me out. I had the impression that he was curious about what I had discovered.

'I didn't expect you'd be able to help me with Tony's death,' I said. 'But I wanted to ask you about the gardener.'

'I've told you, I had nothing to do with that,' said Hoyle.

'I know.' I paused. Outside, a helicopter skimmed low over a cruise ship, which was manoeuvring in the cramped harbour. 'Did you know that Owen killed Dominique?'

Hoyle's eyebrows shot up and his fleshy mouth dropped open. 'Owen did?' Then he pursed his lips, pondering for a moment. 'I thought it might have been Guy.' At last he was venturing an opinion of his own.

'No, it was Owen.' I told Hoyle what Guy had told me about that night. Hoyle listened closely. 'And I think that it might have been Owen who killed the gardener, Abdulatif. He was in France around about the time the body was found, seeing Tony. Do you remember talking to him about Abdulatif?'

The fat lawyer hesitated.

'Oh, come on, Mr Hoyle. We're on the same side here. We both want to know who killed Tony Jourdan. I think what happened to Dominique and the gardener might have some bearing on it.'

Hoyle thought it over. In the end he spoke. 'Yes, I do remember talking to Owen. He came to see me in this office. He brought a contribution towards the money to pay off Abdulatif.'

'Did you give him Abdulatif's address?'

'I didn't have it.'

'Did you tell him anything about Abdulatif?'

'I don't think so. But I was planning to make a payment to Abdulatif whilst Owen was in France. He knew that: that was why he'd given me the cash.'

'Where was the drop?'

'Outside a bar in a seedy part of Marseilles.'

'Did Owen know which bar?'

'No. But I think he probably knew when I was going. He could have followed me.'

'Did you hand over the cash to Abdulatif directly?'

'Yes.'

'Is it possible Owen could have followed you and then followed him? Followed him and killed him?'

'I suppose it is. I didn't see him. But I wasn't looking. It is possible. Abdulatif's body was found only a couple of days later. He had been stabbed.'

'And you didn't suspect Owen?'

'I did suspect something. But not Owen. I still thought of him as a kid, even though he must have been, what, twenty at the time. But I thought he was too young. Too much of a computer freak. It was Guy I was suspicious of.'

'What about the French police?'

'They did go to see Tony, but I think it was just as a courtesy to inform him of what had happened to the man believed to have killed his wife. The death didn't even merit a mention in the newspaper: I checked *Le Provençal*.'

'And what about Tony?'

'He wasn't suspicious, either.' Hoyle paused and glanced at me. 'At the time.'

'What do you mean, at the time?'

Hoyle didn't answer for a long time. He was staring at me through his pink-tinted glasses, his huge head nestling in his many chins, weighing things up. It was uncomfortable, but I kept quiet, letting him think.

Eventually, he spoke. 'I think I told you that Guy was anxious that we didn't tell Tony about the pay-off to Abdulatif?'

'Yes.'

'Well, I went along with that. It wasn't something I was happy with, and I became increasingly convinced that it was

341

unnecessary, since Tony was innocent. But having kept it from him to start with, it became harder to mention it.

'Although Guy was in a way my co-conspirator, this whole business had made me distrust him. I wasn't enthusiastic when Tony decided to back him in Ninetyminutes – you know my views on the Internet. I wasn't surprised when the two began to clash. Anyway, Tony was convinced that Guy was doing things all wrong. Tony has always been a great believer in cash flow, and it worried him that Ninetyminutes was never going to produce any. And I think there was some rivalry in it. He wanted to show Guy who was top businessman.'

'I'm sure that's true.'

'After that rather dramatic board meeting where Guy resigned, Tony and I went out to dinner. He talked about Guy and how he was never going to make it as a businessman. He asked me what I thought of him. That was usually a subject we kept clear of. Tony would sometimes talk about how proud he was of Guy, or how frustrated he was by him, but he had never asked for my opinion before.'

'What did you say?'

'I said I mistrusted him, and Tony knew I had some reason for saying that. He pushed me. It was late, we'd both had a lot to drink, he was an old friend and I felt bad about keeping what I knew from him. So I told him about Guy's idea to pay off Abdulatif.

'He leapt at it. He was convinced right away that Guy was trying to divert attention from the real killer, Guy himself. It only took him a few more seconds to suspect Owen of killing Abdulatif. I wasn't nearly so sure, but when Tony got hold of a notion, then it was lodged in his brain.'

'How did he react to the idea that both his sons were murderers?'

'It was odd,' Hoyle said. 'He wasn't shocked. More agitated. He really didn't like Dominique at the end, and he didn't give a toss about Abdulatif. It was almost as though he had half-suspected Guy all along, and I had finally given him the proof he had been looking for.'

'Did he say he was going to talk to Guy about it?'

'No. But he was thinking hard when we left the restaurant. His brain was whirring. I'd seen him like that many times before. He was making plans. I wouldn't be at all surprised if he did talk to Guy. But I never saw him again after that evening, so I don't know.'

'I don't know, either. Guy didn't mention anything.'

'Are you sure it was Owen who killed Dominique and not Guy?' Hoyle asked.

'I think so,' I said. 'Guy was quite convincing, although I'm not sure how much notice I should take of that. Both the brothers certainly felt abandoned by their father, but I don't think Guy was quite screwed up enough to want to kill his stepmother just because he saw her having sex with someone else. Whereas Owen? Who knows about Owen? There's a deep streak of violence in him and he has a warped view of the world. He could have transferred his anger with his father on to Dominique, and become even more angry when he saw her betraying him. Perhaps Guy's right, Owen didn't intend to kill her. But once Guy had realized what his brother had done, it was totally in his character to try to protect him.'

'Watch Guy, David. He's the actor, the schemer, the manipulator.'

'Not a nice thing to say about your client.'

'He's not my client, technically. The estate is. And as I said, Tony was my friend.'

'One last question. How long has Owen been at Les Sarrasins?'

'Only a few days. Guy called me in the middle of last week to tell me he was coming.'

That was just after Henry had changed his mind about the investment in Ninetyminutes. It meant Owen was in England when Henry's family had been threatened. It also suggested Guy might have known about what Owen was doing, and had waited to send him away until after Henry had capitulated. An unpleasant thought.

I stood up to leave. 'Thank you, Mr Hoyle.'

'Not at all.' Hoyle groaned to his feet. 'Did you say you're going to Les Sarrasins now?'

'That's the idea.'

'Be careful.'

As I drove up the winding road in low gear, with the Mediterranean stretching out a brilliant blue below me and the maquis clinging to the hillside above, I began to feel nervous. I had been impelled this far by the conviction that I had to do something to stop Owen. I had successfully pushed all thoughts of the risks involved out of my mind, but now, as I was approaching Les Sarrasins, they seemed all too obvious. Owen would not take kindly to what I was about to say. Owen was bigger and stronger than me, we had already established that. As long as Owen behaved rationally, I was safe. But how could I be convinced that Owen would be rational?

I almost turned back. But the thought of Owen causing more mayhem with other people's lives in the name of Ninetyminutes kept me going. I had to stop him.

I parked the car outside the big gates and pressed the buzzer on the intercom. They swung open, and I left the car by the side of the road and walked into the courtyard in front of the house. It was as immaculate as I remembered it; clearly the Jourdan estate was still paying for the place to be maintained. I pressed another bell on the front door.

I waited and pressed the bell again. Finally I heard movement inside and the door opened.

It was Owen, dressed in grey Ninetyminutes T-shirt and shorts, his white spiky hair peeking out of a Ninetyminutes baseball cap. His feet were bare.

'What the fuck are you doing here?'

'I've come to talk to you.' I pushed past him. I went through to the living room. Although Hoyle had said Owen had only been there a few days, the place was a tip. There were food wrappers, soft-drink cans and pizza boxes everywhere. A sweatshirt was draped over one of the abstract sculptures. And on a desk in a corner in the midst of the greatest concentration of rubbish a laptop hummed. I could clearly see the ninetyminutes.com logo on the screen. Owen was looking at our website.

He chuckled as I walked over to the machine. 'You see, you can't keep a good man away from the office.'

'Are you trying to hack into our site?'

'Hack into it? I go into it, like, every day. Sanjay might not have told you, but I like to keep a close eye on what goes on at Ninetyminutes.'

I turned to him, stunned. How foolish we had been! After Owen had left we had taken no measures to protect the system from him. There was all kinds of damage he could have been doing since he had left, probably had been doing.

'Don't look so shocked,' Owen said, smirking. He was really enjoying this. 'I haven't done Ninetyminutes any harm. In fact, I've been a lot of help to Sanjay in the last couple of months.'

'Does Guy know about this?'

'Probably. We haven't spoken about it specifically, but he knows me. You thought you'd gotten rid of me. But I can control things just as well from here.'

Jesus! But I believed Owen when he said he hadn't done

any actual harm. In fact he probably had done some good. I felt a surge of anger at Guy. He knew what Owen was doing. I was bloody sure he knew.

Owen moved over to the kitchen area, tripping over a pizza box on the way. A half-eaten slice spun across the floor.

'Where's Miguel?' I asked.

'He couldn't handle the place like this, so I told him to stay away. But I think it feels kind of cosy.'

He opened a can of 7 Up and strolled out into the garden. I followed him. It was a brilliantly sunny day, but there was a cool breeze blowing in from the sea. He sat down at a table near the marble railings overlooking Cap Ferrat, and I joined him. Wrappers and cans lay at the base of the lavender bed a couple of feet away. Owen was treating his father's house with the contempt that he had always felt for its owner. His smugness was getting to me, as I was sure he intended it to.

'I know what you've been doing,' I said.

Owen sipped his drink and squinted out to sea, ignoring me.

'You threatened Henry Broughton-Jones. Scared the wits out of his family so that he gave Ninetyminutes the ten million quid.'

'Really? How do you know that?'

'Don't worry: he wouldn't tell me anything. But it's obvious he's scared. And it's obvious who's been scaring him.' I wanted to keep Henry safe from any more of Owen's attention.

'So, Orchestra did invest, did they?' Owen said.

'And you sent the virus to Goaldigger.'

'Technically it wasn't a virus. It was a worm.'

'I don't care what it was, technically,' I said, fighting to keep my frustration under control. 'It was sabotage.'

'Horrible,' said Owen. 'I hope they catch whoever did it.'

'I know you killed Dominique. And I think it's highly likely that you killed Abdulatif.'

'Abdulatif?'

'The gardener who was blackmailing you and Guy.'

'Oh, you mean the dude the police think wasted my stepmother.'

'Yes. Him. You knew Patrick Hoyle was going to pay him off. You followed Hoyle to the drop. You saw him give the money to Abdulatif. You followed him and then stabbed him.'

'Man, you do have some weird ideas.'

'And I think you got your father killed. I don't know how, but I'm sure you arranged it.'

'Have you been smoking something?'

This time I stared out to sea, towards the white craft buzzing round Cap Ferrat.

'You don't have any proof,' Owen said at last.

'No. But I have enough to get the police asking difficult questions.'

'I don't think so. You have nothing to link me with any of this. Half this stuff happened, like, years ago.'

'I want you to stop,' I said.

'Stop what?'

'Stop threatening people. Stop hurting people. Stop killing people.'

'Huh!' Owen snorted.

'I know you're doing all this for Ninetyminutes. I know you think it'll help your brother. But Ninetyminutes can get by without that kind of help.'

'Can it? I don't think so. You know how close Ninety-minutes has gotten to the edge. It's been real lucky to make it this far. I guess sometimes it needs a little help.'

'I'd rather Ninetyminutes went bust than it survived with your kind of help.'

'You know what? I don't give a shit what you think.' Owen's flippancy left him: he looked serious. 'Ninetyminutes means everything to my brother. It's, like, his last chance. It's also his best chance. If it works he's going to be just as rich as Dad, probably richer. If it fails, it's going to be worse than just a disappointment to him. It will totally destroy him. I don't like you very much, but I know you like him. You know I'm right.'

Owen was trying to talk me into seeing his point of view. That was a first. But he was right. I remembered Guy in the Jerusalem Tavern the evening after Henry had turned us down. If Ninetyminutes went under, so would Guy.

But.

'Guy is my friend. I know you're trying to help him. But listen to me. Listen to me carefully.' I leaned forward. 'I would prefer Ninetyminutes went into liquidation tomorrow than it survived by terror or murder, whatever effect that may have on Guy or any of the rest of us. So if I see you trying any more of this extortion, if anyone else gets hurt, I will blow the whistle. I'll tell the police, I'll tell the press, I'll tell anyone else who'll listen. It will finish Guy. It might finish Ninetyminutes. But I'm prepared to do it.'

Owen watched me for a moment. Then he burst into laughter. 'You're just as bad as me or Guy, you know that? You're desperate for Ninetyminutes to succeed. You've looked the other way for so long, why should I believe you'll suddenly become a good citizen? You and me are no different. Except I've got the guts to do something to make Ninetyminutes survive, and you're too scared. Sure, you'll take the millions of pounds from the IPO, but you won't get your hands dirty. You'll let other people do that. People like me.'

There was something uncomfortably true about what

Owen said, at least as it related to the past. But not for the future; I was determined about that.

'You know,' said Owen, 'I never really liked you since I saw your naked butt going up and down on my stepmother.'

I couldn't answer. I stood up and turned to leave.

I felt, as much as saw, a sudden movement behind me. I spun round as Owen grabbed my shoulder and dragged me back towards the railings. I squatted down to prevent myself being tossed over, and jammed one leg against them to try to get purchase. He leaned into me and pushed. He was stronger and heavier than me. I felt my foot slip. I took a swift glance behind me. There was nothing, just air, and then, far off, the sea.

Owen lunged again. My foothold gave way, but I managed to twist so that Owen's forward momentum brought him up against the railings. For a fraction of a second I had the chance to give him that little extra push that would send him on his way. But I didn't do it. I couldn't do it.

Owen saw my hesitation. His eyes gleamed. With his legs far apart now, giving him a secure footing, he reached for my shoulders and pulled. I found my chest on the railings, my face staring down at waves gently shifting in and out over the strip of sand a thousand feet below. It was a long, long way. I was gripped by vertigo; a surge of panic rose like bile from my stomach and I jerked backwards to try to break free, but it was hopeless. I couldn't move.

'You know what happened to the last person who tried to threaten us?' he muttered.

I didn't. I kept quiet.

'Anyway, let's just get straight who's threatening who here,' he said. 'If Ninetyminutes needs my help, and I think it does, then I want you to promise me you won't get in the way. Do you understand?'

I didn't answer.

Owen heaved. For a fraction of a second I thought I was going over the edge, then he grabbed me again. My face smashed against the railings. 'I said, do you understand?'

'Yes,' I said, fighting back the panic.

I heard a grunt, and he pulled me back over the railings. I collapsed in a heap on the ground. I felt my cheek: there was blood.

'OK. Now piss off out of here.'

34

'Where the hell were you?'

I looked up from my desk. 'Morning, Guy.'

'Jesus! What happened to you?' His expression changed from anger to astonishment as he saw my face.

'Someone tried to push me off a cliff.'

'Looks like it. There aren't any cliffs in Munich.'

'I didn't go to Munich.'

'I know. I was trying to get hold of you all yesterday. Your mobile was switched off. They hadn't seen any sign of you in the office over there. Where were you?'

'France.'

'When you say someone tried to push you off a cliff, you don't mean the one by Les Sarrasins?'

I nodded.

'You saw Owen. You picked a fight with him, didn't you?' The anger was returning.

'No. I told him to stop screwing around with Ninety-minutes. I told him to stop threatening the likes of Henry and me. I told him to stop sending computer viruses.'

'He didn't do any of that,' Guy said contemptuously.

'He did. I know.'

'You know!'

'Guy! He almost killed me!' Guy's refusal to see the obvious was getting to me.

'My brother has a bad temper. You know that. If you went over there to hassle him it's not surprising you got hurt. Now just leave him alone.'

'You tell him to leave us alone.'

'What the hell do you think he was doing at Les Sarrasins? I told him to go there. You're the one stirring up trouble, Davo!' He was shouting now. Everyone was watching.

'One day, he's going to kill someone,' I said, just preventing myself from adding the word 'again' with so many ears listening.

'Just lay off him!' Guy was glaring at me.

I got up and left my desk, fuming. Everyone stared. Guy and I frequently disagreed, but we never shouted at each other, certainly not in the office. This was a first, and everyone was aware of it.

I went out on to the street. I heard footsteps behind me. It was Ingrid.

'David, wait!'

I waited. She looked at my face and touched my scratched cheek. 'That looks nasty.'

'It hurt.'

'Owen did this?'

'Yes. He was trying to scare the living daylights out of me. For a moment there, he succeeded.'

'My God.' She fell into step beside me. 'What were you doing?'

I told her about Henry and about my theory that Owen had planted the Goaldigger virus. I didn't mention Owen killing Dominique and Abdulatif. Although I had told Hoyle, Guy had specifically asked me not to tell her, and I felt I should respect that, at least for the time being. She listened with a mixture of shock and sympathy.

'I knew Owen was weird, but I didn't know he was that weird,' she said when I had finished.

'It turns out he is.'

'It was pretty brave of you to go and see him.'

'Or stupid. But I had to. I had to stop him.'

'Do you think you'll succeed?'

'Probably not. But I had to try. I couldn't let him just carry on terrorizing people without doing something.'

'What did you say to him?'

'I told him that if he caused any more trouble I'd bring Ninetyminutes down. Talk to the police, the press.'

'And will you?'

I stopped and faced her. 'Yes.'

She avoided my eye. 'Ah.'

'What do you mean, "ah"? Do you think I'm wrong?'

'Well. Owen has to be stopped, you're right about that. And I don't condone anything he has done, in fact quite the opposite. But if he does something stupid totally beyond our control, that's no reason to ruin Ninetyminutes.'

'What?'

'You said it yourself to Guy. Ninetyminutes means something to all of us. It's not just a means for Guy to prove something to his father. And it's not just your conscience.'

I shook my head. 'Whatever Ninetyminutes is, it's not worth someone's life.'

'Of course it's not,' said Ingrid. 'But that's not the issue here. It's not our fault Owen's a psycho. Ninetyminutes shouldn't have to suffer.'

'But don't you see? The threat of that is the only way to stop him.'

'It won't make any difference.'

'It might. And for me, that's enough.' But I could see it wasn't enough for Ingrid. She had put a year of her life into Ninetyminutes. I had known she badly wanted it to succeed, only now did I realize how badly. It depressed me. Without saying another word, I turned on my heel and walked. This time, she didn't follow me.

*

My trip to France hadn't solved anything. The doubts I had felt before Christmas, doubts that I thought I had laid to rest, were returning stronger than before.

I had thought the situation was clear. I knew Owen was dangerous, but I had thought he was out of the way. Guy, I had thought, was guilty of no more than protecting his brother. And I had thought that I could forget about France and Tony's death and concentrate on Ninetyminutes.

It was now obvious I couldn't. Owen wasn't out of the picture, and neither was Tony's death. My conversation with Hoyle had raised more questions than it had answered. What had Tony done with the knowledge that his sons had been blackmailed by Abdulatif and that one of them had probably killed the blackmailer? Knowing the Jourdan family, it seemed unlikely to me that he had simply offered counsel and support. And I remembered something Owen had said while he had me pinned against the railings at Les Sarrasins. Something about what had happened to the last person who had threatened them.

Was he talking about his father?

I should take Owen's threats seriously. I felt the icy fingers of fear tickle my chest. I was afraid of him.

I knew Owen had killed in the past. I knew he could kill again. He didn't like me, he had probably never liked me, but while I was on Guy's side he would tolerate me. Once I started asking questions, probing into his brother's past, that attitude would change. He was strong, he was clever, he was ruthless. But what was most frightening about him was he just didn't have the same sense of proportion as other people. Nor did he seem to have any remorse. He had bitten off a schoolboy's ear in a rugby match. He had killed his stepmother for the crime of adultery. He would kill me if he thought I was a serious threat to his brother.

So should I just look the other way, as Owen had mocked me for doing up till now?

It was tempting. It wouldn't disrupt Ninetyminutes. I'd stay alive. I might even make some money.

But it was the memory of Owen's taunts that made me realize I couldn't do that. I wasn't the kind of person who got rich on the back of other people's crimes, and I didn't want to become that kind of person. I would find out what had happened to Tony, and I would do my best to make sure that no one else was killed.

The problem was, I didn't have the time.

Guy's optimism had returned with a vengeance. Ninety-minutes had ten million pounds to spend and he had lots of ideas on how to spend it. Offices in Milan and Barcelona to complement those in Paris and Munich. A site dedicated to Euro 2000, which was taking place in June. More recruits: we now had forty employees and the number was climbing week by week. Organizing this stretched all of us.

And we didn't actually have the cash yet. Following his phone call Henry had sent us a letter promising us ten million pounds subject to terms to be agreed. As far as I was concerned, those terms had to be agreed as soon as possible. And that meant talking to Clare Douglas.

Clare was diligent, fearsomely diligent. She wanted numbers on everything: website visitors, on-line sales, costs, budgets, cash flows, advertising revenues, headcount. She wanted these numbers going back into the past and forward into the future. And she asked questions, lots of questions. Although I respected her, all this caused me a lot of extra work when I had other things to focus on. I wanted to sign the damned shareholders' agreement and get on with it.

Guy, Mel and I met Clare at eight o'clock one morning in the boardroom in Ninetyminutes' offices to discuss the agreement. It should have been very straightforward, since the draft in front of us was based heavily on Orchestra's original investment document. The only difficult point would be, as always, the price. How much of the company would Orchestra get for their ten million pounds?

Clare was a small figure, stuck alone on one side of the table facing the three of us. She was a couple of years younger than us, but there was something in her grey eyes that said, don't try to push me around. I noticed how she was fidgeting with a pencil and she seemed more nervous than usual. It wasn't altogether surprising: we were prepared for a tough negotiation session.

What we weren't prepared for was what Clare actually said.

'I'm worried about this investment, Guy.'

'What do you mean?'

'I mean I'm not sure Ninetyminutes is going to make it.'

The three of us stared at her.

'I don't understand,' I said, although I understood perfectly well. 'This money should see us safely through until we do an IPO later in the summer.'

'But what if the stock market gets worse rather than better?'

'In that case, it's possible we might not get the funds at the price we originally wanted.'

'You might not get the funds at all.'

'We've been through all this with Henry,' Guy interrupted. 'The decision's been taken. He's written us a letter promising us the funds. Orchestra can't go back on that, can they, Mel?'

'Definitely not,' said Mel.

'You've just decided this?' said Guy, glaring at Clare with contempt.

'Yes,' Clare said, glaring back.

'And what does Henry say?'

'Henry's still on holiday.'

'You mean you haven't even talked to him?'

'No. But I'm responsible for this investment now within Orchestra. And I've made my decision.'

'And what will your senior partners say about you welching on a deal?'

'They'll stand by me.'

'When this gets out, which it will, it'll ruin Orchestra's reputation.'

'So will investing ten million pounds only to lose it three months later.'

Clare's answers were clear and strong. I admired her: she was doing a good job in difficult circumstances.

Mel coughed. 'Clare, I'd like to draw your attention to this letter that Henry sent us. It clearly states that Orchestra Ventures will provide the funds.'

'On terms to be agreed,' Clare responded.

'Which is what we should be discussing now.'

'Very well. We will make the ten-million-pound investment mentioned in the letter in return for ninety-five per cent of the company and voting control on the board.'

'That's absurd!' said Guy. 'That values the company at next to nothing.'

'It's next to bankrupt,' said Clare.

'With voting control, you could just put the company into liquidation and get your funds out,' I said.

Clare gave me the briefest of smiles. She had thought of that. 'The truth is, as I said at the beginning, if we don't want to invest, we don't have to. Now, I think I must be going. I'd like to talk about how we take the company forward from here. You still have two hundred thousand pounds in your account. But that's a discussion for another time, don't you think?'

She gathered her papers together and left the room.

'Jesus Christ!' Guy snarled as she closed the door behind her. 'She can't do that, can she, Mel?'

'I don't know. We can try and stop her, but it will be difficult. Henry's letter is subject to contract.'

'First Bloomfield Weiss and then Orchestra Ventures! These City guys offer you money and never come through with the goods. I'll tell the press about this. Davo, I want you to get right on to Henry and get him to sort this out.'

I shook my head. 'Sorry, Guy.'

'What do you mean? Call him!'

I glanced at Mel, but decided to talk anyway. 'You know as well as I do why Henry changed his mind. Owen threatened his family.'

'What do you mean?'

'Owen mutilated Henry's daughter's cat and then shunted his wife and children into the middle of a busy road.'

'What is this crap?' Guy said.

Mel looked at me as though I was mad.

'I'm not about to put more pressure on him,' I said.

'All right, give me his number. I'll call him.'

'No,' I said. 'And let me tell you something else. If any more threats are made to Henry, or Clare, I'll tell the press and the police everything I know. And be sure to pass that message on to your brother.'

With that, I left the room and returned to my desk. I picked up a pen and paper and started to figure out how Ninetyminutes could possibly survive without the Orchestra money.

Ten minutes later, Guy returned to his desk. We sat there in silence for a few minutes, opposite each other but avoiding each other's eyes. Then Guy spoke.

'Davo?'

'Yes.'

'I promise you I know nothing about Henry's family being threatened.'

I didn't answer, but turned back to my work.

'And I swear that neither I nor Owen will put any pressure on Clare or Henry or anyone else at Orchestra.'

I glanced up. Guy's eyes held mine. He looked sincere. Of course.

'But, I am going to do everything legal I can to keep Ninetyminutes alive, and so should you. Agreed?'

'I'm not going to persuade Orchestra to do anything, Guy.'

Guy breathed in deeply. 'OK, I'll do that. But are you with me?'

Was I with him? His brother had done terrible things to keep Ninetyminutes alive. But then Guy had just renounced them. And there was the small matter of my life savings as well as my father's. I didn't want to let Ninetyminutes go either.

'I'm with you.'

'Good. Now let me get those bastards at Orchestra.'

I heard Guy harangue the bastards at Orchestra for the next hour. But it was clear from Guy's half of the conversation that they weren't going to budge. They were one hundred per cent behind Clare. Although her actions had placed Ninetyminutes in probably the most difficult situation we had ever experienced, I couldn't help admiring her. She was a brave woman.

I suspected she didn't realize how brave.

That afternoon I went round to Bloomfield Weiss's offices in Broadgate to discuss the possibility of doing an IPO for a reduced amount of funding at a lower price. The banker was not optimistic. NASDAQ was still sliding. All the hot internet stocks were way below their IPO prices and slipping lower by the day. Wait till the summer, he said. We were in

May. I wondered when his summer would start. Not any time soon, I thought.

Back at the office, I described my meeting to Guy. He listened impatiently.

'So what are you going to do about it?' he asked when I had finished.

I took a deep breath. 'I think we should do two things. Firstly, we should talk to Champion Starsat again. Ask them whether they still want to buy us.' Guy scowled. I ploughed on. 'Secondly, we should cut way back on expenses to make the cash we have left last longer. If we cut back far enough, we might be able to last through till October. We might even break even.'

'Great idea, Davo. And what price do you think Champion Starsat will pay? I'll tell you something, it won't be a hundred and fifty million quid. If we didn't want to sell out at the top of the market, why should we sell now? And as for cutting back, I keep telling you, we need more investment, not less. Can't you see that?'

'We don't have any choice. If we carry on as we are we'll be closing our doors in three weeks.'

'Look, I want solutions, not problems. Finance is your responsibility, Davo, so be responsible for it. We are the fastest growing soccer site in Europe; ninetyminutes.com is a brand people know. We're getting there. We're winning. And you're trying to tell me that we've lost. I don't get you, Davo. We used to work together as a team. But now I think you're just trying to look for problems.'

'I don't have to look for them,' I said. I was angry now. 'They're there, staring me in the face every day from our bank statement. I can't make them go away.'

'You could bloody well try,' said Guy.

'Oh, yes? How?'

'Fire Bloomfield Weiss. Get an adviser with guts. You

must still have some mates at Leipziger Gurney Kroheim. And what about all those other people who were falling over themselves to get our business in March?'

'It'll look bad in the market if we fire Bloomfield Weiss.'

'I don't care what it looks like. All I want is a broker who can get us the cash.'

'It'll be hard to find one.'

'How the hell do you know until you've tried?'

I didn't answer. He sounded right. But I knew he was wrong.

'And I haven't finished with Orchestra Ventures yet. They broke their word and they know it. If I can't get them to change their mind, Mel will.'

I shook my head. 'Don't count on it.'

Smiths was crowded. It was Friday, still a big night, even in the current climate. Pink-slip parties were beginning to take over from website launches, but the dot-commers still had money to burn. It was Guy's birthday, his thirty-second, and the drink was flowing.

The funding worries had led to a build-up of tension throughout the whole company and it was as if everyone wanted to take this opportunity to forget present worries and remember past camaraderie. I was drinking fast; Guy was drinking faster. The chatter was frantic, the laughter loud. Time flew.

At about ten o'clock I found myself slumped on a sofa, an empty space next to me. Mel plumped herself into it.

'Hello,' I said.

'Hi.'

'How are you?'

'Yeah, all right,' she said.

'How's it going with Guy?' I asked, without thinking. Although I had spent a lot of time working with Mel over the previous three months, I hadn't spoken about her and him since I had caught them together.

She raised her eyebrows, surprised I had brought up the subject. Then she answered me. 'It's so frustrating. Sometimes he's there. Sometimes he's not. I just never know.'

'Some things don't change.'

Mel sighed. 'No. I just wish they would.'

I suddenly found myself with lots of questions that I had wanted answered for a long time. This seemed the right time to ask them.

'When I came round to Guy's flat that night, why did you show yourself? I mean, you could have stayed tucked up in bed. I'd never have known.'

'I could,' said Mel. 'In fact, that's what Guy wanted me to do. But I get sick of being his secret squeeze. If I'm good enough for him to shag, then I should be good enough to talk to his friends.'

I was taken aback by the bitterness in her voice. 'Of course you're good enough,' I said.

'Well, can't you tell him that?'

'He wouldn't listen,' I said. 'He listens to me less now.'

'He's feeling the pressure.'

'When did you two get together again?' I asked.

'Oh, it's been going on for a while, on and off. It started last year just after he'd had that massive row with his father about turning Ninetyminutes into a porn site. He usually comes to me when he's feeling down. It's all secret, of course,' she said bitterly. 'No one should ever know.'

'Why do you put up with it?'

Mel turned to me. There were tears in her eyes. 'I can't help it. I just can't help it. I know I should have him on my terms or not at all. But the truth is, I need him. When he's not with me I'm so miserable I'll put up with anything to get him back. Anything. And he knows that. Sometimes I think he's a total bastard, but then he smiles, or he touches me and, well, there's nothing I can do.'

I got Mel another drink. And one for myself.

'Thanks,' she said, taking hers. 'It doesn't look good, does it?'

'What do you mean?'

'Ninetyminutes.'

'It never looks good.'

'I can't believe that stupid Scottish cow wouldn't give you the money.'

I sighed. 'She's probably right.'

'Do you think Ninetyminutes will make it?'

'I don't know. I can't quite see how. We'll have to cut right back, and Guy will hate that.'

Mel squinted at me. 'That stuff you said about Owen threatening Henry Broughton-Jones. Was that true?'

'Yes,' I said. 'All true.'

'Did Guy know?'

'I have no idea. But I was serious about going to the police if he or Owen threatens Clare.'

'Bitch,' muttered Mel.

We sat in drunken misery together on the sofa, the hubbub of the party all around us. Guy was a few feet away, talking to Ingrid. He put his arm around her waist.

I felt Mel stiffen next to me. 'There's another bitch,' she muttered under her breath. 'What does he see in her compared to me?'

It was true that Mel was more conventionally better-looking than Ingrid; she was taller and she had a better figure. But Ingrid had something about her, something that Guy could see, and so could I. I decided not to explain this to Mel.

She glanced at me, scowled because I hadn't given her the response she was looking for, and then climbed unsteadily to her feet. I should have stopped her, but actually I wasn't too happy seeing Guy put his arm around Ingrid either.

I watched from my vantage point on the sofa. I couldn't hear, but I could see. It was predictable. Mel swayed up to Guy. Draped herself on his arm. They exchanged words, gentle at first, then sharper. Ingrid pulled herself away from them. Then Guy said something harsh and low that only Mel could hear. It was if she had been slapped. She turned on her heel and marched straight towards the door, blinking back the tears.

There was a slight drop in the noise level as people paused to watch, but it quickly rose again. Guy reached for Ingrid's waist. She pushed him away and disappeared to the loo.

I returned to the bar for another drink. I felt a gentle touch at my elbow. It was Ingrid. 'Can we go outside for a moment?'

'Sure.'

It was a cool May night, and I huddled into my jacket. But the fresh air took the edge off the beers I had drunk. 'Where shall we go?'

'I don't care,' Ingrid said. So we headed east, with Smithfield Market looming on one side, towards Charterhouse Square.

'I saw Mel having a go at you,' I said.

Ingrid shuddered. 'She's never forgiven me for what happened in Mull. That was such a stupid thing to do, I know, but it was a long time ago and she really has nothing to fear now.'

'Doesn't she?'

Ingrid laughed and squeezed my arm. 'No. It's true I used to find Guy fascinating, but he's not my type.'

'Oh, really?'

'Yes, really. I've been surrounded by flaky screwed-up people like him and Mel all my life. Somehow I've avoided becoming like them. I'd like to try to preserve my sanity.'

'I think you're totally sane,' I said.

'Ah, that's the sweetest thing anyone's ever said to me.' She squeezed my arm again.

'Now that is sad.'

We walked and talked. Past St Paul's, silhouetted against the three-quarter moon, past the Georgian columns of the Mansion House and the Bank of England, through the narrow streets of the City, alternating between stretches of deathly quiet and patches of noise and light where people spilled out of crowded bars on to the pavement. Eventually we ended up by the river approaching Tower Bridge. Not far from Guy's flat in Wapping.

Ingrid halted. 'I think we'd better stop now,' she said.

'Yes,' I agreed.

'Thank you for walking with me. I needed that.'

'So did I, I think.'

We were in one of those quiet stretches. Lights were everywhere, yellow and orange, illuminating the tower beside us and the bridge ahead of us, and dancing on the swiftly flowing river. I felt the urge to kiss her, but I hesitated, confused. Was Ingrid my friend? Or something else? Did I want her to be something else? Did she?

Ingrid saw my confusion and her eyes creased into a smile. 'See you tomorrow,' she said as she reached up to peck me on the cheek. Then she hurried off up the hill towards the busy road, in search of a taxi.

I watched her go, feeling pleasantly disoriented. I wondered what had happened that evening, if anything. I found my own cab, but as I was climbing into it, I realized I had left my briefcase at Smiths. It was late, but I thought I would check to see if the place was still open. It was, just. I found my briefcase and then made my way to the gents before heading for home. I passed a dark corridor and noticed two figures in an embrace. One was Guy. I peered into the darkness to see who the other was. Michelle.

Poor Michelle.

35

The next day was Saturday, for us a workday. There were a hundred and one urgent things to attend to, but I took advantage of the fact that I had no meetings arranged to put them all on one side for a couple of hours and concentrate on Tony's death. While Guy was plotting his public revenge on Orchestra with the PR people, I called Detective Sergeant Spedding. He remembered me instantly and invited me to come in to talk to him that afternoon.

I met him in a bare interview room at the police station in Savile Row. A friendly freckled face beneath red hair. He brought me a cup of coffee and we sat down.

'I've become a big fan of your website,' he said.

'Excellent.'

'But I think you're wrong about Rovers getting a new manager for next season.'

'I'll pass that on.'

'What we really need is someone good in the air up front.'

'I'll pass that on too.'

'Thank you.' He stirred his coffee and sipped it. 'So now we've got the important stuff out of the way, talk to me.' He smiled encouragingly.

'Do you have any idea yet who killed Tony Jourdan?'

'Now why is it that every time I talk to you, you ask the questions and I answer them? Isn't it supposed to be the other way round?'

'Sorry,' I said.

Spedding smiled. 'We don't know who killed him. We can rule out a contract killer: running someone down in a street like that is very messy. All kinds of things could go wrong. So that makes it most likely that it was someone who knew Jourdan.'

'I see.'

'Of the immediate family, Sabina Jourdan was in France at the time and I doubt very much she paid the man you saw, Donnelly, to kill him, for the reasons I just gave you. Besides, he's not that kind of hired help. We probed the two sons' alibis pretty thoroughly but they stacked up. Jourdan had some old business enemies that bore him grudges, so it's just conceivable that one of them may have been involved, but we haven't been able to uncover any useful leads there. So our official best guess at the moment is that it was a drunk-driver hit and run. But in such a small street that seems very unlikely to me.'

'So Owen's alibi held up? He couldn't have tampered with the CCTV or anything?'

'No. He was definitely in the Europa a couple of minutes before his father was run down.'

'And Guy?'

Spedding looked at me closely. 'What about Guy?'

'Did Guy's alibi check out?'

'It seemed to. He went for a drink with his brother in Camden and then went to see a girlfriend in St John's Wood. He got there at nine thirty, only five minutes after the murder.'

'And she confirmed that, did she?'

'Not just her. She had a friend staying with her that night who saw Guy as well. There wouldn't have been time from when Guy left the pub in Camden to when he arrived in St John's Wood for him to drive to Knightsbridge. He claims he didn't have his car with him that evening, anyway. We checked it. Clean.'

'Do you know whether he saw his father that day?'

'He saw him the day before, at Jourdan's place in Knightsbridge. According to Guy, it was quite an upsetting meeting.'

'Did he say what they talked about?'

'Yes. The future of Ninetyminutes. He was trying to persuade his father to change his mind.'

I hesitated before asking my next question. 'Did they talk about anything else?'

'Not according to Guy,' Spedding said. 'He and his father were the only people there, and of course Tony Jourdan can't tell us anything.'

'I see.'

'Why?'

'Oh, I don't know. I'm just trying to get an idea of what happened.'

'Do you have any information for me?'

'Oh, no,' I said.

'I've been quite forthcoming with you. Can't you be the same with me?'

'I don't have anything to tell you.'

Spedding looked at me for a few long seconds. 'This case doesn't add up. You know that and I know that. I think there's something wrong with what Guy Jourdan told me. I think you might know what that is. I don't know whether it's just a suspicion, or whether you have some concrete proof, but if you do, you should tell me. I know Guy is your friend and your business partner. But murder is a serious business, David. And so is withholding evidence.'

I met Spedding's eyes. 'I know that,' I said. 'That's why I came here.'

Spedding nodded. 'Fair enough. If you want to talk to me again, call me. Any time.' He passed me his card.

I left the police station clutching it tightly in my hand.

*

I left work at five that afternoon. Guy was still in the office, and I was confident he would be there for another hour at least. I took the tube to St John's Wood and walked through the leafy streets to where Mel lived.

I had been to Mel's old flat in Earls Court a couple of times many years before, but never to this one. It was on the first floor up a narrow dark staircase. She invited me in to the living room. It was very tidy and quite soulless: bland framed posters and prints, cool grey walls, very few knick-knacks, a row of books in a neat bookshelf, a tiny CD collection, a solitary photo frame. It looked more like a temporary corporate flat than a person's home.

'It's nice to see you, David,' she said politely.

'I hope you don't mind me just showing up like this, but I was worried about you. After last night.'

'Yes. Last night. I'm sorry, I got a bit drunk.'

'Didn't we all?'

We were standing in the middle of the living room. Mel closed her eyes and leaned forward into my chest. I held her. She began to sob. Gently I stroked her hair.

Eventually she pulled back. 'I'm sorry,' she said. 'It's just, I think I might have finally lost him.'

What could I say? That she'd be much better off without him? That she shouldn't worry; he'd probably be round at her place one night when he'd been turned down by another woman and fancied a shag? I touched her sleeve.

She smiled quickly. 'I know what you're thinking,' she said. 'And I'm sure you're right. I just . . . I don't know. I feel so miserable.'

'What happened?'

'He told me to piss off and leave him alone.'

'You were drunk. He was drunk. That doesn't mean anything.'

'But he was with Ingrid.'

'She left a few minutes after you. Guy stayed.' I didn't tell Mel about Michelle.

A flicker of hope sparked in her eyes. Then she ran her hand through her hair, visibly trying to pull herself together. 'I'm sorry. I feel such a fool. Do you want a drink? I don't think I could face another one after last night.'

'No thanks,' I said, sitting on a sofa. There was a photograph on the mantelpiece beside me, of Mel and Guy. I recognized Guy's flat in Gloucester Road from several years before. It must have been taken just before the fateful Mull trip.

'Nice picture,' I said.

'Yes,' she replied. 'Those were good days.'

I quickly scanned the room. There were no other photos, no parents, no pets.

Mel started to talk. She wanted to talk. 'You know, I fell for him the moment I first saw him. We were only fourteen. Fourteen! God, it seems so long ago.' She laughed. 'I was taller than him then.

'I didn't do anything about it at the time. I was starting to realize that I wasn't just a pretty little girl any more. Boys were beginning to notice me. Older boys. I went out with a lot of guys who were sixteen or seventeen.'

'I remember.' It wasn't just older boys who had noticed Mel.

'It gave me a kick. I seemed to have this power over them. I used it. And I never let them get very far. You know I went through school a virgin. I enjoyed the power of saying no.'

'But you never went out with Guy?'

'Not until the very end. I was used to being chased rather than chasing. I thought he would come round in the end, and he did. I knew how to play him; I was a real expert by that stage. But, as I think I told you in France, he was the one.

'Then I went and messed it up by sleeping with that bastard Tony Jourdan.'

'Did you ever get over that?'

'No, not really. It's not like he raped me, or anything. But I was going through a really bad patch at home. My father had walked out, and he and my mother were trying to manipulate me against each other. I was always Daddy's beautiful girl. I worshipped him. And then it turned out he was having it off with some tarty secretary only a few years older than me. Six months later and I end up having sex with someone his age and losing the boy I loved. I felt cheap, worthless, stupid.

'I changed. Reinvented myself at university. Got rid of the tight jeans. Ignored men. Worked hard. I didn't have many friends. I used to brood, get depressed. It was a miserable time, until I met Guy again at that Broadhill do. The rest you know.'

'Do you think you'll be able to leave him behind you?'

Mel smiled. 'I should, but I doubt it. I know he doesn't respect me after what happened in France, and he's right. It was a terrible thing I did. That's why he treats me like he does. But I keep hoping that if I show him just how much I love him, he'll forgive me. He'll have to.' There was desperation in her voice.

I smiled at her weakly. It wasn't going to happen. The harder she tried, the more Guy would take advantage of her. But I didn't have the heart to tell her that.

'I worry about Ninetyminutes,' Mel went on. 'If that blows up it'll destroy him. Even if he drops me, at least I know I can help him with that.'

'Last night you said you started to see him again just before Tony died?'

'That's right,' she smiled. 'It was the day before. Guy came round quite late. He'd been drinking. I have no illusions about why he came; he just wanted a shag. But afterwards. Afterwards he lay in my arms and we talked. He told me everything. All about his worries about what his father was going to do to Ninetyminutes, everything. I comforted him.'

'Did he tell you about the gardener in France? About Tony finding out about it?'

'Yes, yes he did.' Mel looked at me, puzzled and a little put out. 'He said he hadn't told anyone else about that.'

'He hadn't,' I said. 'At least, not then. I found out from Patrick Hoyle later. I spoke to Guy about it a few months ago. He was worried about Owen, as usual.'

'Tony was trying to persuade Guy to stay on at Ninetyminutes. Guy didn't want to, of course – he didn't want to be Tony's gopher. But Tony was threatening to go to the French police about the gardener and Owen's role in his death.'

'He was going to expose his own son?'

'Guy couldn't believe it, either. He thought it was a bluff, but he couldn't be sure. I think he was as upset that his father would do something like that to Owen as he was about being forced out of Ninetyminutes.'

'So it was lucky Tony died when he did?'

'Very lucky,' Mel said firmly. 'Guy was heading for self-destruction.'

'You say Guy told you all this the night *before* Tony was killed?'

'That's right. But he came round here again the following night. You probably know he was here when it happened.'

'Yes. Apparently a friend of yours was here as well?'

'Anne Glazier. We were at uni together. She works for one of the big British law firms in Paris. She was just staying here for the night.' Suddenly, something clicked in Mel's brain. 'Why are you asking all these questions?'

'Oh, I don't know,' I said casually. 'I'm curious about what happened to Tony Jourdan, I suppose.'

'You don't think Guy had anything to do with it, do you?' Mel's eyes flashed with anger.

'Oh, no, no, of course not,' I said hurriedly. 'I know he didn't. I just don't know who did, that's all.'

'Well, it's best forgotten about, as far as I'm concerned. In fact I wish I could forget about Tony bloody Jourdan. I hated that man. I still do, even though he's dead.' The phone rang. 'Excuse me,' she said, and went to pick it up.

She turned towards me, her eyes alight. She carried on a short conversation with some yesses and noes, coolly delivered. Then she said: 'Well, if you really want to come over, that's all right . . . About half an hour? . . . I think I've got some food in the fridge. Do you want me to cook some dinner? . . . OK, see you soon.'

She put the phone down in triumph.

'Guy?' I asked.

She nodded.

'I'd better be going.'

She smiled, a radiant smile, her misery banished. 'I've got to go out to the shops and get some food for dinner. Thanks for coming, David. I'm sorry to burden you with all that, but it's nice to talk to someone. You're about the only other person who's close enough to Guy to understand. Apart from Owen, of course, and I try to have as little to do with him as possible.'

'Do you mind if I use your loo before I go?'

'No, not at all. It's down the hallway.'

As I returned I passed the open door of Mel's bedroom. On the wall was a large frame holding a collage of photographs. There must have been twenty of them. Twenty cynical images of Guy, smoothing their way into a vulnerable woman's bed.

'Have a good evening,' I said as I left. But despite Mel's sudden change in spirits I hoped, for her sake, that she wouldn't.

I went back to my flat, flopped into the sofa and turned on the TV. I was tired. Thoughts of Mel, Guy, Ninetyminutes, Tony and Owen tumbled over and over in my mind. I knew I should try to sort them all out, but my brain just wanted to shut down.

Eventually, I went to bed.

I kept my computer in my bedroom. I didn't like it in the more public spaces of the flat, like the living room or the spare bedroom. Since I had joined Ninetyminutes, I had barely used it; I did most of my Ninetyminutes-related work on my laptop and I didn't have time for much else. I probably hadn't turned it on for two weeks. But, as I opened my bedroom door, I heard a low hum and saw a flickering glow.

Strange. I moved over to the small pine desk that supported it. Everything seemed as it should be, as I had left it. I grabbed the mouse and clicked to shut the machine down.

The hard drive whirred. A familiar animation flickered on the screen. A golfer. A golf club. My head with its idiotic corporate brochure smile. The impact. Blood, brains, that horrible squelching sound. It may have been crude, but it was so totally unexpected it shocked me. I leapt back from the keyboard and watched. The red gore slid down the screen to be replaced by shimmering orange letters.

JUST MAKING SURE YOU HAVEN'T FORGOTTEN ME.

I pulled the computer's plug out of the socket. The image died, my bedroom returned to darkness.

Owen! In my flat! How the hell had he got in?

I turned on the light and scanned the room. Nothing was out of place. I checked the other rooms, all the windows, the front door. Nothing broken, nothing open, nothing moved, no sign of a forced entry.

I wondered whether he could somehow have planted his sick little program remotely, over the Internet. But that was impossible. The computer was switched on. That could only have been done by someone in the flat. Owen had wanted me to know that he had been there. Physically. In my room.

I glanced at the door to the flat. That was the only way in. The security at the front entrance of my block was pathetic: it would be easy to get in. But my door? He must have had a key. Instinctively, I pulled the key ring out of my pocket and checked that I still had mine. I did. He must have copied it. I could easily have left my keys unattended on my desk or in my jacket for a few minutes some time in the months we were working together. I shuddered. First thing on Monday morning I would change the lock. And I would never let the new key out of my trouser pocket again.

36

I dragged myself into work the next morning. I didn't mind working on Saturdays, but I hated spending Sundays in the office. In Ninetyminutes' current crisis there was no choice.

'So what do we do?' I asked Guy.

'Get money from somebody else.'

'Champion Starsat?'

'Not bloody Champion Starsat.'

'I know we won't get a hundred and fifty million, or anything like it. But if we came out with a profit on our investment, that would be a result.'

'No it wouldn't. It would be a disaster. We'd lose our independence, they'd take control, it wouldn't be our site any more.'

'So what do you suggest?'

'Did you try some other brokers?'

'I spoke to a couple on Friday. My contact at Gurney Kroheim thinks there's no chance of anyone taking us up in the current market, especially if Bloomfield Weiss drop us.'

'Make some more calls tomorrow.'

I sighed. 'OK. I take it Orchestra won't change their mind?'

'No. Derek Silverman's been on to them, but they're adamant.'

'Then we'll have to cut back.'

'No.'

'We have to, Guy! If we follow our current spending plans we'll be out of cash in three weeks. If we're tough enough we can make our cash last through the summer.'

'No.'

'Have you got any other ideas?'

'I'm going to Hamburg this afternoon.'

'To see Torsten?'

Guy nodded.

'There's no point.'

'Yes there is,' said Guy. 'He sounded interested.'

I snorted. 'You go to Hamburg and I'll come up with a cost-reduction plan.'

I spent the day working on the numbers. I needed to make our half-million quid last the summer and beyond. It was a depressing exercise. Cut, cut, cut.

Retailing had to go. It was a long way from profitability and the more clothing we sold the more cash the business swallowed. We would have to close the European offices we had opened, even Munich. No more hiring, in fact we would have to fire fifty per cent of our journalists. The WAP company in Helsinki was on its own: the widespread use of WAP-enabled phones was too far off into the future. All that was left would be the original UK site. It would mean a loss of momentum, the quality of the site would probably suffer, but the cash would last well into the following year.

Ninetyminutes would survive.

The next morning, with Guy still in Hamburg, I decided to take an hour or so to track down Anne Glazier, Mel's friend who had been staying at her flat the night Tony Jourdan died. Ninetyminutes' situation was worsening by the day, and so was my relationship with Guy. I needed to know where I stood with him. And I couldn't do that until I had cleared up my doubts over what had happened to his father.

A few minutes' work on the Internet gave me the names and numbers of the major British law firms with offices in Paris. I picked up the phone and worked my way through the list. I was only on number three, Coward Turner, when the switchboard operator recognized Anne Glazier's name. I tensed as I was put through, but the line was answered by her English-speaking secretary. Ms Glazier was away from the office for a few days, and wouldn't be back until the following week.

So I returned to the numbers.

Guy arrived back in the office late afternoon. He smelled of alcohol.

'How did it go?' I asked.

'Good,' said Guy. 'Torsten will do it.'

'Really? How much?'

'Five million, I think.'

'You think?'

'Yeah. I've still got to pin him down on details. But he said he'd do it.'

'Pounds or marks?'

'Pounds, of course.'

I eyed Guy suspiciously. 'When did he say he'd do it?'

'Last night. We went out. It was a good night.'

'Was he drunk when he said it?'

'Well, maybe.'

'Had he asked his father?'

'Not yet. But he will. He says he's going to stand up to his father this time.'

'And he said this at what time, precisely?'

'What is this?'

'What time of night did Torsten say he would stand up to his father?'

'About midnight.'

'That's worth nothing,' I said. 'Last time he said he'd do it, the Internet was booming. If he couldn't come through then, what makes you think his father will let him invest now?'

'Trust me,' said Guy, his voice slurring. 'He's a mate.'

'Have you been drinking?'

'Jesus! I had some champagne on the flight. To celebrate. And I might just go out and have some more. Want to come?'

I ignored the sarcasm. 'No. I really need to go over some figures with you. I think we can survive into next year. Provided we cut right back immediately.'

Reluctantly, Guy looked at my numbers. It took him a couple of minutes to figure out what I was proposing; it was clear his mind was far from razor sharp. Then he pushed the papers to one side.

'This is crap,' he said.

'We have no choice.'

'Yes we do. Torsten.'

'Oh, come on. We can't leave the company in Torsten's hands again. We did that once before and look what happened.'

Guy was about to answer me, and then he stopped. He looked down at my figures. When he did speak, it was quietly.

'Ninetyminutes means everything to me,' he said.

'I know. It means a lot to all of us.'

Guy stared at me with his piercing blue eyes. 'I'm not talking a lot. I'm talking everything. You know me as well as anyone, Davo. Anyone apart from my brother, maybe. You saw me when I was pissing about pretending to be an actor. I told you about LA, how I cracked up. You knew my father. You know what I felt about him; still feel about him. I have spent most of my life this close to falling apart.' He held up his thumb and index finger to show how close.

'But this last year I've felt I've been back on track. I've built something that's good. Better than good, remarkable. Something that will be worth tens of millions of pounds. Something that thousands of people use each day. A team that works together. Something unique.' He was spitting out the words. 'And now you want to destroy it all.' He shook his head. 'If Ninetyminutes goes, I go.'

I knew that Guy had been feeling the tension over the last few months, but this was the first time I had seen him facing it since that evening in the Jerusalem Tavern after Henry had turned us down. Since then he had been in denial, looking the other way from bad news, losing his temper, drinking, taking solace in Mel, or Michelle, or God knows who. But now he was facing it again, he didn't like what he saw.

'That's just it,' I said. 'We have to save Ninetyminutes. Cutting back is the only way of doing that.'

Guy slammed his palm down on his desk. 'You don't bloody get it, do you? I'm not talking about the survival of Ninetyminutes as a legal entity. I'm talking about the idea. The big idea. Your plan would kill that stone dead. We'd never get to the number-one site slot. We'd be lucky to show a profit to investors on their money. We'd grind to a long slow death. As soon as we implement that,' he waved my figures in the air, 'Ninetyminutes is over. And I think I'm over too.'

I knew what Guy was getting at. But he needed a dose of realism and the only place it would come from was me.

'There is no other choice.'

'There is. Come on, Davo. We've done so much together. But now's when I really need your support. This is the culmination of all that hard work, all the good times and the bad times. You can destroy Ninetyminutes. Or you can help me save it. But if you try to destroy it you should know I'll do everything in my power to stop you.'

We stared at each other. He was calling it all in. Our thirteen years of friendship. For most of that time I had never been sure whether I was a true friend of his at all. Now, he was saying, it was up to me to decide.

He was tempting me. But one of the reasons I had gone into Ninetyminutes was to prove that I was more than a bag-carrying yes-man. That I was capable of making up my own mind, taking my own decisions. I could succumb to Guy's force of character, or I could tell him what had to be done.

I took a deep breath. 'I insist that we undertake these cost reductions immediately.'

Guy looked at me hard, the disappointment and anger written clearly all over his face. 'Insist?'

'Yes. Insist.'

He drew a breath. 'OK. Well, I'm the Chief Executive. And I say no.'

'If you refuse, I'll talk to Silverman,' I said. 'And Clare Douglas.'

'Are you threatening me?'

'I'm just telling you what's going to happen.'

'Well, I'm having dinner with Silverman and Clare this evening. I'll put forward your point of view.'

I started. 'Dinner? You didn't tell me about that.'

'I thought you said you didn't want to be involved in putting pressure on Orchestra?'

'Yes. But you're going to be talking about much more than that, aren't you?'

'Possibly.'

'I want to be there.'

'You're not invited.'

I glared at Guy. He glared back.

'I'll tell you all about it in the morning,' he said. 'I'm going now. I think there's something to celebrate and I'm going off to celebrate it. You'd better stay here and take inventory of the paperclips. I'm sure Amy uses far too many.' With that he left the office. And he didn't come back.

*

I waited anxiously for him the next morning. He didn't roll up till ten. He looked dreadful – he hadn't shaved and his eyes were puffy and unfocused. Guy could cope with a heavy night pretty well. This must have been a very heavy night. I was sure he hadn't done that much damage with Clare and Derek Silverman: he must have carried on long after they had disappeared home.

'How was dinner?'

'Clare won't budge,' Guy said as he switched on his computer. 'But they were pleased to hear about Torsten.'

'Has he contacted you?'

'Not yet. Give him time.'

'Huh.' I picked up the papers I had been working on. 'I want to talk to you some more about the cost reductions.'

Guy strained to focus his eyes on me. 'Oh, yes. I want to talk to you about that too.'

'I've done some more figures, and –'

'Forget the figures. Let's talk principles. Are you still determined to cut the foreign offices and the journalists and the retailing?'

'Yes.'

'Even though that was what we set up Ninetyminutes to do?'

'Yes,' I said. 'There's no other way.'

'And there's nothing I can do to change your mind?'

'No.'

'Are you quite sure?'

'Yes.'

Guy was silent. For a moment he looked uncertain, almost sad. Then he seemed to come to a decision.

'You're fired,' he said quietly.

'I'm what?'

'You're fired,' he said more clearly.

'What!' I looked around. No one else had heard. The bustle

of Ninetyminutes continued as if nothing had happened. I couldn't believe it. 'You can't do that.'

'Of course I can. I'm CEO. I set the strategy. You've just told me that you insist on doing something that will permanently cripple that strategy. You won't be talked out of it. You're fired.'

'Silverman won't let you.'

'He will. We discussed it last night.'

'And he went along with it? Clare went along with it?'

He nodded. I had been stuffed. Outmanoeuvred. I couldn't believe how persuasive Guy could be. 'We should talk about this.'

'We have.' For a moment his eyes softened. 'Do you want to reconsider your recommendation?'

Did I? If I did, he might keep me on. If I did, then our friendship might remain intact.

But I had gone too far. Guy was wrong. I had told him many times and I believed it with all my soul. I couldn't go back on that.

I shook my head.

'We'll pay you your month's notice,' said Guy. 'And I'll get Mel to arrange an emergency resolution of the board to remove you as a director. But I suggest you leave today. There's not much point in hanging around.'

He was right, there wasn't. I wanted to get out of there as quickly as possible. I didn't want to say goodbye to anyone. I opened my case and stuffed my few personal possessions inside it. Then I closed it up and headed for the doors.

I passed Ingrid's desk.

'David!' she called. I slowed. She leapt up and fell in step beside me. 'David. What's wrong?'

'I've been fired.'

'You've been *what*?'

'He's just fired me.'

'He can't do that.'

'He just has.' I looked at her. I had lost Ninetyminutes to Guy. At that moment I wanted to know if I had lost Ingrid as well. 'Are you coming?'

'What do you mean?'

'I mean, are you coming? With me?'

'I'll talk to Guy,' Ingrid said. 'I'll get him to change his mind. I'm sure you two can sort something out . . .'

I turned on my heels and walked out the door.

I went home. Home in the afternoon on a weekday was a strange place to be. I felt angry. Deeply angry.

I resisted the temptation to get plastered, and went outside again instead. I headed for Kensington Gardens and walked. Walked and thought.

I remembered the moment when I had read Guy's plan for Ninetyminutes and decided to drop everything and go for it. The delicious feeling of resigning from Gurney Kroheim. Guy's enthusiasm as he talked Gaz round into joining us. The first day in our new office in Britton Street. The excitement of launching the site. The thrill of seeing it succeed. The sense of achievement in creating so much from nothing.

It was a warm afternoon, the warmest of the year so far. I found a shaded bench and sat on it. A large family of Italian tourists walked past, arguing. They frightened away a squirrel that an old lady on the bench next to mine had been trying to tempt with a piece of bread. She frowned in momentary annoyance, and then held out the bread again, making clucking noises. She had all day.

Where had it all gone wrong? Of course part of it, probably a large part, had nothing to do with Guy or me. It was beyond our control. We were unlucky the market had crashed just before we raised the forty million instead of just after. We were unlucky that the internet bust had been quite so vicious. But Guy and I working as a team could have dealt with that. And even if we had failed, it wouldn't have seemed quite as bad if we had failed together.

I was reminded of that flight up to Skye. I had trusted Guy in the storm, almost trusted him for too long as he had flown up that glen. I had wrested the controls from him with seconds to spare. This time, he had hung on to them.

Ninetyminutes had meant so much to me. It had been my chance to prove to myself that I was more than a risk-averse accountant. But in the end, was I? I had failed as an entrepreneur. At the last minute the accountant in me had tried to rescue things, but that had been too late. I was out of my depth. I should face facts. There was nothing special about me after all.

I was sure Ninetyminutes was going bust. I would lose my investment. That I could handle. I would have to try to find another job, probably in a big bank. That would be true defeat. And, of course, I would have to tell my father that I had failed him. That he had been foolish to back me with everything he had. That he now had nothing.

I left the bench and the old lady, who by now had become good friends with the squirrel, and wandered for another hour or so. When I got back to the flat I turned on the TV and watched rubbish. I cracked open a beer, but just one.

Then the bell rang.

It was Ingrid.

She stood in my doorway. 'Hi,' she said.

'Hi.'

'I'm leaving Ninetyminutes.'

Something melted inside me. I smiled.

She opened her arms and we held each other tight.

'Why?' I said.

She plopped down on to my sofa. 'Can I have a glass of wine or something?'

I opened a bottle of white and poured us both a glass.

She took hers eagerly and drank from it. 'Mmm, that's good.' She answered my question. 'It was when you asked me to come with you and I didn't give you an answer. I waffled on about reaching some kind of compromise with Guy. Well, once you'd gone, I knew I was wrong. I knew I was hiding from the truth.

'You know how determined I've been to make Ninetyminutes succeed. I'm proud of what I've achieved there. I suppose I thought Ninetyminutes was like a test. I was under pressure and the important thing was to try harder and not give up. And to support Guy. And then I saw you walk away from him because you believed he was wrong, and suddenly I saw things differently. I know Ninetyminutes is in deep trouble. I know Guy isn't going to get us out of it. And, well . . .'

'What?'

She looked embarrassed. 'I thought for once I'd rather go with you than go with Guy.' She smiled shyly at me. She ran her hands through her chestnut hair. 'I don't know. Maybe I'm doing the wrong thing.' Then she smiled again. 'But it feels right.'

'I think it is right,' I said.

'I'll tell him tomorrow.'

'You haven't told him yet?'

'No. He left early. I only really decided on my way home. So I came here instead.'

'I'm glad you did.'

We sat in silence, drinking our wine.

'Some more?' I asked her.

'Sure.' She held out her glass and I refilled it. 'You know, I'm not sure Ninetyminutes ever could have worked.'

'What do you mean?'

'I mean, Guy got pretty close to achieving his aim, didn't

he? A few more months of growth and Ninetyminutes will be the number-one soccer site in Europe. Most people know the brand name now. Lots of people want to buy the clothing and the merchandise.'

'That's true.'

'So what's the problem?'

'The problem is we haven't got any cash and we aren't likely to make any any time soon.'

'Precisely,' Ingrid said. 'And that matters. Now. It didn't seem to matter a year ago. A year ago the Internet was a gold rush, a land grab. Once you'd got the eyeballs gawping at your site, the money would roll in. Advertising, e-commerce, no one knew exactly how it would happen, they just knew it would happen. If Ninetyminutes had reached the stage we're at now a year ago, we'd all be worth tens of millions.'

'That's true.'

'But the world's changed. It turns out the Internet is a lousy way to make money. People expect it to be free. People expect to buy goods over the Internet more cheaply than in the shops. Advertisers want tangible results and don't have bottomless budgets for an unproven medium. There's just not that much money in it. So Ninetyminutes is worth virtually nothing. That's what Guy doesn't understand.'

'So what are you saying?'

'I'm saying we did succeed in what we set out to do. It just didn't make us the millions we thought it would. I suppose if we'd been really smart we'd have realized that at the time. What you've done is realize it now. But I think we should be proud of all we've achieved. All of us: you, me, Guy, Amy, Gaz, everybody. It's not really our fault the numbers don't stack up.'

I saw what she meant. Looked at her way, it hadn't been a waste of time. It hadn't been a disaster at all.

Ingrid picked up her glass. 'To Ninetyminutes.'

'To Ninetyminutes.'

We both drank.

'What are you going to do now?' Ingrid asked.

'I don't know. I've got my savings in Ninetyminutes. So has my father. I really don't want to see it all pissed away.'

'It's not just the money that worries you, is it?'

'What do you mean?'

'I mean Guy.'

'You're right. It is Guy.' I tried to explain. 'When Guy showed me his vision for Ninetyminutes he was showing me not just a good job or a good investment, but a new life. A life that I had always wanted but had been too scared to go for. He talked about creating something new and exciting, taking risks, breaking the rules, building the new economy. He inspired me. He made me believe I could become a new person. And then . . . and then he let me down.'

'But we just said it wasn't his fault that Ninetyminutes is going under.'

'It's not that. In fact, if Guy and I had led Ninetyminutes to a glorious end together, it wouldn't have been so bad. Sure, I'd have lost some money, and it would have been a disaster for my father, but I would have felt I'd achieved something. Become a better person, a different person. As it is . . .'

'As it is, what? I don't understand.'

I looked at Ingrid. My promises to Guy meant nothing any more. 'There's some stuff about Guy you don't know.'

I told her all about Owen and Dominique and Abdulatif and Guy's efforts to cover everything up. And I told her that I still didn't know whether Guy had murdered Tony.

She listened closely, at first with disbelief, then amazement, then anxiety.

'So you see I have no idea who Guy is,' I said at the end. 'I know he's a liar. I know his brother kills people. But I don't know whether Guy kills people too. I don't know whether the only reason Ninetyminutes has lasted this long is because Guy killed his father.'

Ingrid sipped her wine thoughtfully. 'You might be right about Owen, but Guy?'

'I know. That's what I thought. But he's an actor. A good one. And when he's in a tight spot over his brother or Ninetyminutes, who knows what he might do?'

'God.' Ingrid shook her head. 'I can't believe it.'

'I need to know. About Guy. What kind of person he is. Whether what I've been doing for the last year means anything.'

'So what do we do? We can't just walk away.'

'You can,' I said. 'In fact, I'd recommend it.'

'I'm not going to,' Ingrid said. 'We'll sort this out together.'

My emotions had been in turmoil for weeks: hope, despair, anger, frustration. For weeks I had been at war with these feelings, trying to control them, trying to control Ninetyminutes. I had fought this war alone. I had thought I had lost, but now Ingrid was with me perhaps I could win after all. We gave each other comfort, strength and, in an as yet undefined way, hope.

We went out to a small Italian restaurant round the corner for dinner. We drank more wine. We discussed what we could do to rescue Ninetyminutes and find out about Guy once and for all. But as the evening wore on we talked about other things, about each other and about life outside Ninetyminutes.

As we left the restaurant, Ingrid linked her arm in mine. 'Do you mind if I come back with you?' she asked.

'No,' I said. 'I'd like that. I'd like that very much.'

37

I awoke to the sensation of a hand stroking my thigh. It was six thirty. Ingrid was lying next to me in my bed, and I didn't have a job to go to.

I rolled over. The sunshine poured in through my bedroom's puny curtains, painting stripes of pale gold on to Ingrid's skin. She was definitely one of those women who looked better the morning after.

'Good morning,' she said, with a languid smile.

'Good morning.'

Her hand moved upwards.

Half an hour later I went through to the kitchen to make some coffee. By this time I would usually be in the shower. But not today.

'Are you going straight in to Ninetyminutes?' I asked, carrying two mugs back to the bedroom.

'There's no hurry. Guy's always late these days. And besides, I quite like it here.' She took her mug and sat up in bed. She tasted the coffee and pulled a face. 'Yuk! That's disgusting. If I'm going to come here again, you're going to have to get some decent coffee.'

'What do you mean? It is decent coffee.'

'It's crap. I'm Brazilian. I know.'

'I knew I should have made tea,' I muttered.

Despite her grumbling, Ingrid took another sip. 'What are you going to do today?'

What was I going to do? It was tempting to spend my first day of freedom from Ninetyminutes in bed with Ingrid. But I couldn't.

'Go and see Derek Silverman for starters. And then Clare. I must make them realize Guy has got it all wrong. Then I'll see if I can get hold of Anne Glazier again. She should be back in her office today.'

'I'll come with you to see Silverman,' said Ingrid. 'Once I've told Guy I'm quitting.'

'Thanks. I could use the support.'

'It's going to be frustrating, though, isn't it?' Ingrid said.

'What do you mean?'

'Sitting on our hands watching Ninetyminutes go down the tubes.'

'Well, I hope we'll be able to do something to stop it. But they'll find it hard without you.'

'Gaz will manage.'

'I'm not so sure.' Gaz would be able to keep the content coming, but without Ingrid the whole editorial and publishing process would soon unravel. Especially if it was necessary to cut back and reorganize. 'Maybe you shouldn't resign.'

'What do you mean? I told you why I want to quit.'

'Yes. And all that makes sense. Believe me, I value the support. But I think you'll be more use still working at Ninetyminutes. Things will be bad enough as it is without you leaving. And it will be useful to know what's going on at the company. If we are going to save Ninetyminutes, we should do it together. Me on the outside and you on the inside.'

'You don't expect me to go along with Guy?'

'Absolutely. For the time being. Until we get Silverman and Orchestra to see our point of view.'

Ingrid sipped her coffee. 'Maybe I should stay,' she said. Then she frowned.

'What's wrong?'

'That means I have to go to work now.'

'I'm afraid it does.'

She put her coffee down and leaned over to kiss me.

'Well, perhaps not quite yet,' I said.

After Ingrid had left, I had a shower, put on a suit and went to see Derek Silverman at his town house in Chelsea. He showed me into a study at the back with a view over a perfect herbaceous border, blooming powerfully in the sunshine. He was very civil and offered me a cup of coffee. I told him that in my opinion Ninetyminutes had no choice but to retrench and Guy had been mistaken to fire me. Silverman was polite, he listened and he seemed to understand my point of view. But he was firm.

'Guy is confident he can raise more funds. He's the Chief Executive. I'm not one of those people who believe in dumping the Chief Executive as soon as things get tough. You're putting me in a situation where I have to choose between you and him. I have no choice but to go for him.'

'But we've got ourselves in trouble before by relying on Torsten Schollenberger,' I protested.

'Guy and I discussed this at dinner on Monday night. He says the deal is ninety per cent done.'

'He's wrong.'

'It's possible he may turn out to be wrong. But from my standpoint it seems to be the best chance we've got.'

'But . . .' I hesitated, and then went ahead anyway. 'Ninetyminutes has been in a similar situation before. Last year, when Guy had that argument with his father and resigned.'

'And?'

'And, well, a few days later Tony Jourdan was killed.'

'That was a hit-and-run driver, wasn't it?' Silverman said.

'Perhaps. The police don't know who it was.'

'What's your point, exactly, David?'

What was my point? Was I going to accuse Guy of killing his father? Once I had suggested that to Silverman there would be no going back. And I had no proof, yet. Even if I did suggest it, what would I expect Silverman to do? Change his mind in my favour? Fire Guy because he might possibly be a murderer? No. That would be unfair. Not just unfair, wrong.

'Nothing, Derek. Nothing. Thanks for your time.'

Silverman saw me out. 'I'm sorry that you felt you had to leave. I've been very impressed with what you've contributed to Ninetyminutes over the last year. One of the saddest things I see is when good teams split up under pressure.'

I wanted to protest, claim I hadn't wanted to leave at all, that it was Guy, not me, who was feeling the pressure, but I realized there was no point. Guy had got to him. So I went.

Once out on the street I pulled out my mobile and dialled Orchestra's number. Clare Douglas reluctantly agreed to see me in her offices in an hour. But she said she'd only have ten minutes between meetings.

I was shown into a conference room, where I waited for half an hour before Clare arrived. She looked flustered.

'I'm sorry,' she said. 'This doesn't seem to be a great time to be a venture capitalist. No sooner do I put out one fire than another starts.' She looked at her watch. 'I'm already late for my next meeting. I've only got five minutes.'

'OK,' I said. 'You've heard I've left Ninetyminutes?'

'Yes. Guy has explained it all to me.'

'Did he tell you why?'

'He said that you wanted to cut back on costs drastically to conserve cash. He said he'd found another investor so he could continue growing the business.'

'He hasn't,' I said.

'Well, he says he has. I have to believe him.'

'It's an old friend of ours from school. He's let us down once before. He'll let us down again.'

Clare looked doubtful. She was not her cool Scottish self that morning. She frowned. 'That's not what Guy said.'

'I know.'

Clare hesitated. 'Look, I've spoken to the Chairman. I'll be sorry to lose you, but I trust Derek Silverman. People here have known him a long time, and if he wants to stick with Guy on this I'll go along with him.'

'Can't you reconsider?'

Clare's expression became firm. 'We've made our decision. Now I really must go. Can you see yourself out?'

Once again I found myself out on the pavement.

When I arrived home I rang Anne Glazier in Paris. She was back from her trip. I had decided I needed to talk to her face-to-face. If there was some vital detail to be gleaned from her about Guy and the night Tony died I'd never get it from her over the phone. I was prepared to go to Paris to speak to her, but she had a meeting in London the following week and she was willing to see me for half an hour before that.

The next call was much more difficult. My father was at work: his building-society office in the Market Place. We skated over some small talk, before he asked the question I dreaded.

'How's Ninetyminutes?'

'I have bad news,' I said.

'Not again! This thing really is a roller coaster, isn't it? I'm sure whatever it is, you'll work out a way round it.'

'Not this time, Dad.'

'Oh.'

'Guy and I have fallen out. He fired me.'

'Good God. Can he do that?'

'I'm afraid so.'

'Oh, Lord. I am sorry. How awful for you.'

'It is, actually.' I appreciated my father's concern for his son. But that wasn't what I was most worried about. 'I think it's awful for all of us. Ninetyminutes is running out of cash and I want to do something about it. Guy wants to ignore it. I fear this time the company doesn't have long in this world.'

'Oh.'

Silence. I knew what my father was trying to work out a way of saying. I put him out of his misery. 'I think it's quite likely that you'll lose your entire investment. We all will.'

'Oh God,' he whispered.

'I'm sorry, Dad. I'm really sorry.'

I heard an intake of breath over the phone line. 'That's all right, David. It was entirely my decision. Don't blame yourself.'

'I won't,' I said. Although, of course, I would. He had trusted me and I had let him down. He'd never hold it against me, but I'd always know. It was my fault.

'I would feel better if you were still there, though.'

'Believe me, so would I.'

'Yes, well. I have to go now.' I could hear his voice cracking, almost as though he were about to cry. I had never seen my father cry.

'Bye, Dad.'

'Goodbye.' And he was gone, leaving me feeling angry, sad and very, very guilty.

I met Ingrid that evening in a pub round the corner from my flat. She smiled broadly when she saw me, and kissed me quickly on the lips.

I checked my watch. A quarter to six. 'Coming in late. Leaving early. What will people think?'

'They won't know what to think. Anyway, I don't care. I was eager to see you.'

'Likewise,' I said.

'And . . .' She reached into her bag and pulled out a small brown package. 'I bought some coffee.'

I smiled. If having my coffee insulted was the price of Ingrid staying another night, I was quite prepared to pay it.

'Did you manage not to resign?' I asked.

'I did. In fact, I hardly spoke to Guy all day. He seemed rather preoccupied.'

'I'm not surprised. No news from Torsten?'

'Not that I could tell. But Owen came into the office.'

'You're joking!'

'No. He spent most of the day on his computer. But he talked to Guy a bit.'

'Watch out for him, Ingrid. You know how dangerous he can be.'

'Don't worry. I'll avoid him.'

'Do be careful. Please.' I was surprised how apprehensive I suddenly felt. I had lived with the persistent threat of Owen's violence for the last six months. I didn't like the idea of Ingrid putting herself at risk as well.

'I will be,' she smiled, grateful for my concern. 'Also, Mel was there.'

'Mel?'

'Yeah. I thought Guy had had enough of her. But obviously not. She didn't seem very pleased to see me.'

'I'm sure she wasn't. What was she doing?'

'I don't know. She was sitting at your desk doing it, though. It was kind of weird.'

'It sounds it.' The idea of Mel sitting at my desk was uncomfortable. But it made sense. She would be able to do as good a job as anyone in picking up my work. She might have other clients at Howles Marriott, but if Guy said jump, I was sure she would jump.

'No luck with Silverman or Orchestra, then?' Ingrid asked.

'No. Guy has got to Silverman. Clare was harassed and was happy to follow his lead.'

'Oh.'

'But I'm seeing Anne Glazier next week.'

'Do you think she'll be able to tell you anything?'

'Probably not. But I have to try.' I drank my beer, feeling the disappointment crowd in on me from all sides. 'What now?'

'I don't want to just give up,' said Ingrid. 'Sit by and let Guy screw it all up.'

'Neither do I. But if neither Silverman nor Clare will listen to us I don't see how we can get Guy to cut back on costs.'

'And you're quite certain Torsten won't come up with the cash?'

'Positive. I'm sure Guy is convincing, but that doesn't mean anything. When Guy wants to believe something, he can make other people believe it too. You know that. Torsten will flake and Ninetyminutes will go under.'

'What about Champion Starsat?' Ingrid said.

'I thought you voted against the idea of selling out to them?'

'I did then. But this is now. I'm not sure we have a choice.'

'Guy would hate it if I went to them behind his back.'

'Guy fired you yesterday.'

I took a deep breath. 'You're right. I'll call them tomorrow.'

This time I didn't meet Jay Madden at the Savoy. This time I met him in his large corner office on the South Bank with a view of the river. Madden sat behind an impressive desk; I sat opposite.

'Now, David,' said Madden with a friendly smile. 'What can I do for you?'

'Firstly, I should tell you that I've left Ninetyminutes. Guy Jourdan and I had a disagreement over strategy.'

Madden raised his eyebrows. 'And does that disagreement over strategy have anything to do with Champion Starsat?'

'It does.'

'You know the market's changed since we last spoke. So have our plans. We've started up our own site. We don't need Ninetyminutes any more.'

'Ninetyminutes has the best site on the Internet.' I was surprised at the pride I felt as I said this. Whatever Ninetyminutes' problems, that was the truth and Madden couldn't deny it.

He didn't try. 'Running out of cash, are you?'

'If Ninetyminutes is to make the most of its potential it needs investment. Serious investment. You can provide that. The markets can't.'

Madden thought for a moment. 'It's true you have an excellent site. Probably even better than ours. But, as you point out, we have the cash and you haven't. And that means we'll dominate the space. You'll fold soon. Goaldigger have a bit more funding than you, so they'll last longer. But we'll win. You know that.' His tone was matter-of-fact, not aggressive, which just made what he said sound even more credible.

'You may be correct. But at the right price it would be worth your while to incorporate our site into yours.'

Madden smiled. 'I take it Guy Jourdan doesn't know you're here?'

'No, and I'd rather he didn't.'

'Is this a way for you to get your old job back?'

'No. Absolutely not. But I think it would be good for Ninetyminutes. I'm still a shareholder.'

Madden picked up a pencil from his desk and tapped his chin with it. 'If we were to make an offer, what makes you think Jourdan would accept it?'

'He might have no choice.'

'Are you suggesting I call him?'

'No. Call Derek Silverman. And please don't mention my name.'

'All right,' said Madden. 'I'll think about it.'

'Thank you,' I said, and left, feeling guilty as hell.

38

Without Ingrid, the weekend would have been unbearable. With Ingrid, I found it extremely bearable. She worked on Saturday, but we went to see a film together that evening. We spent Sunday morning in bed, getting to know each other, ambled down the street to a local café for lunch and wandered round Hyde Park during the afternoon. Summer had come early, the air was hot and heavy, the grass inviting. Then Ingrid returned to her own place to sort out the week's domestic loose ends.

I didn't see her again until the following evening. She came straight to my flat from work. I was anxious to hear what had happened at Ninetyminutes: we had agreed not to communicate while she was at the office. With Owen there, you never knew.

I was also anxious just to see her. At this stage of our relationship a day seemed a long time, especially when I had nothing to do but stew.

She kissed me, and tucked herself under my arm on the sofa.

'Well?' I said.

'Well. Interesting day, today.'

'Tell me.'

'Guy was in a worse mood than usual this morning. I'm pretty sure he's ignoring me, but maybe he's just ignoring everyone. Anyway, I asked him about Torsten. He looked pissed off and said he would handle it. I demanded to know whether Torsten had come through with the cash: I am still a director, after all. Guy admitted he hadn't.'

'What did I tell you? So Torsten's father said no?'

'Torsten wouldn't admit that to Guy, but that's what Guy thinks. Guy was furious. I thought he was going to jump on a plane to Hamburg and kill him.'

'Don't say that,' I said.

'What do you mean?'

'You know. Tony Jourdan has died. I was put in hospital. Henry's family was threatened. It's getting dangerous to thwart Ninetyminutes these days.'

Ingrid shuddered. 'You're right. I'm sorry. Guy didn't jump on a plane, and before you say anything, Owen was in the office all day too.'

'Did Madden call Silverman?'

'I think he must have. Silverman came round about lunchtime, and he and Guy shut themselves in the boardroom for a couple of hours.'

'Did Guy tell you what it was about?'

'No. I asked him if there was anything I should know. He said there would be a board meeting tomorrow morning. Apparently Clare is in Leeds or somewhere today. He said it was to confirm your removal as a director from the board. But there's something else, I'm sure.'

'Madden's put an offer in.'

'It looks like it.'

'I wonder what the board will say.'

Tuesday morning was tough. The waiting was becoming more difficult by the day. I had spent many hours trying to work out who had run Tony Jourdan down, with little success. For all I knew, it could have been Guy. My best chance for a breakthrough was my forthcoming meeting with Anne Glazier, but that was still twenty-four hours away. Ingrid and I had decided to meet for lunch so that she could tell me about the board meeting, but by nine o'clock I was already stir-crazy. I was just about to leave my flat and go for a walk when the phone rang. It was Michelle.

'Hi, Michelle. How are you?'

'I'm good,' she said. But she sounded tense. It took a lot to make Michelle tense. 'I've got a message from Guy.'

'Really?'

'Yes. He'd like to see you this morning. Ten o'clock, if you can make it.'

'OK,' I said. I was intrigued. And besides, it was good to be able to actually do something. 'I'll come round straight away.'

'He'd like to meet you at Howles Marriott.'

That was a surprise. But I supposed in his current mood Guy wanted to keep me away from Britton Street.

'All right. I'll be there.'

Howles Marriott's offices were in a warren of narrow pavements and cramped squares off Chancery Lane and behind Fleet Street. This was once the labyrinth of streets described by Charles Dickens, but those overcrowded dwellings had been flattened by bombs and bulldozers to be replaced by red brick, plate glass and flagstones. I found such soulless quiet in the middle of London rather eerie.

I waited in the reception area. I had been to these offices dozens of times before, and usually Mel would come down to meet me. Not this time. I was shown up to her office by her secretary.

She was there with Guy. I smiled at her. A mistake.

'Sit down, please,' she said, her voice unfamiliarly cold.

I took a seat at her small conference table, on which she and I had strewn papers many times in the past. She sat facing me, next to Guy.

Guy stared at me coolly. He seemed to have aged in the last few days, the lines around his face had deepened. His forehead was creased in a frown of worry. There were bags under his eyes.

It was finally getting to him.

'Hello, Guy,' I said.

He didn't answer. I sat down.

'We want to speak to you about your role in the unsolicited offer Ninetyminutes has just received from Champion Starsat,' Mel said.

'I see.'

'Do you deny you spoke to them?' Mel's voice was dispassionate, lawyerly, precise.

'No, I don't,' I said simply.

Guy snorted. 'What were you thinking of? You know Champion Starsat are the last people in the world I'd want to sell Ninetyminutes to. We discussed this a couple of months ago. The board voted to tell them to get lost.'

'I went to them as an independent shareholder.'

'You're still a director of the company,' Mel said. 'You should have abided by the decision of the board.'

'But Guy fired me last week.'

'Technically you remain a director until you are removed by a resolution at a board meeting. We haven't had the board meeting yet. It's scheduled for later on this morning.'

'Whatever. It's still the only way out for Ninetyminutes. How much have Champion Starsat offered?'

'Eighteen million pounds,' Guy said.

Eighteen million. I ran the numbers in my head. At that level we'd all get out whole, Orchestra, me, Guy, Owen, Ingrid, my father. In fact, we'd make a small profit.

'That's not bad.'

'Not bad? It's bloody awful! Two months ago this business was worth two hundred million. It's grown since then and now it's worth a poxy eighteen. I don't know why I ever hired you as a finance director, Davo. You're really not very good at sums.'

'I can do the sums,' I said. 'In a couple of weeks' time

Ninetyminutes will be worth precisely zero. Eighteen million pounds is eighteen million pounds more than that.'

Guy sighed in frustration. 'You make me sick. I chose you as a partner because I thought you were one person I could rely on. Someone I could trust. I thought you understood the vision. I thought you got it. Instead, you're just as bad as the rest of them. Worse. You betrayed me, Davo. I won't forget that.'

He had touched a nerve and he was pressing hard. I was determined not to let it hurt, or at least to ignore the pain.

'You need more than imagination and vision to be a successful businessman, Guy,' I said. 'You have to be able to see what's around you. The world has changed in the last few months. The Internet is not the way to make money. I can see that. The smart money can see that. If you can't, that's your problem.'

'Christ, Mel, you talk to him. I can't,' muttered Guy.

Mel spoke. 'David, I am giving you notice that you are obliged to sell your shares in Ninetyminutes back to the company at their nominal value.'

'What? Sell them? Why?'

'Because you were dismissed "with cause".'

'What does that mean?'

'It means that since you were passing confidential information to another company to be used against Ninetyminutes, Guy had cause to dismiss you. Under the terms of your contract, in those circumstances Ninetyminutes can require you to sell your shares at their nominal value. Which is one p, by the way.'

'One p?'

'That means you get fifty thousand pennies,' said Guy, with an unpleasant smile.

'That's ridiculous. I didn't talk to Champion Starsat until after Guy had fired me.'

'You were gathering confidential information while you were at Ninetyminutes with the intention of using it against the company.'

'Bollocks. You can't prove any of that.'

'Oh, can't we?' said Mel.

'No. I'm getting a lawyer.'

'It had better be a good one.'

'It will be.' I stood up. 'You're dragging Ninetyminutes down, Guy, and screwing me won't save it.'

I left the building, seething. Guy couldn't get his hands on my fifty thousand investment for five hundred quid. That would be totally unfair.

As I thought it over, I realized that Mel and Guy almost certainly had no case. They were trying to intimidate me, or infuriate me, or both. But I would go and see that lawyer.

Mel was clearly enjoying the whole thing. She was sitting where she wanted to be, next to Guy. Ingrid was right, she was filling the role of trusted adviser that used to be mine, and she was loving it. Mel and I had historically been on the same side. It was sad to see her as an adversary. But if I was Guy's enemy, I was hers too, I could see that.

I met Ingrid for lunch in a café near Baker Street, only a few tube stops from Farringdon. We didn't want to run the risk of bumping into anyone from Ninetyminutes. I told her about Mel and Guy, and asked her how the board meeting had gone.

'It was tense,' Ingrid said. 'Guy was in a foul mood after seeing you. We began with the resolution to remove you as a director. It should have been a formality, but Guy wouldn't stop ranting about what a traitor you were. Silverman had to calm him down so we could focus on the offer from Champion Starsat.'

'Was Clare there?'

'Oh, yes. There were the four of us: Guy, Silverman, Clare

and me. And Mel was there as the company's legal adviser.'

'So, what happened?'

'Silverman told us the deal. Champion Starsat are offering eighteen million in cash for the whole company, subject to due diligence on their part. Guy can stay on if he wants, but their plan is to integrate ninetyminutes.com with their existing internet businesses. The offer expires at midnight on Thursday.'

'Midnight on Thursday? But that's only two days away!'

'Yep. Madden is piling on the pressure.'

'Did the board go for it?'

'Guy made an impassioned plea for independence. You've heard it all before, but he was pretty eloquent. Then Mel started trying to pick holes in the Champion Starsat offer. Clare would have none of it; she said it was very straightforward and there was no reason to doubt it. She and Mel had a real fight; Silverman had to break it up. Clare won, though. Mel had to shut up.'

'So Orchestra want to sell?'

'Yep.'

'Yes! What about Silverman?'

'You know the way the shareholders' agreement is with Orchestra. In times like this, they call the shots. Silverman knows that and he went with Clare.'

'Which left you?'

'I abstained,' Ingrid said, smiling. 'It seemed the best thing to do in the circumstances.'

'So they've accepted the offer?'

'Not quite. They've agreed to let Guy see if he can find an investor before Friday. If he has a firm unconditional offer on paper before then, they'll reconsider. Otherwise they'll accept.'

'He'll never manage that, will he?'

Ingrid shrugged. 'You should never underestimate Guy,'

she said. 'He's going to see Mercia Metro TV in Birmingham this afternoon. He reckons they'd be an ideal fit.'

Ingrid was right, you never should underestimate Guy. But I felt a huge surge of relief. It looked as if my investment was safe. Much more importantly, my father wouldn't lose any money. And I would be proved right. Guy would be devastated, of course, but after that morning's meeting that didn't concern me too much. In fact, I was rather pleased. I was also pleased for the staff, especially Gaz, whose website would continue.

We left the café to head back to Baker Street tube. As we paused to cross the road, Ingrid turned to check for traffic and grabbed my arm.

'My God!'

'What?'

'Look!'

I looked. About twenty yards behind us a large figure in a Ninetyminutes T-shirt and baseball cap was shambling along the pavement towards us. Owen.

He stopped and stared at us, his face devoid of expression. A cab with its light on was approaching us along the Marylebone Road. I thrust out my arm and the taxi screeched to a halt. I bundled Ingrid inside.

I turned to look for Owen.

He was gone.

39

Anne Glazier was a small, harried woman of about thirty wearing an English suit and a Hermès scarf. The rapid clack of her heels on the hard stone floor echoed around the cavernous foyer of Coward Turner's new building as she approached me, bulging briefcase weighing her down on one side. We perched uncomfortably on the leather-clad slabs that were supposed to act as seats for the big law firm's visitors.

'Thanks for seeing me,' I said.

'Not at all,' she answered briskly. 'A murder is important.'

'It is indeed.'

'I take it the police haven't discovered who killed Tony Jourdan?'

'Not yet.'

'You know they spoke to me at length?'

'Yes, yes, I know. But as I told you on the phone, I'm Guy Jourdan's partner. The uncertainty over the whole affair is damaging our business, so I'm trying to get to the bottom of what happened myself. I wanted to talk to you in person: I'm sure you know how important it is to get the details right.'

She frowned for a moment, but then nodded. She looked like the sort of woman who spent a lot of time getting the details right.

'Can you tell me what happened that evening?'

'All right. Mel's an old friend from Manchester. We studied law together. Every now and then when I visit London I stay on an extra night with her. She does the same in Paris. We see each other perhaps a couple of times a year. Anyway, that afternoon I went to her office to pick up her key. She told me she'd meet me at her flat later. She also said her boyfriend might be there.'

I picked up a note of distaste in Anne's voice. 'You weren't happy about that?'

'Not exactly. Especially when I heard who it was. I remembered Guy from several years ago. He wasn't good news. I know he's a friend of yours, but I'm sure you understand what I mean.'

I nodded. I did.

'Also, I wanted to spend the evening with Mel myself. I mean, that's why I was staying with her. But Mel was so excited it was embarrassing. You know her, she usually seems so cool. Apparently, Guy had stayed with her the night before and she was clearly convinced this was going to be the beginning of something serious.'

From her tone, Anne was less convinced.

'So you were in Mel's flat all evening?'

'Yes. From about seven o'clock onwards. I dumped my stuff there that afternoon and went for a walk. I got back about seven.'

'And then Guy showed up?'

'Yes.'

'At what time?'

'I can't remember exactly. I did tell the police. It was quite late.'

My interest quickened. 'So you're not sure when it was?'

'Not now. It's six months ago, isn't it? But I was sure then. I gave them a precise time.'

'Nine thirty?' I said, remembering my conversation with Spedding.

'That sounds right.'

'How could you be so precise?'

Anne's eyebrows knitted together as though she didn't like the implication that she was ever anything but precise.

'I was watching the clock. Mel wasn't back from work. I was annoyed. As I said earlier, the whole point of this was to see her. I thought we'd go out to dinner or something.'

'So she wasn't there when Guy showed up?'

'No. I let him in.'

'How was he?'

'Drunk. Not just drunk. He was in a state. He looked manic. He didn't say anything to me, just, "Hello," and "Where's Mel?". He searched the flat for alcohol, found a bottle of wine, opened it and slumped on the sofa to wait for her.'

'What happened when Mel came back?'

'She wasn't much better. I mean, she did have a few words with me, but she was all over Guy. Comforting him, pouring him more drink. She ignored me! I left them to it and shut myself in my room. I was on my way to the airport when Mel called me on my mobile to say that Guy's father had been killed. She said the police would want to speak to me.'

'Do you know what Mel and Guy talked about?'

'No. They didn't want me to hear.'

'Could it have been about Tony Jourdan's death?'

'No. They didn't know about it then.' Anne looked me straight in the eye. 'As you can tell, Guy Jourdan is not my favourite person, and to be frank neither is Mel when she's with him, but nothing he said or did suggested he was plotting to kill his father. And according to the police, it would be impossible anyway, given the time he arrived at Mel's flat.'

'That's true,' I said.

'I hope I've been some help,' Anne said, looking at her watch. 'Now I really must go upstairs to get ready for my meeting.'

I watched her march to the bank of lifts, her heels rapping her progress on the hard floor, and thought about what she had said.

It was looking increasingly unlikely that Guy could have killed his father. He didn't have the time to do it himself, and Sergeant Spedding's conviction that Tony's death was not the work of a professional effectively ruled out the possibility that Guy had hired someone else to do it.

That, at least, was good to know. Or it should have been. But my feelings about Guy were becoming more confused, not less, especially after the way he had accused me of betraying him and tried to take my stake in Ninetyminutes away from me. Was he the friend I had always assumed he was? Or was he someone else entirely? Had I really wasted the last year of my life and ruined my career by following him?

And if neither Guy nor Owen had killed Tony Jourdan, who the hell had?

I was wary of letting Ingrid go back to Ninetyminutes now Owen had seen us together, but she was determined to do it. She wanted to see what was going on.

What was going on was that Guy was desperately trying to get Mercia Metro TV interested in Ninetyminutes. He took Ingrid, Gaz, Amy and Mel along with him to Birmingham on Wednesday. According to Ingrid, he put on a good performance and she had no doubt he caught Mercia Metro's interest. He persuaded two of the senior people to come down to Britton Street the following day, although they weren't confident that they would be able to put in an unconditional offer by the midnight deadline.

Nothing from Owen. Ingrid said he was in the office, but he gave no indication that he'd seen the two of us together the day before. Not that that meant anything. I was worried about her. Guy had his back to the wall. Whenever that had happened in the past, someone had got hurt. This time I prayed it wouldn't be Ingrid.

I spent the next day, Thursday, the day of the deadline, at home climbing the walls. Ingrid called at eight o'clock that evening.

'I'm leaving now.'

'You're what? I thought you'd be staying till midnight. Has Guy given up?'

'No. But he's sent us all home.'

'What happened?'

'I'll explain.'

She did, when I saw her half an hour later.

'The Mercia Metro TV team came down this morning: the Managing Director and the Finance Director. Guy showed them around the office and there's no doubt they were keen. All kinds of talk about synergies, and internet space and all that mumbo-jumbo. But then we sat round the table to talk about the deal. They didn't seem to think there was much chance of coming up with an unconditional offer. They'd have to do their own due diligence, get an accountant's investigation, convene a board meeting and God knows what.

'Guy argued with that for a while, and then Mel suggested that a conditional offer might work. After all, Champion Starsat's offer is conditional on due diligence, so if Mercia Metro come up with a better deal with the same conditions, the Ninetyminutes board will have to consider it.'

'What price are they talking?'

'A valuation of twenty-two million pounds. But Mercia Metro wouldn't buy the whole company. The idea is that they invest eight million of new money and become a minority shareholder. Guy will still run the show. The strategy will still be all-out growth.'

'Will Mercia Metro bite?'

'I don't think there's a chance, no. It's true the Managing Director liked the business, but the Finance Director was sceptical about the practicalities, and he had some pretty good arguments. Also, I suspect they would need a board meeting of their own to authorize the offer, and there doesn't seem much likelihood of them calling one in time.'

'So it's all over?'

'Not according to Guy. He still thinks they might go for it. He organized a conference call with Clare Douglas and Derek Silverman to discuss accepting a conditional offer. I sat in on it.'

'Were they receptive?'

'In a word, no. Silverman said it would be a mistake to throw out a solid deal for a flaky one at this stage. And Clare was adamant that it was unconditional or nothing.'

'Good for her.'

'Yes. But she didn't sound happy about it at all.'

'What do you mean?'

'You know Clare. She always seems so cool and in control. Today she sounded tense. Very tense. Almost afraid.'

'Really? Maybe something else is going wrong at Orchestra. I remember last time I went to see her there she looked stressed. Said something about putting out fires.'

'Perhaps. Whatever it was, there's no way she's going to change her mind.'

'And you? What did you say?'

'I voted with Guy.'

'For appearances' sake?'

'Partly. But I have to admit it would be nice if we could bring in Mercia Metro TV as a minority shareholder and Ninetyminutes could continue growing.'

'It would be very nice,' I said. 'But it's not going to happen. You said it yourself: the Internet doesn't make money. This is our chance to get out whole. We won't get another one.'

Ingrid sighed. 'You're right, of course. But I can't help feeling sorry for Guy. He's a brave man, you know. He's fighting to the bitter end.'

'So what happens now?'

'We wait. Guy sent everyone home, he said there was no point in doing any work. People wanted to stay, but he insisted. It was as if he wanted to be by himself at Ninety-minutes at midnight.'

'Strange.'

'Yeah.'

'What's he like? Is he holding it together?'

'In a manic kind of a way. While there's still hope.'

'But when the hope goes?'

Ingrid shuddered. 'Who knows?'

The door buzzer rang. I opened it. It was Clare. A dis- traught Clare. Her hair was a mess, her grey eyes, usually so cool, were wild, her face was flushed.

I showed her into the living room. Her eyes widened when she saw Ingrid.

'Don't worry. Ingrid and I are together.' I said this without thinking through the implications. It was simply the truth.

Clare's eyes darted between us. Ingrid smiled reassuringly.

'OK,' Clare said, accepting the fact. 'I need to talk to you.' She was shaking.

'Here, sit down. Do you want a drink? A cup of tea. A whisky?'

Clare sank into a sofa. 'No, it's all right,' she said. Then she smiled quickly. 'Actually, a wee whisky might be a good idea.'

I got her one. Lots of whisky, not much water.

She took a gulp. 'Thanks.' She winced at its strength. Her hands were still shaking. 'I need your help. Henry suggested I talk to you.'

'Henry?' I wondered what she could possibly want to talk

to me about. Then I knew. 'You've received a threat, haven't you?'

Clare nodded. 'Two.'

'What happened?'

'Yesterday I got this.' She handed me a single sheet of A4 that had been folded three ways to fit into a standard office envelope. I read it:

> *As you know, Ninetyminutes has received an unsolicited offer from Champion Starsat to purchase the company. You should reject this offer in favour of pursuing discussions with other potential investors. In addition, you should make a one million pound bridge loan available to Ninetyminutes until another investor is found.*
> *If you don't reject this offer by midnight on Thursday, you will die. Your colleague, Henry Broughton-Jones, received a similar threat in April. He took the right decision. You should too.*
> *By the way, if you contact the police, or anyone else for that matter, you will still die.*

The note was unsigned. It had been produced by a computer, of course, but the font was slightly different from the letter Henry had received.

Ingrid was reading it over my shoulder. 'Oh, my God,' she whispered.

'Did you show this to Henry?'

'Yes,' Clare said. 'The bastard told me all about what had happened to him and his family. I can't believe he let me take Ninetyminutes over from him without warning me. The coward.'

'He was worried about his family,' I said.

'What about me? And he said he'd told you all about it. Why didn't you let me know what was going on?'

'I'm sorry. I had promised Henry I wouldn't. I did try to stop it. I went to France to try to warn Owen off.' I touched my cheek, where there was still a small scar. 'Obviously that didn't work.'

'Obviously,' said Clare.

'So that's why you sounded so shaken this afternoon?' Ingrid asked.

'Absolutely right. I decided to ignore the note. But I was rattled. And then I got this.'

She handed me the printout of an e-mail. This message was much shorter.

You have eight hours. Say no to Champion Starsat or you die.
I'm serious.

I tried to decipher the internet routing gobbledegook. The message had been sent to Clare at Orchestra. Where it had come from was impossible to determine: I didn't recognize any of the forwarding addresses.

'Will it be possible to trace this?' I asked.

'I doubt it,' said Clare. 'It's easy to send anonymous e-mails once you know what you're doing.'

'Anonymous?' I snorted. 'I don't know why Owen bothered.'

'Do you think it is Owen?' Ingrid asked.

I nodded. 'I'm sure it's Owen. It's a last-ditch attempt to protect Guy.'

Clare shuddered. 'That man gives me the creeps.'

'So he should,' I said.

'What are you going to do?' Ingrid asked Clare.

'I know I'm not going to give in to the threats,' said Clare, her hand shaking.

'Henry did,' said Ingrid.

'I know Henry did. But I'm not going to. If I do, Orchestra Ventures will lose millions. I'm just not prepared to be responsible for that.'

'It would be quite understandable if you did pull the deal,' I said. 'You should know Owen is quite capable of carrying out his threats. He's killed at least two people that I know of.'

Clare looked at me, eyes wide. 'My God, I've dealt with some shady people in the past, but never a murderer.' Then they narrowed. 'He's not going to mess me about. I'm not that easy to push around.'

I exchanged glances with Ingrid. Clare was a brave woman, there was no doubt about it.

'OK,' I said. 'That leaves you with three choices. You could say nothing and hope, you could go to the police, or I could go and see Owen.'

'Last time you did that you nearly got yourself killed!' Ingrid said.

'I know. But Clare's right, someone has to stand up to him.'

'What do you think about going to the police?' Ingrid asked Clare.

'I don't know. I'm nervous about that. The threat was pretty explicit. What do you think, David?'

I considered it. 'Knowing Owen, if you talk to the police there's a good chance he'll carry out his threat.'

'Whereas if *you* talk to Owen,' Ingrid said to me, 'he'll kill you first, and then Clare.' She quite clearly didn't like that option.

'What if I talked to Guy? Guy could talk Owen out of harming Clare.'

'He might,' said Ingrid. 'But you and he are hardly best mates at the moment, are you? He blames you for all of this. And he's not in the most stable frame of mind.'

'I think he'll listen to me.'

'Are you sure?'

'I'm willing to take the risk. Short of Clare calling Silverman to say that she wants to reject the Champion Starsat deal, I can't see what else we can do.' Ingrid and I turned to Clare. 'Well?'

She thought for a moment. 'If you're prepared to talk to Guy and Owen, then do it,' she said, eventually.

'All right,' I said. 'We'll give it a go. You say Guy's at Ninetyminutes?'

'He said he'd be there all evening,' said Ingrid. 'And I'm coming with you.'

'Oh, no you're not,' I said. 'It might be dangerous.'

'Of course it's dangerous,' said Ingrid. 'But if you two are going to risk your lives, I don't see why I shouldn't too.'

I could see there was no point in arguing with her. 'All right. Where will you be?' I asked Clare.

'Mel wanted me to meet her at Howles Marriott. If we don't hear anything from Mercia Metro TV before midnight then Derek will send a fax from his house to Champion Starsat accepting their offer. We've already drafted it. As the company's lawyer, Mel wants to be involved. Since she's in Guy's pocket, neither Derek nor I are too happy with that. I think she's hoping that if I'm with her and a deal comes through from Mercia Metro, we can draft whatever papers are necessary on the spot. I don't know. She was pretty insistent, though.'

'It's not a bad idea,' I said. 'Lawyers' offices have plenty of security, even at night, so you should be safe from Owen. We'll come and pick you up when we've had a chance to talk to Guy. Depending on what he says, we can figure out somewhere safe for you to go.'

'OK,' said Clare, downing her whisky. 'What are we waiting for?'

Clare took the first passing taxi to Howles Marriott's office off Chancery Lane and Ingrid and I took the second.

'Are you sure Guy will be there?' I asked her.

'I think so. Hang on. I'll check.'

She pulled out her mobile and dialled a number. 'Hello, Guy, it's me ... Any news? ... Nothing? ... OK, just checking. Bye.'

'He's there?'

'Yes.'

'How'd he sound?'

'Tense.'

'Do you think Owen's with him?'

'I don't know. He left with the rest of us. I suppose he might have come back. I could hardly ask Guy, could I?'

'No.'

In silence we pondered the possibility that Owen might be in the office with Guy. It was a risk we would just have to take.

We were taking big risks. People had died. More people might die. Including Ingrid and me.

I worked through the logic of what we were about to do. It held together. Just.

I thought I understood Guy. He would be pretty strung out. I knew that Ninetyminutes meant everything to him. But I also knew that our friendship meant something. He wouldn't callously kill me. Or Ingrid. Nor would he stand by and let Owen harm us. I was pretty sure of that. Wasn't I?

I would just have to trust him.

The taxi turned right off Clerkenwell Road down the much quieter Britton Street. We stopped outside the familiar building and I paid the driver. He disappeared, leaving Ingrid and me on the empty pavement looking up to where Guy was sitting, we hoped, alone.

I glanced across at her. Her face was pinched. She was as nervous as me.

'You really don't have to do this,' I said. 'I can go in by myself.'

'I know.'

'It might be dangerous. You might get hurt.'

She turned to me and smiled, a small nervous smile. 'So might you. I'm coming with you.'

'OK,' I said. 'Let's go, then.'

We took the stairs up to the fourth floor. We pushed open the door bearing the ninetyminutes.com logo and entered the large open-plan room.

Guy was sitting there, staring at his computer screen where a half-finished game of Minesweeper was displayed.

Alone.

We walked towards him. He turned. He looked worse than I had ever seen him, and I had seen Guy pretty bad. His eyes were set deep in dark shadows, their habitual bright blue now dulled. Stubble sprouted out of his chin and pale puffy cheeks. His yellow hair was greasy and uncombed.

'Hi,' he said, his voice flat, defeated.

'Hello, Guy.' I walked towards him.

'Sit down.' He waved distractedly at my desk. I sat in my old chair. Ingrid perched on the desk next to me.

'Heard anything?' I asked him.

'No.' He looked at his watch. 'Ten past ten. I'm not going to hear anything, either. If Mercia Metro were going to do it, they'd have done it by now.'

'They never were going to do a deal, Guy,' I said.

He looked at me vaguely, his eyes unfocused. 'No,' he said quietly. Then he glanced at Ingrid. 'Are you two . . . ?'

I nodded.

'For how long?'

'Not long. Since you fired me,' I said.

He smiled. More to himself than to us. 'That's nice.' Then he seemed to notice us again. 'Are you going to wait with me?'

'Maybe.'

'Because I wanted to be alone. Here. At midnight.'

There was something in what he was saying that scared me. 'Why?' I asked. 'Why do you want to be alone?'

Guy didn't answer. He stared at his screen. He clicked the mouse. We let him play. Then he swore to himself as he clicked on a mine.

He pushed the mouse away. 'Ninetyminutes is over, isn't it, Davo?'

I nodded.

'All that work. All those hours. All the worry, the arguments, the triumphs, all crumbling away into nothing.'

'The site will live on.'

'Yeah, but that wasn't what Ninetyminutes was about,' Guy said. 'It was about you and me becoming new people. Better people. And for a time I thought we'd made it. For a long time. I was the entrepreneur who could make anything happen. You were my right-hand man who made sure that once it happened it didn't all fall apart. We were good, Davo. We were really good. It shouldn't have gone wrong.'

'No, it shouldn't.'

'But it did. Tonight we sell out. Tomorrow? Tomorrow, there's nothing.'

'What are you going to do?' asked Ingrid.

Guy didn't seem to hear her at first. Then he smiled a small quick smile, and bent down to open the bottom drawer of his desk. He straightened up. In his hand was a gun.

It was silver-grey, quite large for a handgun, I thought, not that I knew anything about handguns. It was one of those that have a magazine in the handle. He weighed it in his hand. It looked quite heavy.

'Where did you get that?' I asked.

'Owen got it for me,' Guy said. He chuckled. 'It's amazing what you can buy over the Internet these days. Shootsomeone.com. Why didn't we try that one? Or www.blowyourbrainsout.co.uk. Not many repeat customers, though. And it's all about repeat customers, isn't it?'

'What are you going to do with it?'

'Use it,' Guy said. 'On myself. Don't worry. I won't take you with me or anything. I was going to wait till twelve. But if you force me, I could do it now.'

Ingrid let out a short gasp.

'Let's wait till twelve,' I said. 'There's still a couple of hours.'

Guy contemplated the gun in his hand. 'I don't know. Two hours is a long time to wait with you two staring at me.'

He lifted the weapon.

'You were a crap businessman, you know,' I said. I had to say something. For a second a spark of anger lit up Guy's eyes. But then it died down.

'I know.'

'Nowhere near as good as your father.'

He lowered the gun. I had caught his attention. 'You're right.'

'You're good at the big-picture stuff. The vision thing. But you never really understood that it was all about money, did you? I did, but you fooled me too.'

Anger smouldered in Guy's eyes.

'Your father knew about profit, didn't he? Let's face it, if we'd done what he'd suggested and linked up to a porn site, the money would be rolling in. Sex 'n' soccer. The tabloids would be queuing up to buy us. And the NASDAQ could just go screw itself.'

'I could never have run a site like that,' said Guy.

'Neither could I. Could you, Ingrid?' She shook her head. 'But that's our problem. You'd never have made it in property, either.'

'What do you mean?'

'I remember reading an article in *Private Eye* about your father. How he had bribed a local council to allow planning permission for some shopping centre in the north. And how he screwed his partner in the seventies.'

'That was all libel!' Guy protested. '*Private Eye* settled out of court. They paid Dad a substantial sum and printed an apology.'

'Course they did. Just like they did to Robert Maxwell. I wouldn't want to mess with your father in court.'

Guy sighed. 'So what are you getting at?'

'You built something much greater than your father could ever have done. Ninetyminutes was one hell of an achievement. Not financially, maybe. But I don't know anyone else who could have created the best soccer website in Europe from scratch.'

'Big deal.'

'It *is* a big deal. It impressed the hell out of me. And Ingrid. And Gaz. And Michelle. And every one of the people who work here.' I leaned forward. 'Guy, you've always impressed the hell out of me. For a while I thought that you would be a great entrepreneur. So you're not. So what? I'm still impressed.'

'You're just saying that because I've got a gun in my hand.'

'I'm not, and you know it. I knew your father. I know you. Believe me, Guy. You're a better man than him. You don't have to prove that to me, and you shouldn't have to prove it to yourself any more.'

Guy looked again at the gun. Very slowly he placed it on to the desk next to him. Even more slowly I got to my feet and reached across towards it.

Guy snatched it up and pointed it somewhere between me and him. 'I'm not sure what I'm going to do with this thing, so don't rush me.'

I eased back into my chair. 'OK,' I said.

We sat in silence, the three of us. But I was thinking about a fourth person. Clare.

Slowly, I pulled the note she had received out of my jacket pocket and handed it to Guy.

'What's this?'

'Clare got it yesterday. It's from Owen. Read it.'

Guy read it, frowning. 'You think Owen wrote this?' he said, when he had finished.

'I know Owen wrote it. And he sent an e-mail to Clare today, telling her he's serious.'

Guy was silent, staring at the letter. Eventually, he spoke. 'I don't think this is Owen.'

'Of course it's Owen,' I said. 'It was Owen who threatened Henry. Owen who planted the computer virus in Goaldigger's system. Owen who has been threatening me. You know yourself Owen killed Dominique. I think he killed Abdulatif as well. And now he's going to kill Clare. Unless you stop him.'

Guy looked confused. Unsure of himself. Unsure of his brother.

'You are the only person who can stop him,' I said.

Just then the door to the office banged open. We turned. Owen.

He pushed his way through the door carrying a flat brown carton. 'Hey, Guy?' he called. 'Guy? I got pizza! Pepperoni feast.'

Then he saw us.

'What are these people doing here?' he demanded, placing the pizza box on a nearby desk and moving over to his brother. 'I thought you said you wanted to be alone?'

'They came to talk to me about this.' Guy handed him Clare's letter. 'They tell me you wrote it. Did you?'

Owen read the letter. He chuckled softly to himself.

'Did you?' asked Guy again.

Owen shrugged. 'Maybe.'

Guy's eyes narrowed. He glanced at Ingrid and me. 'Owen, if you did write this, it's pretty dumb. If Ninetyminutes does get sold, killing Clare isn't going to bring it back.'

'Did she fold?' Owen asked.

'No,' said Guy. 'We haven't heard anything from her. Or from Mercia Metro TV.'

'Then I guess it was pretty dumb,' said Owen.

'There's no point in harming Clare now,' I said. 'Ninety-minutes is going to be sold to Champion Starsat whatever you do to her or anyone else.'

Owen glared at me. His small black eyes gleamed with anger. He was about to say something when he noticed the gun on Guy's desk. He reached over and picked it up.

I tensed. Owen was dangerous enough. Owen with a gun was lethal.

'So, you had a use for this after all,' he said to Guy. 'I was scared you were going to, like, top yourself with it.'

Guy looked uncomfortable.

'You *were* going to top yourself.' Owen pulled up a chair next to Guy's desk and lowered himself into it. 'That's why you wanted to be by yourself tonight. Then these jerks disturbed you. I knew I shouldn't have left you alone.'

'What about Clare?' I said.

Big mistake. Owen exploded. 'Screw Clare! I don't give a shit what happens to her. She's given Ninetyminutes away.' He jabbed the gun towards me, using it more as a finger than as a weapon. 'And screw you too. Can you see what you've done to my brother? It was you who totally fucked up Ninetyminutes. If it hadn't been for you, he'd be fine now, not sitting here planning to blow his brains out.'

'Give me the gun, Owen,' Guy said quietly.

'So you can use it on yourself? No fuckin' way. I'm gonna use it. On this bastard.'

He raised the gun and pointed it towards me. He was aiming now, not jabbing.

'Owen, wait!' Guy protested.

'No. This fucker deserves to die. He's gonna die.'

Ingrid let out a small scream.

'You too, baby. One goes, you both go.'

'Don't do it, Owen. It's stupid.'

'Of course it's not stupid. If I hadn't shown up just now, you'd have shot yourself. And all because of him.' Owen stared at me hard down the barrel of the gun. He was angry, but he wasn't out of control. He was very much in control. He knew what he was doing and he was determined to do it.

'I'm telling you. Give me the gun.'

Guy's voice was firm. But Owen ignored it. He didn't move his eyes away from me. I heard the click of the safety catch. He was going to pull the trigger.

'OK, OK.' Guy ran his fingers through his hair. His expression changed. From a state of confusion, he suddenly became focused. Angry. 'You're right, Owen,' he said. 'It is all this bastard's fault. But let me think. There's no point in shooting him and waiting for the police to arrive.'

I stared at Guy. Had he gone mad? He looked very sane. Angry, but sane.

Owen stared at his brother too.

'Guy?' I said.

'Shut the fuck up.'

'Guy. You can't let Owen do this.'

'I said, shut the fuck up!' Guy screamed. 'Owen's got it dead right. I should never have hired you. I shouldn't have listened to you whining about Owen and Henry and my father. I shouldn't have let you sell Ninetyminutes out from underneath me. I should have fired you months ago.' He leapt out of his chair, placing his face inches from mine. It was full of hate. I had never seen him like this, even in his worst moments.

Guy had cracked.

'You speck of shit. You're going to die, Davo, and I'm going to enjoy it when you do.' He stepped back and spoke to his brother. 'But we've got to think about this, Owen. Give ourselves time. Kill these two and then get out of the country before anyone realizes they've gone.'

Owen nodded his head. He didn't actually smile, but you could see him swell with pleasure. His big brother was on his side. They were going to run off together, just the two of them, looking after each other as they should have done all along.

'I'm gonna shoot the fucker,' he said. Just to be clear.

'Yeah, I know. But not here. Not now. We need to take them away somewhere.'

'We can shoot them and move the bodies.'

'Hey, let me do the thinking, will you?' snapped Guy. 'I sorted things after Dominique, I can sort things now. People will see us shifting bodies around. I'll go and get your car and bring it back here. We'll put them in alive, and take them somewhere a bit more remote. Maybe somewhere on the way to Dover. Give me the keys.'

Owen thought for a second and then reached into his pocket. He threw Guy a bunch. 'I'll get your passport while I'm at it. I've got mine here.' He reached down into the bag by his desk and pulled out his own passport, showing it to Owen. 'I won't be long. Keep them covered. And if they try anything, shoot them. It'll be messier, but we'll figure something out.'

He was gone.

40

Ingrid and I were left facing Owen and a gun.

How long would Guy be? Owen's flat was in Camden, not too far away. It wouldn't take him long to fetch the car if he took a cab there. Twenty minutes maybe? It would be a long twenty minutes.

Ingrid was still perched on the desk, beside me. She moved her hand out to mine. I held it.

'How cute,' said Owen. He shifted his aim slightly away from my head and towards our hands. 'But let go, or I'll blow your fingers off.'

We let go.

I cursed myself for allowing her to come, even though it would have been impossible to stop her. Owen wanted to kill me. He didn't care about Ingrid, but now she would die too.

I still couldn't believe the transformation I had seen in Guy. He had turned from confused and suicidal to focused and murderous. Something had snapped. This was a Guy I did not recognize, a Guy I did not know.

I wondered where they'd take us. Probably to some woods somewhere in Kent. They'd shoot us, dump us, and drive on to the ferry and the Continent. Would they escape? Between the two of them, they were pretty resourceful. They might.

I thought about dying. About my parents, how distraught they would be. About what I had achieved with my life. To my surprise, I found myself thinking about Ninetyminutes. That was something. Something good. Then I realized it was all going to be over. Sometime in the next hour or so, it was all going to be over.

I glanced at Owen. He saw the fear in my eyes. He smiled.

I tried to get a grip of myself. I had no intention of giving that bastard any pleasure.

We sat there a long time. It seemed longer than twenty minutes, but I didn't want to check my watch in case it provoked Owen. He sat solidly still. If he was impatient or jumpy, he didn't show it. His eyes never left me. He had the ghost of a smile, a complacent, self-satisfied smile. He liked to watch me sitting there in fear. He was enjoying this.

Then Ingrid spoke. 'Owen?' she said softly. 'You could just leave us, you know. You could easily get away, just the two of you. We wouldn't call the police until the morning.'

'Quiet,' Owen said. 'Don't even try to talk your way out of this.'

'But, Owen –'

'I said, quiet!' He raised the gun.

Just then, we heard the sound of Guy running up the stairs, two at a time. He banged open the door.

'You took your time,' Owen said.

'Come on,' said Guy. 'Let's go. Give me the gun. I'll cover them.'

'No, I'll keep it.'

Guy reached out towards the weapon. Owen pulled it away. 'I said, I'll keep it. If anyone's gonna shoot these fuckers, it's gonna be me.'

Guy stared at his brother, who stared back. He wasn't going to budge. Guy shrugged. 'OK. The car's outside. Let's go.'

Owen waved the gun at Ingrid and me. Reluctantly we stood up and followed Guy out into the hallway and down the stairs, Owen a couple of feet behind us.

Guy was first through the door on to the street. Everything

was quiet. I looked for Owen's black Japanese four-wheel drive, but I couldn't see it.

'Where's the car?' Owen asked.

'Just round that corner,' Guy replied, pointing to an alley on the other side of the road.

We crossed the street.

Then several things happened at once. Everything exploded in a bright whiteness. Guy screamed, 'Down!' He dived to the ground, pulling Ingrid with him. As I dropped too, pressing my face against the hard road surface, I heard the sharp crack of two shots, then a sharp scream from Owen behind me, and the clatter of his gun falling to the tarmac.

I rolled over. I saw Owen slumped in the road, an out-stretched hand reaching for the gun, only inches away from his fingertips. I scrabbled over to it and snatched it away from him. All around me I could hear the sounds of running.

I pulled myself to my feet, still holding the gun. I looked down at Owen, illuminated by the bright lights. Blood seemed to be pouring out of two holes, one in his shoulder and another in his side. Policemen wielding rifles and handguns and wearing bulletproof vests bent over him. A siren wailed with increasing intensity as an ambulance barrelled down the little street towards us.

I turned to look for Ingrid. She seemed unhurt, but she was shaking violently. Wide-eyed, she staggered towards me and I wrapped my arms around her. She clung to me, tight.

Guy was hovering behind the group of policemen who were surrounding his brother, watching them as they tried to stanch the flow of blood. I recognized one of them: DS Spedding. Seconds later they were joined by paramedics in green overalls. Within a minute, Owen was on a stretcher and being lifted into the ambulance.

'Is he going to be OK?' Guy asked Spedding, whose hands were covered in Owen's blood.

'He's still alive. He's bleeding heavily, but he's a big strong guy. He's got a chance.'

Guy tried to get into the ambulance with Owen, but Spedding stopped him. There were questions to answer.

I walked over to Guy. There were tears streaming down his cheeks. Spedding stepped back.

'Thanks, Guy,' I said.

He tried to smile. 'Did I fool you?'

'You fooled me. I knew you were a good actor.'

'I had to be to fool Owen.' He turned to watch the ambulance disappear up the road, siren blaring. 'I hope he lives.'

I hoped so too. For Guy's sake.

'I had to do it, Davo. When I saw he really meant to kill you, that even I couldn't talk him out of it, it all suddenly clicked. He may be my brother, but he's evil. I've tried to hide from that fact all my life. Blame my parents, blame anybody but Owen. So it was up to me to stop him.'

'I thought you were away a long time.'

'I called Spedding. He was pretty quick in the circumstances. I knew I couldn't keep Owen waiting too much longer.' He shook his head, looking along the street to where the ambulance had long since disappeared. 'I wish he'd given me the gun.'

Spedding approached us. 'I'm sorry, Guy, but I have some questions I have to ask you.' He drew Guy a few yards away and began asking them. Other policemen talked to Ingrid and me. After half an hour or so, they let us go.

'I'm off to the hospital, now,' said Guy. 'To see how Owen's doing.'

I glanced at Ingrid. 'We'll come with you,' I said. I didn't give a damn what happened to Owen, but I did care about Guy. He needed all the support he could get.

'Thanks,' he said, and turned to the small group of

policemen who were still busy milling about the road. Sped-ding had already left, so he spoke to a uniformed sergeant.

A moment later he rejoined us. 'Owen's been taken to St Thomas's. The copper said they could give us a lift, but we'd have to wait a few minutes. So let's just grab a taxi.'

He headed off rapidly towards Farringdon Road, and we followed him, keeping our eyes out for black cabs with orange lights on. There were none.

'Damn,' Guy said. He was getting impatient, and began walking down towards Smithfield. He waved at an empty cab with its light off, but it ignored him and drove on. I was reminded of Hoyle's prayers for a recession.

We paused at a crossing. Guy was suddenly struck by something. He turned to me, frowning. 'You know, you were wrong, Davo.'

'About what?'

'About Owen. And the note to Clare.'

'What do you mean? He admitted he wrote it.'

'No, he didn't. When I asked him, he said, "Maybe." He was trying to be mysterious. Having his own little joke.'

Guy saw my scepticism. 'Think about it. Think of the words in the note: "unsolicited offer", "purchase the com-pany", "pursuing discussions with other potential investors". That's not Owen.'

It was true. They didn't sound like Owen's words.

'Did you see the note Owen wrote to Henry?' Guy asked. 'Yes.'

'Was it anything like that?'

'No. It was just a couple of lines. I can't remember it exactly, but it was something like: "Give Ninetyminutes the money, or else."'

'And another thing. I know Owen didn't kill my father.' I opened my mouth to protest, but Guy stopped me. 'It's not just that he was with me at the time, I know he didn't hire anyone else to kill him, either. He was genuinely surprised when he heard what had happened. But someone murdered Dad. Someone ran him down, on purpose. And someone wrote that note.'

Out of the corner of my eye I saw a taxi with its light on speeding past us. But I was too stunned by what Guy was saying to react.

Guy's frown deepened. 'Where's Mel?'

'She's with Clare,' said Ingrid. 'At Howles Marriott.'

'Oh, my God,' I said. Suddenly, I saw it. Guy was right. Of course Owen wouldn't have written a letter like that: it was written by a lawyer. A lawyer who would do anything to help Guy. Anything.

'What time is it?' Guy asked.

I checked my watch. 'Ten to twelve.'

'Jesus.' Guy looked up and down the street. No sign of any more free cabs. We were now quite a distance from Britton Street and the remaining police. 'Come on! Let's run! It's only half a mile to Mel's office.'

Guy set off, with Ingrid and me in hot pursuit. We ran along Charterhouse Street, across Holborn Circus, down Shoe Lane, and into the rabbit warren of streets and squares between Fleet Street and Chancery Lane. Guy ran fast and it was all I could do to keep up. I wasn't as fit as I used to be; my heart was soon pounding and I was gasping for air. But I kept up, just. Ingrid wasn't far behind us.

We reached the entrance to Howles Marriott. A security guard looked up from his desk, startled.

'Have you seen Melanie Dean?' Guy asked, fighting for breath.

'She just left a moment ago.'

'Alone?'

'No. With another lady.'

'Shit!' said Guy. 'Look. Call the police. Tell them there's a murder about to be committed. There's a dangerous woman out there and she's almost certainly armed.'

The security guard's jaw dropped. He didn't move.

'I'm serious. Do it!'

Guy and I ran out of the front entrance. Ingrid arrived panting.

'Which way?' I said.

'God knows,' said Guy. 'She could have gone anywhere.'

'I thought I saw two figures back that way,' said Ingrid, pointing towards the alley from which we had come. 'It's not far.'

'OK. Show us.'

Ingrid set off again and we followed her. She dived through a passageway under an office block and into a tiny square paved with flagstones. The red-brick lawyers' buildings that surrounded it were still. No traffic. No people. Just Mel and Clare, illuminated under a yellow streetlamp.

'Mel!' Guy shouted.

At the sound of his voice, she stopped and turned. Clare was right next to her, looking very frightened. In Mel's hand was a gun.

Ingrid and I stopped. Guy slowed to a walk. He approached the two women.

'Now, Mel. Let her go,' he said calmly.

'No,' Mel said. 'I warned her that if she didn't turn down the Champion Starsat offer she would die. Derek Silverman faxed through the acceptance ten minutes ago.'

'I'm asking you to let her go,' Guy said, taking a further step towards her.

'Stop where you are!' Mel shouted. Her eyes were bright. She was wired. On the edge.

Guy stopped.

'I'm doing this for you, you know that, don't you?' Mel said.

Guy nodded. 'I know.'

'I've done so much for you.'

'I know.'

'Do you? I don't think you do. I got rid of your father. Did you know that? Do you remember that night when you came round to see me after you'd had a fight with him? After he had insisted that Ninetyminutes become a porn site. Do you remember that, Guy?'

'I remember.'

'I was so angry for you. I wanted to help you. So I decided to force him to keep you on, to keep doing things at Ninetyminutes your way. I waited for him in my car outside his flat. I was going to tell him that if he didn't do what I wanted, I'd accuse him of raping me in France.

'Then I saw him. Coming out of his flat into the narrow street. I thought it would be so easy just to put my foot down on the accelerator and finish him off. I remembered what he'd done to me in France, how he'd ruined my life. I couldn't let him ruin your life as well. So I put my foot down.'

I remembered what Anne Glazier had said: Mel had arrived back at her flat that evening *after* Guy. She had driven home straight from running Tony down. No wonder she had seemed so agitated.

I couldn't see Guy's face, but Mel could. 'Don't look so shocked. Owen killed Dominique, didn't he? And you stood by him. Well, I killed Tony. For you.'

'There's no need to kill anyone else,' Guy said. 'Let Clare go. For me.'

Mel grabbed hold of Clare and lifted the gun to her head. 'No. She destroyed Ninetyminutes.'

Clare whimpered. She was terrified.

'Did Owen know?' Guy asked.

'He worked it out. He's clever, your brother. And I knew he was trying to help you too. We both did our best.'

'Is that where you got the gun?'

'Yes. He came up to me a few days ago and said he'd got one for you and did I want one? I think he knew what I'd use it for.'

A siren sounded. Mel looked round the square in panic. The police. If she was going to press the trigger, she might do it now.

Guy took a step further forward.

'I'm going to shoot her! I mean it.'

More sirens, louder. Guy took another step. 'Let her go.'

'I said, I'll shoot her.'

Another step.

The gun moved away from Clare's head towards Guy. Clare bucked and yanked herself away from Mel's grasp. Guy lunged forward. There was a shot and a cry from Guy. He slid to the ground as Mel jumped backwards. Clare ran off somewhere to the side. I dashed towards Mel and Guy. Mel turned and ran down an alleyway.

I ran after her. I knew she had a gun, but I was angry and I was determined to stop her. I rounded a corner. She turned and fired. She was only a few yards ahead of me, but she was holding the gun unsteadily and the bullet whined harmlessly over my head. I ducked back out of sight.

Mel ran on and I followed. She was not a good shot and at that moment I didn't care too much for my own safety. But I would have to figure out how to get close enough to disarm her. How many bullets did she have in her magazine? I had no idea.

Another corner, another alleyway. This time at the far end was Fleet Street, with its traffic, busy even at this time of night. Mel stopped and turned towards me. I was closer to her now. She raised her gun towards me. She was so near it would be hard to miss.

I thought about trying to run back to the corner. But she would fire then for sure. And she might hit me.

So I walked on.

'I'll shoot!' she said, her voice catching with hysteria.

'Don't, Mel. Put the gun down.'

'No!' She was grasping the gun so tightly in front of her that it was shaking. But at least part of the time it was pointing straight at me.

'There's no point, Mel. You've shot Guy. He's back there lying on the pavement in his own blood. He's not coming with you.'

Mel bit her lip. Her shoulders hunched as she tried to control herself, tried to keep the gun pointed at me. 'Is he dead?' she said, in little more than a whisper.

'Perhaps,' I said. 'I don't know. Give me the gun.'

I took another step forward.

Mel braced herself and stared along the barrel of the gun straight at me. Then she slumped backwards into the wall. The gun dropped to her side.

I walked swiftly up to her and prised the weapon out of her fingers. The barrel was warm. She slid down to the ground, put her head in her hands and sobbed.

A policeman arrived breathing heavily. I left Mel and the gun with him and ran back to the small square.

Guy was lying where he had fallen. Ingrid was with him, as were three or four armed policemen.

I pushed my way through to him.

He had a single wound to the chest. Blood was pumping out. He was finding it very difficult to breathe, but his eyes were open. His skin was pale under his stubble, so pale.

He saw me.

'Davo.'

I knelt down beside him.

'Is Clare OK?' he asked.

I looked up. She was standing a few yards away, her face white, her hand to her mouth.

'Yeah. You saved her.'

'And Owen? How's Owen?'

'I don't know.'

He tried to speak, but could only cough. Blood dribbled out of the side of his mouth.

'Easy,' I said. 'The ambulance will be here soon.'

'Can you find out? About Owen?' It was little more than a whisper.

I looked up. Spedding was standing over us, catching his breath, splashes of Owen's blood still on his clothes. I raised my eyebrows. He stepped back and spoke into his radio. After a few seconds he caught my eye and shook his head.

I looked down at Guy. He hadn't seen Spedding.

'He's fine,' I said. 'He's going to make it.'

Guy smiled. Or tried to smile. He coughed. More blood. He coughed once more, and then he was still.

Ingrid wept quietly. I put my arm around her and squeezed her tight. As I watched the paramedics cover his body and load it on to a stretcher, I realized that in the end I had trusted Guy.

And he hadn't let me down.

41

The twenty-six-year-old ex-investment banker finished his PowerPoint presentation with a flourish and sat down expectantly. I glanced at Clare. This was the third Wireless Application Protocol deal we had seen in a month, and easily the worst. By a slight twitching of an eyebrow, Clare signalled that she agreed with my assessment. We asked the two-man team some questions for the sake of politeness, and then kicked them out.

'We were never that bad, were we, Clare?' I asked her as we made our way back to the small office we shared.

Clare laughed. 'Not quite. But those guys were geniuses compared to some of the bozos we used to get in here a year ago.'

The dot-com bubble may have burst, but the venture capitalists lived on. They now counted me as one of their number. I enjoyed the job: finally I had found something that played to my analytical strengths and allowed me to take the occasional risk. Orchestra Ventures was doing well, partly owing to one of Henry's deals, a chain of coffee shops that had been bought by a multinational for tens of millions. So Henry was still a partner; it is amazing what venture capitalists will forgive someone who makes them money.

I sat at my desk and stared at my computer, remembering our own pitch to Orchestra. I called up the web browser and typed in www.ninetyminutes.com. The familiar bubble design appeared, although one of the bubbles now bore the words *Number One Soccer Site in Europe*. I smiled. With Champion Starsat's funding, Gaz's writing and Ingrid's editorial skills, Ninetyminutes had wiped the floor with the opposition. Sure, retailing had been closed down, and there were prominent links to Champion Starsat services all over the site, but none the less Guy would have been pleased. I was glad Madden had succeeded in persuading Ingrid to stay on. I still saw a lot of her. I was glad of that, too.

The legal machinery was grinding on towards Mel's trial. I wasn't planning to attend, but I assumed I would be called as a witness, something I was not looking forward to. Mel had spent most of her adult life feeling guilty. I hoped she would plead guilty now.

Guy was lying next to his father and brother in the village churchyard, but it seemed to me that he had finally broken free of both of them. All his thirty-two years he had been at war with himself to prove that he could make something of his life. And he had: I was staring at it. For the hundredth time since his death I felt a wave of sadness wash over me.

Then I heard his voice whispering in my ear: 'Get on with it, Davo!'

I smiled to myself. With a couple of clicks of my mouse I left the Ninetyminutes website. And got on with it.

Author's Note

None of the characters in this book represent real people. The explosion of new internet companies over the last few years has made it virtually impossible to find a company name that is both plausible and hasn't been used before somewhere, some time. Although a few real companies have been given peripheral roles in the book, Ninetyminutes, Goaldigger, Babyloves, Lastrest, Sick As A Parrot, Orchestra Ventures, Bloomfield Weiss, Howles Marriott, Coward Turner, Leipziger Gurney Kroheim, Champion Starsat and Midland Mercia TV are all fictional.

A great many people have helped with the writing of this book. In particular, I would like to thank Will Muirhead of Sportev, Sheona Southern and her colleagues at Teamtalk, Eldar Tuvey of Mailround, Anne Glover and her colleagues at Amadeus, Toby Wyles, Peter Morris, Tim Botterill, Troels Henriksen, Saul Cambridge, Douglas Marston, Jonathan Cape, Richard Horwood, Simon Petherick, my agent, Carole Blake and my editors, Beverley Cousins and Tom Weldon.

This book is dedicated to Hugh Paton, a skilful and safe pilot. I miss him.

Michael Ridpath
London
September 2002